SIGURD HOEL

MEETING
at the MILESTONE

~~~~~~~~~~~~~~~~~~~~~~~~~~~~

Translated from the Norwegian
by Sverre Lyngstad

MASTERWORKS OF FICTION (1947)

GREEN INTEGER
KØBENHAVN & LOS ANGELES
2002

GREEN INTEGER
Edited by Per Bregne
København/Los Angeles

Distributed in the United States by Consortium Book
Sales and Distribution, 1045 Westgate Drive, Suite 90
Saint Paul, Minnesota 55114-1065

(323) 857-1115 / http://www.greeninteger.com

First Published by Green Integer in 2002
©1947 by Gyldendal Norsk Forlag
Published originally as *Møte ved Milepelen* (Oslo: Gyldendal Norsk Forlag, 1947)
English language translation ©2002 by Sverre Lyngstad
Published by agreement with Gyldendal Norsk Forlag
Back cover copy ©2002 by Green Integer
The translation of this book was made possible, in part,
through a grant from NORLA (Norwegian Literature Abroad)

Design: Per Bregne
Typography: Guy Bennett
Photograph: Photo of Sigurd Hoel
(courtesy Gyldendal Norsk Forlag)

LIBRARY OF CONGRESS CATALOGING IN PUBLICATION DATA
Hoel, Sigurd [1890–1960]
Meeting at the Milestone
ISBN: 1-892295-31-8
p. cm — Green Integer / EL-E-PHANT 54
I. Title II. Series III. Translator

Green Integer books are printed for Douglas Messerli.
Printed in the United States of America on acid-free paper.

Contents

The Storm Trooper   9

PART ONE: *Notes from 1947*   11
  The Lodger   13
  The House   16
  Crackup   23
  Epilogue and Prologue   47

PART TWO: *Notes from 1943*   55
  Hans Berg   57
  An Old Album   80
  Gallery of the Damned   87
  The Spider Web   106
  Prayer for Love   107
  Gunvor   109
  High Up and Deep Down   117
  The Room   120
  Conversation with My Father   128
  Meeting after Twenty Years   136
  Kari   139
  Ida   154
  Vacation   163
  Evening and Night in August   168
  A Baby?   175

PART THREE: *Notes from Sweden, 1944*   179
  Around in Circles   181
  A Secret Mission   187
  A Nocturnal Conversation   199
  A Slip of Paper   205
  A Walk in the Dark   214
  Deep Underground   228
  Shadows from the Past   240
  Flight   256

Postscript 1947   261
  The Anthill   263
  The Fourth Time   275

The Storm Trooper
~~~~~~~~~~~~~~~~~~~~~~~~

He got eight years.

He has served two years already. Six to go.

He was, let me see, twenty-one in 1943. So, in 1947, he's twenty-five. If we figure in the usual reduction of the sentence, he will be twenty-nine when he comes out. Still a young man, but set in his ways, hardened, full of hatred and thoughts of revenge. Though all sorts of things can happen. They are allowed to read the Bible.

It happens that they become religious.

On May 7, 1945, late in the evening, his father jumped off the dock. He had filled his pockets with lead. Nobody knew anything ahead of time, and he left no letter or message.

Her I haven't spoken to since the summer of '45. She didn't answer the letter I wrote her when I learned the verdict. I won't be writing her again.

Eight years. If I had come forward as a witness and reported what I knew, it would have been quite a bit more.

None of this concerns me, I know. The lives of strangers, that's all.

Still, I think I must try to sort out these papers.

Part One · Notes from 1947

The Lodger
~~~~~~~~~~~~~~~~~~~~~~~~~~~

It began one day in the middle of August 1943.

They brought him in one evening at dusk. The bell connected to the garden gate gave the prearranged signal, and when I appeared, there they were. Anyway, I had been notified beforehand.

They were the usual two men, with a third in tow.

I unlocked the lattice gate and led them up the driveway, through the heavy wooden gate, across the back garden and over to the old coachman's lodge. I unlocked the door, showed him in and told him what he needed to know, as I had done with so many during the last year and a half. Showed him the bell wire, the lighting plugs, the emergency exit, and the secret gate in the garden fence. Meanwhile the two men, who had heard it all many times before, stood quietly by.

Had he had his dinner?

Yes, he had eaten. Thanks.

Then he would be brought some supper around eight-thirty.

He said thanks again.

I saw to the blackout curtains, making sure that not the least streak of light could get through. This was something I always did myself. I had been burned once on the blackout. It's incredible how sloppy people are with that sort of thing—even people in mortal danger—when they are away from home. Oh well, we got away with a scare and a fifty-kroner fine that time.

He stood still in the middle of the floor, listening attentively to what I was saying. He gave a nod or two to show he understood. He had put down his little suitcase but was still carrying his rucksack.

He was a man between forty and fifty. Closer to fifty perhaps, though it was difficult to decide such things in those days. A little over medium height. Of rather slight build. Fairly well-dressed, but his clothes were out of fashion. Well, that applied to us all. Narrow face, straight nose, blue eyes, as I believe it says in the police reports. There were deep lines in his face, running from the wings of his nose to the corners of his mouth and down. The bushy eyebrows, darker than his hair, shadowed his eyes. His hair was a slightly sandy-colored light-brown, typically Norwegian. It was thin on the crown and a shade gray at the temples. At first glance, his heavy eyebrows made his face look stronger than it really was. If one looked more closely, his eyes had a mild expression and his mouth was sensitive. He looked like a typical intellectual. I knew I'd seen the face before, but couldn't offhand say when or where.

He had to be a man of some importance since they had brought him here—they set store by this place and didn't use it out of season.

He stood there very politely, listening attentively also when I repeated the instructions, and thanked me again as I left. But all the time, even when he looked straight at me for a moment and surprised me by the perplexed, helpless expression in his eyes, I had a feeling that he wasn't really there. That he was listening for something—something from within himself rather than from without. That somehow, for whatever reason, he was so absorbed in thought that only a small part of him was present—was polite, well-bred, and attentive. He didn't seem really nervous, only—if I may say so—lost.

All sorts of people had stood in this room during the last eighteen months. I only noted, quite superficially, the things I have just mentioned—they didn't really concern me, or concerned me only insofar as, indirectly, at worst and in the end, my life might depend on them.

The two men followed me into my office. Remained standing until I offered them a seat. Sat a few moments without speaking. Took the cigarettes I offered them (they were their own cigarettes, some had fallen to me for—what shall I call it?—rent). Then one of them cleared his throat, the one who always did the talking and always cleared his throat before he spoke, "Hmm!"

Then he cleared his throat again, and I understood that this time it was not quite the usual thing.

At that very moment I remembered the face of the man back there, remembered when and where I had seen him, and knew his name.

Why, he had the reputation of being an out-and-out Nazi sympathizer!

The man cleared his throat a third time. Then he said, "It's like this. Could you put him up for the time being? We don't know how long it might be. A week, perhaps. Or maybe two."

"That's okay."

"You'll get provisions as usual."

"Okay."

Then my curiosity got the better of me. In a breach of etiquette I asked, "Is he—for across the border?"

The man looked down at his cigarette. "Maybe. It hasn't been quite decided yet."

Then he added, on his own account, I think, "He's not exactly in the danger zone. But he's had a difficult job and his nerves are a bit frayed."

He was about to say more but checked himself. The two men finished their cigarettes, got up, said goodbye and left.

The House

~~~~~~~~~~~~~~~~~~~~~~~~~

It was my house that had gotten me involved in this work. The house was the protagonist, I myself was only a supernumerary who came and went with a tray.

I may just as well give a brief account of this house, with a forewarning that I'll change a few details. It wouldn't do me any good if outsiders should recognize me by the house. In other words, I wish to protect myself. But I also wish to protect the house—it did yeoman service in its day. Who knows whether it won't be of service again some time?

In the same vein, I may mention that I'll use my own names for the people I refer to. In other respects as well I intend to camouflage the individuals sufficiently to safeguard their privacy.

So picture to yourself a white-painted villa in a small quiet side street. It sits peacefully in a relatively narrow but quite deep garden. The house is in the middle of the garden.

In the old days, before the First World War, there was a regular cluster of such villas in the neighborhood. Now this house is one of three or four that still remain. The villa to the left, as well as the one in the back, has been torn down, and a small apartment house has been built on each of the two lots. Strictly speaking, the area is zoned for residential villas, but we all know how slick builders with the right connections can get around that sort of thing— they just call the lowest floor a basement and the top floor an attic. Well, anyway the two apartment houses were there. The previous owner of my house could presumably have sued. But he didn't, for lo and behold—the owner was the same company that had built the two apartment houses.

I bought the house in the spring of 1939. I had been rather lucky and felt a desire—vanity, no doubt—to celebrate my fortieth birthday on my own soil.

The builder who negotiated with me was a big, burly fellow of—well, of the builder type. Endless amounts of builder cutlets and meat patties and beer and aquavit must have passed through his gullet to make him into what he was. His face was fiery-red and he was jovial, with a booming, slightly hoarse laughter, but with small, cold eyes in the midst of his rather beefy exuberance. At times he made me think of a big simmering pot of beef: you were constantly afraid he might boil over. He perspired profusely even in relatively cool weather, his blood pressure must have been very high. Cause of death when the time came: apoplexy.

The house had two complete floors, with an attic. A broad driveway led up to the main entrance, located in the right-hand short wall as seen from the street. A heavy wooden gate with two leaves had been added as an extension to the house; it concealed the entrance and the rear of the garden from passersby in the street. Opening the gate, you entered a small graveled courtyard, which was surrounded by lawns, flowerbeds and trees on two sides. The house and the gate made up the third side, and on the fourth, to the right on entering, stood a long, low, brown-painted wooden house (the main building was brick).

Well, I bought the house. The place suited me fine. It was difficult and expensive to maintain, but the purchase price was reasonable. The house was rather large by Norwegian standards, but there were more of us at the time and we liked the spacious rooms, which were nicer than anyone would suspect seeing the old crate from the outside.

I never regretted the deal. One of the reasons for my purchase was the garden house. It hadn't been used as a dwelling for many years, scarcely since the First World War. Servants nowadays insisted on living in the house proper, and some room or other—that of the former mistress, I imagine—had been converted into a room for the two maids one was obliged to keep.

The old servants' lodge had gone to seed somewhat, it was full of cobwebs and mice droppings and the sort of junk that collects in the course of time— things that none of the successive owners had bothered to take with them and that weren't worth putting up for sale. Incidentally, I found a perfectly lovely old oak chest with iron fittings in the middle of the pile of junk. When it had been mended and touched up (eventually costing me a pretty penny), it became one of my showpieces.

Anyway, I cleared out the old house. I had discovered that its foundations were good and solid and hadn't been damaged noticeably by the shocks from trolleys and automobiles in the surrounding streets. I had figured out that I could set up a small lab there, and I did. This business with the lab was my hobby. I was not a professional physicist, but I had taken it into my head—or played with the idea—that it was what I ought to have been. But enough of that. I modernized the old servants' lodge. I had just managed to lay on electricity, put in place a proper waterpipe, drainage, external conveniences and so on, and figured out a way to have both the lab and the main building partially heated by electricity. I had arranged everything so nicely that my family complained I was keeping too late hours back there; they asked me if I had acquired scientific ambitions in my late adolescence. Then came the Occupation.

On the surface it didn't at first bring any great changes to our lives. Some Germans came and looked at the house but didn't find it suitable for their purposes and let us keep it.

Our daily life went on much as before.

In reality, of course, everything had changed. We ourselves had changed, through and through. We breathed differently, our heartbeats were no longer the same, nor were our skins. I dare say that every cell in our bodies, with that tiny bit of soul that it had, knew that the country was in the hands of its enemies.

Later the surface changes came too, and they were greater and more numerous than I had really wanted. I came into the limelight for a while, lost my job and was locked up for a few weeks, and an accident occurred that caused me to lose those nearest and dearest to me. But these are all private matters which have nothing to do with what I'm going to relate here.

On the other hand I may mention, as a matter of some interest, the nickname the members of our group gave me afterward. They called me Mr. Spotless. It was intended as a joke, and they used it partly to tease me. But I may just as well admit that I appreciated that nickname.

It also had a certain importance that the Germans took the two apartment houses that were located behind and to the left of the house. One seemed to have been converted into a kind of school, I don't exactly know what they used the other for. There were some offices there. A few officers lived there too, and sentries were stationed outside.

It was strange to have them so close. When I stood in my inner garden in the evening I could hear muffled roars and yells, rhythmical clamping and tramping, and besides that a number of sounds I couldn't account for offhand—it sounded somewhat like blows or bangs, but that wasn't quite it. And I could hear some brief roars or groans that came from a living creature. The sound was stronger than a human voice, but it resembled a word, though I couldn't make out what it was. It sounded like—*oll!* Time and again I would hear that bang, followed by a groan: *oll!*

It was as though they were torturing someone—I fantasized that they had found a troll someplace up in the mountains and, having tied it up, were now harassing and tormenting it, yelling at it and beating it—many of them beating it at once. That could be the bangs I heard. Until the troll groaned its brief cry of woe—*oll!* Was the troll in his distress calling to his mate for help?

It was uncanny to be surrounded by all those muffled sounds that I couldn't

18

figure out. It was like being encircled by a nether world, something bestial—no, something even more oppressive and more primitive. Rage and helplessness, confused words of abuse and wailings. And it was all in rhythm.

Later—I don't recall when—it gradually dawned on me that it was the very spirit of Hitlerism I was listening to, that the brief yells were shouts of command, that the bangs were presumably twenty to thirty pairs of heels clicking together at once, and that the wailing troll was twenty or thirty throats saying, "*Jawohl!*"

Funny. But it didn't strike me as funny. It was like standing at the entrance to hell without being able to see, so that you received only confused reports through your ears from some of those damned, tormented souls.

For they *were* tormented, though they didn't know it.

When the Occupation had lasted nearly two years, I was visited one evening by a man from the Resistance. He was one of those who could pull quite a few strings. We called him Andreas.

We were sitting in the lab—I spent more time there now. Partly because I had more time to spare, partly because I didn't feel comfortable anymore in that big, empty house.

Suddenly he displayed an intense interest in this room and in the entire little house. I had to explain everything to him—doors and exits, its location in relation to the surroundings, the nearest streets and so on.

We looked it over inside and out. Little by little I was overcome by the same feeling I always had as a boy when my father for some reason or other became interested in something I was doing. I believe I had the same thought as then: This bodes no good!

Nor did it, when you come right down to it.

My friend asked me whether this lab was absolutely necessary to me. Of course it wasn't. No one had asked me to do the work I was doing there. It was even possible it was all nonsense. Besides I could presumably do it just as well in my own office in the villa. And there was also the fact that Andreas was one of those people you couldn't very easily say no to. For one thing, I looked upon him as a sort of superior. But it was more than that. Andreas was an exceptionally nice and lovable man. Far, infinitely far, be it from him to use threats and big, heavy words. He was friendly to almost everybody. But now and then you would have a slightly unpleasant feeling that, when the chips were down, his affection for you didn't mean a thing to him. The *cause* was all that mattered to him.

And when it came to the cause, we were in such close agreement that there was nothing to discuss.

He himself was devoting all he had to this cause—time, money, energy, everything. The worst of it was that he didn't even seem to think that what he was doing was anything out of the ordinary. Risk? Pooh! If the Germans came and questioned him, he would twist them around his little finger, you bet.

And—worst of all—I believe he would have succeeded. He always made such a disarmingly calm and sincere impression.

He had no great knowledge of human nature, and it happened he was grossly mistaken in people. But this didn't affect him. It was the fault of the people concerned if he was mistaken in them!

In reality he was, as will be evident to anybody, a thoroughly hard and ruthless fellow, strictly speaking quite insufferable. The trouble was, I liked him so much. Quite apart from the fact that I admired him.

Was the lab absolutely necessary to me? he asked. And my answer came back as it had to: No, it wasn't.

He went nosing about the room a little more. Then he said, "In fact, this place is exactly what we've been trying to find for a very long time."

Then he explained.

For several months now he and his group had been on the lookout for a place where people could go—one or several—when they had to lie low, but where they could still be easily contacted. This was the very place. Protected by the Germans themselves, so to speak. Who would ever get the idea of looking for people right in front of their own door? The only thing lacking was an emergency exit, in case an accident were to occur, in spite of everything.

But after looking around a bit, spending half an hour or so nosing about in the neighborhood, he came back in a state of great excitement. Even that problem had been solved. If we just sawed an invisible door in my board fence directly behind the garden house, it would give access to the garden of the adjacent property. After three steps you found yourself on a gravel path leading up to the house next door. A few steps down this path took you to a walk behind that house, lined by hedges tall enough to hide a man, and ending in another little side street fifty yards away. It would be quite impossible for anybody who wasn't initiated even to imagine an emergency exit there.

"Ideal!" he said. "Almost too good to be true. And this," he said, looking around the lab, "is much too nice to be a lab in times like these!"

Suddenly he came to think of something.

"By the way—that suit of yours!" he said. "You haven't heard anything more about it, have you? It's done with, dismissed, isn't it?"

I answered that I had that impression.

"Well, I should certainly think so. Even those fellows must have a sense of shame. No, that's just what they do not have, as we all know. But—oh well. So you think it's been wound up. That's good. I should say you had enough troubles, hard hit as you were!"

I knew damn well he wasn't thinking of me. His thoughts were fixed upon the house. He was part of a campaign, and people, houses, arrests—these were all pawns in the game.

He was a lawyer, and an exceptionally good one. We said every once in a while that, if he'd been a general, or Minister of Defense, much would have been different. (Well, many of us probably had such thoughts in those days about some of those closest to us.) He had been told so too, but the very thought made him shudder. He a public figure? To stand there like a monkey and...

No—but to stand behind a cabinet minister and pull the strings, so that the minister went through the right motions, that was a different matter, that he might consider—.

Of course he never said anything of the sort, but I knew it was what he was thinking. In general, as time wore on, I came to imagine that I knew most of his thoughts. It was an amusing game, one of the things that made me like him.

And so there were workmen in the house again, but this time they were workmen of a special sort. They tinkered with the electrical wiring so we could have the necessary connection between the main building and the backyard. They laid secret wires with bells all over the place. They installed an interphone between my office and the lab. They sawed through the board fence at two points from top to bottom, making up a door that was invisible to anybody who didn't know about it. They put in place a latch and hinges and painted everything over.

There is no point in going into further details. When they were through, I felt as if I were in a fortress, surrounded by visible and invisible walls.

But, despite everything, the fortress could be forced. Suppose the Germans became suspicious. Suppose they wanted to surprise us at night, when the outer garden gate was locked. They could bring it off using ladders, or in some other way. But they couldn't get into the house or the rear part of the garden except by opening the heavy wooden gate, and if they did so when the electric circuit was connected—and they had no way of knowing about that— a bell would ring in the lab, which had now been furnished as a small apartment again. Then the individual concerned had only to grab his valise and rucksack, slip out the back door, open the invisible door in the fence and wait on the other side until he knew whether there was really any danger.

In the house itself there was extra space available. Arrangements were made for a tenant, who took over most of the guard duties and provisioning. One of the maids, fairly new to the house so I couldn't entirely vouch for her, was replaced by someone else who had been carefully selected. And as I've said, I myself was reduced to a supernumerary.

Everything was worked out as carefully as in the best American Indian tales. But it had still to be tested in practice. After a couple of incidents where people fled because the wind tore open the wooden gate, we introduced a few improvements.

But at the time I mentioned at the beginning—August '43—everything was working without a hitch. And the regulations were gone through again and again. There mustn't be gaps or faults at any point.

There were some all the same. One day the whole thing cracked, and the house, along with the backyard apartment, the bell circuit and all, fell into the wrong hands. But about that later.

I proposed and carried through a few small improvements that the workmen hadn't thought of. I had a hole drilled in the board fence at a suitable place, and into the hole we fitted a small periscope that looked like the outlet of a gutter. It was very simple, but it enabled us to stand on our side of the fence and see whether anyone was lying in wait on the other side.

And then I made them saw another extra exit in the fence facing one of the buildings occupied by the Germans. For I figured that, if worst came to worst and my house was surrounded on two sides, it wouldn't occur to anybody to station sentries near the German houses themselves.

There was an alleyway leading to the street between the two houses. And a narrow passage ran between my fence and the two apartment houses. At the very worst, a man could steal out through this other door and, innocently whistling, walk between the two houses into the street.

Now afterward, there may be a certain satisfaction in knowing that it was all very cleverly thought out.

Crackup
~~~~~~~~~~~~~~~~~~~~~~~~

One evening when I dropped by at my new lodger's, he lay prone on top of the bed with his face buried in the pillow. He hadn't answered when I knocked, but when he heard my footsteps in the room he jumped up and politely apologized. He kind of stood at attention before me, as if I were his superior.

I said I'd just looked in to see if everything was all right,

Oh sure, everything was in order, he said, with a wry little smile.

I noticed that his dinner sat on the table, untouched.

I took care of the blackout and left.

He looked like he had been crying.

I didn't give it much thought. I had seen a good many upheavals and witnessed a good deal of misery during the last few years.

But the following evening, about an hour before I used to take my customary walk, the interphone rang. It was he.

Again he apologized very much. But—could I possibly spare him a few minutes—maybe an hour? He couldn't imagine it would take more than an hour.

This sort of thing, too, I had experienced a few times. I said I would come over right away.

It turned out to be somewhat more than an hour. It took two evenings.

He was pacing restlessly up and down the room when I entered, but stopped at once and apologized afresh. It almost looked as though he were apologizing for his very existence.

It took some time before he got going. He had found a seat for himself, but he just sat there picking at the tablecloth, looking down all the while. At last he began, rather haltingly.

It wasn't so easy, he said. There were so many things.

He fully realized that he hadn't been brought here because he was in any special danger. At any rate, he knew of many who were in greater danger than he.

"I'll tell you—they're afraid I'm going to pieces!" he said, suddenly looking straight at me. "They're afraid that my nerves may snap, or…that I might crack up in some way, which would make many others suffer. Therefore, I think, they've decided to wait and see awhile and then perhaps send me across the border. Well, no, I really don't know.... I've tried to explain to them how I feel. I've had a rather risky job, a taxing and unpleasant job actually.... I'm worn out, it may not be anything more than that. I need a little rest, there may not be anything more to it than that.

"Though I don't know—it may very well be that I've gone a little crazy. Just a tiny wee bit crazy. Oh, I'm sorry!"

Suddenly he laughed—laughed outright, without merriment, a long while, "Ha-ha-ha, ha-ha-ha!"

It came in fits and starts. His nerves were in pretty bad shape, all right.

Then he began to talk again, more to himself than to me at first.

He had tried to explain himself. But it wasn't so easy. Evidently people had some difficulty understanding him. And rightly so, perhaps. He himself was probably a weak person, as he had come to suspect more and more. And the others were so strong, so sure of themselves. No doubts or scruples of any kind.

Well, I probably knew Andreas? he said, suddenly looking at me again.

I felt uncomfortable. Did he want to interrogate me? What sort of person had they sent me this time?

I replied coldly that I didn't know anybody called Andreas.

"No, no." He nodded. Then he suddenly laughed, but now with a touch of good humor in his laughter. "Oh, you must forgive me! I had no intention of examining you. But I've had my own ideas, of course. And the fact that you've placed this house at their disposal, and one thing and another...."

But what he really wanted to say... He had talked to a couple of people, and he had a feeling that they didn't quite understand.

If he had talked to Andreas in this way, I could well understand that he didn't get through. Andreas wasn't one of those who were patient with weak souls during this period.

But, he said, today it had occurred to him that perhaps he could try to talk to me. I must belong to the group in some way or other—"Oh, I apologize!" And then, of course, he knew me—knew who I was, he quickly corrected himself. But I didn't know him, most likely.

Oh yes, I knew him. This country was so incredibly small. Everyone knew everybody else, and had heard something about one and all.

I knew who he was at any rate, and what his name was. Here we shall call him Indregård. He was a few years older than I and had been a student in a different department at the university, but someone had pointed him out to me and told me something about him. He studied mathematics and was considered to be very promising. A future scientist, people said.

But nothing had come of that. He had taken up something practical, I thought I'd heard. Something to do with insurance. As far as his present situation was concerned, he had certainly had a risky job, if what I started to suspect was true. An unpleasant job. And so his nerves had given way.

It was a good thing he thought I didn't know him. It provided a basis for increased confidentiality. The secrecy of the confessional and all that.

He sat for a moment again. And then it came, the explosion.

"The fact is, I've begun to hate the Norwegian people!" he said, banging the table.

I just said, "Really? That's quite something."

He gave me a hostile look.

Yes, he knew it sounded ridiculous. And if I felt like laughing I shouldn't hold back. He himself would laugh at it so hard that—

And he laughed again. Laughed by fits and starts, without mirth, the unpleasant laughter of a robot. It ceased as suddenly as it had begun.

"I'm obviously out of my mind," he said, very calmly.

From now on he spoke more coherently.

The point of departure was his work. He'd been—and this I couldn't very well have guessed—an insurance man. And that led him to... Well, he couldn't explain himself without giving me some information about himself and his work. And that was wrong, he wasn't so mad he didn't understand that. But in this case it scarcely mattered; he had seen it in the eyes of more than one person: the decision had been made, they no longer trusted him, he had to be exported. With fine references and papers, he realized that too. "'Has shown himself to be unusable, is recommended very highly.' For a big position in London, ha-ha-ha!"

But anyway—he became very matter-of-fact all of a sudden—he had traveled around the country a good deal at one time, had organized the work for his company and had many connections from that period. In certain quarters it had been considered practical that he use those connections during this time. He was released from his work in Oslo and took to the road again. In particular, he called on the Nazis all around the country. Well, that meant he had to pose as non-political, of course. Or rather as favorably disposed toward the new order.... Oh yes, all the necessary arrangements had been made in that regard.

Travel permit? That was easy enough. It was simply a matter of going to the right person and explaining that you were an insurance salesman and so on, and that you were unpolitical and of the opinion that insurance and such must at any rate be kept outside politics.

They nearly fell on your neck. It seemed as if they thought a sympathetic non-political person was much more wonderful than someone who shared their own views.

That was the general rule, in fact—most of those so-called new people couldn't stand their ideological partners. The only sound instinct they still had, so to speak.

Well, he traveled around the country. Selling insurance. And trying to obtain information. Supposedly *that* was the purpose of it all.

Had he managed to obtain any information of importance? Hmm. He didn't quite know. He hoped so. Especially in view of the fact that the insight he gradually gained was making him so damned uncertain.

Stop. I mustn't get the idea that he'd developed any sympathy for the Nazis per se. Most of them were people of the sort who, should they be removed from the surface of the earth, would make the earth breathe a sigh of relief.

The majority of them were coarse, soulless people. Derailed, obtuse, brutalized—so much so that you often had to wonder. They, too, must have been children once, must have laughed and cried and stretched out their arms to someone they loved. They must have enjoyed cats and dogs and baby lambs, they must have watched the wagtail in spring and found it pretty, they must have been in love in their youth, they must have laughed and cried and thought: I'm happy! The world is mine!

But no. Most of them could scarcely have experienced those things. The brutalization went deeper than that. Sometimes it went so deep that you felt like asking yourself whether they had ever been human beings. And at other times you asked yourself whether there wasn't something wrong with the nation as a whole, since it could produce such creatures.

And yet, how sentimental they were! After five to ten drinks, that is. Then they felt so sorry for themselves. They were so misunderstood.

And they were intensely interested in insurance. Many of them. Because you could never know.

As a rule one or more members of the family didn't belong to the Party. And *they*, at least, must be able to take out an insurance, eh? Could it be arranged as a secret insurance? Payable at the end of the war? And in such a way that, if the right people won, Mr. N.N. would collect the money himself, but if the others won, then the money would go to his wife? Or his son?

Many strange questions cropped up, betraying a mentality to match.

Oh yeah, they would talk about all sorts of things as the evening wore on. Sometimes they bragged about things they had done to the point that you sat there thinking, And these people call themselves human beings!

But none of all this was such as to wear you down, not in the least. In fact, it was simply amusing. Apt to fortify your faith—not in those people, those so-called people, but in the others, their opposites.

But then there were all the other things. For example, there you were in a small railway town, staying at the so-called hotel. You remained for a few days, arranged an insurance or two—oh yes, it came to quite a few insurances. Many of them would likely be declared invalid in due time.

But then there were a few who came—well, they came up to the hotel at dusk, cautiously and on the sly, or stole up to you on the road at night. People who didn't belong to the Party. Oh, far from it. Decent people, good Norwegians. Freeholders, the backbone of the nation! Or city people, for that matter. But couldn't city people too be a part of the nation's backbone? It looked like it, anyway.

A backbone affected with rot, but—. Sure, it was the rotters who came, that was plain to see.

They came at night, like Nicodemus to Jesus, asking so cautiously, touching so delicately on this matter of insurance. They might be well-to-do people, or even better. With their papers in order, of course. Well, they had dutifully delivered to the Germans all that the Germans wanted. They had perhaps done a bit of work for them on the quiet, directly and indirectly. Providing them with lumber and boards and planks and victuals and odds and ends. But the farmer had to live too! Or didn't he? And, of course, they had also made deliveries to Norwegians. At black market prices, sure—but what else could one do in times like these? The farmer had to live too, right? And considering all the lean years the farmer had suffered, why shouldn't he be allowed to take advantage of a good thing when it came his way? After all, the only ones to get hurt were those worthless city fellers—for the Germans, well, they took what they wanted anyway.

No, all in all, this Nicodemus said, he knew in his heart that he'd done the right thing by everybody. So the new Nazi sheriff—who was a congenial fellow, by the way, you couldn't say anything else; well, he'd taken a few schoolteachers and such and sent them up north, where quite many seemed to have kicked the bucket, that was so. But he had, after all, done only what the authorities told him to do—anyway, as he was saying, that new Nazi sheriff wouldn't get anything on *him*, oh no. As long as one's own people didn't blab, anyhow. For he'd been a good Norwegian, that was plain to see; he had, for example, contributed a good many kroner to pay the parson, who had declared a strike and just sat there—strange what people like that could think up. But surely it must've been *safe* to make such a contribution? Surely, you could *trust* those who collected that money, that they wouldn't give any *names* if they were arrested and beaten a little—it would be just too bad if you had to pay for it to boot, for having acted like a good Norwegian, that is. But he would say this much: when that tramp—for he was a sort of city tramp—when he came here begging money a second time, well, all he got was a flat no, you bet.

Anyway, you would get that money back, with compound interest, people said, as soon as the King came home again. *If* he did come, that is. Otherwise that bit of cash was probably lost. But it was an old story—they bled the farmer, and when did he ever get anything in return?

But what he wanted to say, Mr. Nicodemus continued, if those scoundrels should win—well, Hitler and his gang—how much would come to light, not too much, eh? It had happened, supposedly, that people were denounced by friends and neighbors! And sometimes scapegoats were picked, he'd heard.

Oh well, all in all and without offense to anyone, it could probably do no harm to take out an insurance—on the wife—in case worst should come to worst and—yes, if worst should come to worst....

No one among the farmers had expressed himself quite so clearly, of course, Indregård said by way of explanation. They were more cautious than that. After all, he was himself regarded as somewhat questionable, and one such didn't trust another very much. But he had his secret contacts—that was fifty percent of his work—and they were able to fill in the picture, if one might say so.

And besides it happened that people were so shrewd that their whole sordid reasoning was written on their faces in letters of fire.

Oh yes, he got to know a good many people. It was—well—unpleasant.

How they found out that he was in the area? Oh, they had their secret channels. They were good Norwegians, as stated, but hadn't altogether broken with *those others* either. It was important to keep one's options open. Put a little on both horses. Not quite the same on both obviously, because one did have a sort of idea who would win, but—a farmer was only a farmer, after all, and he had to keep his eye on himself and what was his, and it wasn't so easy for him to know what either party was hiding. One could have the wool pulled over one's eyes in no time at all—so a small insurance as he'd said...

"I can't quite understand why you take these things so much to heart," I said. "After all, you must have known beforehand that there were rotten elements in this country too.

"But I suspect your biggest mistake is that you demand far too much heroism from the average man. Most people are not heroes. If we reach a point where one man out of ten is decent—in this instance, that one man out of ten is prepared to take a risk, ignore his own interest, perhaps even stake his life—isn't that sufficient reason to be satisfied? The rest of them straggle along, and brag a little in their cowardice. That's the way things are.

"The percentage of good people—let alone heroes—isn't any bigger than that. If it seems bigger in some nation at a particular time, it's because people have been whipped into being heroic in one way or another—frightened, coerced, harassed or hypnotized into it. But it's not a natural state. And we haven't been in a position to frighten, harass, hypnotize or use coercion."

"Hmm!" he said. "I wonder about that. I think there are quite many who with gentle coercion—not always so gentle either, for that matter—have been frightened into being a bit more heroic than they really are. But I won't dwell on that. For that's not the main thing.

"No, the main thing—for me, that is—are those Nazis I've run into whom I can't get myself to regard as scoundrels.

"Misled, sure. Wrong-headed people, sure. Self-centered, narrow-minded people, sure. Grumblers, sure.

"But now and then—well, after saying goodbye to some of them I would catch myself thinking, That one was actually a little better than average. Yes, I really mean that. A little more honest, more stiff-necked and stubborn, a little less crafty. It's very sad, but it happened—a few times too often.

"I recall one man. A farmer. He wasn't doing very well. He wasn't exactly in dire need, but—.

"He had a neighbor. This neighbor was a good Norwegian. I mean—well, that can wait.

"This man, the one who later turned Nazi—let's call him Per Vestby—had owned one half of a small waterfall. He and his neighbor each owned one half. Nothing to brag about, it just had an old flour mill sitting there, half tipped over. There had been talk of developing this waterfall and putting a sawmill there, but it had never come to anything. The neighbor—the one who later was a good Norwegian, let's call him Ole Østby—didn't believe in it and refused to put any money into it. And Per Vestby, well, he certainly didn't have the money to go it alone. Nor did he have the right to do that, the two of them had to join forces. But, as I've said, it wouldn't pay.

"You know how it is with the tillage of such neighbors. A partition took place sometime long ago, with a result that was often rather odd. Per Vestby—the later Nazi, that is—had a field that went all the way to the river. But above that field, closer to Per's buildings, his neighbor, Ole Østby, owned a piece of land that was a bit larger and every bit as good.

"One day—this was ten years before the war—Ole came to Per and proposed a trade. If Ole got that piece down by the river, Per could have the other, which was, in fact, both bigger and better. When Ole proposed this, it was, as he said, to round off his property. To have it in one piece. And to avoid the long cartage. And Per, too, would prefer to own the field that stretched nearly up to his buildings, wouldn't he?

"They came to an agreement, and Per thought he'd made a good bargain and that Ole was an all-right fellow.

"Then one day Ole Østby began carting materials down to the river. Boards and lumber, stones and cement. And then he began to tear down the old flour mill.

"Per went down and asked him what he had in mind.

"Well, Ole replied, he had thought he'd try to build a sawmill there.

"Really? A good idea, for sure. But why hadn't he mentioned it to him beforehand, so that Per could have found the time to contribute his part?

"Then Ole laughed a hearty laugh. Didn't Per know that he no longer had any right to that waterfall? That right went with the field he'd traded away, oh yeah!

"The sawmill went up. It provided Ole with a good income. Now during the war he has expanded, by the way—he's making trap doors for German airports and crates for German shipments. But so what? Someone has to do it. And why should *the farmer* let slip every chance he has in times like these?

"It was Ole who came and talked about a small insurance for his wife, in case Hitler and his gang were to win.

"But he wasn't entirely happy at the thought that our own people should win either. Didn't quite know how the King and his men would look upon this business of the trap doors and the crates, if they ever came home again, which he, at least, hoped as sincerely as anybody. But they'd been away so long and didn't, maybe, quite understand what the situation was here at home—. And for that matter, those fellows had never given much thought to *the farmer*—.

"So—well—a little insurance, just in case…

"But I was talking about Per.

"He'd been sitting there for ten years listening to the screeching noise from the sawmill every day, and watching his old field filling up with piles of boards. He was really going places, Ole was. And little by little Per seemed to go slightly off his rocker. Ole sort of grew bigger and bigger in his eyes, he turned into wickedness incarnate, the very root of evil in this world. If only the Lord would do him the great kindness of killing him! But even that wouldn't help; the sawmill sat where it was and Per would never have any part or parcel of it.

"When the Occupation came and the waters began to divide, Per sat stock-still waiting. There are signs that suggest he was praying that Ole would come to grief. But no, he didn't. And then, one day, Per knew what *that* meant. It was the new order that happened to be right! For it wasn't possible, not in this world, that the side on which Ole stood was the right one.

"Once he had realized that, it didn't take him long to become a fanatic Nazi. And he was one of those who had arguments. His thoughts made sense too. A cantankerous sense, clear and subtle.

"Basically, the only fault in his thinking was that an offense near at hand had assumed vast dimensions in his mind. He lacked perspective. What was near became big, and what was far away became so small that it almost disappeared.

"That was a fundamental defect of a great many of the Nazis."

At this point Indregård looked at me. It was obvious that he thought he'd found a good formulation.

I said nothing. I was, and still am, a friend of academic thinking. But here, it seemed to me, it was pushed to an extreme.

Those Norwegians who lent the Germans a helping hand, denounced their countrymen and delivered them to torture and death, even took part in the torture and the executions—did they do it just because what was near had grown big and the faraway small?

Indregård went on talking about that Nazi of his, Per Vestby.

"But insurance, no, *he* wanted none of that! Come hell or high water. But if all went well, he had a sort of hope of doing that deal over again and getting back the sawmill.

"Those were the words he used—getting back the sawmill."

"That sort of thing will always happen," I said. "There will always be grumblers, and their story is almost always tragic. For it begins almost always with their suffering a real injustice. But a country cannot build its system of justice on a concern for grumblers."

He shook his head. "That's not my opinion either. I only think that the more one sees of such things, the clearer it becomes that the whole disaster the Norwegian Nazis represent, both to themselves and others, falls apart into a chaos of individual disasters. And no case completely resembles any other.

"Well, there is the big bag—which contains most of them—of people so obtuse and coarse that they cannot be helped.

"But then there are people like Per. And a number of others I've run across. Not quite so few either.

"I have been thinking: Those people ought to be helped!

"But the law—decreed by the government-in-exile in London—lumps them all together. No one is helped. They'll be consigned to the bottomless pit. There are thousands like that.

"And I keep asking myself, Can we afford that? We are a small nation. Do we have the right to make ourselves even smaller?

"Sure, if we could really clean up everything, down to the bone.

"I realize of course that we'll manage to weed out a great many, all those shitheels who bet on the wrong horse. But what about all those ditto heels who bet on the right horse?

"We'll never be able to weed out rotters like Ole Østby. So what's the use?

"Yes, I really mean it. What's the use?"

I thought, somewhat aggressively, Rotters are each other's worst enemies!

He looked at me. "Would you like to hear some more about Ole? He worked that sawmill of his very hard, as I've said. He spent most of his time down at the saw. He had hired an agronomer to run the farm.

"Ole's main building was a huge affair, quite a mansion. More than twenty rooms. It was handsome—built during the good period a hundred years ago. It rose up like a tower on its height. A long avenue lined by ash trees led up to the farmstead from the road. Altogether one of the handsomest farms I've ever seen. And well-cared-for. He was able, Ole was.

"Right. But down by the road, at the start of the avenue, a few hundred yards below the mansion, sat a little house about fifteen by twenty feet. It looked like a sort of porter's lodge. It was occupied by an old man who had worked his whole life on the farm. He was married, and they had brought up eight kids in that tiny shack. Fine fellows and pretty girls, by the way.

"One day—about a year ago now—the agronomist discovered that the following day it would be exactly fifty years since the old man had started working on the farm. He spoke to the cook and they agreed that she should bake a cake for him. The agronomist had some white flour, and a little milk and cream could be found. A bit of sugar too. But what about eggs?

"Ole himself controlled the eggs.

"The agronomist went to Ole and asked if he could buy four eggs from him. But he got a flat no. The Germans were so particular about their egg deliveries—.

"Then the agronomist mentioned what it was all about.

"'Hmm!' Ole said. And then he said 'Hmm!' again. And then he said he would think about it. And one hour later he came up and said that, since that was how things were, he would himself like to have a hand in it by making a present of the eggs. But surely three ought to suffice…."

Indregård stopped for a moment and looked at me.

"Well?" he said.

"Well?" I said.

"The miracle," he said in a truculent tone of voice, as if I had contradicted him, "is not that there are so many Nazis, but that there aren't a great many more! That old man, his wife and their eight children—not one of them was a Nazi."

"All right," I said. "So you ran across a crook. And because of him you hate the whole Norwegian people. Isn't that a bit thick?"

He looked at me, flabbergasted. "Me hate the Norwegian people?"

"That's what you said at the beginning."

"Oh no!" He waved both hands in protest. There I had completely misunderstood him. Hate the Norwegian people—he?

On the contrary, he regarded it with open-mouthed admiration. That more had not revolted! For surely I had to admit that Nazism was a kind of revolution gone astray. A revolution on the wrong path, well, a revolution backward, reaction carried to an extreme. But it was violent, a blind, furious protest against the status quo.

And the status quo, that which had been, wasn't entirely admirable, was it? So if some people had protested, they... But when the chips were down, what happened? People put their protests aside and rose in defense of their country; they rose to the occasion and stood upright, refusing to be cowed. Oh, he'd seen such splendid things that... Sometimes he felt so small—like a worm— he could've crawled in the dust.

His voice dropped to a murmur. He buried his head in his hands as he rocked back and forth in his chair.

His murmur gradually turned into short gasps. He broke down and cried. I could see the tears trickling down between his fingers.

About the worst thing I can think of is men that wet themselves—whether it occurs at one end or the other.

It turned out that he was crying over his own misery. But he also cried at the thought of all the wrong-headed people who refused to be helped. He felt so sorry for them! Oh, if only he were strong enough to make people see things in a wider perspective. A day would surely come when we valued someone who'd turned traitor from misguided idealism higher than someone who had remained loyal out of sheer fright!

I spoke soothingly to him, but I had to keep myself in check. Those banalities of his were irritating beyond words.

In the midst of his tears and sniffles he repeatedly apologized. I had a feeling that if I could have squeezed all the water and mush out of him, so that what was left was something firm, he would be a wee little man.

I said I thought we'd talked enough for one evening. If he wanted to go on, he could just call me on the interphone tomorrow.

I went my way, relieved to be rid of him for a while. But I was uneasy as well. I wasn't sure how this thing would develop.

We all of us had our ups and downs. But the case of Indregård seemed to me somewhat worse than the usual thing. Good old Andreas had assigned the wretched fellow to a job that overtaxed his strength.

What if he should go off his rocker? We couldn't very well keep watch over him.

It was a chilly starlit night. I stopped for a moment. I just stood there.

The city was in darkness. A streetcar rattled and screeched a block away, a flicker of bluish light appeared where it passed. Down in the street I could hear some people groping their way. One of them tumbled off the sidewalk and cursed heartily.

The streets used to be illuminated in the evening at this time of year— rows of store windows shining warmly with ripe fruit.

From the building to my left came the usual noises: muffled yells, rhythmical tramping, dull bangs, screams and groans. In the other house some officers were having a bottle party; I heard a boisterous clamor from several people talking at the same time, loud laughter, clattering of glasses and bottles, and squeals of women. That sort of thing had gotten worse lately.

After standing there a moment I went up to my room.

He called again at dusk the following evening. Could I possibly give him a little more of my time?

I went over to him.

He looked if possible even more tortured and careworn than the day before and avoided my eyes at first.

We began with the usual ceremonies. I must forgive him, he was afraid he'd given me the wrong impression, an impression of defeatism and hopelessness. But nothing could be further from the truth. He'd lain awake thinking about all that until well into the night.

But he had thought about something else too.

Suddenly he looked up and met my eyes. "We're going to win!" he said.

"We know now that we're going to win.

"Have you considered what a crucial thing that is?

"Oh sure, we believed all along that we would win! He who fights believes he will win. There's a victory in the struggle itself.

"But we didn't *know* we would win. It was the others who knew that about themselves. We—we learned every day how it felt to be the weak ones, we had to hold back, put up with humiliations, insults, intolerable things. We managed it, because we—oh well, I'll skip all that. But every day, *every day*, we could see the others strutting about, could see—if we bothered to look at them—that they soothed their wretched consciences with the magic words: *We're going to win!*

"They don't believe that anymore.

"We know it now: they lie tossing in their beds at night, having nightmares, sweating and waking up, taking pills and drinking. I wouldn't exactly say that their conscience has awakened. It's something far simpler. They think, *We're going to lose*—and what will happen to me then?

"Mark my words—I don't feel sorry for those people. Not for *those* people. Most of them—almost everyone—are what I would call a blotch on the face of humanity.

"I'm not thinking about them. It's us, ourselves.

"We shall still have to put up with malice and humiliations. Worse than before, in fact. But now we know in the midst of it, *We're going to win!* And the others know while tormenting us, We're going to lose!

"It entails a lot of changes.

"A lot? A total change.

"It didn't happen in a day. Actually, I'm not able to say when it happened. It wasn't Stalingrad or El Alamein, though that was important.

"I think I know when it struck me the first time. It was that morning it was reported that Cologne had been bombed by one thousand planes. The news spread from one end of town to the other in no time at all. We walked the streets watching the German soldiers and officers, and our own traitors. Our faces were impassive, but in our hearts there was jubilation as we watched their sad faces, their bowed heads.

"It was a happy day, but brutal.

"Afterward they were probably ordered to hide their feelings. They laughed and joked demonstratively in the streets. But we weren't fooled. We heard about crackups, about suicides. Several of us received secret communications—from Germans, from Norwegian Nazis: 'Don't forget me! I was never one of them, not really!'

"We noticed a hectic element in their mirth. We saw that they got drunk more often than before.

"Little by little we knew: From now on it's just a matter of time. *We're going to win!*

"That's the unfortunate thing…

"There's always—or often, no, almost always—something pathetic about the one who loses. And often there's something—something—about the one who wins.

"It's not easy to win with dignity.

"Have we learned enough? Have we experienced enough, thought enough, felt enough, understood enough—so that we can win with decency? So that we won't lose—as we're winning—the dignity we gradually attained while we were the weak, the downtrodden, those who were trampled on?

"It's things of that sort I've been pondering."

I said, "It's no good looking ahead for trouble, you know."

"You're right, of course!" he said. "Yes, of course you're right. But—."

He had stood up and began pacing back and forth again.

It was just that—well, he thought there were several things that suggested we weren't going to win with dignity—"not with the desirable degree of dignity," he quickly corrected himself.

By this time it was generally admitted—or wasn't it?—that we (and not only we but the democracies on the whole) had been in a slump on the eve of this war. Morally, politically... Well, many things seemed to show that we were working ourselves out of it. But there were some traces left here and there. Our government-in-exile in London, for example.

How strange. There we had a man whom the Lord in his great wisdom had created and formed to be chairman of the township board at Hommelvik—and what a chairman! And then, by a tragic misunderstanding, he became Norway's premier in the nation's hour of destiny.

And he wasn't the worst one.

But now he—well, that township board—sat over there and reintroduced the death penalty in Norway. And gave the law retroactive force. Borrowing from Hitler. Borrowing twice from Hitler. His first real triumph in Norway. The Norwegian government in London helped him win that triumph.

Ah, what a government!

But that we had known all along, of course. We just thought, Government—is that so important?

Then came a day when it was important.

But we were made in such a way—since olden times—that once we had, through some complicated slippage, gotten a government so strange that most sensible people would have been embarrassed to be seen with its members— once we'd gotten such a government, we weren't the sort who made a secret of it man to man. The air was thick with scorn and derision.

It was possible that some young man or other had heard a good deal of this derision. It was also possible that he shared in the public mood during the Finnish War, a crusading mood that grew so strong that a young man who didn't volunteer would feel like a kind of traitor. Further, it was possible that this young man loved his father and that his father subsequently joined the Nazi Party. As a result this family got pushed out into utter darkness, cut off from social intercourse (except with such as Ole Østby), without access to

36

our news, only to their own, which strengthened them in the belief that they'd done the right thing. That they were a small minority among the people might be sad, but not apt to weaken the faith of a Norwegian who had read his Ibsen and adopted his view of the majority.

Well, to get back to that son. He was too young to go to Finland as a volunteer. But now he had a second chance. He could volunteer for the Eastern Front, fight against the same enemy the Finns had fought and were still fighting and that he'd heard people refer to as the devil himself since the time when he was a little boy. He was hearing it again now, all the time, and he was cut off from his former friends, who might have suggested another way of looking at it. He signed up. He went to the Eastern Front. It was no holiday trip. It was toil, frost, hardships, lice, and mortal danger. Maybe he got killed. But if he came back, whether unhurt or wounded, he would be called to account when the war was over and could look forward to several years in prison.

Indregård had been sitting down. Now he got up again and began to pace the floor in great agitation.

"I'm not saying that all who go to the Eastern Front act from such noble motives. But I do maintain that many of them do. And in the same breath I say that these are first-rate young men, idealists, romantics, men without ulterior motives, valuable men for the Norway of the future, if only we treat them right, explain their mistakes to them, put them on the right path. But we are going to give them several years in prison, punishing them for their naïveté and good faith. That is barbarism, I tell you, it's miscarriage of justice before the fact, at the very start. We'll punish them, and thereby shove the responsibility away from us. It's hair-raising. I've seen some of these boys, and I know."

He sat down again and remained seated awhile without speaking. I thought, When is he going to stop?

"Anyway, that isn't the worst either," he said, suddenly weary. "But—I've reached the point where I've had to ask myself, Who among us is without blame?

"Who among us is so pure that he can stand up in public and say, I'm innocent? I'm not a Nazi, neither openly nor secretly, neither inwardly nor outwardly, neither in thought, word or deed. Nor am I to blame for anybody else having become one.

"Who can say that?

"Not the government. Well, I've already referred to that.

"Not the political parties either.

"Not the Communists. They scared many over into the camp of the traitors and were on the verge of ending up there themselves.

"Not the Labor Party and the Liberals. They abolished our defense. How many haven't joined for that reason?

"Not the Conservatives. They saw Hitler, as long as they could, as a defense against the greatest peril of all: Bolshevism.

"Not the Farmers' Party. They thanked God for Hitler, even more ardently than the leader of the Oxford Movement, that fellow Buchman.

"Not the press. Did it keep well informed? Did it keep watch?

"Not the intellectuals. Did *they* keep well informed, did *they* keep watch?

"And when the disaster had occurred, not the Norwegian broadcasts from London. Oh, what a lot of rubbish! Two men walked three miles in twenty degrees below zero to listen to the radio; they lay in an open fox cage turning the knobs and listening. What did they hear? A half-hour report on a Christmas celebration in Cardiff.

"But first and last, not I. Quite the contrary. I know today that I'm directly to blame for another person, in fact a whole family, going to hell—because it means going to hell, in my opinion. I'm to blame for it."

He buried his head in his hands for a moment, but checked himself immediately and straightened up.

"I apologize!" he said.

They had become his magic formula, those two words: I apologize!

He evidently found it difficult to go on. Beads of perspiration stood out on his forehead, and he wiped his face again and again with a handkerchief he held balled-up in his hand.

Then he began, beating a general retreat.

He was not the kind of man who was justified in criticizing the government-in-exile. Or the political parties. Or the press and the intellectuals. What had he done himself? Nothing, less than nothing, as it turned out.

Pause.

It concerned a man, he said haltingly, a man who—. Well, he was pretty sure that I too knew that man.

He mentioned his name. Hans Berg.

Sure, I knew him. I knew him, I should think, far better than he did, that broken-down man sitting at the table directly across from me.

Hans Berg had been one of my closest friends for a few years when we were students together.

About a year ago I had learned he had "crossed over."

Here I sit, in 1947, writing this down on the basis of some scattered notes and my recollection of what happened. And I can't help thinking, What a strange time that Occupation period was! It was only a couple of years ago and yet it somehow feels foreign to me and far away. Romantic—but that's a lie, I know—and dreadful. Dreadful—that too may be a lie. But it was so *different.*

I know that much of what is associated with that period has already been forgotten. People just can't remember. It's their blessing and their curse.

I for my part remember. I think so anyway. Not figures, not statistics, but—at least I think so myself—things that are more essential. That's my curse and my blessing.

I know that this peculiarity will cause me to be lonely in the years to come—humdrum years, new years of crisis, maybe new years of occupation. People will say, Well, I never!

I have already experienced that loneliness. I anticipate it more and more. It's all right.

I remember the day I learned that the friend of my youth had let us down. Remember how I erased him from my life, as you brush away a blowfly. Without any feeling, soberly. You simply noted a fact. So that's where he ended up! Through with him. How, why? Of no interest. Sometime later, maybe. From that moment on Hans Berg was more dead to me than if he'd been in his grave for twenty years. Automatically, as if an electric circuit were closed, a whole cluster of youthful memories were enveloped in ice. If I'd heard the following day that he'd been killed, I would've noted that too as just a fact. It wouldn't have meant more to me than a strange telephone number.

But he seemed to have been of some importance to this Mr. Apologize. Well, let's hear.

I noticed that I turned cold—even colder than before. I know now, afterward, that from that moment on I'd written off this man, too. The other things he'd said were just idle chatter. Poor nerves, needless doubts. What was the government in London to us? We knew that it wasn't very remarkable. That was not the issue. What was this or that rotten farmer to us? It was all about other things. And those oddballs and grumblers he talked about—sure, too bad for the oddballs. But there were bigger things at stake. Didn't he know, the worm, that our nation was finding itself again during these years? Perhaps more than at any time for hundreds of years?

I had sat there listening to him as I expect a doctor will listen to a patient. Tough on the guy. Used-up. Sad for him; but the time we lived in wasn't nice to anybody.

I thought, Let's get this wreck over to Sweden!

"Sure, I know Hans Berg," I said. "What does he have to do with you?"

I could tell that my voice had grown polite.

He didn't notice that. He was too wrapped up in his own thoughts.

Then came his real story.

*

He looked as though he was going to jump off somewhere. I saw him tense his every muscle. But once he'd started, he told his story calmly, objectively, almost dryly.

Perhaps I remembered, he said, that there was a shortage of teachers in Oslo in the years around 1920. Many years of underpayment eventually avenged themselves. The state and local authorities were caught completely unawares. But the situation was a windfall to many peasant students, who got to teach a few classes in some school while completing their studies. He for one found a job like that. It was in the spring of 1921. A science and math teacher at one of the junior colleges had suddenly taken sick. He himself was then completing his studies in mathematics. He and Hans Berg shared the position. Hans Berg was a chemist, a very promising chemist. He was expected to have a future as a scientist, but it turned out otherwise.

He himself taught mathematics, Hans Berg physics. The two of them were friends, or passed for such; but they didn't particularly like each other.

"I believe I saw the two of you together," he said, "so you must know that Hans Berg had a rather brusque and taciturn manner. 'Keep out!' seemed to be written all over him."

There was an exceptionally attractive girl in the science graduating class. She was also exceptionally gifted. And strangely enough, though a girl, she had a special aptitude for science and math.

Her talent for math was well above average. She aroused his interest both as a mathematician and a teacher. He corrected her homework with special care and sometimes wrote long explanations just for her. She was grateful for that, as was to be expected. A couple of his classes were right before the noon recess. After those classes she would sometimes come up to the teacher's desk and ask an extra question or two, and they would sit and talk until the bell rang for the next class. Her blend of girlish coquetry and a genuine interest in mathematics was perfectly charming.

She was nineteen years old, Indregård was twenty-five.

Then, quite by chance, he discovered that Hans Berg was going for walks with her in the evenings.

"As you may remember," he said, with a slight change of subject, "Hans Berg looked quite striking at the time—dark hair, a sharp acquiline nose, and dark-blue eyes so deeply set below his black eyebrows that it looked as if they too were black. I have sometimes wondered whether there weren't a few drops of Gypsy blood in him. Well…"

He discovered them quite by chance one evening up in Sogn Road. They were talking together. Once or twice he had the impression they were holding hands.

They didn't see him.

He went home and thought the matter over. The more he thought, the angrier he got. There a friend of his was abusing his position as a teacher to seduce an innocent young girl!

He looked at me, slightly embarrassed. "I was brought up strictly and can well imagine I was quite a philistine at the time. For that matter, maybe I still am.

"Anyway"—he got up and paced back and forth a few times in great agitation—"I still think he behaved improperly. What would happen if parents couldn't be sure that their children—. Oh well!"

That outlook, that opinion, would have to serve as an excuse for what he subsequently did. After a sleepless night and a most disagreeable day—he was at the school and taught her class—he made his decision. That evening he went up the Sogn Road at the time he'd seen them—a bit earlier, to be on the safe side—and lay in wait for them.

They came. Came slowly strolling past the thicket where he was hiding. They were talking, they joked and laughed. They were holding hands. Nothing worse was taking place as far as he could see.

But it could be enough. He got terribly worked up. The whole thing appeared too scandalous for words. He was so worked up that his whole body trembled. He swore he would put an end to it. To abuse—but he could no longer remember the words he used in his thoughts.

Next day—he hadn't slept very much that night either—it turned out that Hans Berg and he taught her class by turns. Hans Berg's period came first, then came his own, and then the noon recess.

He was on the lookout for Hans Berg as he left his class. He asked to speak to him. Hans Berg went with him, reluctantly. They liked each other only so-so, as he'd said before.

He came straight to the point. Scandal, irresponsibility, abuse of a pupil's natural attachment to a teacher of a major subject…

Hans Berg was pale by nature. Now his face turned white. From indignation, obviously. But scarcely that alone—he must have become scared too. This was a fine, button-down school, and the principal was an old sourpuss. And the young girl came from a well-known, genteel Oslo family. Her father was one of the leading Conservatives in town. It could turn out to be a nice kettle of fish, no doubt about it.

"So that's the sort of man you are!" Hans Berg contented himself by saying. Then he turned his back on him and walked away.

Indregård interrupted his story for a moment and looked at me. I saw him turn red even now, more than twenty years later.

"I didn't feel comfortable about it," he said. "But I was as worked up as ever. The contempt in his voice made me boil. After all, I had only acted in his own best interest. I decided to pursue the matter."

He got up again and crossed the floor, came back and sat down again.

"Oh well," he said.

After the math class—a difficult period for him—he asked the girl to stay awhile. She did so, with a coquettish little smile. As they left the room, several of the others also smiled. It made him feel uncomfortable—and more indignant than ever.

Again he came straight to the point, told her what he'd seen, pointed out the impropriety of it, and said he'd spoken to Hans Berg and warned him.

She gave in at once. She said amid sniffles and tears that she'd known it was wrong all along. But Mr. Berg had been so nice, and so she'd thought it didn't really matter very much. She'd thought that... And nothing had happened, nothing at all. And...

He said he'd only wanted to warn her. If the matter came to light, it might be unpleasant. More unpleasant for Mr. Berg than for her, to be sure, but... He figured she could scarcely have fully realized what the consequences might be. That was why he...

She uttered a barely audible thank-you, dried her eyes and slipped out of the classroom.

A few minutes later he saw her leaving the school premises. Headache...

He didn't feel comfortable about it. Not a bit. The smiles of the other pupils as they left bothered him. The expression in Hans Berg's face as he turned his back on him continued to haunt him.

Had he known what would happen later on, he would've felt even less comfortable.

Because a scandal developed. A hushed scandal, so-called. Triggered entirely by his warnings.

After three or four days he was summoned to the principal's office. The principal gave him a reprimand, which, however, gradually turned into a warm appreciation. He was reprimanded for not having gone straight to the principal himself with the matter. This was not the sort of thing a young teacher should take into his own hands, and so on. As the school's principal he had a right to be kept informed about everything, and so on. At the same time he could well understand that a young man felt reluctant to inform against a fellow student and friend. Indeed, all things considered, he felt inclined to believe that if he'd been in a similar situation at the same age, he might well have acted in exactly the same way.

It was a praise that hurt. All teachers agreed that the principal was a most unpleasant mixture of a dry stick and a snob.

That the matter had come to light was the girl's own fault. Her mother had noticed that she wasn't her usual self. Having caught her red-eyed a couple of times, she went after her, gently but with female guile. The truth came out in a trice. Unfortunately it became apparent that the girl had fallen more deeply in love with Hans Berg than she herself had suspected. Well, the mother went to the father, and the father to the principal.

Hans Berg was dismissed at once. Since it was just before final exams, it could be done quietly. But, in addition, the principal had told Mr. Berg that he might spare himself the trouble of applying for another job in Oslo. If he didn't declare himself willing to do so, the principal would inform all the schools of his conduct. The upshot was that Hans Berg gave in.

Small-town morals were evidently less of a concern to the principal.

Incidentally, the girl did considerably worse at the final exam than either she or the school had expected. Shortly thereafter she went abroad for a while, accompanied by an aunt. In those days such things were taken very seriously in certain Oslo circles.

Indregård's eyes had been turned away. Now he suddenly looked at me—embarrassed, but with a sort of bitter defiance.

"Believe me or not," he said, "but the fact is that during the whole period when this was going on I hadn't realized for a single moment that I was madly in love with the girl myself. You may tell me that you find that to be strange or incredible. I can only answer that it's incredible to what extent a human being can deceive himself."

I asked, "And when did you finally realize it?"

The answer came without hesitation, "Two years later. When I saw her wedding announcement in the paper."

My next question took me by surprise. It stemmed from sheer curiosity. "Are you married?"

I felt ashamed as soon as the question had escaped me.

"No," he said, slowly turning red. He added, after an uncomfortable pause, "But that, of course, has nothing to do with that little story of more than twenty years ago."

I nodded. Of course not.

There was another silence, which I broke.

"So you went into the insurance business. But wasn't there—I seem to remember that somebody referred to you once as an up-and-coming scientist."

There I made a slip of the tongue, disclosing that I knew him. But he didn't notice. He just said, "Oh well. I may have seen myself taking that path. But then I received that offer from the insurance company—a good salary from the start and quite speedy promotion, and so I thought—."

He didn't say any more.

Another silence. Then I said, "But I still don't understand—"

Maybe I understood a bit more than I wished to let him know. Sitting there, my mind had gone back to the spring, summer, and fall of 1921. A number of things about Hans Berg which I hadn't understood at the time became suddenly clear to me and fell into place.

"I'm coming to that," he said. And he continued, "I didn't see Hans Berg again for over twenty years. He married that fall, as you probably know. I—I had of course had opportunities of meeting him. But I—avoided him. He got married, as I said, discontinued his studies and applied for a teaching job in one of those small coastal towns. He's still there. It was there that I met him—a week ago now."

He was once more picking at the tablecloth.

Something wasn't going quite the way it should in that small town, he went on. There was some leak or other down there. It became evident by a couple of arrests. One of them was really unfortunate. There were also some signs that the Germans were learning things that were known only to the inner circle of the Norwegian resistance. As time went on, a really unpleasant situation had arisen. Everybody started suspecting everybody else. And so he was sent down there, on the pretext of selling insurance. It was hoped that an outsider might be able to look at the situation in a fresh way.

"I didn't know when I arrived that Hans Berg had a job there," he said. "I had probably heard about it at some time, but forgotten it. 'Repressed,' I guess it's called today."

He wasn't able to solve the problem, he went on. Didn't find the leak, didn't find anything. But he did meet Hans Berg.

It wasn't a complete surprise, despite everything. He had heard some gossip about him. Down there, that is. He was talked about in both camps.

He wasn't at all well regarded down there. Not by either side. The good Norwegians felt resentful naturally—and disappointed as well. They certainly hadn't expected *that* of him.

Those on the other side were also disappointed. He had joined the Party, but that was all he'd done.

In fact, he'd been a disappointment all around. Had never felt at ease in the town but was somehow stuck there, with his unfinished degree.

He had always been a poor teacher, they said—in both camps. Uninterested, lethargic—and so absent-minded that there were stories about him. Kept mostly to himself, moping around with *Keep out!* written all over him.

On the patriotic side they said that when he finally joined the Party, it was probably in the hope of becoming principal of the school—his wife was ambitious. But there he was fooled. One of the other teachers, an out-and-out go-getter with his degree in hand, joined the Party posthaste and became principal. He—the other one—had also taken over the local cultural propaganda. Berg just sat there staring at the wall, they said.

Then one day Indregård ran across him.

He paused a moment at this point.

"I don't think I've ever seen a less happy man," he said after a while. "We stood for a moment without speaking. Then Hans Berg said, 'Well, well, imagine meeting a man like you in these parts!'

"And then he continued, 'Anyway, you may as well come home with me. I suppose you'd like to see how a traitor is doing.'

"I went home with him. I—I didn't feel I could do anything else.

"Anyway, I wouldn't call it a home. It was just a place to live.

"I don't think he's happy with that wife of his. To put it mildly. By the way, she didn't show herself.

"He offered me a drink. 'We traitors have got liquor,' he said.

"And then, slowly and calmly, he began to rail at me as I'd never been railed at before in all my life. 'You are an old mathematician,' he said. 'If I now tell you that you are the reason for my being where I am today, will you accept the proposition, or do you want proofs?'

"I said I refused to accept such a proposition.

"Then he produced the proofs—good, cantankerous proofs.

"He thought I had conspired with the principal. I don't know whether he still believes that. He thought I had gossiped about him in Oslo. He thought I had slandered him to the girl.

"'Envious, microscopic soul that you are!' as he put it. 'But that didn't wash!' he went on. 'I had a letter from her, but then it was too late. I had another letter from her, then it was definitely too late.'

"'Take a look around!' he said. 'Make yourself at home. Strictly speaking, it's your home, this place here. You're the one who created it.'

"'You've made good, I've heard,' he said. 'That's as it should be. The likes of you are supposed to make good.'

"Then he said something which is the direct reason for my being in hiding today. He said, 'People say you're a Nazi sympathizer. That makes me laugh!

No, a guy like you surely takes care to be on the right side. I'll let you in on one thing: I know perfectly well what sort of mission you're on. But don't worry, I have no intention of turning you into a martyr. And as for being an informer, I'll leave that to you—once more!'

"Here in Oslo, where they don't know him, they are afraid that he may give me away. *I* know that my secret, however he may have got hold of it, is as safe with him as—well, as the gold in the Bank of Norway, we used to say at one time. That will be his triumph over me."

"I see," I said. "So that was the excuse *he* had cooked up. Tell me, do you accept that sort of thing?"

He wiggled his head. "I don't know," he said. "I realize, of course, that he always had a difficult disposition and that he easily fell out with people—and with society, as they say. No, I don't know."

He sat in silence awhile. Suddenly he said, "By the way, the same day I came back from that little town I met her—the young girl—in the street. Well, she's married now, as I've said, with three children, and is past forty— well, just. I hadn't seen her since before the Occupation. In those days— before the war, that is—we would sometimes exchange a few words when we met. I said hello now too. She looked at me but didn't return my greeting. I figured—"

Another thought occurred to him. "Perhaps she'd heard that I was a Nazi sympathizer," he said.

Strangely enough, this explanation seemed to cheer him up. "Actually I'm beginning to wish I could get over to Sweden," he said. "Have a clean record again, and clean work…

"It's quite a strain in the long run to pass for a Nazi sympathizer, take it from me. I feel quite weary."

For the first time he spoke with a certain calm dignity.

He continued in the same tone of voice, "I must thank you again for being willing to listen to all my chatter. It has just been confused nonsense, much of it anyway. Idle talk by a weary man. You were annoyed by it, I noticed that anyway—."

"I apologize," I said.

Epilogue and Prologue
~~~~~~~~~~~~~~~~~~~~~~

A few days after this conversation the two men came and picked up Indregård. He was sent to Sweden.

I was probably partly responsible for that—I had submitted a report on him and his condition. But what I had to say tallied perfectly with what Andreas had decided beforehand.

"Used up!" was all he said. "A weakling! Well-meaning, but... He turns everything into a matter of conscience. I bet that even when he goes to the john he first asks himself if he can justify it to his conscience. No, we'll send him over!"

I talked with him for a few minutes before he left. He had asked to see me—*tête-à-tête*, as he said.

Something was weighing on him again. He stammered and stuttered and blushed like a schoolboy, but managed at last to say what was on his mind. Could I possibly find an excuse for looking up that girl—I could probably figure out whom he had in mind. After some more stutterings and stammerings he mentioned her name.

It was a well-known name. Her husband was one of the city's big businessmen, from an old upper-class family and all. After her forays among the intellectuals the girl had evidently returned to the flock.

Incidentally, her husband had shown himself to be an all-right fellow during this period. I used to fantasize that the likes of him were courageous from snobbery, ignorance and lack of imagination. What? Did someone dare come and speak in a tone of command to *him*? That "those people" could even take it into their heads to arrest anything so grand, didn't occur to him and his peers for the longest time.

But maybe I'm doing him a rank injustice. Later, when he was arrested and sent to the Grini concentration camp, he behaved well from first to last, from what I've heard.

But back to Indregård.

So, would I look her up and tell her he'd been obliged to go to Sweden? That he was not a Nazi sympathizer, in other words. Naturally, I didn't have to say that I had put him up. It must be possible to figure out something, some white lie, which didn't endanger either me or this place.

We came up with a white lie between us, and he went off, more contented than I'd ever seen him.

A few days later I made a call from a public telephone and, luckily for me, she herself picked up the receiver. I expressed myself in suitably vague terms—didn't give my name but hinted that I had a message I would like to bring her about that fishing trip. I assumed that she was familiar with the jargon. And it seemed she was. She asked me to come at once. She was nervous at the end of the conversation, her breath betrayed a tremor once or twice.

How lucky I was with the word "fishing trip," I was soon to know.

I went directly out to the villa.

She must have been waiting in the hall, for she opened the door almost before I had rung the bell. I had barely time to say I was the one who had telephoned before she bundled me off to the living room, at the same time asking me, breathless with suspense, "Has something happened to him?"

I told her that, as far as I knew, nothing had happened that she needed to be nervous about.

With a somewhat excessive movement she threw herself onto a sofa and burst out, "Oh, I became so scared! My boy, you see! He—"

I said she didn't have to tell me anything about him. After all, she didn't know me, didn't even know my name, nor did I intend to tell her.

It took some time before she understood. But then there dawned—again somewhat excessively—a light on her, and she nodded energetically to signify that she understood. That she understood perfectly. She repeated, "It's just that I was so preoccupied. The fact is, my boy—oh, never mind!

"But sit down anyway. Would you like a cigarette? Go ahead, just take one. We had a bit of foresight, thank God, so we have a modest stock on hand."

She took one also and drew a deep breath.

"So it had nothing to do with my boy? You have no idea how scared I was! For let me tell you—oh, never mind again!"

I told her the reason I'd come, white lie and all. For the occasion I worked in the same field as Indregård and had helped him arrange some papers when he had to skip out in a great hurry. And so on. And so he asked me... He had met her in the street—well, the whole story.

She broke into a laugh, clear as a bell, now relieved in earnest. "Oh, that's all! Just think—him!" She didn't say any more at the moment, but an expression came into her eyes as if she had an amusing little private secret.

No, she had not heard that he was a Nazi sympathizer. Nor would she have believed it if she'd heard. And not returning his greeting, well, that was simply because she was so preoccupied with her son that she didn't realize till several moments later that a man had said hello to her. Then she also remembered who it was and turned around, but too late.

"And so he thought I didn't want to say hello to him? Poor fellow!"

She felt—faintly smiling—sorry for him.

"I would hate to cause him any worry," she said. "He's so sweet."

And now I couldn't stop her any longer. She felt she could trust me implicitly, as she said. And this boy of hers—he was eighteen—well, he caused her *so* much worry. Three weeks ago he'd suddenly appeared in full sports gear, with a packed rucksack and everything, and said, "Listen, Mother, I'm going fishing. With Peter."

That was the first she had heard of any fishing trip.

And since then she hadn't had a single word from him.

So when I mentioned the word 'fishing trip' on the telephone... It was just too strange, wasn't it?

I said that 'fishing trip' was a good word during the summer months.

Certainly, but....

She gave me a searching look, as if wondering whether I sat there with some secrets, in spite of everything.

Of course, she had noticed during the last year or so that he'd been up to all sorts of things, with his friends. And she thought that was fine. She did think, though, that he ought to have felt free to confide in his mother, at least. She'd said as much to her husband, but he just replied, "There is a time for everything, my friend. Confidences are a fine thing in peacetime."

As if she didn't know as well as he that a war was going on, and that she could keep a secret too! But maybe I shared the opinion of her husband and her son, that women should be kept out of it?

And she looked doubtfully at me, with a certain ambivalence in her glance— trusting, sure that I was on her side, but with a certain mild reproach in reserve in case it turned out that I agreed with the other men.

I said that her son had doubtless had an inner conflict. On the one hand, no doubt, he had wanted to be completely open with her—who wouldn't have wanted to in his place? On the other hand, if that fishing trip was something more than an ordinary fishing trip, he was duty-bound to keep silent.

Sure, she understood that. All in all, she would be the last to stop men from living dangerously these days. If only it hadn't been so risky!

And her own son at that!

She raised her arms and let them fall—with somewhat excessive helplessness.

She was still a very beautiful girl. Not a quite young girl anymore, to be sure, but—stylish. A young woman of the Oslo upper class, well-preserved and well-trained, in tip-top form. A little tennis in the summer, a little skiing in the winter, a little massage all year round. Nobody looking at that figure could have guessed that she had given birth to three children.

But her face was no longer the soft, dreamy face of a young girl. Though very well-preserved, that too. And beautiful. Slightly matter-of-fact perhaps, in spite of her obvious delight in displaying her feelings.

I couldn't help thinking of a sentence from *Niels Lyhne*: "She probably loved scenes."

God only knew where they still got their creams and powder and make-up and lipstick from, I suddenly thought. That secret arsenal called *under the counter* must be pretty big.

Strange to think that she once had a special talent for mathematics and physics. If, indeed, it was the case.

I wasn't the only one making an appraisal. I felt a pair of experienced eyes giving me the once-over a couple of times. But what conclusion they came to I couldn't say. I suppose I was filed away until a more suitable occasion, if it should turn out that way.

When I got up to leave, my eyes took in the walls for the first time. Surprisingly fine paintings, not likely to have been selected by her husband. Some by young painters, too.

Oh, Indregård! I pictured him again as I walked out through the hall. Poor Indregård!

Once outside I thought, with heartfelt sincerity, Done with that!

Strangely enough, I walked around thinking about Indregård during the next few days. Should I have taken better care of him? Could I have helped him in any way?

The upshot was that I asked myself, somewhat impatiently, if I'd been infected by his doubts and scruples. That I flatly denied.

Deep down I knew very well what it was all about.

It was what he had related about Hans Berg.

To tell the truth, I had often thought about him in the years before the war.

We had hung around together at the university, well, actually from high school on. For a couple of years he was one of those I spent most time with. But there was always something about him I couldn't quite understand. That sort of thing can start you ruminating.

I never found an answer to his riddle, if there was a riddle. Something was always left unexplained. .

Yes, I often thought about him at one time.

He was, of course, very gifted.

But that I should be thinking of him now, that—well, that I found annoying.

I had long ago arrived at the realization that it was impossible to understand every Tom, Dick and Harry. Not even one's friends. Not even oneself—no, that least of all.

It was now many years since I'd stopped ruminating on Hans Berg and his presumed riddle. Anyway, as I've mentioned already, he had left Oslo, had married and buried himself in that small town, where he had apparently gone to seed.

It turned out that he'd gone bad as well.

Done with him!

But then it turned out that I was not done with him, and that was what I found annoying. Wasn't I the one who brushed away the thought about that kind of renegade as one brushes away a blowfly?

As a matter of fact, I'd always done so, up to now.

Well, it didn't take me very long to discover that it was not the phenomenon Hans Berg per se that preoccupied me. To hell with him! But somehow or other Indregård, in all his confusion, had started me thinking. All at once some years of my youth came so strangely alive. Some years of my youth, and the people I knew and associated with at the time. As a rule our ways had parted later on, I didn't even know what had become of a number of them. About others I knew they had fared this way or that. Not always so well. A couple of them had gone straight to the dogs. I had, of course, thought about them off and on—had asked myself, as one tends to do: Why did it go that way with them? Did it have to go that way? Rather useless questions.

Three or four of them had become Nazis. Those I had wiped out of my consciousness entirely, as I've said.

Until they, too, could now suddenly be annoyingly present. I caught myself wondering about them too. Why did it go that way? Did it have to go that way?

It was in 1921 that the dispute over that girl between Indregård and Hans Berg took place. And that year was a rather strange year for me as well. For many reasons the spring, summer and fall of that year stood out very vividly in my mind.

By the way, unbeknownst to him, Hans Berg had played a certain role in what happened to me then. And in some way I myself was, though merely as a supernumerary, mixed up in what happened to him.

My thoughts refused to calm down. They continued to circle around that year and the many things that had happened then. And—oh yes, also around Hans Berg and his bleak fate.

When I now, afterward, try to explain why I was chewing over things that way, I'm always struck by one main reason: the deadly monotony that lay, like a gray fog, over that whole period of the Occupation.

Those years do, of course, have other features which are easier to remember and are more often mentioned. The pressure under which all of us lived. The fear that—whether we were willing to admit it or not—was our daily companion. The camaraderie which sometimes sprang up from one day to the next and is probably the main reason why that period is already enveloped in such a romantic aura to many people. The all-absorbing faith that gave the day its warmth and was our bulwark at night; otherwise the nights could often be troublesome enough. The simplicity of the whole situation, the feeling of being part of a struggle for something completely elementary, the right to breathe, talk, think, live, something so simple and so grand that all doubt had to fall silent. As when a ship is in distress, but all on board know that it can be saved if everybody does his utmost.

Yes, even if everyone says so, it's still true—it was a heroic time, a time of visitation, a swell time, a happy time. We'll never experience anything like it, we hope.

I hope so for many reasons, among other things because I've seen how others were worn down by that time, giving me some idea how I myself was worn down by it. To be out in a tempest year after year—great, as long as it ends well. Capital when, all told, you succeed in saving the ship in distress. Marvelous, in view of all the fine qualities that often popped up where they were least expected. But it was wearisome.

Enough of that.

The reverse of the medal was the pressure, the fear and the monotony.

For my part I perceived the magnitude of the pressure and the fear during my first night as a refugee in a Stockholm hotel. A motor was raced, and a car stopped right in front of the hotel. I started up, every muscle tensed, ready to grab my clothes, rush out the rear entrance and look for the emergency exit—then I was awake and knew: there's no longer any danger. The Gestapo can't get at you here! My body relaxed in a feeling of incredible relief and I sank back on the pillow. To be sure, only to fall asleep and dream that I was in the clutches of the Gestapo.

But the monotony…

It's a condition that is difficult to recall, but I do recall some of my thoughts. I would think now and then: The pressure we live under can be bad enough, the fear can be awful, the dread of what may happen to others and oneself can be abominable, degrading, intolerable. But the monotony is the worst of all. It's the decisive proof, if it should still be needed, that what we are fighting is *evil itself.* The monotony produced by total bondage—the others' internal, our own external bondage. The coercion, doing its utmost to put an end to all intellectual life, spreads like an everlasting November fog over days and nights, seeping in and permeating everything, even our fear, our revolt, struggle, heroism, so that we cannot help yawning with boredom in the midst of the world's most exciting days and weeks. The monotony is the worst of all because in the long run it spells death. With perfect logic. Because it emanates from people who, out of fear, are mortal enemies of all that is free, multifarious and unpredictable—of life itself.

I still think it was the monotony that caused the above-mentioned thoughts to become so importunate, even troublesome, at the time. The fact that this period was relatively quiet may have played a part. The war was taking its course, but without any great sensations. I myself had people in hiding all the time, but just then they were rather ordinary cases.

Enough of that too. The upshot was that I began to write. Those thoughts about Hans Berg annoyed me, as I've said, and so I wrote about him first. But other things crowded in upon me as I was writing. My pen rushed ahead on its own. I stowed away a fresh chapter, or whatever it should be called, every day.

I noticed that I was writing under a sort of internal pressure. Why I suddenly just had to write, I didn't know. I'm not sure I know why even now. But I remember the explanation I gave myself while it was going on.

You used to know Hans Berg, I said to myself. And not only him. You knew a number of people who have become Nazis. There must be some reason why. Perhaps there is a reason common to all. Perhaps you can discover it, or at least get somewhere near it, as you write. If so, the work you're doing is important. It's important to clear the matter up—just as important as to clear up the causes of cancer. You cannot save the individuals who have become Nazis or traitors. You wouldn't do it even if you could. In that you differ from a cancer specialist, who needless to say would cure every sick person, if he could. But in one respect your work resembles his: you search for the cause— or causes—however fumblingly. If you could find them, there is a possibility that such dreadful things might be prevented in the future.

Yes, such vain and grandiose thoughts did, in fact, cross my mind. Not altogether consciously, of course, or I would have brushed them away. But there they were, in the dark recesses of my consciousness, driving me to go on writing.

That the actual force that drove me was a quite different one, of that I'm fully aware today.

And, of course, I didn't find the causes.

After a while they weren't what I was looking for anyway. I noticed fairly soon that the pen itself had taken control, so to speak.

I sometimes asked myself, a bit surprised, But what does this have to do with the matter in hand?

It *did* have something to do with the matter in hand, as was to appear later. And I must have suspected as much as I was writing.

No, I didn't find what I set out to find.

But I did find something. Not what I was looking for. No, something else altogether. And not by writing either. No, by stumbling across some unexpected, surprising and incredibly unpleasant experiences. But what I had written was in some strange way connected with what I experienced. And what I experienced was of the sort that—. Well, I won't try to describe it beforehand. Let it speak for itself.

Nor do I know whether it has made me any wiser. No, I know nothing about that. But I do have a hope, a mad hope, that what I myself cannot explain may, perhaps, be explained by others and thereby make them, and in due course the rest of us, wiser, less self-righteous, more...

But enough of irrelevant talk. To the matter in hand.

Part Two · Notes from 1943

Hans Berg

~~~~~~~~~~~~~~~~~~~~~~

He was a couple of years older than I. We went to the same school, but he was a class ahead of me. Then one day he moved into the same cheap, scrimpy boarding house where I was rooming with three of my friends. He didn't speak to us very often, and we didn't dare say very much to him. That's how it was, how it had to be—he was in a class above us, he was upper-class, we were lower-class. Though we were rebellious enough in different ways, we bowed to the hierarchy. The problems we sat and sweated over, he had solved a year ago, and now he was climbing higher and higher, up to the peaks of knowledge and learning. We knew we would never be able to catch up with him. No matter how long we kept at it and how high we rose, he would always be one bend ahead of us, one year closer to the brink of heaven.

Besides, he was not very easy to get along with. He was reticent, reserved, locked up within himself in a way that seemed dangerous. Anyway, that was how I looked at it. It's a long time ago, but I can still find no other word for it.

His looks were quite peculiar, striking. While not particularly tall, he was lean and strong. Dark, with eyebrows that met over the bridge of his nose, and eyes so deep-set that they appeared black, somber, threatening—as if they were brooding over dark things.

He didn't have a cheerful disposition. He did laugh at times, but usually when the rest of us saw nothing to laugh at. His laughter was short and merciless, and completely joyless, as if he would rather have cried over anything so stupid. But to cry, well, that was simply not done.

His voice was hoarse and hollow. Or rather, it somehow sounded half-choked, as if it came from deep down, from a cellar or a well where he was lying unable to breathe. His voice also had a coarse edge to it, as if what he really wanted to say was something so hard and grim and bitter, something so impossible to say in respectable society, that he managed with some effort to choke his words at birth and mumbled something else instead.

To me it seemed an unexpected favor when he suggested one evening that we take a walk together. I really didn't have the time, knowing it would be that much later into the night before I finished my homework. But saying no was just out of the question—just think, an upperclassman!

He didn't say much on that walk. Once he muttered something about a poor school and poor teachers. A little later he squeezed out a sort of question. After all, we were practically neighbors as far as where we came from. Was my parish just as awful as the parish where he came from? I replied that I couldn't possibly know, since I'd never been to where he came from.

"Well, well! A logician!" he mumbled with a sort of friendly mockery. Whereupon he went on to say it might be six of one and half a dozen of the other. Anyway, they were both awful places. About the worst in the whole country. True, he hadn't been to very many other places, so there might, for that matter, be some that were even worse. Anyway, how people could stand living up there was quite beyond him. But then they weren't really people, he added confortingly.

Well, I don't intend to give a day-to-day account of our association, it would serve no purpose. We became friends of sorts. That is, he put up with me in a gruffly humorous way. He would sometimes look me up; in fact, as I'll relate later, he even asked my advice. But I don't think he ever heeded the advice he received from me—or from anyone else, for that matter. It was simply a kind of conversation he made while thinking things over.

But first a slightly more detailed description.

He was from the country like the rest of us. He admired and hated the city, like us. He'd had a Christian upbringing, like us. But it had all become more intensely engrained in him. The hamlet he came from was more confining, and the same was true of his father's Christianity. For this same reason his ambivalent feelings about the city and urban life were more intense than ours—so I believe, in any case. Who can know such things!

He hated his father. When he started on that subject, there was nothing half-choked about his speech. Then curses and coarse words gushed from his mouth in torrents.

It took a long time—several years, I think—before I formed some notion, from utterances squeezed out at intervals of weeks and months, of how he'd felt while growing up.

His father belonged to the pietists. He seemed to have been a lay preacher at one time, but normally he made his living from the farm. He was also a politician, as far as I could understand—had apparently been put up as a candidate for the Storting once but lost to the Labor Party. The Socialists, as they were then called. The devil won, as his father had put it.

Hans Berg summed up his childhood in two words: slaps and Scripture, he muttered. There were joint morning prayers with hymn singing, joint evening prayers with ditto, joint grace before and after meals. The slaps came in-between.

His mother walked around silent and powerless, kind but weak. Trying to mediate and reconcile.

He asked me once, "Is your mother alive?"

My mother was still alive at that time.

When he heard that, he stopped to ponder a moment. Then he blurted out, "Thank God, *my* mother's dead!"

He thought it was the best thing for her. She was too kind and too weak for this world.

"Poor stupid fool!" he said. It was the closest thing to an expression of tenderness that I ever heard from his lips.

One Sunday—he must've been around eleven—something happened to him which I imagine turned out to be—what shall we call it?—the crucial experience of his childhood. I conclude this because he related it playfully, with a *gaiety* as bitter as gall. And because at first he tried to hide the fact that it concerned himself. It was just something he had heard about.

It was in the spring, just before the summer vacation, and we had taken off a Saturday and Sunday to go hiking in the woods. We were both university students at the time.

We had walked ourselves warm, and when we came to a tarn we decided to take a swim.

Then I noticed that he had some white streaks across his back, scars from something or other. I asked him what he'd done to get hurt that way.

"Burned myself!" he replied, possibly a bit more shortly and sharply than usual.

Several moments later—we had dressed again and were about to continue our walk—he muttered, "By the way, it happened on a Sunday."

At our next stop, as we rested leaning against our rucksacks, he suddenly said, "I once heard about a boy who experienced something really fine one Sunday. Let me tell you about it."

Then came the story.

It was a Sunday morning. A lovely summer morning with dew on the grass, fresh and nice, made for an extra dose of Scripture and slaps. Then this boy came rushing into the kitchen, glad and eager, stumbled on the threshold and cursed a blue streak. He didn't see his father. But of course his father had to be there, right behind him. It was always like that. The good Lord was the sort of guy who took pleasure in arranging little things like that. The big things belonged to the devil, the whole world was bound for hell, as everyone knew. But the little things... Well.

There stood his father, and chastising righteousness—the Lord himself in the guise of his father—grabbed the boy by the nape of his neck before he had time to get up again. What? Was he cursing? He, the son of Christian parents? Cursing on a holy Sunday morning? Then he would—

Off they went to the side room, where the rattan started swinging.

At first he didn't scream. Then he did. Then he howled. His father stopped. And now the boy had to crawl on his knees up to the picture of Jesus hanging there on the wall and ask forgiveness.

He refused.

Then his father kneeled in his place and prayed a long prayer whose refrain was, Oh, Lord, look with mercy upon this wicked child.

Then it started again. This time the boy thought his skin and flesh were cracking open and sticking to the switch. Sheer delusion, of course. *That* only happened in the afternoon.

The mother, stupid fool that she was, walked about the kitchen wringing her hands. There was nothing else she could do. There wasn't much else she could do altogether. To disturb her husband, the lord and master of the family, was strictly prohibited. And most of all when he was taken up with a sacred act such as this.

But the second time, when the screams finally turned to baby whimperings, she plucked up courage—and not so little courage either. It must have felt as if a tiny human was voluntarily entering the cage of a ferocious gorilla. In any case, she went in, tears streaming down her wrinkled face. (It was as wrinkled as a dried-up winter apple. She was thin and wasted and later died of T. B.) She managed to stammer out, "We'll be late for church, John!"

"Oh yes," Hans Berg commented. "His name was John, like the disciple the Lord loved. Do you know, by the way, that my name is also John? But when I entered junior college I re-christened myself and took the name Hans. I thought that would suffice."

"What the…" said John, the Lord's beloved. He was within an ace of cursing himself now. Then he flung the switch at the wall but, checking himself again, picked it up and hung it in its usual place beside the mirror. He took his stand in front of the crucifix and prayed once more. It was something to this effect: "Forgive me, O Lord, my fiery temper. But Thou knowest that all is for Thy glory. And so I pray Thee, O Lord! Mollify the heart of this hardened child!"

All this time the boy lay prone over the chair and saw and heard everything only in glimpses. But what he did see and hear etched itself into his soul.

His father said, "Well, let's go! But"—and he turned to the boy—"you stay here and think about what you've done till we return. Then we'll come back to the matter."

They left. He heard the key being turned in the lock. He scrambled down from the chair, but his legs refused to support him and he collapsed on the floor like a rag. A moment later he heard the carriage as they drove off.

Then a sort of holy wrath came over him. He prayed to the devil with all the oaths and curses he had learned from the farm hands out in the field, that he had to keep an eye on that father of his, overturn the carriage and let him fall into the river, let lightning strike the church and burn everybody alive— no, not Mother, she should be allowed to escape in the nick of time. But all the others should burn, burn alive, burn, burn, burn in all eternity. The flames should rise high in the air, the rooster on the church steeple would be flaming red, the bells would ring of themselves, the parson's cassock would catch fire, it would flare about him like a burning wheel, and his clergyman's ruff would shine like the sun. And his father's beard would be on fire, it would sputter like hot iron in cold water, and smoke would come out of his ears when he began to burn internally. Because he must burn internally, he must catch fire internally, and he should squeal like a stuck pig. "Oh, Satan, sweet Satan, let it burn, let it all burn!"

When he'd finished cursing he felt a kind of relief, vomited profusely and fell asleep.

When he woke up he thought at first that the bird song had awakened him—a bird sat on a branch right outside the window, and it was singing so beautifully. But then he realized that he had just heard the rumble of the carriage wheels.

So the church had not been burned down. His father and mother had come safely home.

At this point Hans Berg gave up pretending he was telling a story about someone else. He looked at me and said, "When I realized that the church had not been burned down, I understood once and for all that the world was evil."

The sound of the carriage wheels paralyzed him. He wanted to stand up but couldn't. Lying on the floor, he heard every sound and could follow what was happening. Now his father unhitched the horse, now he led the horse to the stable, now he wheeled the carriage into the wagon shed, now he put away the Sunday harness, now he was coming, now it would all begin again.

He could see no end to it. Something had gotten jammed inside him, he didn't know exactly what. Knew only that he just couldn't crawl up to Jesus and ask forgiveness. Just couldn't. A knot had formed inside him, and when he heard his father cross the kitchen floor with heavy steps as he lay there on the floor, the knot tightened again, tightened and tightened. It wasn't he who couldn't do it, he would gladly have crawled from there to church to avoid another caning. It was something else, something alien inside him.... Outside, on the branch, the bird was singing. Through the keyhole came the smell of boiled meat. Sunday dinner. They always had a good dinner on Sundays, for the glory of God. Now his father turned the key in the door, and the knot grew so tight that he thought something would go to pieces inside him.

It didn't start straightaway. First he had to clean up all the vomit, wash his face, carry out the water, wring out the rag and hang it up.

Then came the question: Would he go and kneel before the picture of the Savior and ask forgiveness? He didn't answer. And so it began.

In the middle of the second round his mother came rushing in, she'd had a fit and cried out something to the effect that he mustn't beat the boy to death. She was chased out again—chased out in a hurry and locked up in the other room that had a key, locked up in the office, the room with that strange chair which could spin around on a corkscrew, and with the bookshelf where the Bible and Johan Arendt's book of sermons and several more such books were kept, books that filled him with fear, books that in some way or other hailed from the place he was more afraid of than anything else—from heaven itself. And heaven, well, that was something like the Sundays here at home.

On weekdays, as a rule, his father had his hands full and didn't see a lot of the children. Between them and him there was a protective wall of servants, men and women. They might threaten with *the boss*, to be sure, but the threat never went beyond empty words. Because they, too, were afraid of him.

But on Sundays he had time to spare. Then he could take the children in hand—and he did. Then the prayers and the hymns were longer and the slaps more numerous.

He wasn't yet old enough to doubt what he was told. He believed in his father's god and his father's heaven. But he had formed his own opinion of what it was like up there. In heaven every day was a Sunday. And up there the father who swung the rod and gave the slaps was much bigger and stronger than *his* father. And there everybody had to go to church early and late, and God help the one who didn't mind his place at the table or forgot to fold his hands when God said grace. But now and then in the evening, the blessed souls could amuse themselves by sitting at the edge of the abyss listening to the lamentations of all those who were in hell. And then they would nudge one another and whisper, "They're worse off than we are!"

So his mother was locked up with those books. And he himself was given a third round. He couldn't scream anymore, just whimper. And it was then that bloodstains began to show up on the rod. Blood that had soaked right through his shirt. He noticed this the moment his father put away the switch to go in and have his dinner. He hung up the rod and said, "Now you can think it over till I've eaten." Then he went. It was quiet as the grave in the kitchen, although there must've been quite a few people in there—two maids, the hired man and the parish pauper, and the shepherd boy from the cotter's place. But never a sound. A Sunday silence reigned in the kitchen.

His father went out and across the hall, unlocked the door to his office and came back with the mother. Sound carried easily in the house, he could hear every footstep.

Then grace commenced. Outside, the bird was again singing on its branch. Had it been sitting there all along? His head felt hot and his ears were buzzing, but two sounds came through, drilling their way into him: that never-ending grace and the song of the bird, those four or five notes that were forever drilling their way into his brain. Then he dozed off again, lying prone over the chair, and didn't wake up until his father stood over him with the switch in his hand. "Well? Have you thought it over? Are you sorry now? Will you ask forgiveness?"

Then it started again. He probably fainted a couple of times. The whole thing seemed a bit hazy, but he thought he must have fainted. Because once when he came to, the knot inside him was gone. He had solved the problem— he couldn't understand why he hadn't done so right away. It was so simple, after all. He could just ask forgiveness but make an agreement with himself that each word meant the opposite. "Please, forgive me!" meant *Go to hell!* "I'm sorry" meant *I don't give a damn and will spit on you as long as I live.* "I know I am a great sinner" meant *When I die I want to go to hell, because I'll never want to be where you are.*

He asked forgiveness. His prayer sounded something like this: You are the worst thing I know. You're even worse than Father, but that's impossible, but you're just as bad as Father. And you stand there with a sneer curling your lips, just like Father when he is at his worst. I wish you were burning in hell, but if you don't go there, I'll go there, because I want to be as far away from you as possible for all eternity. Amen.

Then he fainted again, most likely. When he came to, he was lying on his belly over his mother's lap. She was washing his back with lukewarm water and crying, and it hurt—her tears dripped down on his back and burned like fire. Later she applied some solution to his back and it burned even worse, iodine she called it; it was like having your whole back put into an oven, and he screamed and passed out again.

Later still he sat at the table trying to eat but unable to get anything down. He tried twice but only threw up. Then they gave over. Both his mother and the old housemaid gave over. They paced up and down between the stove and the table, both equally red-eyed; but neither said anything, and now they let him alone. He got up and went out. He scarcely recognized his own body, it was—it was tremendously big, it was tiny, but he sort of floated above the ground. Once or twice he fell and stayed down for a moment, but got to his feet again. At last he reached the back of the stable. There he stopped. And then he began to curse. He used all the curse words he'd heard out in the fields, all he'd heard in the servants' quarters, all he'd heard in the kitchen when his father was traveling. And finally he made up a few of his own, the sort that spewed fire and stench. In the end he couldn't come up with any more and stumped in again.

It was peaceful in the house. His father was at a prayer meeting.

He stayed in bed for several days. When he got up again he noticed that something had happened to him. What it was he didn't quite know. But he could remember feeling he'd grown old. And that feeling had never left him since. He felt—usually without thinking about it—that he was old, old. Older than the oldest people he would ever see. Old as a rock, as a moss-grown tree stump. Old. No, he didn't know what the reason was. Hadn't thought much about it either. He just knew—he was old. Oh, but wait—perhaps it had to do with something he'd heard: youth and folly. No. Youth and frivolity. No. Youth and... Oh, carefree youth, that must have been it.

"Something else happened to me that Sunday," Hans Berg said at last. "I noticed that in some way or other my will had tied a knot so hard that I've never been able to untie it.

"I didn't want to go to my father's heaven. Everybody else wanted to go there, as far as I could see. All right, then I didn't want to go where everybody else wanted to go.

"I've noticed it since, noticed it all my life, to this very day. If I see that everybody else wants a certain thing, then I want the opposite. Something rises up inside me that I can't control—even if my reason tells me that this time the flock of sheep are right. This something that rises up is too strong for me."

I heard Hans Berg tell this story deep in the woods one quiet spring evening in 1920. Many years later I read a similar account in a book by an American writer. The endings of the two stories are not very different. The American boy becomes a murderer later on and is himself killed in the end.

So it appears that such things happen all over the world.

The circle which Hans Berg and I were part of—it was only one of the circles that I was loosely associated with—consisted almost entirely of rural students. From all around the country. Most of them poor, most of them awkward and clumsy as seen with city eyes. Most of them harboring a stranger's feelings about the city: envy, impotent admiration, self-assertion, and hatred. But first and last a vague fear. The city roared like an ocean outside our poor furnished rooms. We sat there staring out. It boiled, it roared. Screams, laughter, shipwrecks... The breakers leaped up toward our windows. We were not good sailors, had no oilskins, were not able-bodied seamen; people laughed at us in the streets, the girls stuck their little noses in the air.

Meanwhile we dreamed about sailing to kingdoms nobody had ever seen, to supine chocolate-colored girls beckoning us, to gold coasts and emerald isles. *The future* was ours, of that we were never in doubt. The outlook for the present was not so good.

Most members of that circle are scattered now. Scattered to the four winds. Some were shipwrecked, others made it to the shore of some remote island or other. A few were successful in a modest way and are now acting like petty tyrants with a swelled head. That great future of ours just went to hell. But most of us are still alive. That alone is no small thing.

Hans Berg was probably one of those who privately were most afraid of the city. Little or nothing of this ever came out, but...

Once, however, something burst out of him. We were on a measly little student spree, the two of us. Measly—well, it cost us three or four kroner each. But that was a lot of money, we couldn't very often afford such things. As a rule it would mean going without dinner for two or three days afterward. But we were used to that. Bread is good, the man said—he didn't even have bread.

That evening Hans told me about his first encounter with Oslo.

The very first thing which happened to him that fall day when he came to Oslo to go to junior college was that his pocketknife got stolen.

That knife of his was a fine Swiss Army knife with many blades and things, given to him at confirmation. It was the next most precious thing he had. His watch, also a confirmation present, was the most precious.

A friend who had lived in town for a year had helped him find a servant's room in a tenement building on the East Side. At the moment, the friend was negotiating with the landlady about something. Meanwhile Hans went down into the street. He just couldn't wait to see the town.

He was seventeen years old, but small and thin for his age. It was the first time he'd been to a city.

He stood there looking up and down the street. A street, a paved street. With sidewalks, and with gutters where dirty water was trickling down. It had rained during the day, but the rain had stopped.

"Hey, you," he heard someone say. When he turned around he saw a grown man and a woman. They were standing in the entrance to the next house. The man had a bottle in his hand. Thinking back later, he realized that the fellow could scarcely have been more than twenty-three or twenty-four. But in Hans's eyes he was a huge, middle-aged man.

"Hey, you! Do you have a corkscrew?" the man asked.

Hans had that Swiss Army knife with a corkscrew and many other curious things. He went up to him and held out the knife. The fellow uncorked the bottle and twisted the corkscrew out. He took a good look at the knife.

"A fine knife!" he said. He turned it over in his hand. "Would you like a swig?"

"No, thanks," Hans said. He didn't touch the stuff, he said.

His speech, his accent, what he said—it all seemed terribly funny to the two people. They laughed and laughed, they were bent double with laughter.

"You don't say! Never touch it, eh? Haw-haw-haw!"

They took a swig each on that and laughed even more. "He doesn't touch the stuff, did you hear! Haw-haw-haw!"

Then the man slipped the knife into his pocket.

"Well, then you don't need a corkscrew, do you?" he said. The woman beside him snickered admiringly.

They took another swig from the bottle. Then they went off, arm in arm.

"Thanks for the knife!" the man said.

"That was the face of Oslo the first time I saw it," Hans Berg said after telling me that story. "And to me it's still like that. Let me tell you something! (He was a bit tipsy.) This city doesn't spell anything good for me. Just wait, and you'll see!"

I ask myself: If a man goes around being absolutely sure of something—let's say, that a brick will fall on his head, or that all women will deceive him—won't he find some way or other of making it come true? It may not be a brick exactly, he may be hit in the head by something else one day. Most of us are hit in the head by something at one time or another. But *he* will say: What did I tell you? A brick on my head, that's what I said! And should a girl deceive him ever so little, sort of accidentally on purpose, what does he say? What did I tell you? All women betray me!

Well, maybe the city was not particularly kind to him.

But he set the stage for it. I've asked myself, Could he have been saved? And I must answer, Perhaps—but in that case he would have to be saved in spite of himself. He was strangely self-destructive. If all went well for a while he became uneasy: something must be wrong somewhere. And so he would usually think up something or other that made things go a bit awry again.

66

Then he gloated; it was as though he blared out to the four corners of the earth, What did I tell you?

And then he would see to it that things went even worse. A bit awry wasn't bad enough, it failed to satisfy his strange, twisted, enormous vanity.

He made a point of not being liked.

As I've said, he had a striking appearance. He was quick-witted and anything but stupid. When he forgot himself for a moment, he could be cheerful and happy. The girls especially couldn't keep their eyes off him. But as soon as he noticed that he was liked, he would be sure to blurt out some hurtful and offensive remark. No, he was *not* liked, and he would be man enough to prove it.

Sometimes we went after him for this. But then you should hear him! Haw! Hadn't the guy done him wrong? Hadn't he forced his company on him—obviously just so he could badmouth him behind his back afterward! So now he could stew in his own juice! And she? Hadn't she been giving him the glad eye only to make a laughingstock out of him if he swallowed the bait? But now she, too, could stew in her own juice!

That was his stock sentence. All sorts of people could stew in their own juice. The poor who let themselves be cowed, the weak who let themselves be trampled on, the sick who succumbed, the failures who were ridiculed—all of them could stew in their own juice.

Why we put up with him?

Because we knew—or rather suspected, and as time went on saw proven more than once—that all this was nothing but a monumental defense. A defense that was so deep and complicated and had so many entrenchments, one behind the other, that he often got stuck in his own barbed-wire barricades.

We had seen enough to know that, deep down, he was dangerously sentimental, and more so with regard to others than to himself. If he caught himself at it, he grew snappish and hostile in earnest, even brutal. What did they imagine? That they could trick him into crying like a girl, maybe? No, let them just sit there! They had brought themselves to this pass on their own, so let them stew in their own juice!

He felt that the dialect of his native district was about the ugliest in the whole country. Haw! That hideous dialect—it was the spitting image of the place!

Yet he often used that dialect in Oslo. Not so much when he was with us, whom he regarded as his friends in a way—though friends, he? He had no friends. Didn't count on any friends. Nobody had friends, nobody should count on friends, and he who did and was fooled, which invariably happened, could just stew in his own juice. Well, in any case, with us he seldom used his dialect.

But if he bumped into some polite portly gentleman from Oslo's best society, of the sort you could swear never used a folksy expression even in his sleep, then he would use his broadest dialect. Especially if he wanted something from the man. If the man didn't understand what he said, or became snooty and condescending so that his whole purpose came to nothing, then Hans Berg would be gleeful. There you could see! If you used the language your mother had taught you, everything went to hell. But all the worse for him, the other one—he himself could always manage. So let the damn fellow stew in his own juice.

He threw all discretion to the winds when he took it into his head to annoy people who annoyed him. Once he and I attended a lecture given by a well-known professor. It had to do with monogamy and polygamy, and the lecturer tried to continue Bjørnson's battle for purity in life and literature. He claimed that men were the cause of all immorality in the world. Man was polygamous, woman—finer, more tender and innocent—was monogamous. The men went around like roaring lions looking for prey. As for the women, poor things—their only fault appeared to be that they couldn't run fast enough. Consequently, they were sometimes overtaken and forced to take part in the unspeakable. He painted a bleak picture of the world. It could only be saved if the men turned over a new leaf, so to speak, and tried to be as much like women as possible.

The lecture was followed by loud applause. The hall was packed with women of fine, older vintages. There were practically no other men there than the two of us, besides the professor, and I thought I noticed angry glances—what were two members of the enemy of our sex doing there?

When it was announced that the floor was open for discussion, Hans Berg stood up and said, in a voice that here, in this gathering, sounded, if possible, even more brutal than usual, "Hasn't it ever occurred to you, Professor, that as a rule it takes two, one from each sex, to do the thing you have all along been thinking of?"

There were shouts of "Phew! Out with him! Phew!"

Hans Berg was delighted.

"Are you mad?" I whispered to him. "Don't you know you'll have him for an oral in two months? Don't you know that he never forgets something like that? It's the one thing that's still left of a quick head—a memory that saves up everything and is dead certain to revenge itself, if only he gets the chance."

"Sure, I know," he whispered back, looking as pleased as Punch. "But I annoyed him. He will have a restless night. Oh sure, I know how revengeful he is. But that's exactly why I did it. If he's so small-minded that he lowers my grade, he can stew in his own juice."

The professor *was* that small-minded.

I can imagine that someone who happens to read this will ask, All right, granted that this fellow was sort of puzzling, there is another, more striking puzzle: How come decent people were willing to put up with him?

The very fact that such a question arises tells me I've given a lopsided picture of the man. Which was probably unavoidable, since I've crammed together all that was eccentric and strange about him, all that was perverse, twisted and wrong-headed. But there were other sides to him, of course. There's no explaining away that the girls were crazy about him. Nor can it be denied that he often spread an unusual cheer. It was partly due to his being so exceptionally bright. Nonsense, humbug, hypocrisy, and all kinds of propaganda bounced off him, or burst like tiny soap bubbles on contact with him.

But, in part, the cheer he spread had something to do with his being so at home in the wild. Out in the open—whatever the scenery or the weather—he became happy, peaceful, almost friendly. And he had a wonderful knack for finding his way, making the best of a situation, straightening things out— and, yes, for creating a sense of comfort, warmth, cheer.

Here I sit looking for things that may have brought him where he is today. I know him so well—in any case I think I know him so well—that I'm convinced of this: *that* is not a natural place for him. Sure, I know that twenty-five years from now we'll look differently at much of this. But we are living now, today. And so is he.

No, I can't figure him out. But I'm accumulating certain characteristics.

During the first few years at the university we were penniless. We were in the same situation, he and I—our fathers had paid our way to the matriculation examination, however difficult it had been for them. But if we wanted to go further, we had to manage by ourselves. We did manage, in a way. As for me, I dropped by at my old school and asked for private pupils. The principal was my friend and sent me some. It would work out fine certain months, but other times there were sparse pickings. Then I had to skip dinner and sit in my dark furnished room with that perpetual crust of bread.

However, later on I was given regular classes at the school for a couple of years. There was a shortage of teachers in those days, as I've said.

Hans Berg fought his way through roughly like me. But he had a somewhat harder time of it, I think. His manner worked against him. I'm fairly certain there were periods when he had to skip dinner numerous times each month. But he never spoke about those things.

Then he found a friend. An old lady. Well, she seemed so to me at the time. Thinking it over now, I gather she must've been around forty. She was a buxom blonde, of the sort that overflows with female vim and vigor. He'd come to know her by calling at her home to tutor a teenage son.

I met her in his place once or twice. That didn't faze her. She just laughed. There could be no doubt what she came there for. She laughed, red lips and fresh teeth and all, the brassy old lady! I thought she was a shameless woman.

Come to think, he changed his lodging about that time, got himself a better one, with a private entrance.

This lady used to bring him food. Jars of honey, canned goods—once I even came across a pail containing beef and potatoes. I figure she had brought it in a basket. She had presumably arranged to prepare the food in his place and to eat with him. She'd just happened to bring a bit too much.

I thought it was a crying shame. Yes, shame. I felt it made him look a bit like that strange, horrible type I'd seen off and on in the neighborhood where I lived—the pimp who lived off the streetwalkers.

One day I told him so.

I knew very well it might be the last conversation I had with him. All right, then let it be the last.

But he took it differently than I had expected.

He just sat there in silence, with that brooding look on his face which could be so painful to watch, because he obviously didn't feel happy. Then he said, in his hoarse, pinched, suffocated voice, without looking at me, "He who knows he's a pig may feel it does him good to behave like a pig."

We never spoke about it again. I don't know for how long she continued visiting him.

I've pondered those words from time to time in later years. They would pop up again in various forms.

"If I am to be a pig, then let me be a pig."

Those early years contained a little of everything.

The fervent dreams of youth. The body with its clamoring demands. Poverty. Loneliness. And the belief that had been beaten and yelled and preached and sung and sneaked into us that those things were nothing but filth.

And so you thought now and again, All right, let it just be filth then! But it can't be helped. And that woman, she's ugly enough, brutal enough, coarse enough, willing enough, isn't she!

And so you did something that ended up being filth.

I believe that Hans Berg had a worse time of it than most of us. He was more passionate and intense than most, and suffered more severe inner conflicts. Protest, revolt—and submission.

If there had to be filth, then let there be. But filth with a vengeance. Coarse, brutal, disgusting. For since one couldn't help but feel like that and in a way wanted to, one might as well wallow in it and *be* like that.

"Hell, I've met a woman!" he told me once. Afterward I realized he was talking about that married woman; but this was before I'd met her and before he had any idea that I would meet her.

"I've bawled her out and told her she's a damn whore. Then she cries. But she comes back again. In fact, she comes back more than ever then."

"Let me be your whore, then," she says. "Do all the things with me that you do with your whores. Just do it!"

"Oh!" he said, raising his clenched fists toward heaven in a kind of impotent protest. "Oh, life is a pigsty!"

This was in early spring 1921—the spring he fell in love with that young girl.

Once in a while I think, Suppose we had lived in another world, in another country, in another time—a world and a time where that which is natural was called natural, that which is beautiful was called beautiful, and that which is ugly was called ugly, and where one's elders didn't use their energy to forget what it means to be young.

An impossible thought.

Hans Berg had a fellow student who came from a mountain parish. He even looked as though he'd come straight out of the mountain. The city polish didn't rub off on him. He seemed to have been made of granite and old crooked mountain pine shaped with an ax.

I'd gotten to know him and liked him a lot. He was wise and unspoiled and gave me an agreeable feeling of being damn sophisticated.

One Sunday afternoon the three of us met at our mutual temperance café.

Hans Berg was always particularly sullen and taciturn on Sundays. The other fellow was also very sullen and grumpy that Sunday. He barely opened his mouth. Finally it came to seem strange even to Hans Berg, who generally had enough and to spare minding his own silence. He said, "What's eating you today, Croppy Boy? Have you been bewitched?"

We called him Croppy Boy. His name was Trøan.

Then Croppy Boy spoke, "I'll have to move."

"Really?"

Pause. Then Croppy Boy spoke again, "The room I'm giving up is very nice."

"Oh. And so what?"

"And the room I'm moving into is really poor."

"Why, then, are you moving?"

Then we were told the whole unfortunate business. It had happened the previous Sunday. Croppy Boy had been so extraordinarily lucky with his new room. It was large, it was attractive, and his landlady was pretty and clever and friendly. And she kept it squeaky-clean. She'd managed to worm out of him when he would usually get home, and by the time he came home she'd lighted the fire for him so it was warm and pleasant. And once in a while— not so seldom either—she brought him coffee and Danish, which was quite outside the contract. He'd never felt so happy with his lodging before, and had never spent so much time at home since he came to town. Occasionally he'd stayed at home for the sheer pleasure of it, listening to his landlady as she walked about one of the other rooms humming to herself.

Then came the afternoon of the previous Sunday. From old habit he'd dropped by at his café. But then he came to think, Why should I hang around here when it is so much more comfortable at home? And with that he went home.

When he got home his landlady had lighted the fire, and everything was so clean and nice. And then she came in and asked if he'd had his coffee. He'd just had a coffee, of course. And so she just stood there, not knowing what to say maybe, and...

"And," Croppy Boy said, "so I also just stood there, feeling I had to say something because she was so nice to me. But I didn't know exactly what. And so I just kept standing there. But I had to say something. And—and so I gave notice!"

Hans Berg laughed, and how! He laughed with genuine, unadulterated glee, and because he thought the story was typical and good, he laughed again with glee. He exploded with laughter, slapped his thighs and laughed until the tears rolled down his cheeks. Then he suddenly fell silent and glared angrily at Croppy Boy.

This abrupt change was like a shot, and for once it was overwhelmingly clear what was going on inside him. It reminded me of a Chaplin film I had once seen—Chaplin sits and laughs heartily, enormously and cruelly amused by a friend who has received a blow plunk in the head from a policeman's nightstick. He's amused and laughs, laughs and is amused—until he himself receives a blow from the same stick.

It was written on Hans Berg's face, which suddenly became very serious, and on his eyes, which suddenly began glaring angrily at Croppy Boy: Exactly the same could have happened to me!

He glowered at him once more and cleared his throat.

"Oh well!" he said.

As may happen to anybody who has to wrestle with things inside him, Hans Berg was often extremely absent-minded. In the middle of his circle of friends he would fall into such deep thought that he didn't hear a word. When you went for a walk with him, he might be quite talkative for a while. Then he grew silent, and a while later it turned out that he hadn't heard a single word of what you'd said during the last ten minutes.

One morning he dropped by at my place. He came in, put away his briefcase (this was in the spring of 1921, when he had classes at that junior college), took off his coat, placed it over the back of a chair along with his hat and sat down in a chair. There he sat without saying a word.

I had classes to teach myself that year, and it was quite by chance that he found me at home that morning. I was a bit surprised—we usually didn't visit each other in the morning—but I knew him, after all, and thought I should let him take his time, then he would probably come out with what was on his mind.

He sat there for perhaps ten minutes. Without saying a word.

Then he took out his watch, looked at it and jumped up. "Oh, damn it, I'm supposed to be at school this minute! What the hell am I doing here with you? What the flaming, fucking—why do you have to live on the street I take to school anyway!"

And off he went.

He never talked about it afterward. But as I think back, it must have been just at the time when he was having that conflict with Indregård over the young girl.

Had he somewhere deep down meant to talk to me—perhaps ask my advice—however low an opinion he had of my intelligence? Because he did. But that went for everybody. "Sure, you're stupid!" as he said to me. "But you're not as stupid as my fellow students."

I don't know whether his subconscious wanted something from me that time. I only know that a few months later he came once and asked my advice— and paid no heed to it.

It was in the fall of the same year, an evening at the end of September.

That evening he was truly in a state of anguish and doubt. You could tell by just looking at him. His eyes were darker and more brooding than usual. But he wasn't the sort of man who came out with what was on his mind just like that.

"Come for a walk with me!" he said.

Why not? We went out. It was a fall evening, as I've said, and it was dark. He decided where we should walk, and I noticed that he chose the darkest streets. It suited him to walk in darkness that evening. Then he told me the story. He'd got a girl with child. A decent girl. A good girl. Intelligent too. Of good family and all. A bit of money as well. Not much, but something. "Hmm!"

He was in the habit of clearing his throat occasionally.

"But I don't love her," he said. "Not the least. Not in that way. It was she who wanted—that thing. The whole time. Hmm.

"I can get it fixed if I want to," he said. This came in a near mumble. We were in a very dark street just then, down by the Aker River somewhere.

So you can really arrange that sort of thing! I remember thinking. Why didn't I know that before!

I'd had a rough time of it myself that fall.

"If you can you should do it," I said. And I said more—something to the effect that it was a touchy business to get married while one was still a student. There was no telling how that might affect one's studies.

Marriage, it seemed to me—at that time—was like walking open-eyed through a prison gate into a dark cell where some danger or other awaited you. For life, I always thought. Just imagine—for life.

"And you don't even love her!" I said. "For God's sake, get it fixed! Remember—the alternative is for life!"

Said I.

"Hmm!" he said angrily in the darkness beside me. Not only angrily, by the way. Angrily and at the same time thoughtfully. When he spoke his voice seemed to come from far away, as if he spoke to me across a number of rooms—through open doors, one might say, or at any rate through doors that were ajar, but across a number of rooms. Dark rooms, empty or full of things I wasn't familiar with. Those rooms were always there between him and us, dark rooms he knew a little about but not all, and of which he was secretly afraid. He was afraid of the dark, the dark in himself. It was that dark, choked, faraway sound of his voice that gave me this image; and for the first time it struck me that I understood why he was so absent-minded, why he would be absorbed in his own thoughts and lose his way, why he was the way he was. I didn't understand it at all, of course. As little then as before or later. I don't even understand it today. It was just that at the moment I'd found an image that pleased me.

"We did it once before," he said. "We were together about a year ago. But then I broke up. Hmm! She has told me she's willing to do it this time too. But then it will be over between us."

I had an idea who it was now.

All right, I said. But since he didn't love her, he ought to put an end to it anyway, oughtn't he?

"You don't understand!" he mumbled in his choked voice—it sounded as if it were intended for howling or crying rather than speaking.

"You don't understand!" he mumbled again. And then he continued, in an even lower voice, with a sentence that I recognized, "When one has behaved like a bastard, one has to take the consequences."

I recognized that line of thinking, as I've said. He had voiced it before, and more than once. Oh yes, I'd seen him behaving brutally and harshly, and afterward I'd seen him full of remorse. It would come over him in spells. He had a Christian heart, if you like. He lost his faith but kept the sense of sin and guilt. He'd been a strong man, that father of his.

I couldn't help recalling, as I walked there beside him, the one time I'd seen him with his father down here, in Oslo. His father was an old man then, with white hair and beard, but with a pair of strong black eyes. He sat in his son's rented room, a black skullcap on his head. He was a handsome old man, with an air of dignity about him. His figure made one think of the ancient patriarchs, Abraham and Isaac. Well, Isaac of course was blind, but this one was not. His eyes took in everything, dwelling long on an empty bottle that stood in a corner of the room.

Hans Berg showed him throughout a certain taciturn reverence. And I thought, Where is your indignation now?

He walked beside me in the dark, muttering something that I wasn't able to make out. Nor do I think it was meant for me, he was really talking to himself.

"A time comes when one has to pay," he muttered, a little louder.

I spoke again. He listened to me awhile. Then he interrupted me, impatiently, "Of course, you're right, I too can see that. But the time comes, you know, when one has to pay for it."

He walked a few steps. Then he mumbled, "Being that she is a much better person than I..."

With that he clammed up like a hedgehog. Didn't say another word. I just heard a few mumbles and grunts.

He had turned along with me, and we were headed for our part of town again. We walked in silence through the streets. He left me only at my door.

"I think I'll do it!" he mumbled all of a sudden. Then he turned upon his heel and was off. I had no idea what it was he wanted to do.

But a few weeks later I knew. He got married. Abandoned his studies and moved away from Oslo, down to that small coastal town. There he got a job in the local secondary school.

He never completed his degree. He has been there since. He could have continued his studies. He said himself that she had some money. His professor said he was brilliant. I myself knew something about his ambition—it burst out of him like a cry now and then.

He gave up. Didn't make good, as they say. But he really didn't make good. "A poor teacher. Doesn't even bother to maintain discipline."—"Has become something of a small-town character."—"People laugh at him for his absent-mindedness. One day he came to school in scorching heat in the middle of June wearing his winter coat."

These are a few of the things I happen to have heard about him, from people who had been to that part of the country. I myself have met him only in passing once or twice during the last twenty years.

His departure for that small town gives the impression of an act of defiance, an attempt at some sort of revenge.

A revenge on whom, for what? After all, he became the butt of his own revenge! Well, yes, precisely. Because—and this is something else that I know—he hated himself with a terrible hatred.

He systematically made his life poorer, narrower, more troubled than it needed to be.

He wasn't happy down there. Not for a single day. He was just stuck there. In a job he hated and handled with minimum effort, no more. Had lost his drive—was *that* why? He was plagued by financial worries, by domestic worries—the child, a son, turned out rather badly and was sent to sea about the age of fifteen. He and his father couldn't live under the same roof.

There were a couple more children, I seem to remember.

And so, about a year ago, he joined this so-called "party." If I just could figure out why. I only know one thing: it's impossible, logically and intellectually impossible, that he can believe in that so-called gospel. He who had never belonged to any party, who said about every party program, "Away with it! I cannot stomach such highfalutin stuff!"

No, I can't figure him out. Unless his discontent, with himself and the whole world, had become so great that he was ready for anything, just to annoy himself and others.

76

*

Addition the following day:

Still, there may possibly be a certain advantage to writing things down. Suddenly late last night I happened to recall a little episode.

It was during that hike in the woods we took in the spring of 1920, when he told me the story about that Sunday he received a caning by his father.

We had pitched camp and I had lighted a fire to make coffee. It was late in the evening, but we had planned to walk until well into the night. The fire shone nicely against the dark background of the forest.

All of a sudden he came rushing up. He had a bunch of dry twigs in his arms and threw it all on the fire. "Hey!" he yelled—no half-choked mumble then. He rushed back into the woods and returned with a fresh armful of dry twigs. "Hey!" He flung it on the fire. The flames leaped up. Then he ran into the woods again. This time he returned with a big blown-down spruce, dried-up and full of twigs. "Hey!" He wanted to toss it onto the fire. But then I stopped him.

"Have you gone out of your mind!" I said.

It was truer than I realized. His eyes were wild, he was completely beside himself. I was stronger than he and pulled the trunk away from him.

"Do you want to start a forest fire?" I said.

I'd grabbed him quite hard. As I stood there, prepared for a fight, I saw that something was happening to him. He regained consciousness. How can I find the right words for it? It was as if a fire went out in his eyes, he faded, became tired, sort of withered. I recall the image that came to me as I stood there, that of a fire going out and ashes settling on the embers. All in a second.

"It was a good thing you stopped me!" he said. "Sometimes when I see fire I go off my head. Well, let's put the coffee kettle on."

This is what I picture to myself:

He married to expiate a sin—oh yes, he, the pagan, thought along Christian lines. But he did it also to avenge himself on fate, God, the world, himself. Or maybe the defiance came afterward: now he'd done what they wanted, and now the world, his wife, his children, society, his country and he himself— may he be busted, burned and boiled, debagged and consumed in hell— could stew in their own juice!

I've never met anybody who could curse the way he did. It was like opening the door to a furnace at white heat.

I think I know how things gradually turned out between him and his wife. She was just as dissatisfied as he was. Dissatisfied with all and everything— with the world, her husband, his job, their finances, everything. Not with herself though—that was the difference between the two of them. And so there they were, in the same room year after year, he taciturn and brooding but with blowups, she constantly carping, egging him on, her mouth full of venom and gall. There they sat scowling at each other, full of hate but bound to each other for life.

And then came his chance—*she* thought. Her jawing became worse than ever. "Here's your lucky break, if you don't make use of it, then…"—"If you can't understand even this much, then…"—"Oh, those men!"

Until he did what she wanted.

Maybe he believed himself in the lucky break. Getting to be principal, transfer to Oslo—what do I know?

And then it all came to nothing. Because the other teacher, the real go-getter, joined the Party like a shot.

So there he was.

To sell his birthright for a mess of pottage and then be cheated of the pottage.

What was he thinking?

Well, my friend had told me something about that, of course. But surely not all.

Hans Berg was not stupid, nor is he now, and he certainly knows at this moment that his future is dark as the night itself.

I don't think he only grieves over it. I think that when he let himself be persuaded by his wife—if that was how it happened—it was as usual with a double motive. If she was right, well, all the better. But if she was wrong and drove him into this devilment to no purpose, well, then she could stew in her own juice. And he could say, "Haw! Just what I thought! Just what I told her! But she…!"

But mostly, most of all, I believe he allowed his mind to be made up, not by his hatred of her, not even by his hatred of himself, but by his hatred of all the others, and of the path taken by all those others. If all the others wanted to go to heaven—well, then he preferred hell!

And then finally, like an irresistible, compelling power clean through all this: the fire, the blazing fire!

Yes, there must've been kindled an insane little fire inside him. Hey! Now it burns nicely! More twigs for the fire! Let the house burn! Let the forest burn! Let the country burn! Hey!

But he didn't assert himself. Took no part in any agitation, didn't misuse his position. Didn't make the most of this lucky break either, as his wife might say.

I believe he woke up one day and saw something. What, exactly, I don't know.

And then he just sat there in silence. One more time.

He sits there, I believe, somber, dark, brooding, absentminded. Curses now and then perhaps, conjuring up a red glow. And mumbles, with suppressed rage, "Now I can stew in my own juice!"

An Old Album

~~~~~~~~~~~~~~~~~~~~~~~

It turned out as I had already suspected. I wasn't able to solve the riddle of Hans Berg. It became apparent that I didn't know him well enough. I had to guess on a number of points, and more than once I had no basis even for my guesses, couldn't even grope my way but was up against a wall.

I didn't write down all I knew about him, not even most of it. I simply chose things I thought were important. But perhaps I made the wrong choices, perhaps I was groping in the dark. If I'd been wiser than I am, I might have chosen quite differently. Maybe the key to the man's secret is to be found in some trifling situation or sentence that passed me by. I don't know.

Still, I feel that what I've written down contains part of the answer to the riddle for anyone with eyes to see with. Maybe. I'm not sure even of that.

But to me this attempt has acquired another meaning. I can feel how that period twenty-odd years ago has in a strange way come alive in me again.

Figures are emerging from oblivion, faces are showing up. Some I'm glad to see, and I greet them as friends. Others—oh well.

That time, I'm convinced, was important to others as well as to me.

I realize that I'll continue to pry and ponder. I perceive a hope, which I myself know to be wild and witless: namely, that by pondering, probing, and prying into the past, I'll be better able to understand the present.

Yesterday I once again tidied my drawers and shelves. I've done so many times before, on days when I had a feeling that the place was getting too hot for me. Strange to say, each time I find something that may just as well be consigned to the flames. If things were to go wrong, there's no reason for letting them have more material than necessary, about myself and others.

At this time there is no particular danger afoot, as far as I know. I haven't the faintest idea why I suddenly was in such a hurry to tidy up.

But I did find something. On a shelf, at the very bottom, I came across a photo album. I no longer collect such things, and this one was old and dusty. It was from the years around 1920. I sat turning its pages awhile, and my thoughts were carried in a certain direction.

More than once during the last few days I've asked myself, What sort of person was I exactly around the age of twenty or twenty-two? What did I think, what did I feel, who was I? How did I appear to people around me? What did I look like? Well, this last question has just been answered in a way—there were several pictures of me in the album. They'd been made because—well, we exchanged photos, of course! That way I could also brush up on the looks of the young girls—on the photos, that is.

It's quite a strange business suddenly to come face to face with your own past.

Drowned in the river of oblivion—.

I had completely forgotten some of them. Who was *she*? What about *her*? What, where, and when?

The river of oblivion is a strange river. Sometimes it suddenly delivers up its dead, who may even be restored to life again for a little while.

Am I getting old and sentimental? Have I lowered my requirements? I sat for quite a while flipping a few pages of the album, back and forth, and as the past came alive I thought, God help me, that the girls were all very pretty.

Vintage 1920–21.

But if there was a year in which the young girls weren't pretty, I would like to know.

Well, that's all private and doesn't concern the matter in hand.

I noticed there was one—one in particular—I didn't have a picture of.

The photos of myself show a young man who—why, I can easily see the likeness to myself as I am even today. I assume that others too would be able to see the likeness and say—aha, a picture of N.N. when young.

I see a picture of a young man, very young, someone whose features haven't yet, so to speak, been developed by life. Soft lines, or no lines, where a grown man has angles and edges and wrinkles. Masses of superfluous hair on his head. (Ah, there envy's peeping out!) And then, well, then there is that vagueness, which fills me with rather mixed feelings. Which sometimes makes my flesh crawl—I can see in this face something I would call contemptible weakness. A weak mouth, weak eyes. Weakness, anxiety—not malice, not outright conceit either. I'm trying to find the right word—a sort of prolonged childishness. Not an entirely good thing. In a curious way, not seasoned enough. Oh well, the seasoning must have come with time. It's just that if a young man has somehow managed to carry with him into adolescence too much of his childish innocence and then for some reason gets seasoned too quickly, his innocence easily turns into its opposite—into an anxiety that calls itself wisdom but isn't ever that, a dread that calls itself detachment, a fear of new disappointments that calls itself knowledge of human nature and manifests itself as suspicion.

The weakness, the uncertainty, in this only half-finished face troubles me.

I can see now that, face to face with this fellow, a stronger, more resolute man might say to himself, Him I can use!

Why does it trouble me? Let's try to be honest as long as possible. It troubles me partly because in some way I still feel a sense of solidarity with this man, and because I know that weakness is weakness and that it inevitably gets a person mixed up in many stupid, awkward, embarrassing situations—as, in fact, it did. I see the weakness, remember the situations, feel ashamed and unhappy and want to groan with pain, as when we see a close friend disgrace himself and can do nothing to help him. Too late, too late...

But there is obviously something else and more. I look at that young, half-finished face, see the weakness that many, many must've seen and know in my heart: you don't see everything, not the whole weakness, not that part which you still carry inside you. Even now your face doubtless betrays, unbeknownst to yourself, open places, areas lying there without protection, naked to the eyes of those who are happily free of just those weaknesses. Even today, if a man like that looks at you, he knows, Him I can use!

One and all of my friends knew that about the young man.

And the women?

As an older man I can evaluate this young fellow to some degree. Despite my many obvious blind spots and the temporal distance that separates us. But I cannot see him with a woman's eyes. What was there about him that caused him partly to succeed, partly to fail? Well, his being a flop doesn't surprise me. I just remember and groan. But how about the rest? What did those wise, sharp women's eyes see in that young weakling? I wonder.

I ask myself, When, on the whole, do we men cease to have a certain attraction for the other sex? When you look around and see all the strange things that happen, you can only answer, Never.

But there are so many things that can make a woman resign herself to a man's company, even make her think she's fond of him, loves him, and so on. Reputation, money, power...

But that young man had no reputation, no money, no power. No prospects for any of those things either, no career like a beaten track ahead of him. If he was loved, one is tempted to say that it was for his own sake.

At times he was, and that is something of a puzzle. Honestly, I think I'm more of a man than that pale boy. But he was, in his weakness, his green youth, his poverty, his total lack of prospects, more loved (and hated), more sought after than.... Oh well. It's puzzling. It's unpleasant too, but first and foremost it's puzzling.

I happen to remember a little incident that occurred just before the war. I was hiking in Nordmarka one Sunday. I walked fast—it was in one of those periods when for some reason or other one has put on weight and gotten wise to it, somewhat belatedly, feels annoyed and tries to turn it around and, noticing that it won't turn around, does various things to make it turn around—eats a light breakfast, skips supper, goes on hikes to sweat it off....

I went hiking to sweat it off. I walked uphill from Voksenkollen, that long climb up toward the radio towers. There were many people ahead of me, I passed one after the other. One man walked a bit faster than the rest, but I caught up with him too. Then it turned out to be someone I knew, though quite superficially, a man about my own age.

"Out for a walk?" he said, falling into stride beside me.

I couldn't deny it.

"You're walking fast," he said.

I couldn't deny that either.

"Well, I suppose you're trying to get rid of a few pounds," he said.

I still couldn't deny it. And, sure enough, he was there for the same reason. Then he began to philosophize a bit, while we slogged our way up the hill in the scorching heat, past one couple after another, group after group of other perspiring hikers—the sun is strong on that hill, and there's a lot of dust in the air when it hasn't rained for some time.

"How strange," he said, "—strange when you come to think of it—that at one time it was quite unnecessary to worry about this business of one's weight. Now one must always worry about it—or pay attention to it at any rate."

There were several such things that made him wonder, he told me. Previously he'd never felt any desire to take a nap after dinner either—well, for that matter, it wasn't very much of a dinner to begin with. But now? As soon as he'd put away his dinner and smoked a cigarette or two, he was overcome by a nearly irresistible desire to take a little nap.

Several such things—for example, how one loved back then to roam the streets on a mere chance, hoping that something might *happen*—hours and hours every day. Nothing ever happened of course, or almost never. Or this oddity that one regarded almost all effort as fun—for example, to run a dozen miles of a summer evening to some place where there was a dance, although it was much more comfortable and pleasant to stay at home...

Ah, what a strange time youth was. And one of the strangest things was, as he'd said, that one could put away food in great quantities when one was hungry and food was to be had, and it didn't matter at all. Not in the least. But now! Now one had to watch out every hour of the day. If only one could figure out what the reason was!

At Tryvannet Tarn we went our separate ways.

At the very back of the album there are also some photos of my friends at that time. So we, too, traded photos? Of course, now I remember. We were so important, that was the reason. We were going to conquer the world, so it was crucial to trade photos. When each one of us someday reached the pinnacle of glory, he would remember all the others, still struggling down below. Perhaps he would send a rescue party to pick up one or two and offer them seats at his council table....

There are a good many photos here at the back. Some of those men are still my friends. Oh, heavens—is that how they looked? Sometimes I have to smile. Sometimes I laugh. But sometimes, too, my laughter stops rather abruptly.

So that's what he looked like, and that's what he was like. Sure, now I remember.

Innocent. Ah, how innocent!

Life has been quite rough on some of us, I'm afraid.

There are also some pictures of others, of people who are no longer my friends. Hans Berg...

Oh yes. So that was how he looked. I'd forgotten. That is, in those days I looked at him with the eyes of someone his own age and didn't see what I can see now—that he had a childish gaiety in his eyes, although he tried to look so grim and manly. I can also see something else. That—well, that he was still innocent. All hope was not yet lost. Not by far.

There are more. Edvard Skuggen—why in the world did he give me his photo? Of what use did he figure I could be to him?

But perhaps, for once, he was scattering presents right and left. I can see that the picture is from the year he received his university degree. Maybe he took a breather for a few days and decided to please his friends with a picture.

No, not he. Besides, he had no friends. But he was rightfully proud of his degree, and confident that he would go far in the world. Maybe he was thinking of the future.—Hello! This is *Dagbladet* calling. You knew the famous Edvard Skuggen at one time, didn't you? Tell me, do you have a picture of him as a young man?

In the picture he tries to smile, but that was a subject he hadn't studied at the university. It's a wolfish grin.

There's nothing childish or innocent in those hard eyes.

Why, here is Iver Tennfjord. Things are getting stranger by the minute. In full uniform and all. That photo must've cost him at least one krone.

But maybe he regarded it as a necessary public relations expense. Young women, some perhaps with money, often browsed in such books. And then they might ask, Well, who's that lieutenant? Iver Tennfjord? Does he live in town?

And there is Sverre Hamran, handsome, wrapped in thought, with that strange, dreamy look in his eyes—and already with an intimation of that subtle, understanding grumbler's smile which later etched itself into his face, a smile that by no means said, Go to hell, all of you! but rather, Lord, forgive them, for they know not what they do!

And there, if it isn't Heidenreich himself!

*

To the business in hand, you say. But that's just what I'm trying to do.

What sort of business—settling of accounts or whatever it should be called—is it anyway?

It concerns a group of young men and women who more or less accidentally roamed about together, crossed each other's paths, ran foul of one another, and were happy and unhappy together for a few years in their youth twenty or twenty-five years ago, and particularly during one summer and fall that I remember better than the rest. Since then they have been scattered to the four winds, and during the last few years things have taken an unhappy turn for some of them.

It's this group, to which I myself belong, that I'll try to take a closer look at. How life dealt with it—how life threw us all blindly into the world, leaving us to grope our way in the dark, mostly in circles naturally, but now and again offering us a moment of insight. Always when it was too late, of course, always when it was too late!

But first of all this story, or whatever I shall call it, was to be about—if I can bring it off, which is uncertain—about being young. No, I don't know whether I can bring it off. Whether I have the necessary qualifications. The first qualification is that one must no longer be quite young, for as long as one was young one found oneself in the midst of it and had only a faint notion, or none at all, about what one found oneself in the midst of.

But on the other hand one mustn't be really old either, not so old that that there is no spark of youth left.

I have a sort of feeling that if I could explain this one thing—what it means to be young, one's face turned toward the future, sniffing, scenting, hungering, yearning, dreaming, refined and crude, tender and brutal, sensitive and coarse, touchy and ruthless, and longing, longing, while being pinned between forces and powers one cannot understand, see through or master, not even suspecting they're there most of the time, because one has lived under the pressure of them from as far back as one can remember, so that one knows nothing but that pressure, those fences, that wall, which one nevertheless bangs one's head against and then again bangs one's head against until the blood flows—if only I could explain this, then most of the other things would sort themselves out, clear up on their own, so to speak.

Even those among us who later became traitors would find their niche, fall into place, so that we could clearly see: It was at such and such a time, at such and such a place, that they received the hurt which made them warped, one-eyed, blind, so that they swerved off course, more and more, till they ended up where they are now.

Gallery of the Damned

~~~~~~~~~~~~~~~~~~~~~~~~

More than once I've asked myself, Was there a higher percentage of future traitors in the circles in which I moved than in most other circles? I've tried to figure out how many people I know, but that is an impossible task. Then I've considered how many traitors I've known personally, and I get a feeling that the percentage is much too high. *One* percent of the Norwegian people are traitors, we claim. But the percentage for the circles I know comes out decidedly higher. That's my opinion anyway.*

But of one thing I'm certain: the percentage that came from the handful of relatively small circles to which I belonged during my student days is much too high.

Obviously I can't say exactly how many students I associated with at the time, during 1920–1921. But it cannot possibly have been much more than a hundred. Seven turned traitor. With Hans Berg the number is eight.

There must accordingly have been special forces at work in those circles. Which? It's important to find the answer to that.

There were several circles, differing from one another in many ways. But they did have something in common. Almost all the students I associated with were from out of town—from all around the country. Almost all were poor. Most of them were lonely. Some of them were lonely beyond words. They had lost the world of their childhood and hadn't found a new one. I know that, when they sat in their wretched little rooms in the evening, loneliness occasionally howled around them like an ice-cold wind from the black void of space.

Some of them were homesick, others hated the very thought of going home. But most of them never adjusted to Oslo, this hard city which has always turned a cold shoulder to all those droll students shuffling about the streets, wearing the seats of their trousers shiny in the reading rooms and standing in line in front of the cheapest restaurants.

---

* Later note: The allegation about that one percent turned out to be a—necessary—propaganda lie. It was two percent.

The country's future professionals? To which this city of big merchants reacts with, Oh, go to hell!

It was in those days when I wandered about hungry in Kristiania, that strange city which no one leaves before it has set its mark upon him...

These words were written in his youth by a man who later turned traitor. The city has changed its name since, but not its character.

Still, that cannot be a sufficient explanation. Many have gone hungry in this country. Many have been lonely. Few became traitors.

Let me not make myself more stupid than I am, even if we are at war.

I know that there are thousands of different forms of treason and that the motives may run into thousands.

I know that many things will seem different after the lapse of a few years (but after two thousand years Judas is still Judas).

I know that ideologies have partly taken over the role once played by national frontiers. And I know it's being said once again, as so often before: Everything is in flux, the old is no more, the new isn't yet here, we live in chaos.

Some traitors can doubtless find a philosophical defense for their position. After all, every position can be defended philosophically, it is simply a matter of providing for a suitable logical error in one's premises.

We shared the ideals of the aggressor, some will say—in more cautious words, of course.

What was it that drove them to choose such an ideal for themselves?

We were driven by religious faith...

How could they take refuge in such a dark religion?

No, I accept the word treason, knowing full well that it doesn't explain anything and that, like a too big gown, it covers all too many things. The word tells us, at any rate, that these people had become strangers to those nearest and dearest to them.

How and why?

I think I'll have to take a closer look at those seven men.

I used to talk with them, sat with them in our cheap restaurants, quarreled with them, laughed at them. I went on the spree with a few of them, and I've walked the streets with one, hungrily sniffing around for adventure. Three or four I didn't like very much, but one I thought a lot of. We used to laugh at a couple of them in our circle, we thought they were funny.

And now they are damned. That's how I feel, and I think they feel that way themselves. God knows, the rest of us aren't exactly in heaven either at the moment. But when I think of those seven it's like sitting on the edge of the earth looking down into hell. That's where they are—bowing and scraping, licking the dust before their masters, kowtowing to them and turning themselves into doormats; or they are henchmen during the interrogations and the tortures, holding out leg clamps, testicle clamps, and red-hot needles.

Let us look at them one by one.

Lars Flaten and Iver Tennfjord went to the military academy. Then they became officers. Later on both assisted the enemy—Iver Tennfjord straight-away, Lars Flaten after half a year. Iver Tennfjord is suspected of having been a spy. I think he was. Someone who knew him intimately said about him once—and this was before he turned traitor, "He was born too far north. He should've been born in one of the Mediterranean countries, where they have lots of tourists. There he could've stood before the door to his house and sold tickets of admission to his mother."

Lars Flaten was from Toten. He was big and broad and strong, and incredibly simple-minded. He never understood a joke, but he laughed readily and often, and sometimes in such wrong places that silence fell around him. It happened that girls sought him out—what with the uniform and one thing and another. But they quickly abandoned him again, as if they had been burned. I think he bored them to death in no time.

"What do you say to your girls?" he asked me once.

I often found it difficult to talk to girls myself and had no prescription to offer him.

"It depends," I said.

"Yes," he said. "But what do you say?"

I suspect he wanted a jingle. He was good at learning by rote.

His schoolmates at the military academy used to tease him. Once they had led him to believe there existed a Russian cheese called Raskolnikov, which made you so spry—evidently you didn't have to talk to the girls at all if you'd eaten some of that cheese. For several days he went from one shop to another asking for Raskolnikov cheese.

When he tried to think, as it were, he would make the most awful faces. He seemed to believe it might help. Alas, it did not.

Once he was discussing something or other with Hans Berg. Near despair in the end, Hans Berg said, coarsely and brutally, "Tell me, does it hurt to be that stupid?"

I'd lost sight of him long ago—he was not the kind of person one sought out. Then I heard he had crossed over.

Perhaps it had hurt quite a bit nonetheless to be so stupid. During all those years he'd merely been tolerated wherever he went.

I've thought to myself that perhaps the Nazis were friendly toward him. That friendliness was more than his system could handle.

*

Iver Tennfjord was a different sort. From West Norway, short and dark, industrious, rather taciturn, good in school. He was ambitious and wanted to get on the General Staff.

But he lacked the ability to please. It might have something to do with the fact that he was so incredibly stingy. It was like a disease with him. He was no poorer than the rest of us, but I don't believe a day passed without his dodging payment of ten or twenty Øre, which the rest of us had to pick up. It might be a trolley ticket or a pair of shoe laces, or half a cup of coffee at one of our dismal temperance cafés. He'd left his money at home, or had a too large bill that he was loath to break. We would get our money back the next day.

He was a stickler for order. I believe he collected that money in a separate piggy bank.

He begrudged himself food, and once or twice he took sick for that reason.

He told me once with a certain admiration about a farmer's wife in his native parish who sat at her loom all winter on her bare bottom. To save her skirt. She froze herself sick.

Iver Tennfjord said, "She went too far. She could've lighted the fire."

Iver Tennfjord was never together with girls. Not that he had anything against them. But they were expensive—a piece of pastry in a tearoom perhaps. And besides it was a waste of energy, he thought. "A man should hold on to what he's got," he said.

But at the same time he was looking around for a wealthy wife. "An officer should marry wealth," he said. "That's his duty to the fatherland."

He proposed to more than one. He was rather easy to please, by the way. A realist after a fashion, he understood that the very wealthiest were not for him. And besides he came from a poor West Country parish. Fifty thousand was wealth to him. A couple of the girls told me about it afterward; they didn't think it was much of a secret, they said, for it wasn't a real proposal, it was an offer of a deal with a supplemental clause—"of course I'll love you," as he said.

But he couldn't find a girl who was willing to devote her life to the fatherland. He's still a bachelor, and I believe he has held on to what he's got to this very day.

Once he made one hundred kroner in a rather peculiar way. He was going home to the West Country and biked the distance in order to save the train fare. He was a lieutenant then, and possibly the only lieutenant in Norway who was able to save on his measly salary. One evening on the trip he had to put up at a hotel. He took the cheapest room they had.

He ran across some people who were staying at the hotel. One of them was a salmon fisherman. They were drinking in one of the rooms. Little by little the others discovered what sort of person he was. Eventually the fisherman offered him a hundred kroner if he dared to strip then and there and walk stark naked down the corridor to his room. A hundred kroner was a lot of money. Iver Tennfjord took him up on it. "I can pretend that I'm sleep-walking," he said.

Off he went, while they stood in the doorway to check on him. It turned out well for a while, but then the proprietor came up the stairs.

"I'm walking in my sleep!" said Iver Tennfjord quickly.

He got his hundred kroner, but was forced to leave the hotel.

Edvard Skuggen was a few years older than I. He's now pushing fifty. He has done well, is the head of a junior college and a Nazi big shot. It's said that when Quisling reshuffled his cabinet, he was convinced he would get a post. But it didn't happen, and he went to bed in a pique.

That it didn't happen, it's said again, was not because the man was incompetent. It was because nobody liked him, not even in those circles. No one has ever liked him, with one exception—himself.

I think he is the most bald-faced careerist I've ever known. His eyes narrowed with passion whenever he saw a chance for his own advantage. It never occurred to him that others might take it amiss if he pushed them aside. Good heavens, he just wanted to get ahead, after all!

He had a good head on his shoulders, as the phrase goes, but we all know how little such an expression says about a man. It's important for a lumber jack to have a sharp ax, but it's also important whether he uses it to cut down trees or to hit somebody on the head with, or perhaps cut himself in the foot.

Edvard Skuggen had an aptitude for absorbing knowledge. He was a philologist and took his degree with honors. He married, while still a student, a teacher who could support him. She looked like a rake. Thin as a stick, and with a big, broad row of upper teeth. Whether *she* liked him, I don't know. But she did get married.

He sailed through his studies slick as a whistle. Never wasted an hour or a krone on nonsense, as he called it, never went to the theater, never read a book for amusement. Amusement, what was that? His refrain was, "Does that sort of thing really pay?"

Iver Tennfjord and Edvard Skuggen came from the same stifling West Country parish. Now and then they would tell little tales about each other. Either of them could see something of the parish reflected in the other. Not in himself.

From Iver Tennfjord I heard a little about Edvard Skuggen's childhood.

He came from a fishing family (Iver Tennfjord's father was a teacher). His father was lost at sea. His mother was left with four minor children.

She got involved with the skipper of a sloop who dropped by the little fjord a few times each year. He probably helped her some, with money and other things.

The religious bigots in the village wouldn't put up with this relationship. They threatened her. Everyone knew that the skipper was married in his own part of the country. But she didn't give him up. Maybe she couldn't do without his help—or perhaps she loved him?

They prayed for her in church. The parson belonged to the crack-brained sort.

That she couldn't take. She drowned herself. The children became wards of the parish.

That people from the village got together and paid for Edvard's secondary education, may have been meant as a kind of indulgence.

He himself never uttered a word about his childhood.

But he didn't seem to bear any grudges against the parish. Maybe he thought his mother had followed a wrong economic policy. Something *he* would certainly never do.

He was strong in his own way. He could make you shudder—there was a chilly air about him.

He made a good career for himself, in the gradual way the Norwegian school system allows. But for some reason or other that wasn't enough for him. Suddenly he wanted to be a politician.

There he came up against an opposition he could never understand. He kept at it but got nowhere. It's not easy for a man whom nobody likes to succeed in politics.

At first he was a Liberal and a proponent of New Norwegian. Later he became a Laborite and ditto. Thereafter a member of the Farmers' Party and ditto. Finally he became a Communist, while remaining ditto. All along a proponent of New Norwegian. Then came the Occupation and he joined Quisling's party, while still sticking by New Norwegian.

What he wanted was to become a member of the Storting. But he wasn't even elected to a township board.

He is at present the head of a junior college and holds a number of offices of trust. He has started backtracking—never really belonged to that movement, you know, but in order that the school be left in peace and so on...

There's only one thing about him that's unclear. When he continued to be an adherent of New Norwegian straight through all vicissitudes, was it because he really believed in something, or had he discovered that for a Norwegian politician it always paid to be in favor of New Norwegian?

He always spent his summer vacations in his native village. Then he went to call on all those who had helped to pay his way and was systematically agreeable.

Did he feel a sort of gratitude toward those people, or did he feel bound to show them what a big shot he'd become?

He'd long ago repaid the debt he owed for his education—most of it before he took his university degree. "It pays to be free from debt," as he used to say.

Now he no longer visits his native village. The summer after he'd become a Nazi they all turned their backs on him.

Fate decreed that he and Iver Tennfjord were the only Nazis from that parish.

"There you can see what happens when you help young people to get an education," said the poor fisher folk.

Ole Gundersen took his law degree but never used it for anything. He went into journalism. This was partly due to the fact that he got married so early and needed a larger income than a law school graduate could expect right away. And that he married was due to his being so plain and clumsy. He couldn't get a girl in any other way.

He never realized this himself, thinking it was as it should be. The girl he married was anything but pretty, besides being quick-tempered and morbidly ambitious. He thought that this also was as it should be, figuring that all women were like that. He loved her, and overturned her chair or spilled coffee on her in his amorous ardor.

He was incredibly clumsy. Though not particularly big, he managed to give the impression of a mountain troll. His face was warped and crooked, and he couldn't control his body. He was the sort of person who constantly falls all over himself, pulls the tablecloth along with him, forgets to fix his clothes, upsets flower vases and steps on the tail of his landlady's Angora cat. He was prey to the oddest mishaps too—he was once attacked by a rabbit and bitten till the blood came.

His wife was terribly annoyed by him. He perspired and suffered when she fussed and fumed and slandered him in the presence of others. It happened he would jump up and run out, falling all over himself. He had to run to put the calamity behind him. But he always came back after an hour or so, having discovered it was all his fault, and he apologized profusely. His apology was accepted. "He's so stupid," she said, by way of an excuse. "He can't help it."

He thought that strong feelings were like that.

He was the center of the world. Oh well, I suppose all of us felt now and then that we were the center of the world at that time. But Ole Gundersen *was* the center of the world. The sun and the moon and the stars bowed down to him, as to the young Joseph. He saw this but seldom talked about it, and only to his closest friends. And even when he told them, he was rather embarrassed. He realized, in his deep earnestness, that it might appear ridiculous.

He did tell me about it. I was a friend of his in those early years. He was actually a kind and touching fellow at that time, not by any means simply ungifted.

His dream of glory had arisen, as far as I could make out, from the unhappiness he felt because of his impossible body. He told me, in all innocence, about the first time he discovered his true self, as he called it.

His mother was baking bread in the kitchen, and beside the dough stood a wooden tub with flour. Ole wasn't even supposed to be there, and yet he managed to put his foot into the flour tub. It was after this incident, having crept into a dark corner in the attic, that he realized this body of his wasn't really *him*. He himself, the true Ole Gundersen, was wholly different, the opposite in fact. He was harmonious, handsome, elegant, swift and sure of foot. Indeed, when all was said and done, he had wings, like a god!

As the years went by he'd built up this other person in every detail. Finally he became so grand that the splendor of his person was reflected back all the way to his starting point. When I came to know Ole Gundersen he no longer thought of himself as plain, while realizing no doubt that he wasn't handsome in the banal sense of the word. Still, this outer shell did contain the true Ole Gundersen, thereby acquiring a fresh, deep, singular beauty.

That sort of thing could become somewhat wearisome.

But it was his wife who made his social life impossible. She was clearly an unhappy woman, but her unhappiness manifested itself in strange ways. She demanded that her husband's friends make shameless propositions to her which she could turn down—for she was faithful, yes sirree! If they did, she showered them with contempt. If they did not, she made them the objects of her hate.

Luckily—or unluckily—he never saw through her.

In this way he lost his close friends one by one as the years went by. But he also lost his jobs.

His wife, as it happened, had gradually become ambitious on his behalf. She had originally intended to become a journalist herself, and had prepared herself for it by wearing bobbed hair with bangs and by washing herself a bit less than others. But instead she got married.

And it must be obvious that she, who was born nothing less than a Miss

Lunde from Hedemarken, had to have an important man for a husband. Her husband *was* an important man.

He was never treated according to his merit.

Having gotten this far, she would go to the editorial office at certain intervals and abuse the editor. Ole Gundersen was a true chevalier and stood up for her. An editor gets tired of such things in the long run. Ole Gundersen had to change from one paper to another several times. In the end he was without a paper and had to support himself as a free lance. But Norway is hard on free-lancing intellectuals. Gundersen fell on hard times, he had to do lots of hackwork at poor pay. He translated books at starvation wages, wrote articles east and west for wretched fees, and all his great plans drifted further and further toward the horizon—the novels and plays he was to write, the great newspaper he wanted to start, the new spiritual rebirth he was going to bring about.

Oh, I almost forgot to mention that: he was going to accomplish a spiritual rebirth in Norway. What its nature would be and how it was to take place, hadn't been planned in detail. Programs weren't all that important, as he said. But there *was* going to be a rebirth.

That was in his younger, happier days. Gradually this rebirth idea moved far out toward the horizon. Indeed, more and more things suggested that the whole nation was doomed.

There was nothing but coteries, Camorras, corruption and gangsterdom. It almost sounded as if a nation-wide conspiracy had been created in order to keep Ole Gundersen down.

His wife thought the same. As they became more and more lonely and everything went more and more badly, she became more and more ambitious on his behalf. "Ole Gundersen, remember you are a genius!" she would say. Finally she said it every day. On such solemn occasions she always used his full name.

When she called him an idiot, she only used his first name.

To soothe her agitated nerves she began to drink bock beer and eventually grew fairly heavy and bloated. He thought she was beautiful. His and her life was a great tragedy.

When the Occupation came he didn't cross over right away. He took a few months to think it over. There were several things in Hitler's and Quisling's program that he couldn't agree with offhand. There was also something about the way certain people behaved.

Verily, he wrestled like Jacob with his God, a wrestling bout in several rounds. But he emerged a victor. Programs weren't that important. The new order *was* the rebirth he had dreamed of—or could become so with his help.

Yes, God only knew if *that* wasn't the deepest meaning of this whole violent period—to allow him at last to try his wings, give him a platform, a jump-off for that global rebirth whose prophet he now more than ever felt called upon to be. Why, it was for his sake that the whole show was staged! God had tried him hard and let him wait a long time. But now the fullness of time had come!

He crossed over.

And then nothing more happened, not really. He'd thought it over for too long, or whatever it was. Had wrestled too long with his God. The editor-in-chief post he thought he was the obvious choice for was given to someone else. The next editor-in-chief post too. The post of cultural editor too.

His situation was about the same as before. He had to write articles at piecework rates, to translate novels at a measly pay per signature. His articles got scrapped just about the same as before. Ideologically unsound! it was said. Those were some articles about the rebirth.

If anything, the tragedy was greater than ever. Here fate, the laws of nature, the Lord God himself had created a revolution and a world war just to give *him* a chance—only to be cheated of the result.

Recently, after beginning to backtrack, he told his last friend, "Previously my life resembled a play by Ibsen. Now it is like a tragedy by Shakespeare."

Sverre Hamran turned traitor because he loved his country so dearly.

Or was it a particular village that he loved?

He and I went to school together. We were the same age, but he was in the parallel class.

Our clothes had been cut by rural tailors. They looked as if they'd been shaped with an ax and sewn together with shoemaker's thread. The girls nudged each other and snickered at us in the street, "Look at those country bumpkins!"

They snickered most at Sverre Hamran. The rest of us—well, we didn't see that there was anything wrong with our clothes, we weren't accustomed to any other clothes. But his clothes were several notches worse than ours. That village must've had a hell of a tailor. Maybe he was tailor and shoemaker both, for Sverre Hamran's boots were as quaint as his clothes. They were much too big for him—wide, flat snowshoes, good for someone walking in a swamp.

Later—several years later—when he could afford to buy himself cheap ready-made clothes in town, he showed himself to be an exceptionally well-proportioned and handsome fellow.

There was something about his dialect too. He was from up north, somewhere in Møre. At any rate, he had an uncommonly distinctive dialect, and he used it to the full. A couple of the teachers thought it was funny. Many pupils too.

He pretended not to notice. A faint smile would form on his lips, that was all. Little by little they put up with his countrified language.

One day—we'd gotten to be students then—we happened to be standing in the street together. An old classmate of his came along, nodded and went on. Sverre Hamran turned a little paler, and a sort of mild look appeared on his face. His strange smile, which was almost always there, like a faint ripple on a calm lake, grew slightly more noticeable. He followed the fellow with his eyes a long time.

The one who had walked by was nothing to brag about.

"It looked as if you couldn't take your eyes off him," I said.

"Yeah, well. He used to make so much fun of my dialect at one time, in high school. Perhaps one shouldn't remember such things."

He was still speaking his dialect. I won't try to reproduce it.

By the way, on the same occasion he asked me a curious question. "Could you die for a cause?" he said.

The question hit me with a bang. We must've been talking about something or other that put his thoughts on the track. I have no idea what it could've been. I had no idea then either. We were, in fact, discussing something in connection with Latin, which we were both studying just then.

I said, somewhat taken aback, that it probably depended on what kind of cause it was. And what kind of situation. I for my part would prefer to live.

"But don't you see," he said, "that dying for a cause—the right cause—*is* to live! It's the pinnacle of life!"

I thought that was all very fine. A little too fine for me.

"Those who are willing to die for a cause shall carry the day!" he said.

I had an inkling of which cause *he* probably had in mind. He was the most fanatic New Norwegian fan I knew.

I saw him very rarely. He was studying philology, I myself law. We were sort of distant friends, nothing more. He doubtless found me uninteresting, I found him difficult. That smile of his was also rather bothersome. It was now a permanent fixture on his face. An attractive smile, I'll grant that. But it was so friendly, somehow. Perhaps not exactly affectionate, rather mildly compassionate. He reminded me of a picture I'd seen of Saint Sebastian, gently smiling, his body pierced by arrows.

I thought sometimes, "Is he laughing at me?"

The years went by. He finished his studies eventually, and I knew he was a substitute teacher at various schools. He was married to a girl from his native parish. Her I never saw. I asked him about her once when we met at the theater.

"Oh, she doesn't go out very much in this town," he said.

His smile became somewhat more marked when he said *this town*.

Later I learned that she kept herself in their tiny apartment as in a fortress. He even did the shopping for her. She was to be spared walking about alone in enemy country, where they laughed at her dialect.

I also learned the reason why he didn't apply for a job away from the city: he was working on a research project.

He even went abroad once, I heard. Then he must've lived on dry bread for a long time. He went without a fellowship; he had applied for one but been refused.

He went to the Mediterranean countries. He'd learned Spanish and Italian on his own.

In the meantime one of his teachers from secondary school had become a university professor, in his major subject at that; he was a member of the fellowship committee. But he didn't believe in Sverre Hamran's research. Nothing but chauvinism, he's supposed to have remarked. I heard all this quite a while later.

Anyway, the result was a doctoral dissertation—which was rejected. I believe he tried to prove that Christopher Columbus was a Norwegian. Well, Magellan too, apparently. All the great seafarers. God only knows whether they didn't hail from that Møre hamlet of his, every one of them. In any case, he apparently claimed it was people from up there who had discovered Greenland and Vinland, and that most of the Viking expeditions, including the greatest ones, those that had sailed around all Europe, had started from there. Even that every royal family in Europe, all things considered, descended from there—via Rollo, perhaps. And his native village had been in secret communication with Vinland for hundreds of years—via the Faeroe Islands and Ireland, I think. But I'm not certain of any of this, I heard it by chance from another philologist, who thought it was terribly amusing. The dissertation had been flatly rejected, as I've said. Ravings. Feverish dreams of a sick brain. Something like that.

He now applied for a job away from Oslo. That didn't go so well either, apparently. The news of such a rejected dissertation leaks out, it's not exactly a recommendation. Anyway, he was gone, wherever he might have buried himself.

In recent years one could see his name in connection with the language battle. There was a great deal of argument just before the war about modifying

New Norwegian in the direction of East Norwegian speech—out with the *i*-endings of feminine nouns, in with the *a*-endings, moving it closer to the spoken language of the more open East Country, and so forth.

Next to religion, there is, as we know, nothing that sends Norwegians into such a towering rage with one another as the language question. If the same laws obtained as in ancient Iceland, many would've been killed in that battle. New Norwegian enthusiasts are like Communists and fanatic Christians: while they despise the large masses of people who pay no attention to them, they *hate* those who almost agree with them, or disagree on a point or two—the virgin birth, everlasting hell, Trotsky, *i*- or *a*-endings of nouns.

Sverre Hamran wanted *i*-endings. He took part in a couple of newspaper controversies on this question. He wanted *i*-endings with an ardor which made me recall the question he'd put to me once—whether I was willing to die for a cause.

Those brief contributions he wrote were imbued with a smoldering hatred. There was certainly no gentle Saint Sebastian smile in them. He waged the Lord's war for the most sacred thing of all—the *i*-endings of his native village. *Bygdi* was the right form, not *bygda*.

Then I met him again in the late fall of 1940.

"So, you're in town?" I said.

Oh yes, he was in town.

We exchanged a few more words which I don't recall. Then I asked him what he thought of the news reports from London.

His gentle saint's smile deepened a little. He looked me squarely in the eye, and for once I understood that it was I he was smiling at.

"I don't listen to the radio," he said.

I didn't grasp what he meant but forbore asking. That *he* should have crossed over struck me as the most unthinkable ever.

But that was just what he had done. I learned about it a few weeks later.

When the so-called minister of culture and propaganda in Quisling's administration took over his position, he gave a speech in which he said the time had come to stop all this New Norwegian nonsense. But already a few weeks later he had trimmed his sails to the wind and made a complete turnabout. New Norwegian would be restored to great honor. And he didn't even throw over the *i*-ending.

It was a speech that had the sole purpose of tricking the fans of New Norwegian. All in all it did not succeed. But Sverre Hamran crossed over.

He sold his country for a letter and, in doing so, had circumnavigated the globe following his own compass, like one of the great seafarers.

I believe he's right now sitting in some office down in the Ministry, writing *i*'s. Lots of *i*'s.

Is he smiling as he does so?

Karsten Haugen was the son of a sheriff somewhere up in the Gudbrandsdal valley. He majored in philology but abandoned his studies when he discovered that he had talent.

I'm not the right person to judge that talent of his. At any rate, he achieved a sort of breakthrough a few years before the war by a play about piety and original sin. Afterward he received a large fellowship, on which he went to Germany and Italy. That was in 1937.

He came back full of enthusiasm and wrote a couple of articles about his impressions. He was no politician, but down there *big things* were transpiring. Down there they had *faith,* they had *style,* and they had youth. Just to see them marching! And still without taking up a political position (evidently that was beneath the dignity of an aesthete), he felt bound to say that anyone who'd seen and heard Mussolini, *Il Duce,* speaking from his balcony above Piazza Venezia had experienced something he wouldn't easily forget. And anyone who'd heard Hitler, that former painter's apprentice, speaking to a hundred thousand people on the fairground in Nürnberg had known real thunder and lightning.

A number of people were furious about those articles. We who had known him in the old days reacted more calmly. We'd known from the beginning that his instincts were rather queer. You noticed it the moment he entered the room—that tall, slightly stooped figure, those shifty eyes, that pale face with pouches under the eyes and pendulous cheeks, those moist hands; they were always wet, as if he'd dipped them in sticky, lukewarm water.

As far as I know he was not a practicing homosexual. At any rate he had a number of girl friends over the years. But—well, his instincts were odd. He was always so inordinately impressed by power and pomp. His knees became wobbly at the sight of a military parade, he swooned with delight over eloquent table thumpings, magnified by loudspeakers and followed by a brass band's blare—ta-rah, ta-rah. He admired strong men of every ilk and was a passionate spectator at boxing matches.

But there must also have been something in him that protested against these inclinations. He loved to run down people he generally admired. He carried this to the point of a fine art. He preferred to run down people who were in the same room, and his malice was as a rule formed as a sort of eulogy, but with a few little words slipped in here and there which twisted the sense. If the person in question approached he greeted him effusively, often quoting some of the things he'd just been saying. Stripped of the subordinate clauses, it was fulsome flattery. On such occasions he looked out of both corners of his eyes simultaneously, awaiting applause from both sides.

It was unavoidable that he should occasionally be caught at this double game. Then he collapsed immediately. Then he would come out with such declarations of love and such inspired expressions of admiration that no scald at an Old Norwegian court could have done better.

It was these tendencies of his that made some of us eventually prefer circles to which he didn't belong. They were the same tendencies that caused us not to be greatly surprised by those articles.

At the same time there was no question at all that, if by chance he'd gone to Moscow instead of to Nürnberg and had an opportunity to see the First of May parade in Red Square, he would if anything have been even more enthusiastic.

Because he was really a radical. Non-political, but a radical. First of all, the Norwegian literary tradition was distinctly radical—Wergeland and all that, Vinje and Fjørtoft and all that, to make a long story short. But secondly, a liberated, a truly liberated man was after all instinctively radical, wasn't he? Sympathized with the oppressed and so on, at least in principle. Supported revolution in theory. Even though as a man of intellect one naturally agreed with Ibsen when he wrote,

> Until then I sit and wait,
> wearing gloves of the finest make...

How strange that a sheriff from one of our inland valleys, a real square, should have begotten a thing like that.

When he noticed that his articles weren't a success, he withdrew, somewhat bewildered. I beg your pardon? Was there no longer freedom of thought in this country? But freedom of thought or not, he preferred to be popular and wrote a couple of supplemental articles where he spoke ironically about many things in the dictatorship countries. The articles were written in a light tone, which rose to pathos, however, when he touched on the lack of freedom of thought in those great but in many ways so unfortunate countries. The Jews' silent tears behind drawn blinds must tug at the heartstrings of any sensitive person.

Those articles partly restored his popularity. And Karsten Haugen would most likely have had a steadily advancing career, with some alternation of sun and clouds, if April 9, 1940 had not arrived.

The Occupation jolted him out of a number of agreeable habits. The war in Norway annoyed him, even though he went along in principle. Of course we must defend ourselves; but what was the use, having neglected our defense for so many years?

Much worse was the fact that it became so difficult to get advances from publishers, newspapers and magazines. Didn't anyone these days think of *culture*?

At the same time the sight of the marching columns of Germans had its effect on him, slow but sure. Knees trembling, he made his choice in the fall of 1940. He became one of the court poets of the new order.

He ran down his new masters almost from the very first day. He sought out the men in the government that he knew were good Norwegians, that he knew were busy sabotaging—stashing away documents, copying in secret, burning things if they could. They had to put up with him, of course. He told them amusing tales about the latter-day greats.

But he groveled before them in the newspaper. It was difficult to read those articles without imagining the small additions he would've made if he were talking.

Not since Saint Olav laid down his pen—and he never wrote a word, unfortunately—had there been anything to match Quisling's wretched style in Norway.

At the moment he's backtracking at rushing speed. For God's sake, people haven't taken his little blunder seriously, have they? He, a poet... A poet is subject to so many moods. And besides, if he hadn't done it, someone else would. In reality, it was from a sort of sympathy with the inarticulate aspect of this new movement that he... He'd thought that it must, after all, be receptive to a certain culture. To a certain refinement. But unfortunately, in that he'd been mistaken, which he himself was the first to discover and the first to admit. A blunder, as stated. But now, there he was, and... It hadn't been very easy to manage, among other things financially. Anyway, he wanted everyone to know that he'd *never* belonged in earnest to that—those... Never! Never for a moment!

Ah!

And so, at last, we've come to Carl Heidenreich.

I don't quite know why I feel he's the worst of them all. But yes, I think I do know.

Those others—well, anyone can see there was something fundamentally wrong with all of them.

A couple of them were greedy to the verge of insanity. When a tidbit was dangled in front of their noses, it was more than flesh and blood could take.

One went to hell driven by a fixed idea, another by a self-delusion that shattered him, a third by instincts gone astray, a fourth by a stupidity passing all understanding.

And all suffered from a loneliness so great that they couldn't endure it. A person can be so afraid of the dark that he's grateful for the company of a ghost.

But Carl Heidenreich has no such excuse. A physician in a small town—a quite capable physician too, with a good practice and a nice income, according to my informant. Married, with an attractive, very likable wife, according to the same source. Children too, apparently. A well-situated man, and quite talented. Normal, judging by outward appearances. What on earth can have driven him to break out and prey upon his own people?

I haven't seen him in over twenty years. But I think I know.

The man was cold. He was rational to the point of idiocy. He thought all other people were mushheads. For lack of rationality, all others let themselves be guided by their so-called feelings. But not he. To him life was a calculus, a question of practical advantage. He chose, as he said, to study medicine as a necessary evil, a means of making good money. And he did eventually make good money, in that small town of his. Then came the war and the Occupation, that sickening initial period when all sensible people figured that the Germans were bound to win. He was doubtless one of the first people in town to figure that out. And since he'd never given a thought to anything but that which was worth his while, worth his while in a practical sense, that is, he crossed over—with a light regret, I dare say, but first of all with a supercilious, conceited smile and a compassionate thought for all those hopeless mushheads who either didn't want to or just couldn't understand—to the devil.

He's no problem. And now that he cannot help seeing that he has made a miscalculation and that all those stupid people were wiser than he was, now he's *backtracking* naturally—I don't need to have heard anything to know that. And fretting and pondering. Pondering how he can unsay all the things he has said, undo all the things he has done. And asking himself over and over again, How can I get off scotfree?

The only thing he doesn't ask himself is, Who am I, that I was capable of doing such a thing?

No, Carl Heidenreich is no problem.

Is he not a problem?

It's a riddle anyway, how a man can go so completely to hell that he is no longer a problem.

If a person's actions appear to be perfectly simple and obvious, be on your guard; we human beings are not as simple as all that.

The truth, my dear Watson, is that you know far too little about these people.

How about Lars Flaten? He'd managed to get married at last, that much is certain. So, maybe he learned a jingle finally? Or maybe he met someone who knew a jingle herself?

Was she the one who pushed him over the brink?

You have no idea.

If Iver Tennfjord became a spy—which you don't know for sure—who talked him into it and paid him?

You have no idea.

What was it that pushed Edvard Skuggen, that hard, cautious man, into politics, the most uncertain thing of all?

Hmm. There is a hypothesis about that. It's said that he couldn't bear the strain resulting from his suddenly affording to eat something other than oatmeal porridge, while at the same time being able to reduce his working hours from fourteen to seven. He was like a deep-water fish that's pulled up to the surface—the organs of equilibrium burst.

A kind of belated romanticism arose in him. His previous life came to seem like a miracle. Everybody ought to learn about that miracle. The nation's eyes ought to be riveted upon him. He had a message for the Norwegian people: if everybody followed his example, then all Norwegians could become secondary school teachers.

Those who have seen him can relate that, in recent years, he has been unable to speak of anything but himself.

Well, in a way he reached his goal. The nation noticed him.

Is this hypothesis correct?

You have no idea.

How about Karsten Haugen? Why and how did he turn out as he did?

It was said that his father was a tyrant. A fine, handsome figure of a man— rifleman, hunter, brawler, athlete, a convivial person, a ladies' man. And angry and dangerous at home.

Strong father, weak children.

That's not always true either.

Was it true here?

You have no idea.

Are there any common traits that link all these types together into some unity?

I think it is a mess.

I can just see one thing—that it's a long road from a poor little fjord in the West Country or a remote hamlet in the East Country to university, professional school and modern life in Oslo. A person can lose his way many times on that road.

*

And now, at long last, you must've gone around in circles long enough. You are back where you started and have to tell yourself, If it's true that you can understand the present better by digging and delving into the past, then you'd better look into the person you know best, the person you *ought* to know best at any rate—yourself.

Why are you so afraid of that?

You are spotless, after all.

The Spider Web

~~~~~~~~~~~~~~~~~~~~~~~~~

Of course I'm afraid. Afraid to put down in black and white the memories of my own youth. The very thought of it makes me feel a restlessly fluttering anxiety, as if a bat were running riot in my head.

I believe, or at least hope, that it's not merely due to the fact that these memories may not be very flattering to me. I know it's due, in part at least, to something else.

This is not the first time I've thought back to those years, so far away and yet so near. They've popped up more than once in the course of time, in flashes, glimpses, occasionally in a somewhat wider perspective. And I ask myself, This web of faraway experiences, of reminiscence, longing and dream, will it survive being put into clear, brutal words? It's said that in old houses which haven't been inhabited for a long time, things may continue to be as they were when the place was abandoned. But if, after many long years, someone comes in and touches the things with rough hands, then they may crumble under his fingers, collapse and turn to dust.

Will that happen to these memories, which I have approached and moved away from by turns and am now again approaching? Memories I'm partly ashamed of, partly fond of, partly feel like protecting from the eyes of strangers. Will the words turn out to be a too hard mold for the delicate spider web that the years and the days have spun around some small events from a time beyond so many horizons? I don't know and I'm anxious, for in a way I'd become fond of this spider web that I have myself spun.

Prayer for Love
~~~~~~~~~~~~~~~~~~~~~~

Where should one begin, where end? To open the door a crack to memories is like starting a kaleidoscopic film. A welter of images all mixed up.

All sorts of situations. Happy, humiliating, funny—or not so funny, except to everyone else. Alone, with friends, with girls.

But mostly alone. Most of all alone.

I can see it now. I felt small, lonely and helpless, and the city was overwhelming—big, cold, sneering, threatening, venomously revengeful.

An eerie sense of hostile powers, paralyzing us in the presence of women, closing us off from strangers, terrifying us at exams, barring us from the pleasures of life—a sense that there's nothing but struggle, nothing but cruelty, that it's all just a question of being stronger or weaker and woe to the vanquished…

Where is the trust? The child's trust in the mother, the mother's in the child, the simple confidence of childhood?

Yes, I can see it now. I was afraid. I didn't know it then, but the streets from that time have returned in subsequent dreams and they're full of anxiety.

Those streets—I don't need to dream to remember them. Small side streets, most of them quite dark at night. Lusty squeals of women in doorways. A man's coarse words to a woman, a woman's to a man. By a street lamp stand a pair drinking from a bottle; their shadows are so big, they look like two trolls divvying up the spoils.

Late at night—on the way home—the sound of a fight around the corner, the glimpse of a raised arm, the dull, saturated sound of blows to a body, screams, curses, groans. Staggering figures far down some street. A hung-over streetwalker, dark circles under her eyes, inside a doorway. "Hey, you—come with me!"

It was in those streets that I saw *him*, the most mysterious and horrible figure of them all—the procurer, the pimp, owner of a harem and whoremonger in one, tyrant and lover and trader in love.

Desire, desire—and fear of infection.

Fear, feelings of guilt. Fear of infection, fear of pregnancy, fear of loneliness, fear of getting tied down. Lust, want, a burning need—and fear, fear, guilt and fear. Of getting the girl into trouble, of falling short, of appearing ridiculous—and again lust, dreams, yearnings, want, which drove you out of bed, out of the house, onto the streets, through a sleeping city, up and down the street, up and down. And a prayer into the emptiness—let me experience something, let me fall in love let something happen let me experience something let me fall in love who stands there is it a woman let me experience something let something happen I can't bear the thought of going home let me experience something let something happen to me in love in love oh good God whom I don't believe in let something happen to me I can't stand wandering about so empty and full of longing let something happen no matter what no I don't dare talk to her I'm afraid of infection let something happen...

The happy time of youth. The terrible time of youth. And in spite of everything, now I can say it openly, remembering fully all the unhappiness and all the privations which that time entailed—the happy, happy time of youth.

Gunvor

~~~~~~~~~~~~~~~~~~~~~~

One day in the spring of 1921—it must've been around the middle of April, right after Easter—Hans Berg dropped by my cramped north-oriented lodging and said, without any preliminaries as was his wont, "Would you like to have a girl?"

A superfluous question.

"Then you must show up at Heidenreich's tonight at nine," Hans Berg said. "He's giving a party. I'd promised to come, he said he would get me a girl who was game. But I don't feel like it—I can't stand that damned Heidenreich and all those girls of his. So I dropped by and said I couldn't make it but would send you instead. At nine, okay?"

With that he left.

I know more now than I did then—by that time he'd fallen in love with the girl Indregård told me about. His not liking Heidenreich was just a pretext. None of us liked Heidenreich, at least we said so, but we put up with him, and precisely because of the girls. And Hans Berg—well, he used to come to terms with him by calling him names.

Heidenreich was a medical student. He wasn't all that young anymore, to us he actually seemed a rather elderly gentleman. He was pushing thirty. He was educated as a pharmacist, that was the reason he was getting on in years. He was a clever, stylish fellow, that couldn't be denied. We didn't like him any better on that account. More than anything else perhaps we begrudged him his fine silk shirts, a present from a female cousin in America, according to what he told us. They were supposed to have cost up to ten dollars apiece.

Heidenreich was much more of a man of the world than the rest of us. He seemed to have a relatively plentiful supply of money—how plentiful we didn't exactly know, because he was quite tight with his cash. But at any rate he could afford to live in a fine, large apartment and to arrange things with the landlady so that she never made a fuss when he had women visitors late at night. For Heidenreich was keen on girls. More than once the rest of us would follow him with wistful eyes when, brandishing his cane, he whisked by with some smart-looking girl or other that we knew was beyond our reach in every conceivable way.

Ah, Heidenreich and his girls! Witnessing his many conquests contributed to giving the rest of us a prematurely cynical view of women. That old guy! Who wasn't anything much to brag about anyway. No, we couldn't like him—he was boastful, mendacious, and bursting with a self-importance that we felt was very badly misplaced. And besides he came from Kristiansand—or was it Mandal?—and spoke loudly in a dialect that we all agreed was insufferable. But he wallowed in girls. And once in a while, like now, a little fell to the lot of one or more of the rest of us.

Heidenreich dropped by just after Hans Berg had left. He wanted to make sure everything was in order. Tactful as ever, he explained to me that I was a substitute; one of the fellows had been prevented from coming, but he couldn't very well cancel the invitation to the girl in question. As far as he himself was concerned, the whole affair could be regarded as an overture to something. He had made the acquaintance of an exceptionally sweet girl, but she was on her guard and insisted on a party, with several others. The girl who fell to me was quite sweet too, he went on. She'd been engaged, but they'd had a tiff recently, so she was free. The time was nine o'clock, at his place.

As he was leaving, he stopped in the doorway and said, "Tell me, lad, do you have sex appeal?"

I replied, truthfully, that I hadn't seen any signs of it.

No, he said, he wouldn't have thought so either. But it was really a young girl who—a very sweet young girl who—but never mind! Who—what? Oh, just some nonsense. Anyway, I could try my tricks on her this evening. He would keep a sharp eye on me and the girl—that sweet little fancy-free thing…

Then he left. I felt like shouting after him, "Go to hell!"

Lad! he said. I was half a head taller than he was. I thought he was swaggering, tactless, cynical and smug.

But when the clock approached nine, there I was, eager and breathless, on my way to his apartment.

I felt anxious. Those girls of Heidenreich—I'd run across some of them and I didn't like them. I saw them as women of easy virtue, as silly chatterboxes, at times somewhat coarse—and much too experienced. I felt insecure in their company.

No, I did not like Heidenreich, and I did not like his girls. And now I was on my way there. Was drawn there—nervous and scared.

Now afterward I can see several things. Alas, afterward it's easy to see so many things.

I can see now that Heidenreich tried to be nice to me, in his way. I almost think he liked me and felt like teaching me a thing or two. And I for my part—well, after all I couldn't see into the future.

I guess I'll have to face the fact that, all things considered, I liked him. But I was a bit afraid of him too. What at once frightened and impressed me about him was mostly that he was somewhat older than I and that he had a little more money. And then the fact that he was a cynic. He wanted to enjoy the pleasures life had to offer. And they were simple pleasures.

That was where his interests coincided with those of the girls.

They were saleswomen and secretaries, progeny of Oslo's lower middle class with all that this entailed. They had gone to business school, maybe they had graduated from junior high too. They sat in an office or stood in a shop all day long. They had few or no pleasures at home. They were from twenty to twenty-five years old. They had some hope of getting married perhaps, but it might take time. And often whatever hope they had wasn't even definite. They wanted a bit of fun, and they were willing to give something in return for that fun. They came from a milieu that knew one doesn't get something for nothing. Their lives in the shop or in the office had taught them the same lesson, coldly and brutally. And when they'd reached the point where they no longer had their virginity to look after, their girlish heads told them after a little thought that, with every year after turning twenty, they lost some of their market value. In ten years' time they would be old, their chances gone, and they would marry that plain, stinking store clerk—if they could get him.

But to a poor, lonely, scared and completely inexperienced student from the provinces they seemed dangerous, experienced, cynical. He, of course, couldn't see how helpless they were.

Heidenreich's apartment was located in Pilestredet Lane, on the second floor, facing the street. It was large as a hall, with armchairs and couches and writing table and folding screens, and God knows what.

When I entered I found the four girls and the three men already there. The time of the party had been changed to half-past eight, but they hadn't had sufficient time to let me know.

The men I knew from before. The four girls were new to me.

The girl that I gathered was earmarked for me threw me a quick glance, a glance that took me in from head to foot in a flash. It sized me up in an instant from top to toe. I felt cold and hot shivers running down my spine—she was a lovely girl in her way, slight, blond, with curly hair and a round, not particularly remarkable face, but with exceptionally large, dark eyes.

Weighed and found wanting, I thought, as so often in those days. Hide in the darkest corner! Aspire toward the light and get your wings burned! Ah, happy youth! I felt the palms of my hands sweating in anticipation of defeat and shame.

She took another look at me. It must've been just a moment, but to me it seemed infinitely long. I forced myself to look back at her, forced myself to smile, felt I was trembling, felt a hot tingle in my scalp. She smiled back, a tiny little smile.

"I believe you and I are supposed to be partners this evening," she said.

Her voice was soft and warm, a melodious alto. I thought to myself, That too! Had her voice at least left something to be desired, my courage would've risen. But no! That too!

I mumbled something, but my voice refused to obey me; I felt as though I had gravel in my throat, as so often when I wanted to talk to women.

Most often I felt stiff as a rod, my tongue paralyzed by excessive lust. It was all too obvious what I wanted. I was ashamed of it, and of the fact that it was sure to show on me. I hadn't yet learned the simple lesson that no woman will take offense because a man desires her.

And so I became tongue-tied, or nearly so. But women insist, among other things, on words. It's strange to what extent they insist on words. Sure, action too. But words, words...

Pushed to an extreme, it could be said that a man paralyzed from the neck down but with his vocal chords in tiptop condition, could satisfy a great many women by simply telling them in every possible tone of voice, I love you! until they swooned in blissful rapture.

I couldn't do that. If I were forced to, I might perhaps get my peasant's jaws to stammer, I like you!

I looked at her and thought, How will this end!

The food and drinks had been arranged by Heidenreich. He was an expert on pastries, the son of a bitch, and on the table in the middle of the room there was a superb spread of layer cakes, bottles square and round, and glasses of various sizes. We helped ourselves, and Heidenreich commanded in his South Country voice, a slightly nasal tenor, "Disperse!"

My partner and I got a sofa over in a corner. We ate cakes and drank sweet liqueur. Her glass became empty incredibly fast, I had to take several trips to the table and fetch the bottle.

"Let's leave it here!" she said the third time. "The others can come over here if they want some. Anyway, we're the only ones who're drinking the stuff in that bottle."

Heidenreich thought the time was ripe.

"The light hurts my eyes," he said. Then he calmly went and put out the ceiling light. Walked up to the window and pulled up the blinds. A pale half-light fell into the room from the street lamp outside. Retracing his steps, he put out the two corner lamps and went back to his place, as if it were the most natural thing in the world. None of the girls protested. It was perfectly quiet in the large room. What a disgusting guy! I thought, with his glass in my hand.

Then I felt an arm around my neck, a warm breath, a mouth against mine, two breasts close up, and I looked into a pair of half-closed eyes. A kiss that—no, I just can't explain it. Even now, twenty-odd years later, I can feel it. I can't say whether it was still quiet in the room when it was finally over, there was a buzzing in my ears. She was sitting beside me again, quietly flicking the ash from her cigarette into her glass as she said, "Like this—it's real good!" Then she drank up. Looking at me she said, quite softly, "Kiss me!"

I won't attempt to relate any more. We sat there for another couple of hours. I grew wild, intoxicated, light-headed, blissful—and scared. The whole row of my forefathers, puritans to a man, pietists, Hauge followers and what not, looked down upon me from their stern heaven with profound, *profound*, disapproval. How the others in the room looked upon me I learned the following day from Heidenreich.

The other girls were deeply offended and outraged. The other boys too, for the girls had only been occupied with watching us. They didn't reproach me very much—the girls, that is; but they were terribly scandalized by her, their friend. "Just think! To begin like that—right off!" one of them said.

Heidenreich himself was morally shocked. The evening, which had cost him almost fifty kroner, had been wasted as far as he was concerned.

"And all those pastries!" he said. "Layer cakes for seven-fifty!" He flung his arms about in exaggerated despair.

"And all that liqueur!" he said, and now he showed genuine despair. "Couldn't you behave a little more discreetly when you're a guest in someone's house! But she certainly was a shrewd cookie, the little one! Imagine flicking cigarette ash into her glass! That's an old trick if you wish to lose control in a hurry. Whew, there you've met a pretty experienced chick, my lad!"

I heard him, and I heard him not. There was a buzzing in my head. It was buzzing with her. It had happened, it just couldn't have been avoided. In the course of one evening.

A strange time began. She came to my place every other evening and stayed some two or three hours.

I had prayed I would fall in love. Now I was in love—or was I? Anyway, she captivated me, obsessed me—engaged my thoughts and dreams night and day.

But I felt no joy. And what about my self-esteem, which supposedly should increase when one was happily in love—and I was happily in love, wasn't I? I *had* the girl I was in love with after all, but what had become of my self-esteem?

Yes, I had her. She came every other evening.

I was a bit uneasy. I didn't trust my landlady. But Gunvor merely said, "Pooh! Just tell her I'm your sister!"

I must've looked more stupid than usual. She laughed.

"The fact is, I could easily pass for your sister," she said. "Come over to the mirror and you'll see."

We stood side by side before the uneven mirror.

My sister! I'd pictured my actual sisters to myself. She didn't look a bit like them. But as we stood there side by side, I too could see there was something—there was something—. Something about the eyes? Yes, something there perhaps. And the mouth? Something there too perhaps. The forehead? Perhaps something there as well. Overall? Well, she was rather small and I was tall, she was slight and I rather big-boned, she had curly blond hair, mine was brown and straight. But now that she had said it I could, in fact, see there was something—something strange, a kind of resemblance, however different we were.

And all at once I could see that she actually did look like one of my two sisters. I cannot say whether I was glad to notice it. My sisters—it was somehow quite different with them. What *I* took it into my head to do was my own affair. But my sisters? I'm not sure I liked that idea.

"By the way, you look like my brother too," she said. "Sure, and—how strange!—like another guy I know."

Well, I told my landlady that she was my sister, on a visit to the city. I was a bit worried about what would happen if one of my sisters actually came to Oslo. But it's no good looking ahead for trouble, isn't that what they say? Unfortunately I was unable to teach myself that good maxim. Not then, not even today, I fear.

I was worried, but all went well. My sister did not come. But *she* came, of course, and stayed with me a couple of hours, sometimes three.

We didn't talk a great deal. I'd made use of a friend, a medical student who knew a pharmacist, and provided myself with a couple of bottles of liqueur (this was in the era of prohibition). She quickly drank several glasses of it. Smoked a couple of cigarettes—that, too, quickly. She usually flicked some of the ash into her glass.

"Come then!" she whispered.

And I came. And took her home afterward—through streets redolent of spring, late at night, but always before midnight. And wandered home again, alone.

I should've been happy, shouldn't I? But I was not. There was something—I didn't know what it was. Perhaps that she talked so little. Or—I didn't know where the idea came from, but I know I used to think, It's not *you* she wants. She's just using you to forget something. She wants forgetfulness, to be drugged—.

"Come then!" she said.

She didn't look at me very often, she looked away, into vacancy. Or, if she did look at me, I felt as though she looked straight through me at something on the wall behind me.

She talked very little about herself. Quite readily about all sorts of other things, but not about herself. I knew what her name was, that she lived at home with her parents, that she sat in an office in such and such a place. That was nearly all. Who was she? What did she think, feel, wish, what did she dream about, yearn for, worry about, what made her happy, what sad?

Her parents were devout, I learned that much. That's why she had to be home before twelve. Strictly speaking, before eleven. But at twelve o'clock her father got up—he never fell asleep until she came home—and secured the door chain. After that she wasn't let in.

Had she ever been locked out? Oh yes, more than once.

And what then?

She went to a girl friend, of course, she said lightly, without looking at me.

She never mentioned that she'd been engaged. It was from Heidenreich I'd learned about that, as I've said, and he had it from her girl friend. They had broken up a few weeks before I met her. She must have been terribly in love with the guy. It might excuse her behavior at the party to a certain extent, though such things were obviously unforgivable. And the first time at that!

Said her friend.

She herself said nothing. She would sit and look around a little, hum a bit, turn the pages of a book, look into vacancy. Suddenly she might say, "Tell me something amusing, will you!"

That sentence invariably felt like a cold shower. Something amusing? But what was her idea of amusement? I tried, but didn't always succeed. I suspected it already then, and know it only all too well now, I'm sorry to say: I was not what young girls called amusing, I lacked the necessary nerve. Still I tried, and she laughed politely. Meanwhile she sipped her liqueur diligently. And then it came, the moment. She gave me a look, a long look—the first real look she'd given me all evening.

"Come then!"

But even at the peak of passion together—and she was passionate, her abandon sometimes frightened me—even then I had a feeling that she was far away. I couldn't get close to her. Who was she?

I had no idea at the time that this was something she didn't know even herself.

A young, lonely girl with strict parents who had lost all contact with her. Who had tried—in vain—to force her to join their own religious circle. Who revenged themselves upon the rebel by calling her to account for her whereabouts every hour of the day after the office closed. (Which had merely turned her into a virtuoso liar.) Who were suspicious of her girl friends, and more than suspicious of her male friends. Who never gave her anything but jaundiced looks and sour words, which were lost on her. She was forced to live at home to survive, seeing how miserably she was paid. But she had steeled herself, until she neither saw nor heard her parents' sour faces and whining or scolding words.

Then came the break with her sweetheart, and loneliness—which she had tried to keep at bay as best she could—suddenly stared her in the face from right outside her window. Then she met me, and I reminded her sufficiently of her elder brother, who'd run away to sea and whose picture she carried in a medallion on her breast, to fill a void while she was hoping for something else. I was a nice boy, she felt no ill will toward me. And I helped her kill a few hours that would otherwise have been empty and lonely. Maybe something else entered into it too, sexual attraction—let us hope so.

All of this is just something I guess at as I'm writing. I had no inkling of it at the time. I simply felt I couldn't get close to her, that she was only using me for something—where again, presumably, I fell short.

It came as no surprise to me when one day I received a couple of lines from her.

It must end. Thanks for a very pleasant time, and everything.
Your Gunvor

I made no attempt to look her up. I thought—it was my first and decisive thought: Weighed and found wanting.

Unhappy? Sure, I was unhappy. I missed her so much that I literally banged my head against the wall. But that didn't bring her back, of course. And I—well, I did nothing. Weighed and found wanting. Wanting…

My self-esteem fell to zero.

High Up and Deep Down

~~~~~~~~~~~~~~~~~~~~~~~~~

How could I get crushed that easily?

Well, it was partly because of the literature I was reading.

It was a strange time. Great expectations—I was twenty-two years old and there were no limits to what I could accomplish, given world enough and time. Those dreams, longings, expectations had no definite shape, they mostly resembled white, sunlit clouds that were high up and far away and whose shapes were constantly changing. I didn't yet know what I wanted to be. All things considered, I probably knew very little about my own abilities—or did I have some idea of them? I tested them by taking in rather than by giving out. I read greedily everything that came within my reach. Law, of course, since that was my subject. But also mathematics, physics, chemistry, all the natural sciences, history, philosophy, literature. Above all, literature. And I'd come to the firm conviction that, as far as I could see, I couldn't have had a better mind.

Earlier, while in school, I had learned that, with a will, I could remember anything. Shouldn't I, then, be able to go far—in fact, as far as I wished to go? Sometime in the future?

Few things are apt to increase your self-esteem—the self-esteem of a dream—as much as the literature you read in your youth. It's a shortcut to those high, sunlit clouds. You *are* Gunnar at Lidarende, you *are* Skarphedin and Kåre. The next day you are the hero of Hamsun's *Hunger* or Lieutenant Glahn in *Pan* or Niels Lyhne—all his thoughts are your thoughts, his disappointments are your disappointments, and you anticipate them with pleasure. And you die just as he does, despairing but on your feet. You roam about in faraway lands, have remarkable experiences, are in mortal danger, women fall for you and betray you, and you carry it all off in exquisite fashion.

But you also steep yourself in the grayness of everyday life as portrayed by naturalism and take part in innumerable people's dismal and dreary experiences, before jumping on your winged horse once more, to travel over land and sea, toward the high heavens and faraway kingdoms. Nothing human is alien to you, to the best of your knowledge.

The simple fact is: You are full of an inextinguishable vitality. You do the necessary day's work—and then the day begins! You wear out your shoe leather hunting for adventures—that is to say, women—or spend your evenings in impassioned discussions with your peers and intellectual kin; and you use every free moment for rushing through one volume of literature after another. You eat literature, you drink literature, you absorb it the way a dry sponge absorbs water. Unfinished, with every pore and possibility open, you fill yourself with content from all over the world. More and more, more and more…

It all goes into you without friction, all genres, all styles, all literary trends. You are still so unfinished that you contain the seeds of everything, and accordingly you can accept everything. Nothing human is yet alien to you, but a lot is just literature. Vices, ennui, despair, narcosis, anaesthesia? You are so healthy that you don't yet know health by way of its opposite, you live on bread and coffee, dinner at a miserable restaurant, supper at an equally miserable temperance café—and on conversations, walks in the streets, more conversations, endless conversations; you walk with a friend half the night, take him to his door, then back to yours, back to his again, get home at last toward morning, drop into bed and sleep like a log. The following day you read decadent poets with the most profound enthusiasm and understanding.

Indeed, few things are so apt to increase one's self-esteem in youth. And no self-esteem collapses more quickly at the first collision with reality. For it is a self-esteem acquired in private, in an enjoyment devoid of struggle, with only a purely aesthetic pain, a self-testing by way of play. It's a self-esteem of thousands of different roles. But reality rarely resembles to a т what you've read in your latest book, and the role reality gives you to play is never completely like the one you've learned most recently. You participate in a colloquium and aren't quite as well prepared as you ought to be—you were reading books instead of preparing for it—it doesn't go exactly as you had imagined, and you have a troubling sense that you're not cutting a very elegant figure, and that all too many are seeing through you in a way they rather shouldn't. Come, where has this situation been described, and what should you say or do that would give those louts a memory for life? But you can't think of it.

You sit there chatting with a girl and would like to make an impression on her. But however it may be, she doesn't give you the right cues, you can't be either d'Artagnan or Don Juan, not even Abbé Coignard.

Afterward you wander alone through the streets, resembling, as far as you can see, none of these figures, but rather a wet dog with his tail between his legs. And too late, much too late, your brain starts to function—*that* you could've said, and *that* you ought to have done—but you're neither such or such a person, only a shy, slow-witted, lonely and inexperienced student from the provinces, clumsy, stammering, blushing, falling all over yourself, over your own words. You gnash your teeth in shame and anguish, groan and grunt in agony and look quickly over your shoulder, afraid that someone may have heard you. Back in your room you tear your hair, make faces at yourself in the mirror and throw yourself on the sofa; and God only knows if you don't shed a few tears, an added reason for feeling acutely ashamed afterward. Nothing but sheer play-acting! But you find it a little more difficult than usual, later the same evening, to be the cheerful Axel in *The Fall of the King* or the thoughtful Arvid Stjärnblom in *The Serious Game*.

The Room

~~~~~~~~~~~~~~~~~~~~~~~~

I no longer liked my room after Gunvor had left me. For that matter, I hadn't liked it before either—cramped and facing north, looking out on a depressing fire wall. But now it seemed to me like a grave. I was vaguely reminded of the Unknown Soldier. But I wasn't even a soldier, only unknown, or at any rate forgotten. I also had the thought of a well, a dried-out well. I was sitting at the bottom of it.

At the same time I had, incredibly enough, more cash in my pocket. The reason was that the exams were approaching at all the schools. That meant there was a seller's market for private tutoring. Would-be graduates came in droves. For some reason or other I remember one of them, a tall, lethargic fellow in a stiff black hat and mustard-yellow gloves. He entered the room with his hat on, carefully unbuttoned and slipped off his gloves, and insultingly dusted off the chest of drawers with the gloves before depositing hat and gloves there; then he pulled up his trouser legs and sat down. His insipid face said without words: I'm bored! And his passionate soul turned turtle in a long yawn.

He was the son of a big shipowner, and this was the third time he would be trying to graduate from junior college. We were the same age.

For a fee of five kroner an hour I tried to inject into him the necessary minimum, but in vain. His head seemed to consist of nothing but watertight compartments, not the least bit of knowledge could leak in there.

He managed nevertheless to cheat me out of fifteen kroner. When he was to pay his bill after the last lesson, he raised his eyebrows in exaggerated surprise and said, "I see that what my old man has given me is fifteen kroner short. I'll come by with the rest tomorrow."

He never came.

How I hated him! I still hate him. It's cold comfort that he never managed to graduate. He's junior head in the big firm now, and a long-time millionaire. At the moment he resides in America and is a member of various commissions and things. The fate of the world is partly in his hand. He owes a poor student fifteen kroner.

But in spite of him I suddenly had money in my pocket. I looked for a new room and found one almost immediately.

It was the nicest room I'd ever had. It was situated in—oh well, never mind. The street was a steep little side street; the house below was a corner house that faced a small square.

The apartment was on the second floor; but the street climbed quite sharply, while turning at the same time. The rear part of the first floor was practically a basement, with three small shops in a row. Farthest to the rear, with three steps leading down to a door with a bell, was a shoemaker's shop. That shoemaker became my friend. He was a small man with black bristly hair and a stiff leg. He half-soled my shoes for me and wanted to overthrow society.

The house was built so as to follow the curve of the street, which accordingly was reflected in the hallway of the apartment. It was a large apartment with a long hallway, but it turned in such a way that when you entered you saw only the first ten to twelve feet of the narrow, dark corridor. It was extremely long and grew increasingly dark. I believe the apartment must have contained eight to ten rooms all in all. Deep, deep inside lived the landlady, Mrs. Middelthon, a widow with one daughter. A crabby old housemaid was also kept someplace in there. I never got that far. I never got farther than the kitchen, which was to the right behind the turn in the hallway—not farthest back but far enough.

The kitchen was very dark, as kitchens often are in such apartment houses. One single window, facing the narrow, deep well of a courtyard.

But the kitchen was spacious, it had depth. It often smelled temptingly of good old-fashioned food in there. Anyway, I never gave a close look around, looked neither right nor left, just rushed through, embarrassed and unhappy, opened the door leading to the backstairs, snatched the key hanging to the left of the door and disappeared. But from the corner of my eye I sometimes received the impression that the elderly maid was busy with one thing or another somewhere inside the semi-darkness. I think the landlady was there too once in a while.

As a rule they were gone when I passed by on my return.

I remember this kitchen as a large square twilight, and the hallway as a long, narrow, curved twilight, growing darker and darker the farther back you got.

Along the hallway, on both sides, clothes hung on pegs. They were black cast-iron pegs, with two lower hooks to hang clothes on and one upper. Well, they can still be found, here and there.

Am I getting sidetracked? But I have a strange feeling that all this is important, that it's all important for explaining—oh well.

The door to my room was near the entrance and I could come and go as I wished, nobody stood at the turn of the hallway spying on me. Mrs. Middelthon was a tolerant woman, one of the few.

There was also a room with its own entrance, wall to wall with my own. It was situated directly over the gateway and was occupied by a prostitute. She was heavy-set and dark, with coal-black hair, a broad face with large cheekbones, flat nose, and large black eyes. She looked Asiatic. Privately I called her Slava. She solicited customers mostly on Karl Johan Street, but also occasionally in the side streets around the square. Or, if it rained, she might stand in the entranceway. She'd signaled to me several times there, as I went by on my way home at night. It had also happened a couple of times, when I returned home late and was fumbling with my front door key, that her door was quietly opened a crack; I could make out a face and a beckoning hand in the door opening. But I'd never responded to these invitations. While I was thirsting for adventure—thirsting for *woman* like a desert wanderer for water—my fear of everything that a prostitute entailed was even stronger than my thirst. I was as ignorant as a child of the means of defense that were available against those special illnesses. I associated with medical students, but the farm boy's fear and bashfulness were stronger than everything—I couldn't even bring myself to ask them whether such means existed, had only guessed, from the talk of my bolder companions, that there certainly was something.

Then the prostitute became offended. She no longer looked at me. And one night, when a couple of friends and I had been talking till rather late, she knocked angrily on the wall. She wanted to have quiet.

Did Mrs. Middelthon know what sort of lodger she had? I never got wise to that. Mrs. Middelthon was a storekeeper's widow, big, round and pleasant, although somewhat marked by the not very bountiful last few years. Maybe she paid homage to the old adage "live and let live"? Anyway, that room with its own entrance was hardly very easy to rent out—sitting directly over the gateway, its floor cold in the winter, and full of commotion because of the horses and carriages that were constantly passing in and out over the wooden paving of the entranceway, to and from some enterprise or other in the lurid backyard.

Besides the prostitute and me, there were two other lodgers in the house. One was a withered middle-aged man who stole past me in the hallway as if apologizing for his very existence. On the thin, shiny seat of his trousers was written, in big invisible letters: *office clerk for life.*

The other—his name was Halvorsen according to Mrs. Middelthon—lived next door to me. He was a robust, merry gentleman with a commanding voice and a ringing laughter. I liked him a lot, he had such a fresh and vigorous air about him.

Halvorsen was keen on the girls—or rather on his own girl, for I believe it was the same one each time. Sound carried easily in the apartment so I could hear them, and he must've known that I could hear them. But that didn't bother him.

She had an attractive voice, warm and subdued; I couldn't hear very well what she said, but there was no mistaking that they were tender words. Every now and then she moaned amorously.

"Grab my hair!" she whispered once. The words sounded surprisingly clear from where I sat reading *The Temptations of Saint Anthony* in the furthest corner of my room. She went on, in-between a sob and a prayer, "Kill me! Tear me…"

From Slava's room on the other side I heard muttering voices and a deep female laughter. Through the open window came the mixed, buzzing sounds of the city—clanging trolleys, cars revving up, footsteps, conversation, now and then a faraway shout. And again female laughter.

Saint Anthony—some book to be reading just now. I felt as if put on bread and water in a cell of enforced chastity, while life seethed and bubbled around me on all sides.

I cast aside *Saint Anthony* and set to work on Hagerup. But the dry-as-dust jurist wasn't much better than the mad saint. One led my thoughts down dangerous paths, the other left a wooden taste in my mouth.

I looked about me. My room was nice and big, with two windows, cabinets in the wall and a huge mahogany table in the middle of the floor. It had been an elegant piece of furniture at one time. Now it was slightly lame and rheumatic; there were scratches in the polish and, in the middle of the table top, the imprint of a hot flatiron inadvertently left there. But I thought it was pleasant to look at—it looked like a tame brown bear standing on four heavy legs in the middle of the room.

Sure, the room was fine enough, though maybe not very suitable for quiet study in the evening. I got up and went out—down to the corner.

The shop on the corner was a cigar store. I'd dropped by there occasionally for several years. Now I went there every day. In there, behind the counter, sat Fleischer the hunchback—small, with a cripple's bony face and long, lean knuckle-hands. He sat at the till like a huge spider, cashing in our money. With him, behind the counter, were his two shop girls. They were always pretty, but changed frequently. Always pretty, with white, semi-transparent blouses over young, taut breasts. It was whispered that he was a helluva guy with the girls, this Fleischer—insatiable and brutal. He used his girls and cast them aside like sucked-out flies. Fresh ones, always fresh ones.

I shuddered when I walked in there. One of the girls had such fine brown eyes, with a sticky hot glance, like a dog's.

Those white blouses, those round, firm breasts! Did they let that disgusting spider crawl on top of them, groping his way with those long knuckle-hands?

I could see those spider-hands groping, squeezing and grabbing. I felt nauseous. And full of hatred. I hated that sallow hunchback. Hated those young girls. Hated the whole world because it was like that, because it let such things happen.

But he carried good tobacco, Fleischer did. I continued going there every day.

The little square had its own allure for me. A magic light shone from the shop windows during the long evenings. Inside were all the nice things I couldn't afford to buy. On the house fronts, behind the curtains, lamps were lighted, tier upon tier, all the way up to the bright May sky, where the stars appeared like white specks. People strolled by on the sidewalk, singly or in pairs. Now and then the pairs would stop in front of some shop window, and the girl would point at some article she thought was pretty. At the corner opposite Fleischer's shop was a tavern, and a little farther on stood a green house. People would hang about in twos and threes in front of the tavern. On Friday nights there was a steady traffic to the green house.

Late at night, when most of the apartments were dark and the lights were extinguished in the shop windows, the little square appeared larger. The blond nocturnal light filtered down like a pale dusk. A few twosomes were still lounging in front of the tavern, swaying as they talked in thick, slack voices. From the doorways round about came the whispers and laughter of late couples.

I would stand there alone, or walk through the square alone, on the way home to my solitary cell.

A fortnight went by in this fashion.

Then one night something happened. I had run out of the house, but discovering I'd forgotten to take my key, I returned home early. I rang the bell. I heard light steps approaching, the door was opened and—I was completely at sea. I found myself face to face with Gunvor.

We stood there speechless, stock-still, staring at each other. How long? For a second, maybe.

"I—live here," I said.

"I'm visiting," she said, very softly. "I—am—engaged to someone who lives here. I—was engaged to him—before I met you. But then it was over—for a while. You won't say anything, will you?"

She said it so softly, it was almost like a breath. She looked at me, quickly, searchingly. Then she was gone.

Somehow or other I managed to get to my room. A moment later I found myself sitting on a chair.

So *that* was Mr. Halvorsen's friend. And it was her voice I'd heard every other evening now for a fortnight. And I hadn't recognized it.

At first I understood nothing. Then I understood. Her voice had another ring to it now than when she used to talk to me. It had acquired a faintly quavering warmth it had lacked at that time. I recalled something that had occurred to me one of those evenings before rushing out of the house—that for some reason or other that voice reminded me of the quivering air over seaside cliffs on hot summer days.

Now I could hear Mr. Halvorsen's booming voice from the adjacent room, "You're so quiet tonight, baby! Are you feeling out of sorts?"

I remember now. He always used to call her baby, never Gunvor.

I didn't hear her answer. She spoke more softly than usual.

I grabbed my key and rushed out the door, out of the house.

During the next few days I studied Mr. Halvorsen whenever opportunity offered with—what shall I call it?—renewed interest.

I couldn't fathom that I'd previously been able to look at him without dislike, almost with a kind of sympathy.

He was old, very likely pushing thirty. Tall, rather heavy-set, with curly brown hair, intensely blue eyes, a strong, rather fleshy face and cleft chin.

Each one of his round features cut me like a razor. So that was the way I had to look if I wanted to have a chance with women.

I swore angrily that, rather than being like Halvorsen, I would go without women from now on—till my death in a hundred years.

She'd talked about some fellow who looked like me—no, that I looked like, I think it was.

My stomach was turning, but something told me: she'd been thinking of Mr. Halvorsen. I said to myself—hatefully, as if to a secret enemy—that there was no similarity, that I wouldn't allow a trace of similarity. I went up to the mirror and looked at my own thin, lanky body, my hollow-cheeked face with its mop of brown hair that was constantly falling forward over my forehead.

Not a trace of similarity.

Unless he had a resemblance to an elder brother of mine, if I'd had any.

Someplace it whispered: There is something—that, or something like that, is how you might come to look some day if you went into business and had a bit of luck, ate well and drank some, and acquired some of the self-confidence you still have so little of—.

No! I rushed up to the mirror again. Not the least similarity! Thank God.

I found the man to be altogether repulsive: his fat self-assurance, that loud, rather blustery voice, the hint of an incipient paunch, and the heavy, self-important manner in which he trampled through the hallway. I found it all to be common and disgusting—and tried to find out his secret.

But that he looked like her, there could be no doubt. The curly hair, the intense blue eyes, but above all something obscure and indescribable. That must be the way her brother looked. The one she had talked about with such warmth. The one who had run away from home and was now sailing far-off seas.

Mr. Halvorsen looked like a grocery clerk, but he wasn't; on the contrary, he worked in the office of a lumber dealer and had a good job, and in half a year he counted on becoming office manager. Then he intended to get married. To Miss Arnesen.

This and more of the same I learned from Mrs. Middelthon, in small doses, when she brought my coffee in the morning.

Suddenly she seemed to me to be speaking about Mr. Halvorsen and Miss Arnesen continually.

Mr. Halvorsen rented the two rooms next to mine. A sitting room and a bedroom. He needed a relatively spacious place on account of all the people dropping by on business. His bedroom was next to my room—.

I said politely, "Oh really, is that so?"

Miss Arnesen and Mr. Halvorsen had been engaged a long time. Last spring they seemed to have broken up for a while, and Mr. Halvorsen was very downhearted. But now everything was fine again and Mr. Halvorsen was so merry and cheerful. Indeed, Mrs. Middelthon ventured to say that this was *true love.*

Mr. Halvorsen was such an excellent lodger. Always punctual with his rent, and often a little extra, one thing or another. He had so many connections, of course. Mr. Halvorsen was a man with a future, so she believed anyway.

Gunvor's voice had become more muted after we met in the hallway; I rarely could hear what she said anymore now. But Mr. Halvorsen, on the other hand, having nothing to hide, expressed himself very clearly.

To make my happiness complete, I had Slava on the other side. She wasn't always idle either.

Once in a while I thought I could see a grinning devil before me, bowing politely with the words, "Pardon me, Sir, do you prefer to be boiled or roasted?"

I realized that sometimes the hero has to save himself by flight. As the time drew near when Gunvor used to come, I sat waiting, ready to take off. I didn't want to meet her, didn't want to go before she came, but the moment she closed the door behind her I was on the way out of my nice apartment.

Mr. Halvorsen, however, was a man who didn't waste his time, and he was a past master in the use of words. Before I got out of the door he still managed on occasion to say something memorable.

The evenings in the open air were light and long.

The bird cherry was in bloom.

Conversation with My Father
~~~~~~~~~~~~~~~~~~~~~~~

My father was on a visit to town. He was sitting in my nice little apartment. It was afternoon. We had a couple of hours ahead of us and I was rather uneasy: What should we talk about? How could we while away the time?

He had arrived a few hours ago. We had dined together and he had told me the essentials—that everyone was well, that Dagros and Litago had calved, that the crops looked promising but that it was too early to say anything definite, that the timber prices were high, that the wife of one of our cotters had broken her leg.

In the evening he was going to a meeting, he would spend the night in his mission hotel, and tomorrow morning he would be leaving. He never spent an hour more than necessary in the city.

I knew he read his Bible diligently; it had a passage somewhere about the Babylonian harlot. To him, this capital city was somewhat like that—alluring, frivolous, godforsaken, and dangerous. He drew a sigh of relief when he sat in the train on his way home.

We had two hours ahead of us. We hadn't seen each other in two months. What should we talk about?

I looked at him as he sat there in the chair, so quiet and patient. It struck me that he'd aged. I remembered that this had struck me each time I hadn't seen him for a while. Not that he'd become so much older each time. But when I hadn't seen him for some time, other images of him pushed their way into my memory, images from earlier years. It was like coming home on vacation and feeling each time that the rooms at home were much smaller than I remembered them. And weren't, in fact, the servants' quarters farther away from the house? Time had allowed for the yardstick of childhood to pop up. The yardstick of childhood, stronger than anything else.

It was quiet in my room. The afternoon hours were always quiet. Slava slept, and Mr. Halvorsen and Gunvor hadn't yet started. I was grateful for that; there would be no embarrassing questions and no slightly confused answers, and no increased anxiety on the part of my father—as to the sort of life this son of his, about whom he knew nothing, was actually leading here in the capital. The Babylonian harlot....

As I sat there in my room looking at my kind, patient father, I suddenly remembered Hans Berg and *his* father and felt grateful for having grown up in a milder climate.

Oh yes. In a far milder climate, despite everything.

But that Babylonian harlot—

All at once I wasn't sitting in my room anymore. I was in another place, in another time. I was at home, six years ago.

It was the evening my father took me into his office to talk about *it*.

Having graduated from junior high in the spring, I was all set to leave for the city to begin senior high in the fall. It was the evening before my departure. I remember the lamp on his writing table, and Father to the left behind the lamp.

"Come with me, there's something I want to talk to you about," he'd said. I could see he felt anything but comfortable. I went in with great misgivings— that Father wanted to talk to me about something was seldom a good omen. That was the way things were.

Father rarely talked to us. That is, he rarely talked to us about anything essential. He didn't have the time. Nor did he have any aptitude for it. I could see him in my mind's eye—a big, rather taciturn man the children tried to keep their distance from. I could see a little more now, that goes without saying. Could see that he was a shy man, not free and easy. Lonely, silent, hiding behind a stern mask. Liberal, as far as his field of vision reached. With the years conservative—but that he didn't see himself. Little sense of humor— though, was I so certain of that? I didn't know him, after all. He was only my father, a strange man I'd seen every day while growing up.

Here I sit twenty years later, with a sheet of paper before me, remembering that day in my room and the evening six years before. Remembering my father. He's dead now. We never became close. I feel like bawling, but it would be to no avail. The blunders of our fathers cannot be undone. Nor can our own, for that matter.

Afterward I've learned many things about him that I didn't know while he was alive, and I may have understood a number of things that I never thought about as long as I was young. The young can understand many things; in their way, maybe, they understand some things better than we do. Maybe? What nonsense! They are oppressed and troubled, they're drawn toward things and yearn for them and enjoy them in an entirely different way from us.

Youth understands and age understands—but they each understand their own things. Is there a bridge between them? I doubt it.

I didn't understand my father. Do I understand him now? Perhaps. And when I think I understand him, I feel sincerely sorry for him. But acquit him, no, I can't.

He belonged to a generation that knew little or nothing about how to limit the size of one's family. I imagine he prayed to God that it would stop sometime. But it didn't stop. And he was a poor man.

He was forced to look for extra jobs, to toil early and late. Stayed up late at night—but not late enough, one might say. For the children continued to come. Six of us, besides two who died early on. And my mother grew thin and gaunt, with many vertical lines in her face and with a potbelly of the sort that most wives had at that time—like a knot they had tied on their body to help them remember something.

My father wore himself out for us, so that he neither had time nor strength to be with us. "Hush! Father is working!"—that was the word, the refrain, of my childhood. We grew up under it, he grew old. Work, work—for children he rarely saw, except as a disturbance to his work. For children he couldn't talk to. For children who were afraid of him and kept away from him, who never offered him any intimacy and to whom he didn't dare offer any intimacy. There was this business of his dignity, too.

Did he miss it, the intimacy?

He did miss it. After getting old he tried now and then, clumsily, helplessly, to retrieve part of what had been lost and missed. Too late, too late. The children were grown by then, ready to abandon the nest, as they say. They had their own friends, male and female, their own joys—which they couldn't confide to him—and their worries, which they couldn't bring themselves to unload on him. He was so old, after all, and must be spared.

And he didn't make any vigorous attempts either. He was old and tired— oh, so tired. He sat already on the island of his lonely old age.

Oh yes. One could feel like bawling, all right.

He toiled and provided a good home for us. We all knew that—and longed, longed to get away.

Good parents, fairly well-behaved children. Nothing to be said against that home.

I remember I wished them dead. In all innocence, naturally. I would've been horrified if someone had asked me, You wish them dead? But I did!

It might be like this: One day they were away for a whole long day—they'd driven off in the carriage and wouldn't be home until late. Oh, how glorious! A sort of Sunday, although it was in the middle of the week. A holiday. Just imagine, to walk around, sit down wherever you wished, do what you wanted— within certain limits of course, quite narrow limits, but still! They were far away. You could take a breather, stretch, be yourself. You felt like singing, jumping, dancing!

As far as I can remember I never did anything particularly wicked. It was simply that I *could* if I had wanted to.

But then came the evening, and we were supposed to begin looking forward to their coming home. And we did look forward to it. We were good children.

I would sit there looking forward to it. How strange that I can remember all this even today—after thirty years!

Then your imagination set to work. What if the horse bolted, overturned the carriage and threw them out! What if they didn't come back—not tonight, not tomorrow, not the day after, not...

As a rule I checked myself. After all, I was a good boy who was looking forward to his parents coming home. I quickly discovered that they mustn't get killed, just a bit hurt so they had to go to the hospital—for a few weeks maybe.

A few weeks when we could be without them—free of them—free...

I checked myself, as I've said, and really looked forward to their coming home. And if they got delayed and weren't home by the time they'd said they would, I sometimes became wildly apprehensive lest something might have happened to them. I sensed that if something should happen to them all the same (but nothing ever did happen to them, they always came home again, always!)—but anyway, if something should happen to them regardless, I would feel that I was the culprit, the very cause of the accident.

In my anxiety I began to fantasize once more about all the things that could happen to them. *Here* there was a bridge, *there* a little valley which people said was haunted; the horse might get skittish, or there might be Gypsies on the road. I sometimes grew so anxious that I perspired. So anxious that I couldn't sit still but had to take a walk. And I thought feverishly, as by formula, Dear Father! Dear Mother! Dear Father! Dear Mother!

Where was I? Oh yes, that afternoon in my room. No, that evening six years earlier.

He sat behind the lamp, his hands resting on the writing table in front of him. Strong, hairy hands, but old—with thick blue swollen veins running along the back of his hand. His brown beard had acquired some white streaks. I recall thinking, He's old! Old as the hills!

He was just short of fifty.

"There's something I would like to talk to you about," he said again. My misgivings increased. I didn't have a particularly bad conscience, but I never had a particularly good conscience either. And—he would like to talk to me!

The light from the desk lamp fell on his face. He had a regular, rather handsome face—that I'd heard and could see for myself. It looked weary and worn out. That I did not see. I only saw that he was my father, an old, old man, almost fifty.

He sat in such a way that the light fell on his face, while I was in shadow (he hadn't read his Sherlock Holmes, but I had). I saw that he was embarrassed, and immediately felt so myself, without losing my misgivings.

Then he pulled himself together—I could see that he pulled himself together—and began to talk to me about *it*.

I was no longer a child—no longer only a child, he corrected himself. I was going to the capital and would live by myself, be on my own in a sense. He trusted me, he had no reason not to. Said he.

I thought, If he just knew!

I thought this with a cocky and conceited air, full of childish fear and brag.

"Hmm!" he said. And then again, like an order to himself, "Hmm!"

Now then, it was—it was—. There were temptations in the capital. Drinking and—but he thought he could trust me on that score.

I nodded. I too thought he could trust me about that. I had never tasted as much as a glass of wine. I mumbled something, producing some sound or other meant to convey that he could trust me about that. I'd realized long ago what he was leading up to and was nervous, or rather unspeakably ashamed— on his account or on mine? I don't know, I only know that while I was relieved he didn't want to talk to me about anything wrong I had done, I again confirmed what I already knew, that I couldn't expect anything good to come from Father wanting to talk to me. For the whole thing was both extremely painful and embarrassing—painful for him, painful for me, embarrassing to him, embarrassing to me. I perspired with embarrassment, felt like hiding in the darkest corner; and I could tell by his face that, if it weren't for his dignity, he too would've looked around for a dark corner.

But he didn't give up. This was something we had to get through. It was a duty.

I had no doubt heard, he said, looking away, that there were wanton women in the capital. Dangerous women. Women who were out to lure and seduce fellows like me.

I produced another acquiescing sound and felt like laughing aloud—mostly from embarrassment, but not wholly so. I saw in a flash—or rather didn't see but felt—that he was just as innocent, just as out of it, just as unsuspecting as I was. I suddenly felt standing there that *I* was the adult, *he* the child. It was the first time the thought crossed my mind that this might, in fact, be the case. I felt old, wise and experiencd as I stood there face to face with him, while he preached morals and worldly wisdom to me and didn't dare look me squarely in the eye.

There was also something that disturbed me as I was listening to him—a thought came to me again and again, like a troublesome fly you try in vain to brush away.

I was thinking that he and I shared a terrible, forbidden secret.

One day that summer I'd come across a strange book. It wasn't shelved the way any decent book should be; it was hidden in the empty space behind a row of books. It was called *Hunger*. By Knut Hamsun.

I began to read it then and there. But after a while I realized that this was a book I had to take away with me, and as quickly as possible.

I read it under an old apple tree in the garden, I sat with it under a crooked pine tree down in the pasture, or I went off to hide in a corner of the attic with it. I became mysteriously excited by it. I went deep inside the pasture, so that nobody could see or hear me, and whispered against a birch, "Ylajali!"

I hadn't known that such books existed. But one thing made me thoughtful and uneasy. My father had bought this book, had read it, and had then hidden it behind the other books on the shelf. So that none of his children should find it and read it, I readily understood that much. But he hadn't burned it! Did he take it out from time to time to read on the sly, as I was doing now?

My father! I was shocked, but didn't let on. I felt as though he'd done something improper, snooping on us youngsters. I recall thinking, Reading such stuff isn't good for him!

Such books should really be off limits for parents.

I thought all this as I stood before him.

But, as I've said, I produced an acquiescing sound.

He didn't ask, Oh really? Dangerous women? How come you know about that? How do you happen to know anything at all about such things? Not from me!

No, that was for sure. Not from him. This was the first time he talked to me about such things.

But he didn't ask those questions. He was pleased by the acquiescing sound and hurried on. It was then he mentioned that word. The Babylonian harlot.

Yes, there were harlots. But almost worse—although nothing could be worse—but almost worse was the fact that, from what he'd heard, there were wanton, worthless women who gave themselves to a man the first time they saw him.

He shook his head. I believe he really thought the capital was a veritable Sodom and Gomorrah, inhabited chiefly by prostitutes and confidence men. And nearly all people there had syphilis.

He went on talking about dissipation and immorality and what followed in their wake—about sin and sorrow and sickness—terrible sicknesses, as he said. He was right, of course. And I knew he was right, and knew that I knew better than he did—because I was the one with the devil in his blood, wasn't I, torn between desire and fear, desire and fear, till I was all in a sweat at night? I had a rough time of it, all right. And never for a moment did it occur to me that he, too, could've had a rough time of it once. He, my own father? Who was a Christian and all? Unthinkable.

But he had read *Hunger.*

Those sicknesses—. I shuddered. But above all I thought, I wish it were over I wish it were over wrap it up wrap it up!

He wrapped it up at last and received a final acquiescing sound from me. He drew a sigh of relief—I could see that he drew a sigh of relief—and made a gesture with his hand: Well, that was all. And I turned upon my heel and slipped quietly out of the room, still feeling ashamed. On his account or on my own? That I don't think I knew. But I knew, more firmly and more intensely than ever before, that I could never expect anything good to come of it if Father wanted to talk to me.

I stood for a moment in the dark entrance hall. But it wasn't far enough away from the office. I went out into the yard. It was a dark, mild evening in August with big, blazing stars. I took several deep breaths. And then I laughed. Why? Maybe because I still felt ashamed. And to keep the shame at arm's length.

I felt at once relieved and guilty. Relieved because it was over. Guilty because—well, why? Because I was relieved, perhaps.

It was wrong to laugh, of course, I understood that. I felt like a pupil making faces behind his teacher's back—or like that lumberjack who'd once sat beside me in church. He was cursing softly to impress a couple of friends. He certainly impressed me. But I knew quite well he was thinking as he cursed, Will God strike me now?

I didn't even have anyone to perform for. Even so I stood laughing out there that tranquil August evening, feeling that I was a clown and that the starry sky was eyeing me sternly, with knitted brows.

Conflicting thoughts chased one another so quickly that they were gone before I could catch them by the tail and stop them.

Suddenly I discovered that I had become afraid. Of course I was afraid. For basically he was right, wasn't he? He was an old man, after all, and must know a great many things that I didn't know, even though I beat him at chess and knew more botany than he did.

I ought to be rather careful, all right.

I was reminded of that lumberjack again. As I sat in church beside him, I'd thought that if a miracle should happen and a roof beam fall down on his head—no, even if no miracle happened but he cut his foot with the ax a week later and the wound became gangrenous and he had to die, then he would remember his curses and send for the parson—"death and damnation, get hold of that parson pretty damn quick!"

It was all very complicated. I tried to catch my breath again; I still felt relieved, still embarrassed, still guilty—and tremendously glad that I was going away the following day.

I have no idea how long it took for this recollection to pass through my head. A few seconds maybe. Then I was back in my nice little apartment again, and Father sat quietly and patiently in his chair.

How old he's grown! I thought.

Suddenly I came to think of something entirely different. Those words of his that time were anything but lost on me. They frightened me, you bet they did. They lurked at the back of my consciousness like a warning and a threat. The Babylonian harlot! Wanton women! Terrible sicknesses! Sorrow, sickness, and death!

It had taken me years to liberate myself from them, so that I could use my own judgment.

Now I was liberated, of course. Completely liberated.

My father turned slightly in his chair. He was trying to find something to talk about.

"And your studies are going well?" he asked.

I mumbled something to the effect that my studies were going well. I thought to myself, probably for the first time in such a conscious way: Poor Father!

Meeting after Twenty Years

~~~~~~~~~~~~~~~~~~~~~~~

Ah, how small the world is. The day before yesterday I was writing about Mr. Halvorsen. Today I met him in the street.

Mrs. Middelthon was right. Mr. Halvorsen had shown himself to be a man with a future.

I hadn't completely lost sight of him during these years. I knew he became office manager at the expected time, that he got himself an apartment and married Miss Arnesen. Later came two children, one after another. That much Mrs. Middelthon had told me now and then when we met in the street. I had also run across him occasionally over the years and could see he was doing well.

Her I had never seen.

But today I met them both near the central subway station. He stopped and said hello. We stood there talking politely awhile. Groups of German soldiers strolled by. A German column marched briskly up the street. A superior marched alongside, yelling, "Eins-zwei-drei-vier!"

At the word *vier*! the column suddenly became tremendously happy and launched into a cheerful song.

Mr. Halvorsen spoke some hearty words about my firm attitude in the spring of '41—oh yes, he kept informed. One had one's connections, as he said. I'd been lucky to get away with just a few days up there, considering. He pointed backward, in the direction of Viktoria Terrace.

But tragic, very tragic, that it should lead to...

Tactfully, he refrained from completing his sentence, but bowed his head in quiet condolence.

"Well," he then said, not quite so tactfully perhaps, "people like you still have an easier role in some way. The rest of us, well, we have the less rewarding task of keeping the Norwegian economy running."

The task didn't seem to be that unrewarding all the same. He was stout, and his clothes were exceptionally elegant. Everything new too—suit, shoes, hat, duster, and gloves. Her attire was also brand-new, glittering. So it couldn't be altogether true that the German officers and their lady friends had made off with every piece of English fabric in the country.

No, his task had scarcely been unrewarding. I knew something about that.

He was still in the lumber trade. It was an area where many opportunities opened up once the initial shock of the Occupation wore off. Not that Mr. Halvorsen had done anything illegal, or something he could afterward be run in for. He may have gotten fairly close to the borderline, though. In fairly close contact with a couple of barracks barons. But something he could be run in for? He?

"Oh no," my informant said—he had the task, a really unrewarding task, of keeping abreast of these things—"that Halvorsen fellow is really smart. I bet you it won't be possible to get anything on him. The barracks barons will go to hell, that we know. Apart, of course, from what they've managed to stash away—garages crammed with paintings and things. But that Halvorsen fellow? And he too, we know, is stashing it away.

"But he does pay toll. A few thousands to the Resistance off and on. And brave words. Lots of brave words. What a damn shame to be forced to accept such filthy lucre!

"He has a farm too, with timberland and a summer dairy. Young Resistance fighters do their drill there. He has guarded himself nicely, all right."

My informant was something of a fanatic.

Mr. Halvorsen spoke a few brave words now too—after first looking over his shoulder. "Ah, that time at Mrs. Middelthon's," he said suddenly, "was really a very happy time. Without a care in the world and—well, without a care. One was young and merry then, and had no misgivings.

"None!" he repeated, making a sweeping gesture.

While we stood there I had time to observe both him and her.

He'd put on weight—as could've been predicted already then, more than twenty years ago. But it suited him. He was vigorous, healthy, red-cheeked, without a gray hair despite his fifty years. Well-groomed, with a faint fragrance of fine eau de cologne. A broad-chested, wholesome, dynamic exemplar of a good Norwegian businessman from the upper strata. He was nearly bursting with a clear conscience.

Yes, Mr. Halvorsen had risen in the world and would rise higher still.

It struck me that he was no doubt a fairly pure specimen of a type which— oh well, which is presumably inescapable; some even think it is useful, indeed indispensable: the sort of people who profit from everything. Either they make money, or they derive advantage; but as a rule they do both. They make a profit from the nation's good fortune and from its misfortune, from good times and bad, even from their own joys and their own griefs.

And it would be all too simple to view those joys and griefs of theirs as spurious in themselves, as being adapted to making profit. No, when misfortune befalls the nation they sincerely grieve—and profit from it. And when good fortune again smiles on the nation, they're just as sincerely delighted—and profit from it. When disaster befalls those nearest and dearest to them, or next to nearest and dearest, they're moved to compassion—and profit from it. And when their friends are doing well, they rejoice without the slightest envy—and take their well-earned reward.

Did he look like me? Did he still look like me? I couldn't see it. I refused to believe it. I clung to the idea that the likeness must already then have been rather incidental. That we had already then begun to go our separate ways, toward different goals.

With a certain satisfaction I noticed at that moment that my clothes hung rather loose on me.

She—well. She had also put on weight. Not so little either. I suppose that in a house with a good table, where the wife has the responsibility…

But it didn't suit her.

She was elegantly dressed in a dark tailor-made suit, a hat that must have cost a nice bit of cash—even I could see that—and black suede shoes with heels a thought too high.

But she had put on weight, had become high-bosomed and robust. What had happened to that light, delicate figure of hers? It had gone the way of all flesh. And that provocative, dangerous, passionate feature about her eyebrows, eyes, and mouth? All gone, covered up by an even layer of fat, and the face, the figure, the whole woman had assumed a look of—well, she looked satisfied and peaceful and pleased, as if she had reached her goal in life. And behold, it was all very good. Only, she had a dead look in her eyes.

Seeing her now, I thought in wonderment how I'd lain in bed crying and biting my pillow for her sake, while her amorous words reached me like an insult through the wall.

It was like thinking back to another life.

Here I felt as though my conscience plucked my sleeve.

And what about me? How had these twenty-odd years dealt with me? What was left of the young man with whom she had once whiled away the time for three to four weeks in her youth?

Thinking about him was like thinking about a man from another planet.

She brushed me with a glance, indifferently. I felt old, weary, and melancholy unto death.

We took a polite leave of one another and went our separate ways.

Kari

~~~~~~~~~~~~~~~~~~~~~~

It was an evening just before midsummer. I can still remember the sky—pale-blue with high ripply clouds; they were still lighted by the sun—for us it had gone down—and shone like mother-of-pearl. It had been a late spring, the lilacs hadn't yet ceased blooming. Meanwhile other plants had come out, and the residential areas were enveloped by a constantly changing fragrance of flowers.

A friend and I had been out somewhere together. I'd walked him home but we weren't through talking, and now he was walking me home. It had gotten late, the streets were almost empty of people. We strolled about amid the silence and the scent of flowers. We should have been home and in bed, but were too restless for that. It was such a beautiful evening.

I looked at my friend and thought, Lucky man!

The girls were so strangely taken with him. He always had one or more adventures going. A happy, lighthearted sort of person, he approached his studies with astonishing serenity; he was liked by everybody, especially by the girls. Lucky man!

A couple of years later he died—of a heart ailment he'd kept hidden from us all. It went so quickly; he lay there joking and laughing: "You can't imagine how strange it is to have a heart that doesn't know what it wants—ticktock, ticktock—pause—thump, thump!—pause—ticktock, ticktock!"

About the anxiety that comes with such a heart, he said nothing. The following day he was dead.

But it wasn't his story I was going to tell.

We had just reached Wergeland Road, where it skirts the Palace Park.

All at once we heard women's laughter.

That was not, of course, an unusual sound in Palace Park on summer evenings. But this laughter was something special—rippling, beautiful, happy. We both stopped to look where the laughter had come from. We glimpsed a light dress—two light dresses. A fresh cascade of laughter. We turned into the park, toward the two dresses and the laughter.

We are approaching something difficult. I can tell, among other things, by the minor detail that my pen is becoming irresolute—it fumbles, crosses out and stops.

I know I have some scruples about part of what I've already written, but I have more—in advance—about what is coming.

I ask myself, Am I justified in putting this down in black and white, even if it's merely something I'm writing to and for myself?

These notes ought preferably to be honest. If they're not, they have no purpose whatsoever.

But at the same time I realize they'd better not offend too much against my own requirements for good taste.

We all know this much: We may be as liberated as anything, we may have seen through as many of the world's prejudices and doctrines as at all possible and realized they're mostly vanity and listing after wind—still, one of the last things we dare let go are certain rules for good taste.

Although it's perfectly obvious that many of these rules have been established for highly dubious reasons.

Never talk about anything essential. Essentials are often disquieting. Accordingly they are labeled private and stamped *secret*.

Talk about trifles. Talk about the weather.

For God's sake be insincere!

If the devil is the father of lies, then good taste is their immaculate mother. For it goes without saying, it's a virgin birth.

Oh, if only it were that simple. But suddenly you run up against a rule that contains the sum of the filtered-down experience of numerous generations.

For example, the rule that a man should keep to himself what he has experienced when alone with a woman. If it was a real experience, at any rate.

But aren't there, maybe, circumstances where also this rule must be waived?

One of these circumstances may be the amount of time that has elapsed.

Once the day comes, as it has for me, when one must eventually admit—however reluctantly, very reluctantly—that youth is over, when it appears in the distance like blue hills partly hidden by mist, then one and all of us may be overcome by a desire to return to those hills, dream we are back for a fleeting moment, linger there once more for a brief hour. A desire to confirm: that was me! But at the same time the distance, the very remoteness, causes many things that were true then not to be true any longer. The years have gone by—all too many. Things that couldn't have been disclosed then can now be disclosed without further ado. Wishes and dreams that one couldn't acknowledge even to oneself, can now be readily acknowledged before the whole world. Secrets that were then kept as treasures have suffered the inflation of time. While other things, which were forgotten or overlooked, or cast aside as indifferent—well, time has worked on those too and, lo and behold, they've acquired a certain value, a value as a rarity, or even a more genuine value. The customary rules of discretion don't apply, it's such a long time ago. Or they must yield to something of greater importance.

That's what I believe is the case here.

I'm looking for something. Groping my way and looking for the roots of something, the roots of what I myself and others have later become.

We had the seeds of so many things within us. Why did some spring up while others went nowhere or withered?

I'm going to relate an event or two. But around these events I feel or rather know that something has gathered—the atmosphere of the years when they took place. If I could remember accurately enough, relate honestly enough, that atmosphere would envelop the events like the faintly quivering air over the smooth rocky slopes by the sea on a summer day, or like the softly shining orb around a faraway street lamp in misty weather. And this atmosphere would contain part of what has irretrievably vanished but that we are so reluctant, so sadly reluctant, to let go: the radiance of youth, the light of youth.

If it were to succeed I could say, This is what I was like. That—something altogether different—is what I could have been. This is how my life turned out. Such or such or such—infinitely many times—it could've turned out if...

As we wrap ourselves around the little thing we have become, we draw a kind of comfort, a kind of nourishing sap—or fall into a cold dread—from the thought of all the other things we could've been, we could've become. In that time of endless possibilities we call youth.

So we turned into the park, toward the two dresses and the laughter.

They were two very young girls. Eighteen or twenty years old. There was nothing very special to be said about one of them, she was just lively and pretty and average.

The other—.

It was the other one who'd laughed. She'd got a pebble in her shoe, had taken it off and was shaking it. That was the thing which was so funny.

I remember the way she looked as she stood there—if I knew how to draw, I could make a portrait of her from memory.

She was dark. Shiny black hair. A golden skin. Not deeply tanned exactly, it was too early in the summer for that; but you could see she'd been out in the sun a good deal, her skin had acquired a warm tint all its own. Her face was— what shall I say?—a triangular oval. It was faintly reminiscent of a cat's face. Her eyes were intensely deep-blue, her eyebrows dark. Her cheekbones stood out a little and her eyes had a slightly upward slant toward the temples. There was a mild suggestion of a Mongolian about her, a pure Mongolian. But above all she struck you as Norwegian. As Norwegian as a folk ballad.

She was still laughing, that ringing, happy laughter. Her teeth gleamed white against her warm skin.

They were not streetwalkers, even I could see that. They were just two girls on their way home through Palace Park.

My friend broke the ice, as it's called. He had no equal at that sort of thing. You couldn't find a girl who would be offended by him. I'd stood speechless beside him many a time, begrudging him that art. Everything became a matter of course when he did it. So natural.

In next to no time we were involved in one of those conversations that cannot be reported: light words, nonsense, laughter, a girl poking at the gravel walk with the point of her shoe, a brief sideways glance, a hint of a smile. And a brief sentence in a teasing tone of voice. All little things, wee little things. A small black beetle has been roused by our merriment and crawls angrily across the gravel walk to see if it's quieter on the other side. It can't be let out of sight—it looks like a parson in his cassock, it's so angry that it glistens. There it disappeared.

And the electricity in the air. Heaps of it. And the smell of flowers. The little pauses in the conversation. The pale night sky above the green trees. A bird flying with calm wingbeats high in the sky—a raven, or a nocturnal bird of prey on a scouting mission. A few little words again, and laughter—.

I remember thinking, I've never seen a more beautiful girl. And I thought hurriedly, despondent in advance, So that'll be Einar's next!

The other one—well, she was just pretty and sweet and young.

We started off. They had agreed we could walk them home.

We went up Wergeland Road, along Park Road, up Pilestredet Lane. Then the long Therese Street. We reached Ullevål Road and turned left. The sweet pretty one lived in a side street there, far up, almost at West Aker Church.

We chatted as we went along, stopping now and then when we touched on something we thought was important. Then we walked on. We'd known each other for a long time already.

She, the dark one, walked lightly as a gazelle. She surely didn't act like a girl with a stone in her shoe, not now anyway. I remembered a verse from the Bible, "How beautiful are thy feet with shoes, my beloved, my bride!"

And then I thought again, quickly, Oh well, Einar will make off with her, of course!

We hadn't split. I just couldn't bring myself to give up that dark folk ballad. And certainly not Einar; he knew, after all, that he always got the prettiest one. My heart sank when we finally stopped in front of the entrance door of the sweet and pretty one. It wouldn't be long now before Einar did the expected, took hold of her arm—yes, *hers*—and said as the most natural thing in the world, "Come, let's go!"

And to us, "Well, good night then!"

It was always like that.

Then the dark one took a step forward. "Well, goodnight then!" she said, giving Einar her hand. She turned, took my arm and said, "Come, let's go!"

Einar stood there for a fraction of a second and—well, he was gaping. Then he laughed. Or rather smiled. I can still remember that smile of his.

"Good night then!" he called after us.

Neither of us spoke for a while. There was a buzzing in my ears and my heart pounded like a sledgehammer. We headed downtown again, but now she chose another way, down Ulleval Road toward Sankthanshaugen Park.

Quiet streets, perfectly quiet. It was just after midnight. The night was blue but light, almost like the day. It was the shortest night of the year, the day we'd just put behind us was June 21.

The street before us was grayish white and quiet, lined by yellow and red houses, green lawns and dark-green trees. All colors were subdued now at midnight, but they were clearly there.

We'd crossed Collett Street and stepped onto the sidewalk that runs around Sankthanshaugen Park. She stopped under a large tree whose branches extended over the fence and made a roof over the sidewalk; she stood there gazing at me.

There were no people to be seen, no footsteps to be heard; it was quiet everywhere, as if the night were waiting.

She was deeply serious. I thought she gazed at me with such a strange look in her eyes—questioning, searching, a bit uneasy, but trusting too. I returned her look. I knew I felt very serious myself. For some reason or other it seemed to me a very solemn moment.

We stood like that for a while. We didn't touch each other. I felt in a floating, unreal mood. I recall how it flashed through my mind, Is this me?

"Why do you look at me like that, miss?" I said at last.

She replied, "I'm asking myself, Are you the person I've taken you for?"

She spoke as if we were on an intimate footing.

I said, "So what have you taken me for?"

"Oh—only that I felt, every time I saw you, that I've always known you."

And then she added, as if lost in her own thoughts, "It was strange, very strange, that I should meet you exactly tonight."

She was deadly serious all along, but somehow remote, as though listening to something far away, or something within herself.

All at once she seemed to do an about-face. She said, quite simply and ordinarily, "I don't feel like going home yet. Couldn't we take a little walk up that way?"

And she pointed up Collett Street, with the fence that runs around the park.

We walked slowly up the street. Neither of us spoke. I for one couldn't speak, I had no words for what I wanted to say.

We reached the northernmost corner of Sankthanshaugen Park, where Collett Street passes into Gjetemyr Road. The fence around the park was a bit lower at that point. And there was a gate, though now it was locked.

I said, "What if we climbed over and went for a walk inside?"

"Do we dare?"

She spoke softly, as if afraid someone might overhear us, though the street was deserted and empty.

I jumped over and then helped her across.

We stood still a moment, listening. I think we both had a feeling of doing something terribly forbidden and dangerous. But there was nobody around and not a sound to be heard, except for a nocturnal bird that hadn't yet finished its courtship. Sitting in a tree nearby, it uttered the same declaration over and over again.

There was a heavy, rich scent of flowers from someplace nearby. But I didn't see any.

We walked in among the trees. We had instinctively taken each other's hands, like two children alone in the woods.

As if by tacit agreement, we left the gravel walk, which crunched under our feet, and walked along the grassy shoulder so that our footsteps weren't audible.

We had walked like that awhile without speaking and were well inside the park. The trees were close together here, and there was also some underbrush. Then we heard footsteps on the gravel some way off. We didn't see anyone yet, only heard the approaching footsteps. We quickly ran a few steps farther away from the gravel walk and hid behind the trees and the underbrush. She pressed up against me, and I put my arm around her shoulder. I could feel her heart beating.

The steps came closer. There, at the turn, a figure appeared. It was a guard, with braids on his cap and a bunch of keys in his hand. He came down the gravel walk with a heavy, deliberate gait, walking with shuffling steps, his head lowered, lost in his own thoughts. He didn't see us, went by and shuffled on, heavily and deliberately. Then he was out of sight. I don't know whether he was a night watchman or one of the regular guards on his way home.

We stood there a moment longer without stirring. Then she slowly turned in my arm and lifted her face up toward mine. We kissed.

All the playfulness and all the smiles from earlier in the evening were again gone from her face. It was intensely serious, almost stern. Solemn—I had an obscure feeling as I stood there gazing down at her closed eyes that I'd seen this expression in a woman's face once before. But not in that of any woman I knew—it was a picture. A religious painting? A woman praying? I couldn't remember. And so I gave it no further thought.

How to explain it? It was like being in church, it was like being sucked down into a whirlpool. I felt I'd never kissed a woman before. The world vanished, all I saw was a woman's face with closed eyes, and I knew that she too was far away from the world.

I can't say how long we stood like this. Time and the world were no more. When I came to my senses again I was confused and dizzy and wobbly, and had to grab hold of a branch in the underbrush. She clung to me and hid her face at my shoulder. The pulse in my throat throbbed against her forehead. Every once in a a while she trembled, as if an electric current passed through her.

Again I can't say for how long we stood like that. Once or twice she whispered, "You mustn't leave me!"

Is what passes through one's head at such a moment thoughts, or just feelings that surge up and are later recalled as thoughts? I don't know. I only know that I seem to remember a thought that flashed through my head, "This is just a dream!"

I thought that thought several times, or it arose within me like a fleeting dread. I also recall thinking, like a sort of admonition to myself, Now you must wake up!

I was floating somewhere—someplace or other in space, in time. Was this me, standing here with a girl I hadn't known two hours ago? I didn't know. But I did know that soon I must wake up. It would probably soon be morning.

But I didn't want to wake up.

We stood alone there in the park, under the trees, but we were whispering. She whispered my name a couple of times. I hadn't told her my name but she knew what it was. I wasn't surprised. I was past being surprised.

Next we were walking through the dewy grass. We were holding hands again. We walked through open areas, we walked where the trees stood close together. I believe we sat on a bench awhile too. We told each other things, small but important.

"Look, it's growing light in the east already."

"Yes. But it's only one o'clock."

"The night is so short."

"Yes, the night is so short."

"Are you cold?"

"No, I'm not cold, I'm only trembling a little."

"How your heart is beating!"

"Is it? It's beating for you. Does your heart beat for me?"

"Yes, it does. Anyway, am I the person you thought I was?"

"I don't know. I hope so. No, I believe you are. No, I know it. Can you feel my heart now?"

Then we wandered about awhile again. We passed the swan pond and reached the gate facing Ullevål Road. Somehow or other we'd walked straight through the park. It was still night, with a blue sky, but dawn was on the way.

We managed to climb the gate. No one saw us. No people were passing, there were no cars in the street. It was as though the city had been deserted and become our city, our city alone, for this one night.

We were on our way down the street when I must've asked her where she lived, for I recall that she answered, "I live very close to you."

We continued walking down Ullevål Road. Again we didn't meet a soul. For this once the city had decided to be nice and leave us alone.

We were approaching the part of town where I lived. We came to a street corner. She stopped.

Did she live close by? I could walk her to the door, couldn't I?

But she shook her head, and I could see how she turned pale under her tan.

"I don't dare let you walk me home!" she said. "Someone might see us and... I'm not allowed to let anybody take me home."

We stood still for a moment. She swallowed a couple of times. I could see she was about to say something, but she checked herself each time. At last, however, it came.

"I don't dare go home!" she said all of a sudden. I could see she was scared.

"But—"

She looked down, her cheeks coloring up.

"You don't understand—you can't understand—there are so many things. You see, this evening—we'd seen someone to the boat and I was supposed to stay with Annie tonight, I'd been given permission for that. But then I met you and—it was so strange—and just tonight. I've seen you and known about you and felt as if I knew you, and I wanted so badly to meet you. And so I didn't want to leave you right away—and—and so I forgot that—"

"But—"

"I can't go to Annie now. The front door is locked and her room faces the courtyard. And I can't go home. I don't even have a key. And I'm afraid to ring the bell—so late. They're very strict at home. And…"

She spoke softly and calmly. But she was scared. The night was mild but she trembled slightly, I could tell by the hand I was still holding.

When she saw the expression on my face she said quickly, "It doesn't matter!"

She gave a light toss of her head, and with that she seemed to have freed herself of her worry and everything. Her eyes twinkled and her teeth gleamed in a little smile: "I'll just walk around for a while. I'm such a good walker, you know! And at six Annie will let me in."

That was when I made my proposal.

Everything happened so quickly that night, and so unforeseeably, so contrary to all calculation, so beyond all expectation.

Suddenly she was no longer a girl I was in love with. All desire, every wish for myself, had been wiped out, from body and mind, at one blow. She was my sister, and she was in a tight spot. Shouldn't I help her?

I was full of noble feelings, which I probably ought to have seen through. But ought I to, really? Was there, after all, anything to see through? Wasn't what I felt real enough?

That she took it so lightly, with a toss of her head and a little laugh, only increased my magnanimity and made me even more certain I was right.

What I proposed was that we could go to my place. We would walk on padded paws. We didn't have to wake up anyone. If she was tired she could lie down on my bed. I could sit in my chair. I had such a fine chair, a fabulous chair—she'd heard about Frederick the Great, hadn't she? The history books tell us: "His motto was: A king should die on his feet." At seventy he died in his chair. I had a chair like that. And as a matter of fact, I'd slept in it once— one afternoon. But if she wasn't tired, then we could each sit in a chair and talk. For I had two chairs. Well, we would have to whisper, of course, but— we had lots of things to whisper about, didn't we?

He who speaks in perfectly good faith is invincible. She became frightened and backed a step away from me. First she said, "No, no!" Then she tried to make objections, but I swept them all aside: "Just imagine you are my sister!"

Finally she tried, feebly, to suggest that I could of course join her on that walk. But it was obviously much cozier in my place, in that fine little apartment of mine, the finest ever.

Her hand crept once more into mine. "But do we really dare?" she said softly, in a near whisper.

"Of course we do. We aren't a pair of philistines, are we!"

Everything was so simple. There were no ulterior motives. I felt like a responsible, elder brother. I was calm, sure of myself and masterful.

She was still not completely sure.

"Do we really dare?" she said again. But she held my hand and went along.

When I opened the door she grasped my other hand. She whispered almost inaudibly, "But—do we dare?"

Then she followed me up those dark creaking stairs without another word. She was holding on to my left hand now. She clung to it while I fumbled for my key to let us in; she didn't let go of it until we were inside.

Then she simply stood there. Stood stock-still without a word, just staring at me.

I could see she was scared. Her eyes were so large. They seemed to shine like stars, as the saying is.

I went up to her to calm her down.

I was going to tell her, You mustn't be afraid. Just imagine you are my sister. I won't do you any harm, you know.

That was what I'd meant to say. But when I touched her I suddenly noticed that she was not my sister. My mouth sought hers.

"No, we mustn't!" she whispered. But she made no resistance when I took off her dress. Afterward she hung on to me even more tightly than before. I had my arms around her, she had hers around me. She followed me, whispering, "No, we mustn't. It would be wrong. We mustn't—oh, darling!"

She had been caught by the wave, it washed over her and whirled her along. And she herself was a wave washing over me and whirling me along with her.

Long after, in another space, in another time, we were on a beach, washed up there together by a storm. A beach on an island far, far away from other people—a South Sea island, coral reefs, palms and fanning winds.

This image came to me so strongly that I seemed to hear the soft sound of the surf, the whispering of the lace-edged foam slowly being sucked down the sands with a sigh. But it was only the open window sighing on its hasp, and the curtain curving inward and whispering gently in the mild morning breeze.

We lay there on the sands, limp and blissfully happy and smiling to each other.

She hid her head in the hollow of my throat and whispered, "We shouldn't have done it. But now we have done it and I'm happy, so happy...."

*

148

It was the night of June 21, the shortest night of the year. But a man of twenty-two can experience a good deal in such a night.

She was nineteen. She did tell me that; it was virtually the only thing she told me about herself. I didn't even know her name.

"You can call me Kari," she said.

"So Kari is your name, is it?"

That she refused to answer.

She knew quite a lot about me. What my name was, as I've said before. Where I came from, what I was studying. She knew the names of some of my friends too; but she refused to say where she'd learned all this.

She just said, "I know someone who knows you."

She still wouldn't tell me where she lived. She merely said that from where she lived she could often see me from her window.

"You saw me with someone you knew, did you?"

"Maybe," she said.

What she was doing, if she came from Oslo or from out of town, if she lived with her parents or with relatives—I learned none of that.

Had her family come from one of the mountain valleys? I was thinking of that faint suggestion of high cheekbones and the tiny upward slant of her eyes, everything that I called the pure Mongolian in her, when I asked her about that. But she didn't answer. "I can't tell you that!" was all she said. "It's impossible! If somebody found out that you knew me it could lead to— something could happen to me."

She didn't say what could happen to her. But again I saw her turning pale under her tan.

I asked her where she had her nice tan from.

She'd gotten it on walks in Nordmarka.

"He takes long walks in Nordmarka and Vestmarka. On Sundays—twenty or twenty-five miles. He has been doing it every year. And then he takes me along."

"He? Who?"

That she couldn't tell me. But when she saw my face she said quickly, "It's not what you think. He's a near relation of mine. He's old—fifty."

Who was it? I wanted to know. Was it her father? Was it someone she was staying with?

But she clammed up, keeping mum, sorry she had already said too much. "I dare not tell you!" she said. And again I saw she was scared.

It was a strange night. I had never been so happy. And she? She cried several times, without explaining what she cried for. Hugged me and cried. Just wouldn't explain anything.

"It's only that I am so happy," she said.

And I believe she was. At that moment in any case. No, not only at that moment. I saw her face, saw it turn serious, stern, far away from the world, bearing the stamp of a happiness shading into pain. I knew long since which picture she reminded me of—Edvard Munch's *Madonna*. I experienced that night the magical rhythm of happiness that can arise from a woman lifting a man away from the earth and giving him wings, and he in turn lifting her even higher, inspiring her so that she again lifts him, and he her, and she him, until together they climb, climb to the top of the highest mountain, where they can see all the kingdoms of the earth and their glory, and higher, higher, until they see the very heavens opening before them. I experienced what it means to see a person's happiness and joy growing in intensity, as if you first poured a single drop into a vessel, then fresh drops, fresh drops, until the vessel slowly becomes almost full, becomes full, spills over. I experienced what it means to see a flower bud form and take shape, its petals modestly curved around themselves and their own secret, and then to see how sun and rain and warmth slowly cause it to grow, the petals to open, cautiously, probingly, more and more, until the bud suddenly springs out as a rose and you are flooded with beauty, enveloped in fragrance and feeling proud as a god, because this miracle was performed by *you,* and at the same time so humble face to face with God's greatest wonder that you want to cry, and to hide like a tiny dewdrop deep down at the base of the petals.

I saw her apprehension vanish like the last patch of snow in spring, I saw joy spring forth in her like flowers, I saw tenderness grow within her and turn golden, like ripe fruit.

In the course of the shortest night of the year.

I had never been so happy.

"It wasn't true about the pebble in my shoe," she said suddenly. "I saw you and thought, Now or never! And so I hit upon this idea of a pebble in my shoe."

Well, I may have been stupid, but that much I'd half guessed myself.

"But you mustn't think I'd figured on—this!" she said. "You mustn't think that!"

I promised her I wouldn't. She was soothed.

"Still, I probably had figured on it!" she said. "That is, not I, but something in me had figured on it. Oh yes, I'm almost certain of it. There's thinking going on in so many parts of a person. Isn't it that way with you too?"

Of course it was.

She lay thinking it over for a moment.

"But just imagine—the first evening!" she said. "I'm really a bit shocked at you!

"But isn't Norway a free country?" she said. And she repeated it, as though in a sort of defiance—Norway was a free country and we were all free human beings.

She glanced out the window. Up aloft, far above the rooftops, a bird sailed along on a scouting mission. Caught by the early rays of the sun, it shone like gold against the blue of the sky.

"Free as a bird!" She spread her arms as if they were wings.

Yes, the sun was up. The windows outlined two lopsided sunny squares diagonally along the floor.

We had forgotten to pull down the blind.

I whispered to her, "Look, a new day!"

But with us, in our dark corner, it was still night, a summer night.

We didn't talk for a while. Then she whispered, "I fall so terribly in love with myself when you make love to me."

She seemed to think that this might need an explanation. For she added, "A girl by herself, what is that? Nothing. Only when you touch me do I feel how pretty I am!"

It was as if this thought gave birth to a fresh one. She got up, stepped out on the floor and began to dance. She didn't wear a stitch, but she took her hat—it must've been fashionable to wear wide-brimmed, light straw hats at the time—put it on her head at a rakish angle and danced an audacious dance around the old brown table standing in the middle of the room—that tame brown bear of mine. It was there I'd tried to cram Hagerup evening after evening, until I was forced to leave the house. Now the table seemed to look like myself, heavy and awkward, and she was dancing around me, light as a gazelle.

She was quite a sight. Slim and feminine, with long, slender legs. Impertinently well-shaped. And when she danced I could see that she was aware of it herself. Her dance was like a thanksgiving, a worship; it was like a declaration of love—to herself, to us both, to life.

She came and sat down on the edge of my bed.

"Thanks for the dance!" she said.

"That was for me to say, I think. But now we must be careful—listen!"

In the next room, Mr. Halvorsen had so far been grunting reassuringly. But now his alarm clock rang, and we could hear him turn around in bed and sit up with a sigh and a groan. "Humph!" he said.

She wanted to say something. "Sh-sh!" I whispered.

She made faces to me and whispered, "Take care, or I'll start singing!"

But I'd suddenly become scared. Mr. Halvorsen's alarm clock rang at half-past seven. At eight Mrs. Middelthon would bring my coffee.

I told her. We had to get dressed, quick! I had to get her out and be back again before eight.

"But why?" she said.

"What if Mrs. Middelthon came in and found—"

She thought it would be thrilling.

I was anything but a satisfactory lover that last half-hour. She lay there enjoying the situation.

During the last few minutes I stood by the door.

There was a knock. I said, "One moment, Mrs. Middelthon—I'm just now—maybe I could pick up the tray by the door?"

I held out a naked arm and pulled in the tray. The door opening faced away from the bed, Mrs. Middelthon didn't see a thing.

I placed the tray on the table.

"You see, I wanted to have breakfast with you!" she said.

Fortunately I'd bought a whole loaf of bread the day before. And I did have butter. And goat cheese—from Røldal.

How hungry we were!

Afterward she was sweet and obedient and put up with the fact that now she had to leave. She knew when I taught school, she even knew when my classes began every day of the week. There were things that suggested she lived somewhere near my way to school.

We got dressed, listened at the door, discovered that there was nobody in the hallway and sneaked out. I walked her down the street.

She looked about her, squinting at the clear morning.

"Just think—yesterday at this hour…," she said. She turned toward me. Her eyes were dark, like the water in a deep well.

"Now you mustn't walk me any farther. Goodbye—my love, my beloved friend!" She whispered those last words.

I wanted to know when I could see her again.

"Quite soon," she said. "I hope so," she added, very softly.

But how, since I didn't know where she lived?

She knew where *I* lived, she replied, and then she said, quickly, "Stay here. Goodbye."

She left.

I stood there following her with my eyes.

How beautifully she walked, so lightly, the movements of her hips so supple! She floated along, triumphant, as if each step were a delight.

Then she turned the corner and was gone.

I faced about and went home. I had to be at school in an hour.

I felt—but no, I give up trying to explain how I felt. But I think that, if someone had seen me then, he would've discovered that I too stepped rather lightly.

A few days passed. I was constantly expecting her, but she didn't come. I was happy, blissfully happy, and anxious. I raised my head again, breathed more deeply, threw out my chest, and felt as if I owned the whole world—and waited, waited.

I read a little law, a few novels, poetry, plays—and waited.

She didn't come.

I took the necessary turns in the street, but not sneaking along the walls as before, afraid that people should find me ridiculous. I owned the pavement on which I walked, looked up at the sky and owned that too. I made great plans, dreamed big dreams, knew everything, felt capable of anything—and waited for her.

She didn't come.

I waited so hard I felt hollow inside. Two days passed. Three days.

Ida

~~~~~~~~~~~~~~~~~~~~~~

And then I fell in love.

Well, I know it sounds unreasonable, unnatural, maybe revolting. But that's what happened.

It occurred in an incredibly simple manner.

I'd been waiting in my room all morning. Nobody came. Then I went out. I recall thinking, Damn it all, I've got to eat something anyhow!

I stopped to think for a moment at the corner of Pilestredet Lane and University Street. I was trying to decide whether to go straight to the restaurant and get that meal, or whether to allow myself a stroll on Karl Johan Street first. Karl Johan won out. The weather was so nice and it was midsummer time—June 25—and the next day I was leaving town to go home for my vacation.

As I approached the corner of University and Karl Johan Street I saw three people standing there, obviously waiting for something. I knew two of them. One was Hans Berg, the other was a girl he'd gone around with for some time last winter. Not a very exciting girl, if you asked me; and by that I meant—not very pretty and not particularly amusing. I didn't like her—anyway, she was the girl that Hans Berg later married. I was under the impression they had broken up sometime last winter, but lo and behold, there they were.

The third was a young girl I'd never seen before.

They greeted me as though I were a savior. Hans Berg and his girl, that is. The third member of the party, the young girl, stood aside, somewhat by herself, smiling faintly—a bit embarrassed, rather shy, but at the same time with an air of being quietly amused.

Yes, beyond the shadow of a doubt I was a savior. They were going out for dinner. To celebrate. Agnete, Hans Berg's friend, had just got a raise. So they had arranged to meet a fourth party on this corner but had been a little late—they had dropped by the wine bar at Blom's to celebrate—but not very late, barely half an hour; anyway, the scoundrel wasn't there. They'd been waiting for him for ever so long. Well—Agnete looked at her watch—for a full quarter of an hour, but he still hadn't shown up. How inconsiderate! Without the least regard for his friends' time! So now I came as a veritable savior.

Agnete became rather talkative at times after a glass of wine. For that matter, she didn't always need wine either.

She must be allowed to introduce me.

She introduced me. The girl's name was—oh, it doesn't really matter what her name was. Let us call her Ida.

Come to think, what *was* her name? Not that I mean to give it here—I would on no account have used her name. But I simply cannot remember. It's strange how one forgets names in times like these. I'm continually forgetting names. Even the names of people close to me, friends, relatives. It must be in the air, due to stress, something or other—. Her name was—it's on the tip of my tongue. Anyway, it doesn't matter what her name was.

So we'll call her Ida. She was young, slim, a dazzling blonde. Blue, cornflower-blue eyes. Fair skin—right now it was slightly bronzed by the sun, but it was strangely transparent, like porcelain. Golden porcelain. That, too, can give you the strange feeling of being able to perceive the life, the blood, that seems to pulsate under the transparent layer of fine, brittle clay. Because it's suggestive of skin.

She certainly did look rather delicate and brittle.

In that I was mistaken.

Her hand almost disappeared in mine. She was slender, but not skinny or angular. And eighteen—that I learned later.

I thought, Have dinner with them, why not? A couple of hours or so. *She* hadn't shown up all morning.

Besides I could afford it. My private pupils had brought in that much anyway. And tomorrow I would be leaving, and I had taken care of all my obligations. I'd even paid my rent for the summer. As a rule I gave notice before the vacation, to save money. But this time, no—I suddenly felt it was the nicest little apartment I'd ever had. It didn't bother me at all any longer that Mr. Halvorsen had company every once in a while.

And then there was the fact that *she* knew about this apartment. It was there she would come to see me.

I had made up my mind that morning, although I'd already given notice and all, and dropped in at Mrs. Middelthon's to pay for those six weeks. I got off easy, with half the regular rent. Mrs. Middelthon was so relieved. Now she was spared all the uncertainty, putting in ads and being overrun by people you knew nothing about. Me she knew and liked. Quiet, peaceful, no nonsense with girls, as she said.

We went off to the restaurant.

I looked at this porcelain girl walking beside me. I found her attractive. She turned her head and saw that I was looking at her, saw that I found her attractive, smiled faintly and turned red. Not flaming red—a gentle wave mantled her neck and face, right up to her blond hairline, giving her entire face increased warmth and greater depth, making it softer, more passionate. I found her very attractive.

I don't recall very much from that dinner. I only recall that we drank wine, followed by liqueur. Wine was an extravagance for us, and liqueur was good and sweet.

But wait—there are a few things I recall nonetheless.

I noticed that things weren't all they should be between Hans Berg and Agnete. Hans was absent-minded and silent or sat there muttering to himself. Agnete, it struck me after a while, was nervous and talked too much.

But then Hans Berg opened up. "Listen!" he said to me. "You who are such a moralist, what do you say to what Agnete is proposing? Now that she's got a raise, she can support me, she says."

Agnete wasted no time jumping in. "Cut out the nonsense, Hans, will you!"

"Nonsense? Not at all. She can support me, she says. While I finish my studies. Then it won't matter if I get a bit fresh with the girls in the senior class and lose my job."

"Cut out the nonsense, Hans, will you!"

"Nonsense? Not at all. She can support me, she says. That means I can just go on as before. With being fresh. It doesn't matter. She will support me. Just go on, she says. Being fresh. That's her opinion. Or perhaps mine. Because she, well, she can support—."

He was more tipsy than I'd noticed at first. And now Agnete was to pay for something.

He turned toward me. "A man who's kept by a woman—what do you say to that, you moralist and puritan?"

And I was to pay for having talked to him about that married woman.

He turned toward Ida. "And you, little sharpy, what do you have to say? If I get a bit fresh, I mean? For I don't make it a requirement that my girls have graduated, you know. You haven't graduated, have you? Well, I'm easygoing in that respect. I don't require a diploma. And she, she says she'll support—"

"Cut out the nonsense, Hans, will you!"

She managed to calm him down again. We drank a toast and went on with our dinner.

The whole thing didn't make very much of an impression on me. I had seen him disagreeable before.

I kept looking at Ida—talking with her too; but mostly I was looking at her. She was wearing a light dress with a V-neck. Not at all provocative. But when she breathed I could see the skin moving, and I could just barely perceive the incipient cleavage at the lower end of the V. Well, I was looking at that. And at her. I must've been quite wrapped up in her, for I recall Agnete glancing at me and laughing. Then that delicate blush again mantled her face, right up to her flaxen hairline.

I also recall another brief moment. I guess the others must've been taken up with their own things. At any rate, we were sitting by ourselves. She had said something, or I had said something. And we just sat there looking at each other. Then her eyes changed their expression. They grew darker, deep, deep blue. But that wasn't all. They took on an expression that seemed to come from the depths, her glance strayed—I really don't know how to explain it. It reminded me of the look in an animal's eyes—hot, dark, unconscious.

If I'd been a seasoned lady-killer I would perhaps have thought, In this moment you're mine!

But I might have been terribly mistaken. After all, she could've been thinking of someone else.

As for me, I certainly thought nothing of the kind. I just remember that moment.

The dinner was over at last. It had lasted four hours instead of two. Agnete had become quite—well, happy. She made us understand that now our ways would part. I must simply walk my lady home, unless I had a better suggestion. She and Hans would—well, they weren't quite through celebrating yet. "Are we, Hans?"

Ida and I parted company with them. Agnete turned around and shook her finger at us, "Remember, you will be called to account tomorrow!"

They worked in the same office, she and Ida.

When Ida and I were by ourselves we exchanged a few words. We came quickly to an understanding. It made no sense to go home yet. We would go out to Bygdø, to the Bygdønes Baths. But we would take the longest way to get there: the trolley to Skøyen and the rest on foot.

And what about the other one? What about Kari?

She had drifted so far away from me in the course of the last few hours. And this one was so close. So slim, so blond, so transparent and delicate, so golden and with such blue eyes—and so close. Not only was she right there beside me, so close that I could touch her; in another way, too, more difficult to explain, she gave me the feeling that we were very close to each other, so close.

What was really happening?

I can't say I understand it even now. I ought perhaps to content myself with admitting that this was the way it was and feel suitably ashamed. But I've learned in the course of time that I'm not the only one who has experienced such abrupt revulsions of feeling—or rather fluctuations; because there was no revulsion, not at all. I've heard doctors discuss the phenomenon. They can relate—they have to observe confidentiality, of course—that odd things may happen to honeymooners. Mind you, to happy honeymooners, such as are young, healthy, and in love with each other. The most sudden, unpredictable fluctuations may occur, taking the young bride or groom completely by surprise and potentially causing the worst possible remorse, even tragedy. Because the party concerned doesn't have the foggiest notion of what it's all about and therefore feels like a completely depraved person.

The explanation, the doctors say, is that being happily in love produces a state of tension. One goes around like a highly charged battery. And this state, which envelops him or her like an aura, is felt by all those present who are themselves charged to a certain degree. And then something can happen. It's a natural phenomenon.

Well, I have heard worse explanations.

And better ones.

I find it a bit hard to believe in such natural phenomena. I believe some degree of wishfulness, will and intent is also involved.

I was charged and she noticed it. I had gained in self-esteem, and that made me free and natural. She noticed that too. I was riding the crest of a wave generated in me by the other one, by *her*. But I didn't know that.

Didn't know? Of course I knew—had an inkling of it in any case. But it suited me just then to let the wave carry me down another path.

I remember thinking at some point in the course of the evening, After all, she didn't come, either today or yesterday or the day before. So the whole thing was probably just an adventure.

But in reality I knew, with complete certainty, that when she didn't come it was because she wasn't able to.

I suggest we say I had become a little scared.

I had met a human being who, in the midst of her dependency, was freer, in the midst of her fear more courageous, than I was. And in the midst of my enchantment I had become rather jittery.

And so, in the midst of my joy and rapture, I was constructing defenses.

Now and then I've thought, What might man, this strangest of all animals, be like if he was really free? We can dream of it—a sovereign, proud being independent of its surroundings, raised above them, the equal of beasts of prey, the equal of the eagle and the lion, and the equal of the dove and the gazelle (and, if necessary, the equal of the lizard and the snake), full of strength and mildness, of pride and humility, of wisdom and simplicity, the crown of creation, bearer of all of life's most excellent qualities.

We can dream of it, but we know very little about it. Thousands upon thousands of years of tradition, bondage, commands and prohibitions separate us from the primordial—if it has ever existed anywhere except in our dreams. But I believe it has. For once in a while, though very seldom, we meet a human being who partakes of the primordial. And then, due to the power inherent in its nature, it strikes through partitions and walls and penetrates to the innermost part of us. Be the person a black or a Mongolian, a Jew or a Scandinavian, his way of being tells us, tells each one of us, This is you, as you could or should have been.

Then we are torn between desire and fear; for we sense that if we are to become like him, we must forsake many things.

We may fall down and worship him, forsake all and follow him. But if so, who knows whether it isn't the slave in us who follows him—as a slave?

Or perhaps our fear wins out and we cry, "Crucify him, crucify him!"

It's written that he who is freer than others will walk in solitude.

Am I using too big words about a small thing? I wonder.

But let's try to say it with somewhat more common words. Hitch a horse to a horse walk for one year, two years, five years. Every day. Then turn him out into the meadow and say, Now you can walk about freely. What happens? Perhaps he'll gallop around a little, kicking up his legs and showing a helluva mettle. But when he begins to nibble the grass he walks in a circle.

Well, I hadn't exactly been hitched to a horse walk, but I had been kept in leash by a pretty strong tether. I'd gone about tethered without a demur for so long that it no longer mattered very much whether the tether was removed or not. I would no doubt continue to walk meekly in a circle, with an invisible tether around my foot.

I remember one thing. During that night with her, the gazelle as I called her, I suddenly thought I could see my old father sitting in the chair over in the darkest corner of the room. He looked stern and threatening.

I remember one more thing. When I walked back to my room the morning after that night I was certainly happy, overwhelmed and thrilled. But someplace or other inside me there was also, in the midst of my desire to see her again, a coarse puritanical sneer, Well, well, so you were one of those—an easy make!

And a fear, Hopefully you weren't sick at least!

No, one must be engaged for seven long years. And when the seven years are over, then, with God's help, your girl is no longer a sweet Rachel but a sour and squint-eyed Leah.

Oh, my forefathers, grandfathers, great-grandfathers, moralists and paragons of virtue—products of a cold climate and long winters—how oppressive and difficult you made life for yourselves, how oppressive and difficult for your descendants.

Of whom my humble self is one.

But in any case, Ida wasn't to blame for any of this.

We forgot to go to Bygdønes. We kept sitting out there in the Bygdø Woods. We had so many things to tell each other.

Until that evening I hadn't known that so many things were weighing on me, that I had thought so much, felt so much, intuited so much. It was as though a wide gate were thrown open to a spiritual kingdom, full of fruitfulness and desolation, delight and distress.

I'm afraid a great many thoughts, feelings, and experiences that by rights belonged to the books I'd been reading, somehow or other became my own that evening in the Bygdø Woods. But so what? At least it occurred in all innocence, unsuspectingly.

And she? I don't think she had a single dream or longing that she didn't confide in me.

Another thing is that her innermost secrets were perhaps not so very remarkable.

She had the sort of wishes and dreams that a young girl does and should have. She wanted to be an actress. She wanted to travel far and wide, live in big cities, be wonderfully popular, have a train of admirers and be a queen of love. On her travels she would come to Arabia, get lost in the desert and be rescued by a sheik. Whereupon there fell a red, romantic curtain. But above all she wanted to get engaged and married and have children and live happily and faithfully ever after.

We became close, close friends. We became such close friends that I got within an ace of becoming something more, on the spot. No, wait a moment—that, I think, must be an exaggeration. She had her defenses in order when the chips were down. And all things considered, the whole thing was fairly innocent. We gazed at the stars together—those pale, nearly invisible stars that can be spotted in the night sky at midsummer. Faraway spheres. But she let me take a peek at her tits too—two small touching, white, near hemispheres.

"I call them my twins," she said shyly, delighted that I thought they were beautiful.

We talked about life and death, about eternity, about the life of humanity through the ages, about the pyramids. But she allowed me to kiss both her twins, and I felt the nipples growing big and hard beneath my kisses.

"Now the other twin will get jealous," she said.

But she wouldn't let me go any further. Nor did I take a real crack at it.

And then, late in the evening, we walked together toward the city. From Skøyen on we took the trolley.

On our way home we crossed Palace Square. It was just after midnight. But it was light, it was still midsummer.

The square was empty and deserted—no, there was someone there, a man. He stood still on the same spot, turning around, shading his eyes with his hand as if the sun were shining, and peering around him. When we got closer we could see he staggered a bit. When we got still closer, I suddenly realized that I knew the man. He came from my native village, was one of the wealthiest farmers and forest owners in the district. An ordinary little man by the way, but clever and crafty in his field—he had grown rich buying and selling timberland. He was probably in town to pick up his midsummer settlement. An occasion when feelings tended to run high.

He returned my look and recognized me. He rushed toward me with uncertain steps. His face registered fright—fright, and a vast relief at finally coming across someone he knew.

"I've lost my way," he stammered.

I asked him where he wanted to go. He mentioned a hotel in Karl Johan Street. It was staring him in the face, a few hundred yards away. I pointed at the building, we could see it from where we stood.

"Just go straight down the hill and past those two buildings you see there" (it was the university). "Then it's the first building on your left."

He thanked me and left. He was somewhat drunk, but clear and reasonable. Only so scared.

At home he was known for his unique knack of finding his way in the forest.

"Lose one's way in the forest? No, that must be quite impossible," he once said.

I walked Ida to her door. We swore one another eternal love and fidelity. We would write to each other.

Then I walked back through empty streets, home to myself.

And she, the other one—that is, the first one: the gazelle, Kari. What about her?

That I found out later.

Somehow or other she had managed to make herself free that afternoon. And so she ran up to my place. She stood outside in the street for a long time, looking up and hoping I would come to the window. But I didn't come. Finally she climbed the stairs, rang the bell and asked for me. But I wasn't home.

Then she went for a walk, but returned to her post in front of my window and stood there a long time. When she felt she couldn't stand there any longer, she went in at the gate and sat down on the front steps. She sat there for hours, getting up whenever she heard someone coming from outside or upstairs and pretending she was just waiting there for a moment. Meanwhile time passed. Eight o'clock came around, nine o'clock. She went up and rang the bell again, figuring I might've come home when she went for that walk. But no, I was out. She asked permission to leave a message and wrote on a piece of paper, "Regards, Kari," and put it on the table. Then she went out again and stood on the front steps. It was nearly ten o'clock.

Then the door off the front entrance opened. Quietly, slowly. A woman came quietly out, locked the door behind her, turned around and came slowly down the stairs. When she approached the step where Kari was standing, Kari could see it was a prostitute going out for the evening to ply her trade. And she recalled I'd mentioned that a girl of that sort lived next door to me.

When the stranger had reached the step where Kari stood, she half turned toward her and said in a low voice, "You don't need to stand there any longer. He's out with someone else tonight."

Then she turned and walked down the steps and out.

This was such a blow to Kari that she had to sit right down. She remained there awhile, sitting quite still and crying.

Then she pulled herself together. That woman couldn't really know anything. She had only said it out of malice. Hadn't I told her that she was offended? She persuaded herself into believing that the very fact it had been said by this particular person meant it was a lie.

Eventually she perked up sufficiently to get up, walk down the stairs and go out. A moment later the gate was locked. She stationed herself in the street again, strolling up and down awhile. The clock turned eleven, half-past, twelve. Then it was half-past twelve—she couldn't stay out any longer and went home.

Ten minutes later I came back, let myself in and walked up. There I found her note.

Next morning I left town.

Vacation

~~~~~~~~~~~~~~~~~~~~

And then the summer vacation began.

I worked on the farm as a full-time laborer from six in the morning till eight at night.

One day Ida wrote telling me that she was going on vacation. And just think, she would be staying in a boarding house close to where I lived.

Well, close and close—the boarding house was in the neighboring parish about eight miles away.

The following fortnight turned out to be a strange time.

We often talked about how remarkable it was that she should have landed up here exactly this summer. We both felt it was something of a miracle and ruminated together on whether it could be called fate. Neither of us really believed in fate and we were above all superstition, but this was so remarkable that it seemed almost like a miracle. And it was her mother who had found the place!

Oh yes, she was with her mother, that was a substantial minus to the miracle.

Eight miles. But what is eight miles to someone in love? True, I didn't have a bicycle, we'd never been able to afford that. She *had* a bicycle. But she couldn't very well come biking to see me. And so I started from home every evening at half-past eight. I would arrive at our agreed-upon meeting place around ten. We had found a nice spot, an old outlying barn at the edge of the forest a couple of hundred yards from the farmhouse. There was even some hay in it. We used to sit in there when it rained, otherwise we stayed outside, in a birch grove behind the barn. Our trysts usually lasted from shortly after ten—by which time her mother had gone to bed—till shortly after midnight. Then she had to sneak in. She didn't dare otherwise. She had her own room, to be sure, but no, she didn't dare otherwise.

She wanted us to meet twice a week. Not more often—she didn't dare, it might give rise to gossip. And a girl mustn't give rise to gossip, it could hurt her reputation.

But it turned out to be nearly every evening nonetheless. I lent her a botany box, and she said she was going out to botanize. She did, in fact, learn a little botany during that fortnight.

Within the limits imposed by all her concerns, we had a good time. I was in love and overjoyed, though defiant and furious at times, that couldn't be helped.

For her concerns were manifold. There were so many things that a young girl mustn't do. It was a young girl's duty to look out for herself, or else she became cheap. It was a young girl's duty to play hard to get. She should know her own worth. She should deliver herself undamaged and intact into the hands of her future husband; she should value herself that highly. And I—well, she was fond of me, terribly fond of me, but we were both so young, and neither of us could know how things would be in a year from now, not to speak of three years, and I could hardly finish my studies before then, judging by what I'd told her myself.

On the other hand, it was clear that I must be allowed to do *something*, and she herself must be allowed to do something. We were allowed to kiss as much as we liked, or almost as much as we liked. We were allowed to cuddle, get close to each other, very close, only not *that* close. And I could, when we were sure that no one was watching, be allowed to see a little bit of her and to touch her, kiss her and stroke her and—well, God only knew if that was really allowed. But she just couldn't bring herself to say no, because she enjoyed it so much herself, and after all it wasn't the *real thing,* the thing she had to treasure, keep in the bank, so to speak, for her fiancé.

Oh yes, she took a huge delight in exhibiting herself to me. Part of herself, that is. She had a lovely neck and beautiful shoulders and a perfect bosom, which she was in love with and proud of. All this I was allowed to see—not without some fuss, never without a certain resistance, of course. But we were both of us clearly aware that before the evening was over…

In the course of the summer I acquired a very precise knowledge of— what shall I call it?—her geography. The upper part of her geography. I was grateful for that. I'm grateful for it even today. It was a lovely country. I thought it flowed with milk and honey.

To be sure, I forgot myself at times, becoming a touch too violent. She didn't greatly mind, she defended herself. And with her eighteen years she was more experienced in that sort of game than I with my twenty-two. She was no enemy to a merry rough-and-tumble. On the contrary, she would get excited and quite fascinated. But not *so* fascinated that she forgot her last and most essential duty, to protect the holy of holies, which only her husband, her future husband, would have the key to.

She wasn't quite sure whether she didn't let me go a little too far as it was. But on the other hand, as she once said, nobody suffered any harm from what we did, for nobody could prove anything. The other thing, however… And since nobody could prove anything and we both thought it was so delicious— because we did, didn't we? I thought so too, didn't I?

I thought so too.

I'm doing her an injustice.

I can see that, put down in black and white, in gross insensitive words, all this seems cold, calculating, maybe disgusting. But was that really the case? I don't know. In a way I guess it was. But it was also honest and sincere.

And the fact is I thought she was lovely, warm, innocent and full of sweetness.

And I believe she was.

She appraised herself as a commodity. Her body, her sex, was a commodity. She both understood and didn't understand that. But by submitting to this fact and complying with being bought and sold, seeing it not as something degrading, not as a profitable immorality but as good taste, accepted practice, as the way it should be, as morality, she actually managed to behave like a piece of merchandise in the marketplace without, strictly speaking, knowing that she was a piece of merchandise. While at the same time knowing it. This way she succeeded in at once preserving her feminine charm and exploiting it. This way she succeeded in being at once calculating and innocent, cynical and romantic.

And this way her reasoning came to appear as rather sweet and touching and—well, feminine. Rather stupid and featherbrained, but charming. Deliciously featherbrained. When she troubled her little head about morality and its demands more than usual, I called her my broody-bird babe. She put up with that.

Of course, I got worked up. I got worked up nearly every time I saw her. So that was the face of innocence in our time! For that matter, hadn't it always been like that? But at the same time I was touched and charmed. And, I think, really in love.

And what a warm summer it was. Such mild evenings.

It was her mother who had trained her.

"I tell my mother everything," Ida said. "That is"—she blushed—"not exactly each and every thing that we do, but—. My mother is like a sister to me."

I never met that mother of hers. Which I consider a real loss.

I cannot help recalling a little scene I witnessed on a winter day many years later. Fresh snow had just fallen, and all the children on the block were out with their sleds and skis. A small group of little girls stood with their sled on one side of the street, a couple of boys and a girl stood on the other side. The boys called out, "Why don't you come over to us!" The little girls would've liked to very much—they'd made such a fine big snowman over on the other side. But one of them, the sweetest and the nicest of them all—Erna she was called—couldn't, unfortunately. For she had promised her mother she would never walk across the street except with grownups, because a car might come, and then… That's what she had promised her mother, and therefore…

It really looked as if the girls wouldn't be able to get across the street to the boys and the snowman. For one thing was clear: they couldn't cross without Erna, the sweetest and nicest and loveliest of them all.

Then one of the girls found a way. "We'll pull Erna across on the sled! And afterward we'll pull her back over again. Because then she hasn't walked across, and then, you know—."

And so little Erna made it across the street to that nice big snowman.

Did we fall more deeply in love with one another in the course of that fortnight?

I doubt it.

An emotion wants to grow, to move forward, it wants to take in more and more. But we—we simply went in circles around a taboo. She sought the joys that were permitted, I went around charged, more and more charged, fluctuating between devotion and revolt.

Racing home in the summer night, I was so excited that every nerve was tense and all senses doubly awake. I heard the birds, noticed the multifarious life in the grass and the underbrush, saw the flowers folding up for the night and opening again in the morning—I was just a jumble of sensations. Dead tired, my shoes wet and my legs stiff, I got home toward morning, tumbled into bed, slept three to four hours, and was ruthlessly awakened at half-past five. They had to splash cold water over me to wake me up.

Every once in a while—at first only very seldom, but slightly more often as the nights went by and I was still returning home without having accomplished my object—the picture of Kari cropped up, her face, painfully impassioned, beyond time and space.

I dismissed it. It belonged to the past. I was in love with a different sort of girl now, one who had been strictly—no, leniently—brought up and couldn't help having some scruples.

After twelve days in this fashion I went to a dance. It was held in a hall near the boarding house where she was staying. I showed up as an uninvited guest and commandeered the prettiest girl, and on top of that I was from the neighboring parish, which in itself was as bad as being a Swede or a Russian. As the evening wore on there was a fight. I was attacked by two youngsters. I knocked one of them down and traded a black eye with the other, but had to save myself by flight from the National Guard, which advanced in full formation. Thank God, I'd got long legs.

During our rendezvous the following evening my beloved's virginity hung by a thread. She sighed, she begged. Never did anyone plead more sweetly in behalf of the interests of some man she at that point in time didn't even know by name. God knows why, but for a moment I was reminded of old underpaid bank tellers standing up to gangsters and getting a bullet through their heads while defending money that—if the gangsters didn't make off with it—would be swindled away by fat, incompetent bank managers on speculations in oil fields that had never existed.

But that's how the world endures. And since it is the best of all possible worlds, it ought to endure.

That night it got as late as three or half-past three, and at the last moment it was a cockcrow that saved Ida from going the way of the whole female sex. The cock became the guardian of chastity, and I ran homeward like an untrue Peter who at the last moment missed the chance of betraying his savior.

And then her vacation was over, she was gone, and with a deep sigh of loss and relief I lay down to sleep through a long, sunny, and tranquil Sunday.

Evening and Night in August

~~~~~~~~~~~~~~~~~~~~~~~~~

And then came that evening in August.

She had been in town for a whole month, I had just arrived.

We had exchanged letters, of course. Her letters dealt sweetly and touchingly with nothing at all. Still, or for that very reason, they made me uneasy.

They were written in the office. One of them had a scribbled note, "In great haste."

I thought, What does she do after office hours? Is she studying geography—no, botany?

This uneasiness of mine was confirmed—that is, disconfirmed but increased—when I saw her again.

Sure, she'd thought of no one but me the whole time. That is, she'd made the acquaintance of a young businessman. Just imagine, he was junior head already. Well, his father owned the business. He was very free with his money and had sent her oodles of flowers. But there was nothing between them; actually, he was slightly ridiculous.

He was impudent, too. Imagine, he'd proposed a trip to the Mediterranean with her. His father owned ships, cargo ships with a few cabins. And he proposed that he and she should go in one of them. Could anything be more crazy!

"Just imagine, the Mediterranean!" she said dreamily after a while.

But she had told him off, properly too. Imagine the impudence!

Oh, by the way—she'd also become acquainted with a lieutenant.

She mentioned the lieutenant's name but I can't remember it. Let me call him Kjelsberg.

Lieutenant Kjelsberg was a cavalryman. But she'd seen him only a couple of times and there was nothing between them. Anyway, he was about to leave to take part in a maneuver. And so she'd promised to meet him briefly tomorrow afternoon; but he had to be back home by ten, because they were to be off by eleven. So she was free from ten o'clock on.

This conversation had taken place the preceding day. I left, reassured but rather uneasy. And now I was waiting for her at the agreed-upon corner. It was ten o'clock.

We were at the end of August already and the evenings were dark. I stood in the shadow of a kiosk.

I looked at my watch. Five past ten.

A good while later it was ten past ten. This business with the lieutenant seemed to take a lot of time.

All at once, there she was.

That is, not Ida but Kari. She emerged from the August evening and stood directly in front of me.

We hadn't seen each other since that morning of June 22.

I noticed it took her breath away momentarily.

The same thing happened to me.

It took her, I can't say how long, perhaps a tenth of a second, to discover that I was waiting for someone else. It took her a bit longer to find her voice.

"You're waiting for someone?" she said. She couldn't quite control her voice.

"Yes."

To say I was waiting for someone was putting it mildly. I was waiting like crazy and thinking of the lieutenant. I felt like the greatest anti-militarist ever and looked at my watch again on the sly. A quarter past ten.

"And what about me?" Kari said.

And with those words she threw herself, without warning, without any sort of advance signal, onto my breast, clamped her hands around my neck and cried.

And how she cried. Without a sound, only like a silent, trembling explosion of unhappiness up against my chest.

And I? I stood there. I just stood there. Well, I do believe I put an embarrassed arm around her shoulder. And I should imagine I said, "There! There!" Or whatever a man usually says to a girl who clings to him and cries in the shadow of a kiosk.

And then she came. And this time it was Ida.

She emerged from the August evening exactly seventeen minutes late. I remember thinking, in the midst of my confusion and despair, Maybe this will teach you to be on time!

She looked at us for a moment. "Well, I never!" she said.

And no wonder.

I said nothing. Kari let go of me, wiped her tears and slowly turned around.

The two girls measured each other with a look that... But neither dropped dead from it.

"I'm afraid I'm intruding," Ida said.

"No, not at all," I said. I was inspired that evening.

Then Kari spoke up. "Yes, you are!" she said.

She kept staring at Ida. Her eyes blazed. "Don't imagine I haven't known about you two," she said. "But I won't—won't put up with…"

Suddenly she cried again and hung on to me.

"There may be limits to what I'm willing to put up with too," Ida said.

Meanwhile I had freed myself. I'd been rather rough—Kari wouldn't let me go of her own accord. I was angry. The situation was obviously embarrassing; just as obviously, it could neither be explained away nor saved. Anyway, I was angry. And to be on the safe side I was angry with both of them.

"And as it happens, there are also limits to what I will put up with," I said. "Here I am—"

"—waiting for me but having a rendezvous with another girl," Ida said.

"—whom I haven't seen for several months and who—but I can explain that! Come along!"

It was as though Kari had suddenly lost her gumption. She looked at me and at Ida by turns.

"I just wanted to…" she said.

"I just wanted to…"

She got no further. Suddenly she burst into tears, her whole body shaking. She just stood there in tears, her arms drooping.

Ida took a quick look at her. It was not without sympathy. "Come, let's go," she said.

We left.

Neither of us spoke a word. It wasn't easy to begin. And since I had to admit she had reason to be resentful, I became so myself, thinking, I won't say a word!

I also thought, I don't mind her being angry. But she's nosey too. Let her just stew! I can wait.

It was she who had to begin. And that put her at a tactical disadvantage.

"Well, I never!" she repeated. "Here I'm tearing myself away from Lieutenant Kjelsberg, who insisted on spending the whole evening with me. Who was willing to postpone his trip and all. Who wanted to hire a taxi to the Gardermoen encampment tonight, and all. Just to be with me. But I tore myself away and left. Just to meet you. And there you are having a rendezvous with a prostitute! If only I could have guessed, I would've left you there with her for the rest of the evening. Lieutenant Kjelsberg—"

That's as far as she got. For suddenly I no longer *acted* angry. Without knowing how or why, I'd grown furious, real hopping mad.

I believe I called her a cold, calculating hussy. Who kept rows of admirers on a string. And granted small favors to each of them to keep them warm, while letting herself be pawed a bit to keep herself warm. But never so much that she wouldn't be able to enter the married state at her full market value. Untouched! Untouched, my foot! Touched all over, polished to a gloss right down to her middle by male hands. Untouched, indeed! Did she say prostitute? Was it prostitute she said? First of all, the girl in question was no prostitute. But if she had been, so what? Prostitutes plied an honest trade, a very honest trade. They provided something for something and didn't pretend to be any better than they were. And that was a good deal more than could be said about certain others! Certain others who... But anyway, the girl she'd seen was no prostitute. On the contrary, she was worth ten times as much as one of those who... She gave herself, yeah, she did. To the man she loved. Didn't have her teeny weeny bird brain crammed with the multiplication table—*this* I can do but *that* I can't, *this* is permitted but *that* is not, *this* will pay but *that* will not... And it was not a rendezvous, but if only it had been! Then she could've stayed with her beloved Lieutenant Kjelsberg. For she, the other one, she really loved me. I could see that now. And that was more than certain others did. That, too, I could see now.

I was right about that, she said gently. She had possibly thought for a short while that she loved me a little. But she had quickly realized she was mistaken. Just think, to love me! She laughed, a silvery laughter. But anyway, until this evening she'd believed I was a more or less cultivated person. But in that too she'd been mistaken, unfortunately.

Oh, we were thoroughly charming to one another, as one can be at that age when everything comes unstuck and one is carried away by confusion and hurt and anger, and one's tongue utters things one doesn't mean, or didn't know one half meant, and one is too high and mighty to take back a single word, preferring instead to make things even worse and let both her and oneself stew in their own juice.

We had covered the length of a number of streets, I didn't know which. We were now in Wergeland Road, where it runs along Palace Park. It had started raining, without my noticing that either. Neither of us had brought a raincoat. Suddenly it also started blowing. A gust of wind sent a shower of raindrops over her blue summer dress.

"Oh, you'll get wet!" I said.

"Doesn't matter," she said. "Anyway, it's no concern of yours. And now I would like to go home. Without the pleasure of your company, thank you!"

With that she turned upon her heel and left me.

"Give my love to Lieutenant Kjelsberg!" I called after her.

But I didn't call particularly loud, and I don't think she heard me. Nor do I think I wanted to be heard.

I followed her with my eyes as she went her way—light, supple, lovely to the eye. She grew smaller and smaller as she walked away down Wergeland Road. Smaller and smaller, and by slow degrees rather dim in the fine, light August rain. Actually, just a few tiny little drops fell.

Run after her! I thought. Run and stop her, run—.

But I didn't run. I simply stood there, paralyzed, bewildered and unhappy.

I was in despair, thinking that now she was leaving me for good.

But if I had known, really known, that she was leaving me for good, what would I have done? Run after her, fallen on my knees before her on the wet pavement, flung my arms around her knees and begged and pleaded with her—or kept standing where I was, stiff and dumb with despair and powerlessness?

I don't know.

I only know that I kept standing there.

I sensed vaguely that both of us had met up with something we couldn't master. That we were like two children lost in the woods, afraid of the dark and blaming each other for the woods and the darkness. But I was clearly aware I had behaved unpardonably.

I felt like a thorough cad. I'd said some mean things. And crazy things. And dumb things. And wicked, spiteful things.

I can't say how long I stood on the same spot up there in Wergeland Road. I stood there staring at a black disaster. I was in such despair that I was shaking, as if I had a fever.

I came to myself through water trickling down my neck. I was holding my hat in my hand, I don't know why. And now it was raining for real. I was soaked.

I walked homeward.

I wondered if I could write to her. Ask her forgiveness. Take it all back. But I didn't really feel like taking it all back! Ask her to forget about it? But there were a couple of things it might do her good to remember!

Anyway, she *couldn't* forget it. One doesn't forget such things, I knew that from my own experience. Such things stick with you. For life.

Ruined for ever.

I saw the future awaiting me. A cold Sahara. A desert—desolation and emptiness. *Loneliness!*

I saw everything black-on-black. No break, not a glimmer of light.

I felt so alone, as if I were the only living person on earth.

How could it have gone?

After a few sleepless hours I could've gotten up perhaps, written a letter full of regret and despair—genuine regret and despair—which I could've sent to her at the office. A telephone call a couple of hours later—.

And then...

"I ought never to have seen you anymore."

"But darling, don't you see how desperate I am!"

......

"Did you really mean all those dreadful things you said?"

"Not a word of it. I was only so jealous of Lieutenant Kjelsberg."

"Jealous? *You* jealous? What about me? Seeing you with—"

"But I explained to you that I barely know her. You're the only one I..."

And so on. And all would've been forgiven and forgotten—until the next time we had a falling-out.

It could have gone that way, to be sure. But it didn't. Because when I got home and was about to unlock the front door, a figure stood out against the darkness. The figure of a woman who simply stood there looking at me, without a word. Her face grimy with tears.

It was Kari.

I didn't say a word either.

We stood there looking at each other for a while. Then, still without a word, she took a step forward and held me in a clinch again.

I was in a queer state. It was like a dream. Terrible things were happening, matters of life and death. But it all seemed to take place in a kind of somber drama, and while I had a principal role to play I was also a spellbound spectator unable to interfere with the inexorable course of the action.

I recall thinking, We two damned souls...

At the same time I thought, It's easy for women. They can cry.

In the midst of it all I felt terribly sorry for her. An emotion surged up in me that I couldn't find words for. I clumsily patted her back.

We stood thus awhile. She wept and gripped me more tightly. I thought, Why not? It doesn't make any difference. Nothing matters, what's going to be will be.

I opened the door. And still without a word being spoken, I let her in ahead of me.

As we climbed the stairs it seemed to me that, with each step we went up, we took a step down into a dark abyss. We were two damned souls, doomed to death and destruction. As to myself, I felt I would be an out-and-out cad and sneak if I did what I felt certain I was going to do. After that I would be beyond all rescue. And that's how it should be.

It was a strange night. It appeared that I too could cry. She cried, and I cried. We cried and clung to each other. We didn't speak, only made love and despaired and cried together.

We forgot that the apartment carried sound easily. Mr. Halvorsen woke up and said "hmm!" once or twice. Then we restrained our sobs until he began snoring again, which didn't take very long. Whereupon we forgot ourselves afresh. This time it was Slava who woke up. She knocked angrily on the wall, wanting to get some sleep.

It was daybreak at last. I looked at her. We were both a little calmer now. Her pitchblack hair lay spread out on the pillow like a raven's wing. She was no longer crying, she only caught her breath now and then. Her face was grimy and swollen with tears, but suddenly I thought she was even more beautiful than the first time I'd seen her. I kissed the grimy streaks from her face and felt a salty taste in my mouth, I buried my head in her hair and it seemed to smell freshly of ocean and seaweed. With her hands clasped around my neck, I felt, airily, that I was flying high up under the open sky. A blue expanse of air above me, clouds below me. I spread my wings and rested upon them. I didn't see land but flew on, free, calm, soaring.

I was swimming on the high seas. I didn't see land, but it was nice that way. I could swim on forever. The sea was fresh, salty and deep. Ten thousand fathoms...

I must have been asleep already.

A Baby?
~~~~~~~~~~~~~~~~~~~~~~~

Visitors from warmer parts of the world than ours can relate many odd things. For instance, about the weather. Sometimes the clear atmosphere weighs upon you like lead, the perpetually blue sky is like a sea of fire, and everything in nature cowers as if under a curse—the ants disappear from the surface of their mound and bury themselves as deep as possible with their rear ends up, the birds are silent, and the cattle seek shelter; the natives take refuge in their houses and lie down on the floor with mats over their heads, the white women go into hysterics and the men groan, drinking until their eyes are frozen in a blank stare. And then, look—a black cloud appears on the horizon, menacing, with vicious sulphurous-yellow edges, and at the center of the blackness flashes of lightning like pins in a pincushion. The cloud bank approaches, with dark tattered shreds of clouds at the head, like cavalry in front of the infantry; rising, it swallows the sun, changing daylight to darkness—and then it starts, with a fury so great that you believe the deluge is over you, that the earth is about to perish. The thunder roars, the tempest howls, the rain shoots horizontally through the air like billions of spears, crackling against the walls like machine gun bullets—as if dark gods and devils are scouring the earth.

It lasts for an hour. Then the tempest abates, the thunderclaps grow weaker, the rain deigns to fall at an angle, the atmosphere lightens, and suddenly the sun shines again. The landscape smiles through tears, the world is gay and fresh like a newly bathed child, the ants crawl out of hiding and turn their mandibles against anything alive—just come on!—the birds all chatter at the same time, and the natives stand on their heads and feet by turns. But those who belong together find one another and take revenge on their mortal fear by creating new life; the white women calm down, and the men have an extra drink. All is joy, peace and rapture.

Our tempest was not as nice and grand as all that. It was only one of those summer storms that sometimes occur on the coast and which we landlubbers consider quite severe; but the old skippers merely shift their quid and talk about a fresh or strong breeze.

Anyway, when morning came the whole world was smiling. There was no more fear, no shipwreck, no dark abysses that threatened to swallow anything or anybody. The birds were gay, and I dare say the ants were warlike.

And those who belonged together had found one another.

We repeated the venture of our first meeting and breakfasted together, and all went well. We chatted and laughed and, remembering it was prohibited, whispered awhile.

The first time—it was an eternity since then. It was only yesterday. All that had happened to me in the meantime had grown so pale, I could barely remember it.

Sometimes she would get serious all of a sudden and ask, "How could you…?" But *that* I could no longer understand myself, and so it was easy to answer.

My initial love had come back, strengthened by a deprivation I hadn't been conscious of, purified by my faithlessness, bathed in our mutual tears, reborn in mutual despair and unhappiness. There was no more grief or pain, Ida had vanished into the wings like a supernumerary, after walking across the stage with an announcement about the next scene.

It may sound hard and brutal. But isn't love always hard and brutal—toward all else? Young love is, at any rate.

In the period that followed I forgot Ida as though she had never crossed my path. Kari filled my heart to the brim, there was no space for other women, not even for the memory of them.

For some reason or other which I never learned, she was more mistress of her time for a while now. She would come to my room, we went for walks outside Oslo or in the streets at night, and she wasn't even afraid of being seen with me.

"It doesn't matter these days," she said. "Later on it'll be difficult again."

Never before or since have I been so happy as during the following couple of weeks. Never so fit, never so glad, so strong, so able to work, so friendly, so full of faith, hope, and energy. And it all flowed from love and returned to it.

She never told me anything more about herself. Not what her name was, not where she lived, not what kind of work she did. Nothing.

But at the same time I felt now and then that I knew everything about her. That I'd never known any other human being as well as I knew her. At times I felt I knew her every fiber, every cheerful and every sad molecule in her body, every shadow and every glimmer of sunlight in her heart, everything down to her most secret depths, which she herself knew nothing about. I felt I knew her down to bedrock, that I'd followed the vibrations of her mind all the way back to her birth, even further, back to the prehistory of the human race. Thanks to her I could behold a distant past when people were happy, sincere, innocent, with a joy as pure as a child's, like the joy of Adam and Eve on life's first morning.

But she had a secret room. There I was never admitted. She begged me so sweetly, "Don't ask me about that. Believe me, it doesn't concern us. Believe me again—it can only lead to misfortune if you get to know about that. You might get yourself mixed up with it and—no, I don't dare, I don't dare. Later on, perhaps."

She was not a virgin when I first met her. I asked her about that too—if what she kept silent about had any connection with it. She didn't want to talk about that either.

She just said, "The past counts for nothing now. Something happened, but now it is as though it never happened. Please don't ask me about it. I don't ask you, do I? Now that we have each other, what do those things in the past matter? I love you. You love me. Isn't *that* the most important thing of all? Do we need to know anything more?

I often thought she was right.

She loved me in such a way that I discovered—and was delighted to discover—that no woman had ever loved me before. When we were together we forgot everything—past and future, cares and worries, enemies and friends.

Meanwhile I underwent changes. Old grudges vanished, they were no longer of any importance. Old uncertainties disappeared, because I felt certain of the most important thing of all. Things I'd pondered and pondered—my own place in existence, sin and sorrow and shame, morality and the meaning of life—all that resolved itself, unraveling like a tangled skein when the right thread has been found. The meaning of life? But this was the meaning of life—to love and be loved, to be loved and to love.

But my happiness was not complete. There was a serpent in my paradise.

A man wants to know all about the woman he loves. At the same time he wants her to be constantly new and surprising—and of course she is, by the very fact that he loves her and she him. But he wants to know all about her. I don't know whether women are different from us in this respect, my experience pretty much tells me that they are. A woman wants to be assured of a man's affection. If she is, the rest of his life is of minor interest to her. A man wants to know all.

True, I did now and then, often in fact, have a feeling that I knew all about her, as I've said before, all that was of any importance. But now and then it was different. Sometimes when she came I understood she'd had a difficult time. Sometimes I could see she had been crying. Sometimes she latched on to me in a way that told me she was in despair over something, that she had fled from something, that she would like to confide in me but didn't dare to.

Then I was tormented by that locked room inside her. I would feel like Rolf Bluebeard's wife, that this locked room became more important than anything else. Then I tormented her.

Until she made me forget it again. Until she made me feel I possessed her wholly, every nook and cranny, every thought and dream, every fear and desire, all.

Those couple of weeks of my youth have left me with one conviction. I believe—no, I know—that a man who has truly loved a woman and has been loved in return, though he may meet with adversity and misfortune later in life, be lonely and abandoned, will never come utterly to grief. I mean that, internally, in his heart, he will never come utterly to grief; he will always have a territory to fall back on, a fixed point that helps him keep his balance, a treasure that nobody can take away from him.

But I'm quite aware that very few have had this experience.

It couldn't last, of course. What would the world come to if people could be that happy, and if their happiness could last? Just imagine all the vitally important and necessary things that would then become superfluous. There would be no more war, because its basis, suspicion and envy, would disappear, and because people would rather love than hate. The churches would be empty, lay preachers unemployed, because people had other things to think about and discovered the meaning of life on their own. Most courts of law would be superfluous for similar reasons. The world would come to a standstill—for isn't it a fact that what keeps the wheels turning is envy and resentment?

But no fear! It has been ordained that no trees can reach heaven.

Nor did our tree. A day was coming, a day of wrath.

I hadn't seen her for a few days. It had been hard, but I'd known about it beforehand.

Then suddenly she came. It was early in the day. She usually didn't come at that time. I had gathered that she was tied up with work in the morning. I walked toward her, surprised and glad. Then I saw that something was wrong. She was pale in spite of her golden skin, I could see she was on the verge of tears.

I asked, "What is it?"

She held on to me for dear life. She was all in a tremor. Weeping, her body shaken with sobs, which ceased as suddenly as they had begun. She didn't tremble anymore, she was perfectly calm. And then she said, her voice calm too, "Listen—I'm afraid I'm going to have a baby."

From that moment on I've known what people mean when they say that the ground slipped away from under their feet. I tried

Part Three · Notes from Sweden, 1944

Around in Circles

~~~~~~~~~~~~~~~~~~~~~~

In September 1943 I came to Sweden. It's now July 1944. I've been given time off from the work I'm doing in one of the refugee offices and live in a small pension out by Lake Mälaren.

It's a peaceful spot. Besides a number of Swedes, there are two or three Norwegians living here; but they too want to have time off—we talk about the war only three or four hours a day.

This is the first time since I came to Sweden that I have the time and opportunity to continue the bit of tidying up I began back in Norway in the late summer of '43, at a time when, as the saying goes, I was living in a fool's paradise.

I've just read through my notes from then.

I hadn't forgotten those notes. On the contrary, for special reasons scarcely a day passed without my thinking about them. I also believe that, from my very first day in Sweden, I was fully determined to finish them. But with this, that and the other, the work was postponed.

First, the abrupt switch-over from war to peace. For *that* was the upshot. It's all very well for us Norwegians in Sweden to persuade ourselves that we are working away as best we can, that we are sacrificing everything for Norway's cause, as they say in public addresses and after-dinner speeches. But what a difference! We run no risks anymore, or almost none. We are a small part of a large administration. Modest and safe.

We mill around in a backwater, that's the feeling we have. Strange how important personal risk is. As long as our work was associated with danger we had a feeling that we were taking part in something of vital importance, indeed, that we were helping to determine the fate of the world. Even if what we accomplished was so little that it was practically invisible to the naked eye, it was not so little to us. We took a gamble on—well, on something or other. Everything, if all went wrong.

Suddenly we are just sitting in an office, 9-1 and 3-6. Talk about the air going out of the balloon!

"You have to be prepared for something called the Stockholm sickness," my friends said to me when I came. "It's related to all sorts of things. A neutral country. Peaceful conditions. Masses of food. Your own relief at being out of the danger zone, which the next moment turns into melancholy at being excluded. And then—well, the homesickness is terrible at first. You may be sitting with a group of charming people at a fine board and suddenly not be able to swallow another bite, because you pine for sticky, underdone bread and unsavory margarine and rye coffee. The best remedy is to have your hands full of work. If you do, the worst attacks of the Stockholm sickness will be over in two or three months. But then you have to watch out for the emigrant sickness."

Wise words, as I would find out. I went through all the stages as regularly as clockwork.

Nor did I avoid the emigrant sickness, even though I had been warned in advance and had seen its unpleasant symptoms in others before I was myself affected. But prior wisdom like that doesn't help one bit, for the first sign of this sickness is that one thinks oneself fit as a fiddle, while everybody else is sick. And all those sick people have a remarkable ability to get on one's nerves. Indeed, it looks as if they have nothing better to do from morning till night but this one thing—grating on one's nerves, jangling one's nerves.

Ah, all those other Norwegians in Sweden! Careerists, incompetents, cowards, braggarts, intriguers full of themselves—I,I,I!—in the midst of the world's hour of fate. To be sure, a number of them had, in fact, done some fine things back in Norway, had risked their lives as if it were all a game. But no sooner had they been three months in Sweden and found a perch at the edge of an office stool, than it seemed as if this little game was a matter of life and death. They latched on to the stool as if they were in danger of shipwreck. They saw injustice done, intrigues prevail, insolent louts climb to the pinnacle of glory—but they just latched on to their stools and kept their mouths shut. Had they forgotten there was a war going on? Had they forgotten their countrymen faraway and on the ocean? Had they forgotten their own past? Funny, sure. But it got on one's nerves.

And then there was that government-in-exile in London! The incompetence here in Stockholm was bad enough, but how about the incompetence there! The downright incredible things that were going on over there! How had that government come to be at all? Had somebody hunted high and low and collected its members in homes for the mentally retarded? But when those at the top are so indifferently gifted and know it themselves—or rather suspect it, for they *know* nothing, nothing at all—they invariably contrive to surround themselves with the same sort of people, keeping at a distance those who would make them look ridiculous by their mere presence. And the end result is that peculiar London milieu—the paradise of dwarfs as it was christened by a man who had landed there by mistake.

I suppose it must be called a tremendous victory for the nations's undying intrinsic qualities. In the middle of the world's greatest war, living in the world's greatest city, our countrymen managed—hocus-pocus—to create Norway's littlest Podunk for themselves. Funny, incredibly funny. But it got on one's nerves.

And then those Swedes! Who were so neutral that it had pierced them to the marrow. Who believed, most of them—well, many of them!—well, some of them anyway!!—that since the *country* was neutral, it was the duty of each and every citizen to *think* neutrally, that is, not think at all. Who believed they occupied a morally elevated space because they sat safe on their little mound, while the rest of the world was drowning in the surrounding swamp. Funny, that too. But it got on one's nerves.

I had a rather bad case of emigrant sickness, and for quite a long time.

One of the reasons why I was so deeply annoyed with so many for so long, was that I was so annoyed with myself all the time. I knew that I must, ought to and should continue the work I had begun at home. But I put it off and put it off. There were so many things… And anyway, who could find the peace of mind to write when every day brought so many irritations?

This condition culminated and turned around on a particular day, June 6, 1944. D-Day, the day the Allies landed in France.

For us Norwegians in Stockholm that day was a red-letter day without compare. We'd been waiting for it every hour for four years. It seemed to us that the history of the world turned around on that day. We were walking on air.

In the afternoon I was traveling by trolley out to my small emigrant's residence in one of Stockholm's suburbs. I was still faint with enthusiasm. I sat on my bench as if on a cloud, looking out upon all the kingdoms of the earth and their glory.

Beside me some Swedish petit-bourgeois women were talking together. They were talking about the great event of the day.

It never occurred to me that this event could be anything other than the landing. And what they were saying tallied with that for quite a while.

"Magnificent!" said one. "Unforgettable!" said another.

"Too bad about the rain, though," said a third.

Rain? Had they said anything on the radio about rain?

Gradually there were several things that didn't tally. They had *seen* this unforgettable thing. But had the landing been filmed already, and had the film been flown to Sweden and shown the same day? Sure, technology nowadays, but—

"The King got wet!" said the fourth one.

So that was it: This very same day had been the "Day of the Swedish Flag," and the four women had been in town to see the parade. And it was all magnificent and unforgettable, but there was a small shower and the King got wet.

How outraged I was—and how I gloated! On this day, the greatest day in world history, a parade in the street was the big event for these—these—neutrals!

And the fact that the King got wet.

I gloated and felt outraged long and hard, until my own consciousness suddenly turned around and I was able to see the matter from the other side.

These sweet women were so far removed from the world's misery, so wholesomely lacking in imagination, so happily taken up with their own little joys and worries, that this parade became, as it had to become, the great event of the day for them—because it was close to them, definite, and their own.

Suddenly I thought, Lucky Sweden! Lucky Swedes! Who have been able to keep your lives on an even keel during these years, the same as ever. You have missed out on the pinnacles of rapture, but at the same time avoided the abysses of despair. Such drops may make anyone dizzy. In the physical world it's probably the Stuka fliers who know them best; and it's said that their middle ear, the center for the sense of equilibrium, gets damaged.

When I thought in this vein it was partly, I suppose, because I was nervous about the work I had to do, which I realized couldn't be put off very much longer.

My notes from 1943 end thus, *From that moment I've known what people mean when they say that the ground slipped away from under their feet. I tried*

That's as far as I got. And then things started happening. I was overtaken by what I was slowly and hesitantly approaching in my writing. And I was privileged to experience once more what people mean when they say that the ground slipped away from under their feet.

It was strange, now afterward, to reread those notes.

I believe I started them with the best intentions of being honest, ruthless if necessary, cruel if absolutely necessary.

But little by little my task took on a different aspect. I deviated into sentiment. I'm afraid that in the end I came to *enjoy* this tidying-up, about the same way a poet enjoys his hopeless love. Well, give the devil his due. I don't think I lied or distorted anything on purpose. But I did dwell on things, wallowing in my good or bad luck. And again and again I postponed that which I must have known all along, at the back of my mind, to be the essential, unpleasant element.

In the middle of my notes from 1943 I find a loose slip of paper, with no visible date, which I cannot fit into any context. It goes like this:

"It is difficult to speak honestly about oneself. Difficult to speak honestly altogether, perhaps. But about oneself? And one's own youth?

"We forget. We distort. We misrepresent and idolize—and constantly falsify. Even at the moment we experience something we falsify it, tailoring it, trimming a heel here and slicing a toe there, to make it agree with our wishful thinking about ourselves and others.

"But we're worst of all where the past is concerned. For there, as a rule, we don't even have a checker, except ourselves.

"Some checker!

"And we have a good helper in our memory, which gets gradually weaker with use, misuse, or no use at all, and places a merciful veil over our past.

"We all have dark ages scattered about in our lives. Most of all, perhaps, in our carefree youth…"

That's what I wrote. And I didn't even know yet what I was writing about. Knew neither how true it was, nor what a small part of the truth it was.

All this is beating about the bush. Banalities that I have to break through. I dread what I know I shall have to plunge into and therefore I seek a postponement, while hoping at the same time to escape the fear by philosophizing. But that—escaping the fear by philosophizing—simply cannot be done. It's there, in the darkness. It's like opening a door to a dark room, knowing that a viper, a huge one, lies waiting in there. It says "hsss!" and strikes you in the throat.

Then it's not much use to speak about the nature of darkness—that the darkness is really *nothing*, simply the absence of certain waves.

"Hssssss!" it says.

Once in my youth something happened to me. It was a fine experience, and it became a painful one.

I've been cherishing that experience ever since—taken it out of the chest, so to speak, turned it over and around and been happy about it, and sentimental over it, as well as sad. Even despairing. Oh yes, many times. I've reproached myself…. But all in all I was in love with that experience, ecstatic about it; I would sit around polishing it, turning it this way and that in my hand, it was mine.

Then, a while back, it returned. Like a huge snake crawling out of a dark room. It raised its head—"hssssss!"—and struck me straight in the face.

*

Something new happened to me, in other words. Something incredible, unbearable. The sort of thing that usually only happens in feverish dreams or nightmares. But it happened to me in broad daylight, and I was wide-awake.

We all know the expression, I wouldn't touch him with a ten-foot pole!

A powerful and graphic expression.

But suppose you met *yourself*—neither more nor less—and had to say, I wouldn't touch that fellow with a ten-foot pole! Then it would—well, it would be quite a joke, wouldn't it?

But at the same time I feel: This, precisely this, takes me to the heart of something exceedingly important, not only for me but for all of us right now, and perhaps even more so in the future. For it's not a chance thing, it's bound up with what we are fighting for during this blessed, this cursèd time.

Yes, I do have a feeling that, thanks to a singular blend of lucky and unlucky circumstances, I came face to face with an essential truth. It lies there right in front of me like a tied knot, all I need to do is untie it. But I can't untie it, I don't even dare get close to it; I go around and around it because—well, there it is again!—I have a sort of feeling that if I tackle it, if I try to untie the knot, it will turn out to be no ordinary rope but a snake that rears its head— "hssssss!"—and strikes the very moment I've untied the knot.

It's like a dream, a nightmare.

A Secret Mission
~~~~~~~~~~~~~~~~~~~~~~~

Back to 1943...

Andreas dropped by one day while I was writing what turned out to be the last sentence of my notes.

This was a few weeks after we had dispatched our mutual friend Indregård to Sweden. I had other lodgers now, but they were straightforward fellows, they were just waiting for some papers and for a particular guide to be available.

"Things are still going awry down in that goddamn small town!" Andreas said. He mentioned the town by name. It was the same town Indregård had gone to—in vain—to try and clear up that dangerous leak.

"As you know," Andreas said, "Indregård didn't manage to find anything. But something is going on, and something pretty dangerous too. Now they have blown a cover again, and two of our best people down there have been arrested. That sort of thing won't do. We may be forced to suspend all activity in the region for a while if we can't find the leak."

He gave me a searching look.

"You will have to go!" he said. "You know something about the situation already—through Indregård, I mean. And you also know this fellow Hans Berg. We are a bit suspicious of him. We're fairly convinced that the explanation is quite simple and obvious. Something our local people can't see, just because it's too close to them."

Well, a few days later, there I was in the train, equipped with all the papers required, genuine and legitimate, and an excellent, foolproof assignment. I was to examine a number of things in the bank down there, that was the official assignment we'd waved under the noses of the so-called authorities.

The journey was uninteresting. It offered the usual pictures and impressions of that period. German officers in a reserved second-class car. German soldiers bunched together by themselves as far as possible and generally behaving rather modestly. German troops, more or less numerous, at all the larger stations.

There were several farmers on the train. They talked about the weather, the crops and prices. Gradually the conviction had forced itself on me that if we traveled by train the day before the end of the world and, mind you, we all knew that tomorrow the world would come to an end, we would still hear the farmers talking about the weather, the crops and prices.

Anyway, I didn't much enjoy the trip. I kept thinking about Hans Berg. If I remained a few days in this town—and my official assignment, which I had to take care of incidentally, was bound to keep me there four to five days at least—I could hardly avoid running across him, in a town that small.

I didn't look forward to that meeting. What if he was a spy to boot! But that I didn't believe. There must be a limit to how much a man could change in twenty years. But to meet him and have to say hello and talk to him— because my assignment was such that I couldn't avoid the Nazis—ugh!

I might have spared myself that worry. I didn't meet Hans Berg.

As we approached the little coastal town I noticed some of the same pressure in my chest and throat that I still felt whenever I approached Oslo after a long absence. An anxious suspense before the big city dating back to childhood.

German soldiers at the station. German soldiers and officers in the streets. It was well known that, for some reason or other, the Germans were particularly apprehensive about this town in case of an invasion.

I'd been here only once many years ago, but I'd found out about the geography of the place and knew where the hotel and the bank were located, plus where Dr. Haug could be found. He was my secret contact.

No one met me at the station. That was as it should be. I took my suitcase and walked to the hotel, where a room had been reserved for me.

The hotel was old-fashioned but had been modernized just before 1930, at a time when money was plentiful. The lobby, the reading room and the lounge were spacious and rather ostentatious. A couple of German officers came out as I entered.

My room faced the small but rather attractive town square. Directly opposite the hotel was the bank. I'd taken a morning train, so the bank was still open. After fixing myself up, I walked over to call on the bank manager and to present my papers.

The bank manager, a man my own age with a predisposition for obesity and premature baldness, seemed to feel honored by my visit. Certainly, he said several times. Certainly, that was all right. Certainly. Very pleasant to have a visitor from the capital. The work could wait till tomorrow, there wasn't sufficient time today in any case. But if I would do him the honor of dining with him—he'd known about my arrival and made arrangements accordingly—we could discuss things in general at our leisure. Afterward we could take a trip together out to Dr. Haug, who had also been informed and was expecting me.

Here the bank manager gave a knowing wink.

I didn't quite know whether I should be pleased about that wink. It reminded me a little too much of childhood games of cowboys and Indians and of secret societies, or of those early films where the villain sneaked so cautiously along the walls and around the corners of houses that everybody could recognize him half a mile away.

There could be quite a few chances for leaks if all too many townspeople winked too delightedly at one another.

As it turned out, however, the bank manager—once he had shown me that he was in the know—was both a wise and agreeable man. He was interested in law, finance, literature and painting. He had a good library and good paintings—and a wine cellar which, he claimed, could outlast still a couple of years of war.

Moreover, he was a hunter and owned a perfectly lovely Irish setter.

But his rifles had gone the way of all flesh, as he said. That is, they might conceivably turn up again some day.

All in all, the bank manager seemed to be a man who got quite a lot out of life even now.

His wife was feminine and pleasant. I became a great friend of hers when it turned out that her two children took to me. I have a ready-made method when it comes to children—I believe children like all grownups who don't try talking like a child to them.

Naturally the war and politics were topics discussed at the table and over the coffee. But only in general. The distance to Oslo had become much greater during these years, as they said, and they were anxious to hear the latest news. Not news about the war, which they received daily, but the latest news from Oslo. They had the idea, which they could see through but still hung on to, that something extraordinary happened there every single day.

At one point in the course of our conversation I made a mistake—a quite unforgivable one, as it happened. I took it for granted that the mistress of the house was to some extent in the know and started saying something that must've made her curious if she was out of it. But the bank manager saved the situation, stopping me without anybody noticing I was being stopped and switching with perfect ease to a quite amusing hunting story, which made his wife exclaim, "Oh Ivar, really! That one I never heard before!"

My respect for the bank manager grew.

Around half-past six he got up. "All right," he said. "I believe our good friend Dr. Haug is expecting us."

He said a cheerful "So long!" to his wife as we left.

No sooner had we stepped onto the street than his face took on another expression—older, more serious, worried.

"It's a hell of a situation!" he said. "You will, of course, learn everything from Haug and the rest when we get there. But this much I can tell you already now: something smells bad here. Landmark and Evensen were taken four days ago, as you probably know. They are in custody here, and I'm afraid they're not being handled with kid gloves. We just hope they'll hold out. They were taken when the latest cover was blown. Fortunately they realized there was a hitch and managed to get back home. So when the Germans came they were playing an innocent card game. But they did find some weapons in their place—oh yes, we have all the particulars. Colbjørnsen stood just around the corner of the house and heard everything.

"The Germans have access to the inner circle, that much is certain—or almost certain.

"However, that is something we find absolutely unbelievable, even impossible. There are four of us. We have known one another for years. I'm prepared to bet anything whatever on each and every one. But—we can't find any other explanation either. They have found out about things known only to the four of us.

"There *is* a leak. We've changed our code twice recently, but it's no use. They have got us under their thumbs. We must simply assume they have the two of us in their sights at this very moment. Well, that matters less, since we have a perfectly legitimate reason for seeing Dr. Haug, he's a member of the bank's board of directors. But whether we want to or not, each one of us is beginning to have the weirdest thoughts about the other three. Personally I think I've been able to dismiss such thoughts, so far anyhow, but I've caught something in the eyes of each of the other three now and then—we are a bridge club, as you probably know. And I can't really blame them. In sum, the situation has become intolerable."

"Who are the other two?" I asked. "I know about Dr. Haug."

"There's Ole Garmo, in the old days a leading trade unionist around here; now he's working in the plant. And then there's Ragnar Colbjørnsen, whom I've already mentioned. He's a deputy in the city treasurer's office. Both are above suspicion. Though—who is above suspicion? I'm not either, I have to tell myself. In the eyes of the others, that is."

He smiled a wry little smile.

He related further that he and Dr. Haug had been hunting companions and bridge partners for the past fifteen years. They had some land and a cottage in the Valdres area. The third member—of the original club, that is—had been in England since 1941. He was an army captain. The fourth, an industrialist, was incarcerated at the Grini camp and had been there for over a year by now. So they first accepted Garmo and then Colbjørnsen into their circle.

"By the way, Garmo was also at Grini for a while," he said. "But the Germans released him again—there was so much trouble at the plant while he was away. He's a worker there now. Well, the plant doesn't deliver any more goods to the Germans because of that, but things are more peaceful now. Garmo has a quite remarkable hold on the workers. He was a worker himself to begin with, of course, and now he's one again."

"And Colbjørnsen?"

"We're getting to him," the bank manager said. "But what I was going to say—I'm confident I know those two, Dr. Haug and Garmo, like the back of my hand. There aren't another two people on earth that I trust more absolutely. But if from that you draw the conclusion that there must be something wrong with Colbjørnsen, you're mistaken. There simply *cannot* be anything wrong with Colbjørnsen. He has a list of meritorious achievements and a record that is considerably more distinguished than ours. He has risked his life time after time, and it's a wonder that, so far, all has gone well. We have forced him to be a little more careful lately, on account of our group activities. It doesn't come easy to him. Colbjørnsen is a fanatic.

"Besides, the leaks didn't begin to show until about a month ago, and Colbjørnsen has worked with us for more than a year.

"But once our misfortunes began, they came blow by blow. At the moment one may get a feeling now and then that they're giving the four of us the run of the farmyard, that they're playing with us—fattening us up maybe, as if we were a bunch of Strasbourg geese. So they can take us when they need a carcass. A sickening feeling, I can tell you.

"No," the bank manager concluded, "the whole thing is a riddle. If you can solve it we'll bless you."

We were now some distance away from the center of town, had passed a chapel and a cemetery, and were walking down a long residential street that apparently continued as a road leading out of town.

Dr. Haug lived in a large white villa with a wide garden in front. Lawn, tennis court and fruit trees on the sides. Garage behind the garden gate. Everything was well-kept and attractive. Here was one more confirmation of something I already knew: it is only in the provinces that people know how to live comfortably.

Dr. Haug received us in the hall. He was of average height, a powerful chunk of a man, weatherbeaten and fit. He looked more like our idea of an English squire than a Norwegian professional. But as became apparent, it was Colbjørnsen and the bank manager who had studied in England. Colbjørnsen had also spent a couple of years in France and was, everything considered, over-qualified for his modest post; but he felt attached to the town, what with being a scion of an old family and one thing and another. Dr. Haug had finished his studies in Germany. But that was many years before the Age of the Pig, as he expressed himself.

The other two had already arrived. Garmo was a big, husky man with a deep bass voice and with a touch of gray in his thick hair, suggestive of seal fur. His face was tanned due to continual outdoor life. My hand was helpless in the grip of his giant paw.

Both Dr. Haug and Garmo seemed about the same age as the bank manager and myself. Colbjørnsen was considerably younger—he appeared to be in his early thirties. By contrast with the other three, he gave the impression of being bookish. The bank manager had told me that he was a first-rate athlete, but there were no signs of it. He was pale and thin, with a fine narrow face and shiny dark hair, brushed back from a broad, very handsome forehead. His eyes were deep-set and shaded over—his eyebrows were dark, and he had dark circles under his eyes as if he'd been keeping late hours. His face and whole figure appeared tense. The bank manager had called him a fanatic, and he looked it.

Mrs. Haug came in and greeted us, but soon left again. By contrast to the wife of the bank manager, who'd been carefree and gay, she appeared tired and nervous.

For the sake of appearances we set up the card table and dealt the cards, but we didn't play. Dr. Haug took out some bridge pads with scores from an earlier game.

"There! Now the cat can come!" he said.

And then the conversation began. It didn't offer me very much that was new—the bank manager's account had covered the main points, and I was familiar with the rest from Andreas and Indregård. A number of details gradually emerged, but none of them offered anything even remotely resembling a solution.

Three different arrests had taken place during the last month. In all three instances the people involved worked for this group. One of those arrested had talked, as far as they could make out; but that was just a minor disaster, he didn't know very much and had received his instructions from a man they succeeded in sending over to Sweden. A radio transmitter was taken in transit from one place to another. Or rather, it was taken while they were installing it in the new location. Those who were in charge of the move had taken their time and assured themselves that they weren't being shadowed. Accordingly the Germans must've known where it was going. But how had they managed to find this out? Not from the men who did the moving at any rate—they were arrested and handled quite roughly. They could look forward to a court martial, with a dismally certain outcome.

"I tell you," Dr. Haug said, "it could drive a man crazy. All the threads lead back to us. If none of us has been careless—and we swear, every one of us, that we have not—the end result is that, by sheer logic, we must begin to suspect one another!"

I watched the eyes of the four men. Dr. Haug, Garmo and the bank manager were looking at me. Colbjørnsen looked at the floor for a moment; then he, too, turned his eyes toward me.

Garmo said in his deep voice, "That's just the thing to drive you crazy, as Haug says. For we *know*, don't we, that it's impossible. It's as impossible as biting one's own nose."

Dr. Haug and the bank manager chimed in.

Colbjørnsen, who seemed slightly withdrawn, said nothing.

I asked, cautiously, if it was conceivable that someone in any of their houses… If some relation could have—not betrayed anything, but—if someone could have learned something and perhaps been careless? One did, after all, have plenty of deplorable experiences.

The bank manager said, briefly and to the point, that his wife had no idea he was involved in things like that. Dr. Haug said that his wife probably had an idea of something. It made her uneasy, incidentally. But she knew nothing definite.

Garmo and Colbjørnsen were bachelors.

"Not that this exempts me from suspicion," Colbjørnsen said, with a cold little laugh. "But the fact is, I haven't confided in a single person."

Garmo joined in. "One gets out of the habit of confiding in people," he said.

Dr. Haug explained that since most of the meetings took place in his home, it had suddenly crossed his mind the other day that perhaps some devilish gadget had been installed here in his office—a detection device or something of the sort. And so he'd gone through the whole office with a fine-toothed comb—walls, floor and ceiling. But no, nothing, he could swear to that. And without such a device they couldn't hear anything, he could also swear to that. He'd had his doctor's office here during the early years of his practice, before he got himself an office in the Bank Building. And at that time he arranged to have this room specially soundproofed.

"We could shout in chorus without being heard in the rest of the house. And we aren't even particularly loud."

It occurred to me that Garmo at least was incapable of speaking softly.

Then it had occurred to them that someone might possibly be lurking outside and listening in—with some device or other. Therefore one of them had walked around the house at brief intervals during the last few meetings. But there was nothing to be seen, neither people nor devices.

As all but a matter of form I asked if they had any reason to suspect any of the Nazis in town. As a sort of courtesy to Andreas, I mentioned the name of Hans Berg.

They just snorted. Hans Berg was a crank, and also, it had turned out, a rotten individual and a scoundrel. But a spy, him? First of all, he was completely passive—so passive that this alone made it somewhat of a riddle that he'd joined the Party in the first place. But secondly, the man was so absent-minded that he'd been a byword in town long before the war. Could such a scatterbrain be a spy? Unthinkable, they all said. Colbjørnsen, too, agreed with that.

"On the other hand," Dr. Haug said, "if you had proposed Dr. Heidenreich, all right! He's more the type. But he just hasn't had the opportunity."

"And how about the son?"

It was Garmo who asked.

The son was certainly a dangerous fanatic, storm trooper and a member of Quisling's guard and all that sort of thing. But again the catch was—how could he have found the opportunity?

No, it was impossible.

The discussion continued.

For a moment I had some difficulty collecting my thoughts. So Dr. Heidenreich was here in town—.

But, of course, I'd known that!

I simply *must* have known it. He went down this way immediately after taking his degree and settled here. I knew that. True enough, we hadn't been friends since that conversation in the fall of '21—that conversation, yeah. We hadn't talked even once since then. By the way, he got married too just at that time, right before his final exam—what an odd idea! None of his friends had a chance to meet his wife. Then he moved into a villa on the outskirts of Oslo. A strange business.

But I knew, of course, that he'd settled here. We heard about that sort of thing. And now, at this moment, I knew I'd known about it.

But I had completely forgotten.

Later—about a year ago—when I saw the list of Nazi doctors, with his name among them, his address was right there. Now I remembered.

But that, too, I had completely forgotten. I'd only remembered my own judgment on him when I saw the list: Sure, it was in the cards.

I felt rather numb. Such forgetfulness was…

Well, his name was associated with an unpleasant memory. That fall…

I noticed I was still reluctant to think about that fall.

The others had continued to talk about Dr. Heidenreich.

"It's in his house that it all takes place!" Dr. Haug said to me.

"Takes place, what?"

"The interrogations. The torture."

At this point the bank manager intervened. "Tut tut, give the devil his due. One of the first things the Gestapo did was to take that house. Heidenreich was allowed to keep his apartment and his office on the second floor, but he can scarcely be held responsible for that. He wasn't a member of the Party either then."

"They took that house because it has such a solid basement," Garmo said.

"The most solid in the whole town, apart from the bank. By the way, it *was* the bank at one time. Heidenreich bought it at a bargain price when the bank moved into the new building."

"A real nice place to live!" the doctor said.

"Too bad about the wife," said the bank manager.

"What? Too bad about the wife?" Dr. Haug said. "In such cases they're both tarred with the same brush."

"Come, come!" the bank manager said. "You remember, don't you, when we heard about Heidenreich having joined the Party? First of all, it was a shock to us—we hadn't expected that of him, in spite of everything. And then I recall you said, 'Poor Maria!' You always used to like her so much—have you forgotten that too? You always had a great weakness for Maria!"

"Sure, Haug," Garmo cut in. "We all agreed at the time that it was too bad about Maria."

"What I said or did not say the very first moment doesn't matter," Dr. Haug said, dismissively. "In any case I've forgotten. Maria has chosen—"

"She's not a member, you know!" Garmo said.

"Member or not, she still lives with him as before!" Dr. Haug had lost his temper, but checked himself at once.

"No," he said, hesitating a moment but continuing, "If it's too bad about anyone in that house it would have to be the son. Do you remember what a fine boy he was? And now he's become the worst of the lot!"

They all agreed about that. He'd become the worst of the lot.

"Yes," the bank manager said, "that's one case in a thousand where we begrudge them someone they've gotten hold of. Good Lord, we've seen him grow up, after all. Damn it all, I was so fond of him—as if he were my own son. At one time."

"And the cussed thing is," Dr. Haug said, "that I can very well see—though we're at war with him and his kin—that in a way it's the boy's valuable qualities that have made him go as far as he has."

"You'll understand," the bank manager said, turning to me, "that in a small town like this lots of things affect us very closely. The Heidenreich affair has been a sort of personal misfortune—or a personal nuisance, anyway—for more than one of us. After all, he was our close friend for many years. And I for one don't mind admitting that there were several things I valued in the man. I never accepted that cynicism of his at face value—at that time. Well, strictly speaking, not even today. He has shown himself to be a fanatic, after all—in the wrong way, to be sure."

"Is it Carl Heidenreich?" I asked.

A superfluous question. I knew, of course. But I wanted to know for certain.

"Yes. Do you know him?"

I replied that I had known him briefly in my student days.

Colbjørnsen was silent during all of this part of the conversation. His eyes glittered now and then, and once or twice his face twitched. Quite obviously he was at once amused and annoyed by the other three, thinking they were a bunch of sentimental old fools.

But the three men were caught up in their own business and didn't notice anything.

However, the upshot of this digression was that, whoever was to be pitied or not pitied, and whoever was the worst or the best, no one in that family had had the remotest possibility of finding out what this group was doing or talking about.

But the Germans had found out about it. How?

And so we continued going in circles.

Impossible conjectures saw the light of day, only to disappear into the darkness again.

Had Landmark and Evensen...

But Landmark and Evensen had been *arrested* after all, and were right now, at this cursèd moment, being tortured.

Other names were mentioned, to be dismissed out of hand—they didn't *know* anything.

Again the four men sat there avoiding each other's eyes.

It was no fun.

The answer was unpleasant but clear: dissolution of the whole group, a pause, and a fresh start with new people. Nobody said it, but everyone knew.

At long last Dr. Haug got up and said that now we would have a drink. True enough, he didn't have a wine cellar, like certain members of the cratoplucy. But he had spirits, *spiritus concentratus,* and he had—top that one if you can!—pure lemon juice, sugar and soda.

And afterward we would have sandwiches. Nothing to brag about, he was afraid. But a few eggs could be found, from his own hen house. And there was still a can of anchovies in the basement. And a patient had made him a present of a goat cheese! And another patient had given him a veal roll. Anyway, that was only fair, because he'd carved her up in every way, removed a good many of her vital parts and made her as good as new again.

The doctor's humor sounded forced, but his menu was like a dream of paradise lost.

A young girl brought the drinks, and a moment later the sandwiches.

She was an exceptionally good-looking girl. Young—twenty, twenty-two years, maybe. Slim, blond, golden, but with a pair of warm brown eyes. Those eyes were directed mainly at the floor, as it happened, so that one couldn't help noticing her long eyelashes. She was neatly and coquettishly dressed in black, with a white cap and a little white apron.

Garmo started up a booming flirt with her.

"Oh Inga—any new sweetheart since we met last? No? But we can't have that, you know, you mustn't go off and become an old maid! You won't ever see twenty again, eh? Oh well, if everything should go amiss, you know where you can find a friend of mine called Ole Garmo!"

She barely answered him, barely looked up, just smiled a faint smile with downcast eyes. She reminded you of a blond Madonna. She tripped around taking care of what she was supposed to. Then she tripped out again.

Dr. Haug and the bank manager had listened to Garmo's flirtation with a rather embarrassed air. They looked away. Colbjørnsen seemed to be even more unpleasantly affected. He sat still, close-mouthed and narrow-eyed. Two small white spots sprang out on his cheekbones.

"Inga is practically like a daughter to us," Dr. Haug said, turning to me, after she'd left for the last time. "We have no children of our own, you know, and one thing and another. She is an orphan—lost both her parents in an accident out in the fjord when she was fifteen. We took her in and trained her, and we've never regretted it. She's very musical, by the way, and we let her take lessons. She's intelligent as well. And a very sweet girl, as I'm sure you could see. Garmo makes quite a fool of himself over her—well, I guess I don't have to tell you that."

"Ho—ho!" Garmo roared with laughter. "Let's say we all have a soft spot for her! Don't you agree, bank manager?"

"But you have the hardest time of it!" said the bank manager.

Colbjørnsen didn't say a word.

Finally the evening drew to a close. We all realized we wouldn't get any further today. Now it was up to me to think things over, come up with some questions, examine the terrain, so to speak. But they had already told me the main things, and we all realized what the answer was—unless something unexpected should happen, of course.

We broke up around eleven o'clock. The sky was overcast and it was pitch-dark. We walked in the middle of the street and managed fairly well. A couple of times we bumped into other wanderers. Once a German sentry shined a light on us, but didn't stop us.

Garmo turned off first. Then the bank manager, who stopped for a moment: "Aren't you coming this way too, Colbjørnsen?"

But Colbjørnsen had forgotten some papers in his office which he would like to pick up. Besides, he might just as well take the visitor to his hotel.

We didn't talk as we groped our way onward. Once or twice Colbjørnsen said, "Here we turn," taking my arm.

But when we had reached the hotel he said, "If you don't mind I would like to come up for a moment. I have something to tell you."

A Nocturnal Conversation
~~~~~~~~~~~~~~~~~~~~~~~

After we got to my room, Colbjørnsen first made a round of inspection—to the telephone, over which he placed his coat, to the closets and the bathroom, which he examined very closely. Meanwhile he explained to me, "One had better check…"

He had a free and easy manner, as if the room belonged to him. I thought, Excellent. But a little tact—.

"The hotel is in good hands," he said when he was through, "but our situation makes a person morbidly suspicious. And it's very easy to place a bug, you know."

We sat down. He looked closely at me. I had a feeling his suspicion had broadened so as to include me as well.

He may have noticed a certain irritation on my part, for he averted his eyes.

"I've come up here to tell you that I think Garmo is the man," he said quite calmly, eyeing me again.

It was now my turn to look closely. I had used my eyes as well as I could all evening and had decided that Garmo couldn't possibly be the man. There was something about him that inspired implicit confidence. Simple, strong, lighthearted, somewhat of a blusterer. It was unthinkable that a fellow like that could play a double game of that kind. And the doctor and the bank manager—just as unthinkable. Everything about them said it was out of the question. Moreover, they'd been in this group for three years, and the leaks began only a month ago. No, despite his meritorious achievements and heroic exploits and all the rest of it, my thoughts were constantly coming back to Colbjørnsen. He, at any rate, was not simple, and he was the latest to have joined the group. No, Garmo…

On the other hand I knew, of course, that this was exactly the sort of trap one was liable to fall into. It was precisely people who inspired confidence that were picked out for that type of work.

One more thing. I liked Garmo. I didn't like Colbjørnsen. But these were the sort of feelings that weakened one's judgment. It was about time I pulled myself together.

"Do you have any evidence?" I asked.

But the evidence turned out to be extremely sparse. Colbjørnsen himself had to admit that it was purely circumstantial. To me it didn't seem to be even that.

One of the things he attached great importance to was that Garmo had been an enthusiastic member of the Labor Party for many years, including the party's anti-militarist period. In fact, he was particularly enthusiastic at that time.

I asked him whether he didn't realize that many members of the Labor Party were among the best people of the Home Front.

Yes, he realized that, he replied, with a faint smile that said something like, What a banal question! But as far as Garmo was concerned—

"We formed a pistol club down here a few years ago," he said. "We were in despair at the way things were going with our defense, and—well, one thing and another. Garmo—and others as well, by the way—reviled us as fascists. One member of the club had some windowpanes broken, and—"

I asked him whether that club hadn't partly been formed with an eye to possible labor troubles.

"Quite possibly," he said brusquely, as if it were irrelevant to the matter in hand.

"But I can say this much," he said, "that of the ten members of that club"— here he began to count on his fingers—"one fell during the battles in April 1940, two are at Grini, one is a prisoner in Germany, one lost his life as an airman in England, two are members of commando forces, also in England, one had to escape to Sweden, and two are still here and participate in resistance work. Not a single one has failed to measure up—and Garmo called us fascists!"

Those two white spots on his cheekbones appeared again, quite distinctly, as if the bones were straining to pierce through the skin.

Strange, I thought in a kind of distraction, most people got red spots on their cheekbones when they became worked up; Colbjørnsen stuck to white ones.

I said, as soothingly as I could, that it was obviously deplorable that such words of abuse should've been thrown around needlessly in those confused years before the war. For that matter, who could claim to be blameless in that respect? In any case, he couldn't very well call it evidence against Garmo in the present situation.

He was about to jump up, his mouth poised for an angry reply; but he checked himself, shut his mouth, sank back into his chair again and suddenly became quiet and courteous. A bit too courteous, perhaps.

No, of course I was right about that, he said. One should always beware of hasty conclusions (I couldn't tell whether there wasn't a trace of mockery in his voice). By rights, he ought to beg my pardon for mentioning this whole irrelevant affair, which belonged to the past—to prehistory, as he called it.

When he'd mentioned it nonetheless, it was due to the fact that *he* had remembered it, which led him to undertake certain investigations and, in turn, to make certain discoveries.

Having gotten to his feet, he took a turn up and down the room. Then he sat down. Once again he was worked up, but at the same time a faint smile fluttered on his lips. I said to myself, Easy now! For I didn't like that smile. It reminded me too much of a cat playing with a mouse.

It suddenly dawned on me that he *had* something on Garmo, and that this introduction via the pistol club had only been a feeler to see where I stood. Once again I said to myself, Easy now! For now he looked at me with the same smile again. He, too, thought he was playing with me.

When this new situation arose, he said, everyone was forced to think hard about whether he himself had been careless, or which of the others might possibly have been so. He, for one, had given the matter careful consideration and knew he had never been loose-tongued. To be on the safe side, he didn't taste alcohol during this time.

I'd noticed that he only drank soda at the doctor's.

Well, very soon it emerged that it was no longer just a matter of carelessness. It was *treason* pure and simple. And as far as such people as the doctor and the bank manager were concerned, it was practically unthinkable from the start that those two—those two—

"—could be guilty of something like that."

He didn't say those *fools*, but it was quite clearly the word he was thinking of.

Nonetheless he'd made his investigations there too.

"So you've been spying on them?" I said. It escaped my lips before I could stop myself.

"Naturally!" he said in a friendly, slightly condescending tone of voice, as if speaking to a precocious child. Certainly he had; and he assumed the others had done the same, each for his part. The two of them, that is. The third one, well, he didn't need to…

But it had become apparent, as he knew beforehand, that the bank manager and the doctor were above all suspicion. And so he concentrated his attention on Garmo—bearing in mind what had happened earlier, among other things.

"You shadowed him?"

He nodded. With the other member of the pistol club who was still in town, he'd shadowed Garmo for a couple of weeks or so. Obviously he didn't tell this other person what it was all about. Only that he was interested in knowing where Garmo was hanging out.

His smile had become more distinct now.

"The result was in already after a week," he said. "We discovered Garmo having a secret rendezvous with Mrs. Heidenreich. They met one evening around ten on an out-of-the-way path behind the plant. It all looked quite coincidental and innocent. But it was neither innocent nor coincidental; they both came from the same direction. Garmo came first and sat down on a stone. Then she came. They talked for three to four minutes and then went their separate ways. By chance my friend and I were both there and saw it all, but unfortunately we couldn't hear what they were talking about. They spoke quite softly—"

A slightly bigger smile: "Even Garmo spoke softly that evening!"

I ought to have been glad. I ought to have been delighted. The riddle solved, the villain found, my mission carried out, everything in order. To my own amazement and alarm I noticed that, instead, I became deeply depressed. For some idiotic reason or other I felt sorry for Garmo. How strange, indeed uncanny, that one could take such a liking to a stranger in the course of a few hours. It was the best demonstration of the kind of pitfalls… You are not the right man for a job like this, I said to myself.

"When did this take place?" I said.

"A week ago. A week ago yesterday, to be quite precise."

"And you haven't spoken up till now?!"

Those white spots appeared again—quickly and sharply, as if on command.

"The son of a bitch forestalled us!" Colbjørnsen said. "We had a meeting the following evening. I was about to spring the bomb—then he told us he'd had to send two men into hiding. He had received a warning that they would be arrested, but had been obliged to swear never to mention his source to any living person on this earth."

"And then?"

"The next day, sure enough, the Germans were looking for the two men. The next day after that again we sent them over to Sweden. Two excellent men, by the way.

"After that, what could I do? The man has his alibi all set. Strange how smart such a mountain of flesh can be! He has covered himself. I cannot decide whether that warning had been arranged beforehand, according to the rule of give-and-take, or whether they overheard us that evening, careful as we were, and took care of the matter in a hurry the following day. The result is the same. If I'd said something after that affair, Garmo would merely have replied, 'Well, since you force me to talk—Mrs. Heidenreich alerted me to those arrests.' And where would I've been then? You have seen for yourself how united those three are in mutual trust, like brothers, and heard what a weakness they all have for Mrs. Heidenreich. Mrs. Heidenreich! Mrs. Heidenreich! Maria!" He made a face, full of contempt.

"That's the gentlemen's sentimental point. Hence the entire disaster. *The others* have no sentimental points."

I thought it over awhile.

"From a strictly logical viewpoint it may be true, of course," I said.

"What may be true?"

"That she came to alert him."

He looked at me for a moment with raised eyebrows. I knew I was being reduced to zero. But he chose to be polite.

"From a strictly logical viewpoint—absolutely," he said. "But when we know, at the same time, that treason is taking place—"

He eloquently shrugged his shoulders. I couldn't help thinking of what the bank manager had told me, that Colbjørnsen had studied in France at one time.

"We have considered liquidating him," he then said, very calmly.

"What? Liqui—. Are you mad?"

Suddenly all calm had deserted him. I was confronted by a man who called to mind a panther about to jump. And then he jumped. For a fraction of a second I had the impression that he was going to jump at my throat and I instinctively tensed my muscles; but he only jumped out of his chair and kept standing in front of me with raised arms and clenched fists.

"What do you want us to do?" he yelled. "Are we to let something like that continue? Are we to go around like a flock of sheep—baa, baa, we must have legal proof! Haven't we learned anything at all after three and a half years? Are we to go on and on letting ourselves be led up the garden path by these— these—till we're dead to a man? When are we going to learn that we are *at war*? In thirty years, when the war will long since have been won by the Germans? Do you believe, like the rest of them, that we can win by sitting on our hands? Won't we *ever* understand that, as far as warfare is concerned, as far as effectiveness, discipline, self-sacrifice, planning, enthusiasm, bravery, ruthlessness—sensible ruthlessness—are concerned, we have *everything* to learn from our adversaries? *Everything!* What would you do yourself in such a situation—send a courier to London maybe? And get an answer in six months—if those over there should remember to answer at all! Oh, I could— I could—"

"You could perhaps lower your voice a little," I said. "If there should be people in the next room, they would need no detection devices at the moment."

He calmed down at once and quietly sat down. When he spoke again it was in a low voice.

"I apologize!" he said. "I guess I got a bit excited."

I apologize—. I seemed to have heard those words before.

"All right," I said. "I admit I'm in doubt. As you, too, must've been, since you didn't liquidate him in the course of the week."

"We like to have absolute proof!" he said. "We're still shadowing him—fruitlessly so far. And then we were informed that you would be coming."

From now on the conversation was businesslike. The fellow had obviously needed to let off steam. Once that was done, he remembered I was his superior in a way, old and foolish as I was.

We agreed that for the moment liquidation was out of the question. He would continue shadowing Garmo. We would say nothing to the doctor and the bank manager. "They would just crack up!" as Colbjørnsen put it. I might have to go to Oslo to obtain further instructions, but I would sleep on it—we must assume I was kept under surveillance. The odds were that I would stay in town the following day and work in the bank, to see whether something happened that would make the matter absolutely clear. There was no emergency at the moment—a new transmitter had arrived and been installed, and there was no indication that the Germans knew about *that*. Colbjørnsen promised to keep me informed of any news of interest. I promised the same in return.

When we were through I had the impression that my stock had risen again to just a point above zero.

Colbjørnsen picked up his raincoat from the telephone and made ready to leave. Then he hesitated a moment.

"I hope you'll forgive me for getting a bit excited," he said. "But this situation could get on anybody's nerves."

I said it was all right. He gave me a look that almost indicated confidence. I asked, "This Mrs. Heidenreich—what sort of person is she?"

He shrugged again, in his French manner.

"A perfectly ordinary woman."

"Old or young?"

"Hmm—forty or thereabouts, I should think."

Then he was gone, and I was alone.

There was one thing I had to admit to myself, more or less against my will: Colbjørnsen was not play-acting.

And there was another thing that I slowly came to realize: I still felt bitterly sorry for Garmo.

A Slip of Paper

~~~~~~~~~~~~~~~~~~~~~~~

It was by the merest chance that I was able to solve the riddle.

I didn't sleep very much that night. I lay tossing in bed, thinking about Garmo. There was something in me which stubbornly resisted the idea that this simple, blustery man could be a traitor. But I couldn't get around the fact that the circumstantial evidence pointed strongly in his direction. And if it was him, then he certainly was not simple. He was still blustery, but it was nowhere written that bluster was a reason for acquittal.

How could he have stepped out of line like that? The man's past was clear and clean; that he was worked up about the pistol club wasn't that strange, was it? Many of us thought that those clubs were a symptom of incipient fascism.

Mrs. Heidenreich. In love with Mrs. Heidenreich?

A perfectly ordinary woman. Forty.

Hans Berg and his old lady. A married woman of forty. The dangerous age. Forty years in the desert. Forty-four years less a fortnight in the desert.

I was supposed to sentence him. I, the Spotless One, was to sentence him. Garmo, I sentence you to death because you've fallen in love with Mrs. Heidenreich, a perfectly ordinary married woman of average size. Sentence you to...

I must somehow have fallen asleep anyway, for I was in a courtroom and I was the judge. I was supposed to sentence someone to death, he was down in the dock but I couldn't see him. He had something over his face, a towel or— no, he didn't have a face. It became a blur, fog, there must be something wrong with my eyes—I must open my eyes. But the face was still fog. I wanted to say something to the accused, but it bothered me a lot that I couldn't see his face. Bothered me so much that...I wanted to let him speak, but could one ask a faceless man to speak? I would first have to look that up.... Oh, what the hell, I'll let him speak, what does he need a face for, I'll sentence him to death anyway. I turned to him with these words, "What does the judge have to say in his defense?"

No, that was wrong, a slip of the tongue, I had to say it over again.

"What does the judge have to say in his defense?"

No, no, another slip of the tongue. But good things come in threes, so there, "What does the judge have to say in his defense?"

I didn't get any further. And the faces of the public were sheer fog, and the face of the accused was fog. Only the accuser, the prosecutor in his silk robe, had a clear face, Colbjørnsen's face; it turned toward me with a thin smile as two white spots appeared on his cheekbones—the grass snake has two white spots, no, yellow, but it's not venomous, the grass snake is not venomous....

It was not a regular dream, only one of those half-awake, borderland fantasies. I managed to turn over on my other side and actually fell asleep.

I woke up to a gray, overcast day. I was in a bad humor, not properly rested, and with a bothersome feeling at the back of my head that I had to find a solution to something or other, something extremely unpleasant that hadn't even begun to be solved. How stupid that I had promised Colbjørnsen not to say anything to the bank manager or the doctor! I would have to reconsider that promise. Such promises didn't count if you came to have second thoughts. I would have to think about it.

I went over to the window and looked out at the square a few times.

At the bank I was assigned a room behind the manager's office. He brought me the necessary folders and documents himself. Yes, of course, there was work to be done.

"The problem still unsolved?" He looked inquiringly at me.

I had to answer that the problem was still unsolved.

He said no more about it and guided me in the jungle of folders and documents for a while. As he was leaving he said over his shoulder, "I've brought a snack for you. If you don't mind we can take the lunch break right here. Where we're least likely to be disturbed."

With that he left, and I sat there fiddling with the papers while thinking all along about Garmo.

That meeting with Mrs. Heidenreich could've been perfectly innocent. She was not a member of the Party, they had said. Who had said that? Garmo. How did Garmo know? Nonsense, in a little town like this they knew everything about everybody. Garmo just reminded the others of what they already knew.

Surely, that meeting *could* have been perfectly innocent. Not a member, sympathizes in secret with the Norwegian patriots but lacks the strength to break out. Finds out about a planned arrest, telephones to—

But what about the betrayal? One of the four...

If only something, however small, could be pinned on Colbjørnsen—but no such luck, that was the pity.

What's that? What kind of judge are you? Prejudiced against the prosecutor?

But that meeting could've been perfectly innocent.

Arguing in a circle, completely useless.

Around twelve o'clock the bank manager came, accompanied by Dr. Haug. He hastened to explain, "Don't get the idea we're careless. Dr. Haug and I often take our late morning snacks together—he has his office here, you know, and the hospital is only a block away. So his dropping by doesn't attract any attention. And no one in the entire bank knows that we both come here to see you. I've said I will accept neither telephone calls nor visits during this half hour. We felt we had to speak with you."

To be on the safe side, however, he went and made sure the two other doors were locked.

Then we threshed the matter over again, but nothing new came to light.

The two of them had obviously conferred together before coming to my office. I could tell by the fact that, when a pause occurred, the bank manager cleared his throat, exchanged a glance with the doctor and put forward what was evidently their joint opinion.

They both realized that, unless the leak could be found, the whole group would have to be dissolved and a new group formed, by people whose very names would remain unknown to the members of *this* group. In other words, they themselves would be forced to stay completely out of it. Summary dismissal. Wasn't that it?

He looked at me.

I said that something of the sort would presumably be the answer, unless the mystery could be cleared up very soon.

Well, and that again would mean that a certain suspicion would stick to this group for some time to come—it harbored a traitor....

He and the doctor realized, of course, that *they* would get off most lightly. They'd been part of the group from the start, and what with one thing and another—

Here the bank manager interrupted himself: "I'm terribly sorry for Garmo and Colbjørnsen!" he said.

But what he wanted to make clear was this: Speaking on behalf of the group, he would like to say that it was willing to agree to anything, literally *anything* that might contribute to the solution of the riddle.

I thought, Very obliging—and rather obvious.

But what would be the use? False instructions, sent out to ascertain whether they would be passed on, might've been an acceptable method in other circumstances. But here? The situation was too transparent. The traitor, whoever he was, would be lying low now for a while. At best it would take time. But time was just the problem.

Inwardly I knew that, if I couldn't solve the riddle in the course of the next few days, Andreas and those higher up would've had all they could take and a new group would be formed.

Today, however, the bank manager went on to say, the group had done something on its own initiative. Through a secret contact they'd sent the Germans a false report about a camp in the woods.

So now they would see whether those gentlemen reacted, or whether they knew better. Colbjørnsen had been of the opinion that it served no purpose, but…

I thought, O sancta simplicitas!

Colbjørnsen was obviously right. What did a blind sortie matter? It was nothing but an exercise, after all.

But what the bank manager wanted to say—what he and the doctor had talked about today—was that, while they were willing to agree to anything, as indicated, they wanted to impress upon me that it *must* be possible to come up with another explanation than that one of the four… With the sort of past that…

I saw this as a good opportunity to ask if they could tell me anything more about Garmo's and Colbjørnsen's pasts.

They could, but what they related didn't get me anywhere.

Garmo had been badly mauled when he was locked up. He was imprisoned for three months and during that time lost between fifty amd sixty pounds. He had still scars all over from the beatings and was temporarily in danger of losing his sight in one eye, which had become inflamed from a blow. Dr. Haug had saved it for him, the bank manager said, to which Haug replied, "Nonsense! But it did look ghastly!"

The sabotage at the plant? Well, they didn't feel justified in giving any details about that, but it was conducted with a masterly hand. The Germans just weren't able to discover the reason why the deliveries were so small.

I was also told about several more exploits by Colbjørnsen—about the time when he escaped simply because he could ski faster than the German Gaumaster, or whatever he was called, one of his pursuers. About the time when he saved himself and his work group by a pistol shot—he hit the German straight in the heart with his first shot at a distance of some eighty feet.

"The pistol club came in handy that time," the doctor said. "Not even Garmo had any objection then."

So that antagonism was well known. Naturally.

I gingerly asked about Garmo and Mrs. Heidenreich. I had the impression they had been seeing each other. But didn't they belong to quite different social circles?

They were able to tell me that Garmo and Mrs. Heidenreich were distant relations. They hailed from the same village up in Gudbrandsdal or Valdres, or wherever it was.

I thought, Ah, was that so!

And besides there weren't so many different social circles in a town such as this. Moreover, as one of the leaders of organized labor in the district— thousands of men, over five hundred in the plant alone—Garmo was a man of importance in the town. In the period before the Occupation, that is.

"But it never came to any real association between Garmo and the Heidenreichs," the doctor said. "He and Mrs. Heidenreich were good friends, as you must've noticed. But he couldn't stomach Heidenreich—for political reasons, essentially; Heidenreich was further to the right even than our bank manager, so you can imagine the rest! They didn't get along well otherwise either. Heidenreich's cynical jargon, his—"

At this point the bank manager cut in to say that Dr. Haug was a cultural Bolshevik. He himself didn't go that far, but in reality he was a socialist. He looked forward to a social order where everybody had his own wine cellar— or at any rate a cottage in the mountains.

"Give every Norwegian a cottage in the mountains and the social problems will take care of themselves!" said the bank manager.

In my opinion a good many social problems would have to be taken care of first. Anyway, though their banter continued yet awhile, I listened only with half an ear to their social views. What interested me was the information about Garmo.

Strange how one piece of information was constantly canceling out another piece.

The doctor looked at his watch and jumped up. We'd been sitting there for over an hour.

When the office hours were over I declined the bank manager's dinner invitation, nor did he insist. He realized, as he said, that perhaps we shouldn't be seen together too much.

I noticed a few people in the hotel dining room, sad-looking individuals, obviously regular customers.

Two German officers came in and ordered a drink. They glanced at me— a new face—but were soon absorbed in their drinks and a couple of German newspapers. Suddenly they were in the middle of a violent exchange. One of them was particularly excited. He smacked the table with his rolled-up paper, evidently repeating one and the same thing over and over again and getting increasingly more agitated. They had spoken in hushed tones at first, but their voices rose, and eventually the last words of his sentence reached me right across the big dining hall: "...verdammten Italiener! ...noch mehr verdammt als die verdammten Norweger!"

"Aber hattest du was anders erwartet?"

The other managed to calm the excited one with a couple of words in an undertone. They drank up, threw me another glance and left.

They also had their worries. Good. But how could that help me?

Still, it felt good. During the rest of the dinner it even seemed to me that the half-rotten fish was almost edible. But as soon as I got to my room it didn't help anymore.

I went over to the window a couple of times and looked out at the square. I didn't really know what I was looking for. Did I hope to see the solution come walking down the street?

I thought, Time to shake off your obtuseness. A piddling little case like this! Why, the explanation is sure to be staring you squarely in the face somewhere or other! It's just that you are too obtuse to see it! Have a drink and go to bed, and you'll dream the solution!

I took a stiff drink from a bottle I'd taken along, undressed, went to bed and fell asleep at once.

Well, what with enforced widowerhood and one thing and another, I had of course noticed that the young Inga at the doctor's was not altogether as simple as she pretended to be, with her downcast Madonna eyes and her mincing steps. But that she should come to me at the hotel and with unequivocal gestures urge me to commit fornication in the middle of the afternoon, that I had certainly not expected. And that is what she did—in my dream.

Her eyes were still downcast, but she gave me a lightning glance that couldn't be mistaken—its expression was not chaste. She came toward me, a finger to her lips. Obviously this thing between the two of us was to remain a secret. And all along, in the midst of her gliding movements and the inviting gestures of her whole body, she maintained a hypocritical Madonna expression and a false Mona Lisa smile, with her finger to her lips, as if we shared some dirty secret.

I woke up, deeply depressed. So those were the sort of thoughts that occupied me while I was engaged on a vital secret mission. I cursed, took a cold shower, and decided to go for a long walk in order to find, in the god-given open air, the solution that the dream hadn't given me.

I walked over to the window to take a look at the weather. Gray, heavy, with dense dark clouds sailing up and producing an early twilight. Rain was in the offing. I was just going to put on my coat when I noticed that something was happening in the square. Five or six policemen had turned out and positioned themselves along the edge of the sidewalk. In the middle of the square, right in front of the little fountain, some men were adding the finishing touches to an arrangement that suggested a meeting—they had built a platform, a small stage made of boards, and set out a few flowers and things. A Nazi propaganda meeting! Through the open window I could already hear the brass band playing, and now I saw the procession coming up the main street and turning into the square.

It was nothing to write home about. The band consisted of five or six men—the band of the local Quisling Guard, presumably. They tooted and blew some tune or other, I suppose the Horst-Wessel song. That was something I would never know for certain: my brain had managed to block itself off from that tune during all these years. In any case, it was a pleasure to hear that their playing was out of tune.

Behind the band came the procession—first, a couple of German officers, then ten to twelve young men in Guard uniform, followed by a group of eight or ten people in civilian dress, a mix of children and older people. They marched toward the middle of the square where the platform stood. The band gave a final false blare, the guardsmen lined up as a watch around the platform, the civilians in turn lined up behind them, and onto the stage stepped the two German officers—I could now see that one was from the Wehrmacht and one from the Gestapo. A young man from the Guard followed.

The Gestapo man spoke some words in a staccato voice of command, but I couldn't make out what they were—a gust of wind came up at that moment, sweeping dust and straw along the square and making the roof tiles clatter. Then came the first drops of rain. The band struck up a fresh tune, hoarsely and off-key—that one I knew, it was *Deutschland über alles*. It was now raining more heavily, the clouds were growing darker; dusk was settling on the square, deepening from minute to minute.

The six policemen stood at strict attention. Some people had appeared in a couple of windows facing the square, but they withdrew again, one after another, after watching for a few minutes. I myself withdrew behind the curtain—I would rather not appear as a spectator, though I felt like keeping an eye on the scene. Three or four people who were passing by on the opposite sidewalk on their way somewhere received a stern sign from a policeman to stand still while the band was playing. They obeyed, but moved on again as soon as the tune was played to the end. A couple of guys, obviously bums, half drunk to boot, one of them with a bottle sticking out of his back pocket and up over his jacket, just in case, came lurching into the square but were led away by another policeman.

Otherwise no audience, except those eight or ten—or ten to twelve—who had been part of the procession. Considered as a mass meeting, it left nothing to criticize from our point of view.

But now I could see one spectator anyway, a young woman standing half hidden in an entranceway on the right-hand side of the square, not very far from my window. But—unless my eyes were deceiving me or I was still dreaming—it was the young girl from the doctor's place, Inga, wasn't it? I tried to take a closer look but couldn't definitely say. It was raining quite heavily now and the visibility was poor.

She was probably on an errand—if it was she. On an errand and reluctant to cross the square while this was going on. I followed her with my eyes the whole time. I was now almost certain that it was she.

Was she on her way to me with some message or other from the doctor? We had agreed that I would come out to his place this evening. Did she come to cancel the appointment? If so, it was imprudent—damn imprudent.

Over on the stage the young Quisling guardsman had begun to speak. Whatever he was talking about, he cried out every now and then and flung his arms about or smacked one hand against the other. I wasn't paying much attention to him and didn't listen carefully, but individual words reached me— *unity, future,* and *Norway.* It was no doubt the usual stuff.

Now the rain was starting in earnest. It was pouring. The Gestapo man looked up at the sky and gave a shrug, and when the speaker paused to catch his breath he quickly whispered something to him.

Looking surprised, the guardsman too glanced up at the sky—in his zeal he seemed not to have noticed that it was raining—and then said something to the small gathering in a calmer tone. I caught only one word: *The hotel.*

It was obviously a timely word. The gathering flocked in the direction of the hotel—first, the two German officers, then the band, then the guardsmen headed by the speaker, then the ten or twelve spectators.

I'd lost sight of the girl for a moment while all this was happening. When I looked for her again, I discovered she was no longer standing in the entranceway. I became anxious, moved toward the window again and pushed my head forward all the way—and saw her.

It *was* Inga. And she was making for the hotel. She came walking down the sidewalk toward the hotel entrance—but for heaven's sake, why just now? There—no, she didn't go in, she just passed by, walked straight through the procession and on, looking neither right nor left. Was it a demonstration?

Then I saw a little thing I would never have noticed if—well, if so many things hadn't come together and caused my attention to be particularly riveted on her. She passed the hotel entrance while the guardsman-speaker was still one step away from the sidewalk.

In front of the entrance were two tall potted myrtles, one on each side. Into one of these myrtle pots she dropped a rolled-up slip of paper. She didn't throw it, she simply dropped it straight down, without moving her arm. The guardsman didn't stop—he just bent down in passing, picked up the ball of paper as if it were something he'd dropped, and continued into the hotel. *She* was already several steps away. She hadn't looked at him, nor did she turn around now.

I sat down on a chair for a moment. Then I opened the door and went out into the corridor.

My room was on the second floor. The hotel was built in such a way that one row of rooms faced the square and another row, at right angles to the first, faced a small side street. These rooms opened onto a wide L-shaped corridor. On the inner wall of this corridor there was a row of large windows looking out upon an area that may have been a courtyard at one time but had been converted to a sort of winter garden. It reached up through three floors and had a mat glass roof. Apart from a few half-withered palms in pots, the large room was furnished with easy chairs and other chairs, little tables, and a grand piano at one end. I had discovered that the room was used—as such rooms ordinarily are—as a parlor for the hotel guests, as a smoking lounge, and as a kind of bar where people could go if they wanted to have a drink. Further back was the dining room, and to the right—from where I stood—were reading and reception rooms.

I figured that the procession would gather in the winter garden. I was right. They had settled in the chairs scattered about. The two officers and the guardsman stood in the middle.

He was the one who interested me. Not because it was necessary, but I should like to have that proof too: I wanted to see if he opened and read the slip of paper.

One of the windows facing the winter garden was open. The corridor lay in semi-darkness, but in the large room all the lights had been turned on. I could stand in protective darkness and see all that was going on.

I got there in the nick of time. He pulled the slip of paper from his pocket, unfolded it and read it. His face twitched slightly, and he exchanged a nearly imperceptible nod with the Gestapo officer.

Then he resumed his speech.

But I didn't hear what he had to say. I'd seen what I wanted to see—and more. As he began his speech he took a couple of steps forward. The light from the large ceiling lamp fell on his face, as sharply as if it came from a photographer's lamp.

I probably hadn't even needed that album.

It was myself I saw. Myself as I looked in my youth.

A Walk in the Dark

~~~~~~~~~~~~~~~~~~~~~~

I was on my way to Dr. Haug's. I walked and ran by turns. It was pouring. I thought, My raincoat. But somehow or other I had managed to put on my raincoat. I was saying to myself as I went along, One thing at a time! It was a magic formula. One thing at a time! Nothing else would do.

It was getting darker and darker, but fortunately I have a quite good sense of orientation. The important thing was to find the way, no delays, one thing at a time.

I found the way.

The doctor's house was in darkness—nobody home? Hell, no; it was war and blackout, it was no longer 1921. One thing at a time.

It was the missus who opened the door. I asked if the doctor was home, it was urgent. I was shown into the office and went right in, in my raincoat and hat and everything.

I must've looked queer. The doctor jumped up.

"But in heaven's name—"

"Where's Inga?" I said.

"She's downtown. She has a music lesson. But—"

"Inga is the traitor. I saw her pass a message to young Heidenreich. There is some contact between Inga and Colbjørnsen—I saw them exchange glances yesterday but didn't attach any particular importance to it at the time. Colbjørnsen has given her information, perhaps without knowing it himself. You must first of all get hold of Inga. Confront her with the facts, without giving out who saw her. Call a meeting, confront Colbjørnsen with the same facts. I'll be back later, after taking care of some business."

As I rushed out again I caught a fleeting glimpse of Dr. Haug out of the corner of my eye; he'd risen from his seat behind the writing table and was gazing open-mouthed at me.

"But—," was all I heard, no longer in the office. The next moment I was no longer in the house.

The case was crystal-clear. There wasn't an obscure point anywhere. But, why couldn't these people do something by themselves! I certainly didn't have the time.

My business was pretty much that I couldn't stand being with other people for a while. Moreover, I needed some time to think.

The other case was also crystal-clear.

He was me, and yet not completely me. He was a little better-looking, a little darker, and had a somewhat stronger face. But I could see from whom he had that too—I could see it feature by feature.

The moment I saw myself standing down there in the winter garden, I recalled and understood so many things all at once that my brain seemed to grow overheated.

Mrs. Heidenreich—Maria—Mari—Kari.

Heidenreich saying to me that spring, "Tell me, lad, do you have sex appeal? It is really a girl who—a very sweet young girl who …"

Her saying, "I know someone who knows you …"

The day she came and told me the danger was over. Her manner then— and that was the last time I saw her.

Heidenreich who suddenly got married and immediately afterward withdrew from us all …

Did he know about it? That was the only thing I couldn't know anything about.

Everything else was clear, crystal-clear. It became clear to me in a fraction of a second.

The boy's resemblance to me as I was at that time was so striking that I had a feeling—unreal, but more powerful than reality—that *I* was the one who stood down there, that I was a traitor, spy, pimp—because he, that youthful portrait of myself down there on the stage, was precisely *that*. I was the one who…

But this was madness.

I had to try and think it through as a whole. Take a walk and straighten out my thoughts.

"As if that can be any use!"

It was as if someone had shouted the words into my ear.

Use or no use, that was what I intended to do.

The rain was pouring. It was almost completely dark by now. I got myself through the garden gate and continued up the residential street, heading out of town.

When she came up to my room that day—it was at the beginning of September 1921—oh, dear me, it was the same date as today, exactly twenty-two years ago: many happy returns!—she was so beside herself with fear and despair that, after that first decisive sentence, she found if difficult to say anything coherent. At first I tried to soothe her, but that didn't work. Bit by bit she managed to utter words to the effect that it—it—hadn't come. By now it was a week late. And—and—there were other things too—changes—things she'd never felt before—.

"I'm certain!" she said.

Afterward she just cried. Again I tried to soothe her. I said she couldn't possibly be certain. But, in any case, we would find a way out. Fortunately we had plenty of time if worst should came to worst.

All along I had a feeling of unreality. I stood there beside myself, talking to her. It was all a dream, it *had to* be a dream. But someplace or other in my stomach an iron knot had formed. It gave me a piercing pain, and I felt as though this pain was laughing at me: Yes, sirree, this is reality, this is reality itself, you bet it is!

I somehow managed to soothe her. To stop her tears. Even to make her laugh once, I've forgotten at what. She laughed with tears on her eyelashes— I remember how beautiful she was then, though her face was swollen from tears. But her beauty didn't have its usual exhilarating effect on me. It—well, it kind of disturbed me.

When she left she seemed relieved and calm. She had confided in me, I had told her it would be all right, she trusted me.

We had agreed she would drop by again the following afternoon.

After she'd gone I sat straight down in my chair. I couldn't move. I had a vision—it kept flashing through my head—that her despair, the part of it she'd gotten rid of, had been laid on my shoulders as a burden, and that my own despair and confusion had settled on top of it, and together it felt so heavy that I sat there in my chair as though weighed down by a load of rocks, unable to move, unable to breathe—nor could I allow myself to breathe, and not by any means to move, because if I moved all the rocks would also begin to move and crush me.

It was my turn now, to face that which all of us so often dreaded—when we didn't have other things to worry about, that is.

There were three things we dreaded most of all.

I say we, though perhaps I should content myself with saying I. But I think it applied to all of us.

Three things. Three submerged rocks we were afraid to run aground and be shipwrecked on. This dread could at times become so strong that it filled one's days, even one's nights; it would turn up in dreams so painful that one woke up with a scream, soaked with perspiration.

Those three things were called: Loneliness—infection—pregnancy.

I had sailed past the first—at last, at last. I had escaped the second. Then it went without saying that I had to run aground on the third.

I couldn't remember how long I sat in that chair. One hour, maybe. Finally I was able to get up and go out.

I simply walked out of the house without any purpose in mind. But just as previously it had been necessary to sit absolutely still, it was now equally necessary to walk—walk fast, faster....

As soon as I got out of town I began to run. I ran and ran, ran till I was soaking wet, ran till I got winded and had to stop. When I recovered my breath I also recovered some sense, and understood that this was something I couldn't run away from. I turned around and walked slowly down the Sogn Road, back to the city.

The following morning I sat in the waiting room of one of the city's well-known gynecologists.

There had been quite a bit of talk about this gynecologist. Or rather whispers. It had been whispered that no small part of his practice consisted of his doing exactly what I now intended to ask him to do. But he was very expensive, they said. Some mentioned the sum of three hundred kroner, others five hundred. I had neither of those sums, they were as far out of my reach as the sun and the moon. But I thought, If I have to get my hands on them, so be it. It will be all right, it *has to* be all right! While with another part of me I thought—no, knew—that it certainly wouldn't be all right, neither one thing nor the other. And in the midst of it all a constant feeling of unreality, a feeling of standing off on the side watching myself, her, this waiting room, and the others who sat there waiting.

The waiting room was full. Apart from me, they were all women. Of all ages, all classes, all kinds of faces. Some looked quite happy and contented, others looked as if they were awaiting a sentence. But everyone threw an inquisitive glance in my direction every now and then. And I thought they must all be able to tell from my face what I'd come here for. Perspiration broke out on my forehead—that, too, I sat beside myself watching.

Finally my turn came.

My first impression of the man can be expressed in one word: dignity. The second was that he had extremely beautiful hands.

He was carefully clean-shaven, but his heavy growth of beard gave a pigeon-blue tint to his chin. He appeared—well, rather clerical. A court preacher.

I stammered forth what was on my mind. A love affair...couldn't get married yet...studies...strict parents...misfortune, disaster ...

He sat quite still looking at me.

"What's her name?" he said.

"That—I can't say."

I hadn't even given a thought to that side of the matter.

"That's for her to answer," I said, to smooth it over.

Pause.

Then he cleared his throat.

"The reason I haven't already thrown you out, young man," he said, "is because I would like to tell you a few home truths!"

And then they came, those home truths. Oodles of them.

Moral principles. Sense of responsibility. These were two things that he had and I didn't. The consequences of one's actions. That was something I had to draw, or take.

He went on for quite long. Five minutes, at least.

I was no great connoisseur of people, but even I could tell that he was a hypocrite. There was something—he took such pleasure in his own words, I believe it was mostly that. He tasted them before letting them out into the world, caressed them lightly with his hands; sort of fondling them with soft, pretty gestures.

Finally he was through and said sternly, "You can go now!"

But then he checked himself. "Oh, by the way. You've taken up my time. That will be ten kroner, please."

If that last sentence possibly weakened the moral impact of his speech, he wasn't himself aware of it.

After that day I could never again endure dignified men. But perhaps I hadn't liked them very much to start with.

In the coming years I asked myself more than once, Why did he take that tone with me? It wasn't very long before I knew what I then only suspected—that he was actually doing that sort of thing on a rather grand scale; and his fee was five hundred kroner.

Why did he turn me down? Was it because he didn't know me? Or was he ashamed to take five hundred kroner from a poor student? Or didn't he have confidence in my secrecy? Or was it perhaps the fact that I didn't mention her name?

I've never had a clear idea why.

But having said no, he couldn't help treating himself to a sermon. Some people were like that.

When I happened to think about that man many years afterward, I would find myself trembling with hatred.

I did run across him once, at a party. It gave me special pleasure to put my hand behind my back when he held out that beautiful, well-manicured hand of his. It was a totally unsuccessful revenge. He looked at me for a moment with raised eyebrows, registering my lack of manners. At that moment he appeared more dignified than ever. He didn't even recognize me. He had a large clientele.

Kari dropped in at five in the afternoon. She dropped in at five every day for the next six days. I have no idea how she managed it.

I had only a single word to tell her: Failure.

She slumped in her chair as if the bones in her body had turned to wax.

I'm afraid my comforting words were even more tepid than the day before. They went something like, What the hell, it was only my first try! And we had plenty of time. And take it easy, sweetheart, take it easy!

She left after half an hour or so. Her face looked dead—pale, stiff, not there. Her thoughts, if she had any, were far away.

The next few days appear like a sort of jumble in my memory.

Sometimes I would run about the streets at a loss what to do, hoping that something or other would turn up—a poster maybe. Sometimes I would sit motionless in my chair for hours on end. Mr. Halvorsen had callers, Slava had callers. It didn't concern me, they were creatures from another planet.

One day I summoned up my courage—it was an incredible self-conquest—and asked a friend for advice. Once I had made that decision, I thought: I'll ask the first friend I run across. And the first one I ran across was—how absurdly!—Lars Flaten. I obtained his promise of secrecy, and he cursed and swore, very solemnly; but I was fairly certain he would never be able to keep mum about anything so exciting. That didn't matter much, though, because everybody would think I'd been making a fool of him. But he couldn't help me, and that mattered more; he just became wide-eyed, scared on my behalf, and gradually even a bit more scared at the thought that it could've been him. Then he said he'd heard it was supposed to be smart to jump rope. Or lift heavy things. Did she have a piano? I'd better tell her to try and lift a piano.

He looked at me with those stupid eyes of his, eager to help.

From him I went to a midwife. I went blindly, guided by a chance address I'd found in the telephone book. Yeah, sure, here was the right person to help. An evangelical Christian, she looked at me as if I were Beelzebub, Jr., himself.

Every afternoon at five the same story, over and over again. She came, pale, silent, but with a faint hope in her eyes. Every time the same word: Failure. And every day she left my place benumbed, her face lifeless.

After a few days I feared that meeting like death itself.

A couple of times she cried; that helped a little, because then I became somewhat better at consoling her. Once I talked such nonsense in my attempt to comfort her that she couldn't help laughing. Then things were very much better for a brief moment.

Throughout this time we never touched each other. We didn't kiss once. We were both of us so terrified, we didn't even dare think of anything like that. The time of joy was past.

Thousands of thoughts and plans crossed my mind in the course of that week. America—why didn't we both go to America? But there was a ban on immigration, you had to be on a waiting list forever. Why not go home and talk to my father? Immediately a curtain fell, and behind that curtain was fear, all sorts of fear, all the fear I'd stored up in myself from when I was a tiny boy up to the accursed present. No, I couldn't talk to my father. He was the very last person ...

But *he* talked to me. He sat in the dark corner of my room even in broad daylight now, looking at me with a threatening expression and saying—I didn't hear his words, I wasn't quite that far gone, but I heard them all the same, "What did I tell you? What did I tell you? What did I tell you?"

No, it wouldn't do any good to go up there and talk with him. That I was sure about.

Come to think, was there anything else I was sure about today? Maybe it wouldn't have done me any good. And maybe it would have changed everything, everything.

By the very fact that I was thinking of my father, I also had to think of marriage.

But that very word filled me with a fear that nearly matched the fear behind the curtain.

Marriage was the end of youth, joy, love, everything. Marriage was a lifelong prison you entered as punishment for—well, for having been born a human being and permitting yourself to be young and in love. Marriage was kids and diapers, and a double bed with a pot under it where husband and wife lay back to back snoring—and even so the kids kept on coming. And you never made enough money, and the kids had snotty noses and were run over by the trolley and fought in the streets and had nosebleeds and came home bawling— oo—oo! And you yourself became cross and crabby—the porridge burned again!! And the kids never giving you a moment's peace!! Let me work in peace, will you! Marriage was to grow old and apathetic and become a caricature of yourself, and you didn't even notice, it happened so quietly, so quietly; it was to become a sedate man with a potbelly, your pants baggy at the knees and the seat of your pants shiny from wear, and with flat feet you stuck into slippers before going to bed at night, to snore in chorus with your eternally wedded wife. Marriage was to lose your hair and teeth and your zest for life, be elected to the township board, get pensioned off, and be driven to the cemetery feet first, with a black procession behind the coffin and with

November rain changing over to sleet, while the tree branches were splayed against the sky without a leaf. Marriage was like being penned in for the winter, forgetting your youth and slowly getting bored with your truelove, your evenings whiled away staring at the flames in the fireplace and twiddling your thumbs to the words, "So it is! So it is!"

Marriage, in short, was the exact opposite of youth and love. Youth and love, that was the garden of Eden; but one fine day the great watchman appeared and said, "Ha—ha! Now I've caught you! So you thought that life was nothing but song and dance and play, did you? I'll teach you something else, I will! Joy, ladies and gentlemen, brings its own punishment! Happiness brings unhappiness! Out, all of you—out where there shall be weeping and gnashing of teeth!"

But throughout and above and underneath all this, marriage was even worse, something more bleak and more dangerous which I was unable to explain. To marry was like entering a dark mountain cave without an exit on the other side, and deep inside that darkness lay a dragon waiting for you.

I hadn't the faintest idea where I'd gathered all these impressions. But there they were—they came crawling out like pixies and trolls in the fairy tales and danced around me, making faces and thumbing their noses.

As far as Kari and I were concerned, had I really given any thought to our future during those fourteen days of felicity? Well, no; feelings rather than thoughts engrossed us—feelings that swelled and swelled, dreams of heaven itself come down to earth. Any thoughts we had, if they could be called thoughts, were probably to the effect that we would always be like this, never leave one another, never bind each other but always come to one another, freely, trustingly. We would fool them all and be in love and young and happy till the day we died, hand in hand, in hoary old age.

I began to understand that, instead, marriage loomed on the horizon. It was necessary to find some livelihood. My studies would have to wait awhile. Anyway, one could study at night. From the third day on I was reading ads for vacant positions but found nothing. On the fifth day I went down to the school, which had already sent me a couple of private pupils, to ask if they had any substitute teaching posts for the winter. They did not. No, this time it was for real. Young as I was, I had at least learned that troubles never come singly. I was right now in the midst of a run of them. I'd better be prepared for more. How was I to live? One room and kitchen someplace or other. But could I earn enough to support two?

I sat in my room and figured to myself. Rent, bread, butter, coffee, tobacco— no, forget the tobacco ...

She didn't mention the word marriage even once during those days.

On the sixth day I went to Heidenreich.

I was surprised by the fact that I'd dreaded that so much. After all, it was quite a natural thing for me to do. He'd touched on these things once last spring—I never referred to them, I was much too shy, and besides I was afraid. Better not even mention a thing like that, the words might come true.

I was not superstitious, of course. I simply didn't speak about such things.

But then he brought it up, saying that for a medical student it was no problem. A trifle, in fact. He didn't say any more about it.

I went to Heidenreich. In quite a state, absurdly nervous. I thought to myself, Look what you've come to! I didn't know myself what I meant by it.

Heidenreich refused me pointblank. He didn't meddle with things like that. I would have to go to some doctor or other. Which doctor? Oh, someone or other.

Then I couldn't contain myself. One week's despair turned in an instant into such rage that I could have killed him. But instead venom and gall gushed out of my mouth.

I called him a cowardly bastard, a false friend, a status seeker, braggart and wretch. I said that his answer delighted me in a way—now I knew he was the sort of person I'd always suspected him of being. But what I had already suspected and now knew, would eventually be discovered by many others. It didn't always pay to follow the path of profit and loss, as he would find out some day to his own immense surprise.

I uttered a kind of curse at the end: "May you yourself have children where you do not want them, and none where you do! May everything around you wither as if you were an outcast on the face of the earth!"

He stood there pale and speechless as I left him. I never saw him again.

The following afternoon she came and told me that there was no longer any danger.

The street I walked had become a road, with ditches on both sides. I had strayed into them a couple of times.

It was evening and very dark, as in a closed dark room. I couldn't tell the difference between earth and sky; I could barely make out my own hand when I held it up in front of me. I could feel the road, I didn't see it.

In a few places I'd seen a streak of light, narrow as a knife-edge. Poor blackout. But I wasn't thinking of blackout and that sort of thing. Something inside me thought I was walking on the very brink of hell in the dark, and that those streaks were just narrow cracks in the thin wall separating me from—well, from that place.

It wasn't raining quite as heavily as before, but it made no difference; I was soaked to the skin, as if I had lain in the sea for ever so long. My hat was a wet rag, and the water leaked right through it and trickled down my neck, regularly, as from an hourglass.

I thought, rather solemnly, that just like this road on both sides of me, all Norway lay in darkness, as did the whole world. Millions of people sat waiting in the dark, sat helpless and despairing in the dark, hoping for dawn, nearby or far away.

I didn't know how far or for how long I had walked. I turned around. There was still a lot to be done.

"No danger any longer," she said.

My relief was too great, my joy unbelievable. I couldn't understand, I must be dreaming, I didn't believe my own ears and sat speechless for a moment. Then I asked once more.

But she repeated it. The danger was over. It—it had come. Nearly two weeks late, but...

Perhaps that was the moment I suffered my real defeat.

I shouted, I laughed, I jumped out of my chair and went over and shook her. I was so relieved that I was deaf and blind.

She didn't share my exultation. She was tired, she said. I could well understand that. She was exhausted after all the tension and felt poorly, and ...

I was struck by how strange it all was. What had happened to—

She brushed it aside. Her nerves must've been a bit on edge. Then it often happened, she'd heard, that—well, that it was late. One became more and more nervous and—well, then it went like that.

I was a bit surprised that she was so distant all the time. So far away and—well, not as glad as she ought to be. Not as glad as I was.

Oh sure, she was glad, she said. But maybe she needed some time before she really understood it all; besides she wasn't well.

All at once my whole vitality revived. I couldn't get close enough to her, I had to feel her closeness—well, certain things were out of the question obviously, but ...

She fought me off. I noticed she really meant it. In any case, she had to be leaving, she said—had only sneaked off to tell me this.

But when would she be back? She must come soon, soon.

Oh yes, she would be back as soon as possible. She couldn't say exactly when.

She was already standing in the doorway as she said this. She was smiling so strangely—so wistfully, so sadly—as an old person may smile at the thought of a faraway memory of youth.

I remembered that smile afterward; for some reason or other it stuck in my memory. At that moment I didn't attach any importance to it.

I never saw her again.

For the first few days and weeks I didn't understand that anything decisive had happened. I thought, She's been prevented from coming. Later I thought, She has taken sick. I began walking the streets in the hope of meeting her. I walked for hours every day, but she was never to be seen.

And so, gradually, I began to have an inkling of something. It came so quietly, like a cold wind from a coming winter. It increased. I would sit in my room waiting for her; though I knew better, I was still waiting. Then I was sometimes brushed by a thought so cold that I would get up to see whether there was a window open, letting in the October darkness and the sneaking cold.

My thought, cold and inexorable, might be this: She's finished with you. She finished with you during that week.

But how? Why?

It took quite a long time, and a painful process it was, before I gradually, step by reluctant step, understood—not the worst, not that which had actually happened, but something that I myself believed was the worst: that a girl who was in love with me, and with whom I was in love, could be so finished with me that she never wanted to see me again. That realization didn't come to me evenly but in sharp spurts. When it hit me at its worst, it was no longer like feeling a cold wind through an open window, but like standing naked out in the cold and darkness of winter itself.

She had left me because she thought I was a coward. That was the fact I had to learn to live with.

I never saw her again. And as one month went by after another, and later year after year, something odd happened to my feeling for her.

It didn't go away. Quite the contrary, one could almost say.

Not that I went around thinking of her every day. Days and weeks would go by when she was completely absent from my thoughts. Then she popped up again for some reason or other, at times with such force that once more— it might be years afterward—I would walk the same streets where I'd run about at that time, day after day, in an insane hope of meeting her.

I had a sort of wild plan about undoing something I had done. About explaining, clearing things up.

Suppose I had taken the plunge that time? That I had said, Let's take this as a sign! Let's do that! We'll take a place together! We'll get married!

Now I could say it!

At other times it was quite different. The thought of her would pop up, due to forces I knew nothing about. If I happened to be alone I would sit in my chair writhing with shame, with unhappiness and loss. Until I was again able to push the thought of her down into the darkness from which it had come.

Only long, long afterward did I manage to falsify things to such a degree that I could think of that time with a certain wistful pleasure as well.

It was some medical student friends who told me about Heidenreich's marriage. They thought it was odd. It had taken place in such a hurry, too. From one day to the next, so to speak. None of them had seen the girl.

"It's probably someone old and ugly with money," they said.

I didn't pay much heed. Heidenreich didn't interest me any longer.

Heidenreich's marriage—it never occurred to me to connect it with anything having to do with me and my affairs.

Really? It didn't?

I never saw either her or him alone. But I may have seen them both together once.

I found myself on the street one evening. I was wandering around in the hope of meeting her. Some distance ahead of me walked a couple, but I could just barely make them out—it was a dark evening in November and it was sleeting. Then the couple turned into a restaurant, and the moment they became visible in the light from the open door, I thought, That was her! That was him!

The door closed behind them, and the next moment I dismissed the thought as unthinkable. After all, I was used to the fact that half of the women I saw at a distance gave me the feeling: That's her!

The thought seemed to me so absurd that I didn't even go in to check. After all, I didn't suspect that …

I didn't suspect?

Why did it become so important to me, as I sat writing my notes, to include that story about Kari?

And why had I totally forgotten where on earth Heidenreich was living?

Why did I look out of the window time after time today? Was there someone I hoped, and feared, to see?

I didn't get any further. That which had happened had changed the world. I no longer remembered how it had looked before—didn't remember what I'd known or not known, what I'd suspected or not suspected.

One thing alone from that humiliating fall gave me a certain feeling of satisfaction afterward. At that time there was a radical group among Oslo's young academics. It was led by a tall, thin, baldheaded man who, in my opinion, was a kind of genius. Among many other things, he had a strange power: he could express an utterly surprising thing in such an obviously logical manner that you understood it instantly, and a tenth of a second later you were thinking the thought yourself. That way the thought became nearly your own, and you felt you were a hell of a guy.

This group wanted to change the world. Everything old was rubbish, all elderly people were fools, the revolution was imminent.

Way out in the periphery, I was an eager admirer and follower. I thought the world was rather stupid and that most things ought to be changed. At bottom everything was so simple, especially when you were listening to that tall man and thinking his thoughts after a tenth of a second.

But that fall made me doubtful. I had a growing feeling that a great many things were extremely complicated. For one thing I'd come to suspect that my own defeat was not simply due to the wickedness of the outside world but also to the weakness of my inner world. It dawned on me that there was a certain connection between the two—that I couldn't change the external world until my own inner world had grown stronger. I came to suspect that I didn't have the stuff out of which great revolutionaries were made. I quietly withdrew from the circle. I was scarcely missed by anyone, I belonged on the periphery.

That was the only comfort offered by that period. A cold comfort. I never solved my own inner problems so that one day I could say, Now I've gotten over it! All in all, my life never again came to be what it had been during that strange fortnight in the late summer of 1921. That fortnight was my youth.

Things went well for me, everything went splendidly. But it wasn't very important anymore. It didn't really matter. The uncanny thing was that only when *this* had definitely become my fundamental attitude to life, only then did things start going really well for me. From then on it was as though life said to me, Now I can use you!

It had stopped raining, but the night was pitch-dark. There wasn't a ray of light anywhere. Nonetheless I had a sense of where I was. I was coming down a slope, and I knew I had walked up the same slope after leaving the doctor. I groped my way to a garden gate, inched along it using my hands, and read Dr. Haug's name with my fingers.

I ought to go in and take part in the final discussion. But it seemed to me so wholly superfluous—I knew my job down here was done. Well, I would come back later and take part in the deliberations, pretending they were important. But first I would go down to my hotel and peel off my clothes, peel off my entire outer shell and put on a new one, in the hope that some of the inner man would come away with it—my whole self sickened me, like a dirty, stinking shirt.

When I entered the hotel lobby I noticed that several chairs around the room were occupied by Germans. One officer, unless I was mistaken, and two or three privates, or possibly NCO's. I had a feeling that the officer looked at me, and it dawned on me that he resembled the Gestapo officer I'd seen in the square that afternoon. Well, that was nothing to me.

Sitting in shadow were a couple of slightly darker shadows—guardsmen as far as I could see. In other words, the hotel was a nest for that sort of thing. Hmm. There was nothing one could do about that.

When I went up to the desk of the hall porter to get my room key, I noticed that the porter blinked so oddly with one eye. It looked as if he'd got a grain of sand in his eye and was making energetic, but vain attempts to get rid of it. However, it made no more impression on me than anything else—honestly, I had other things to think about. First of all, I wanted to change into dry clothes; all other problems would have to wait. Anyway, they were utterly indifferent, belonging either to the past or to the future, and both those spaces of time were so indifferent to me that nothing in this indifferent world could be more indifferent.

I went up the stairs and let myself into my room.

It struck me as a bit odd that the light was on and the room full of smoke. Then I opened the door wide.

In the chair sat Dr. Carl Heidenreich.

Deep Underground

~~~~~~~~~~~~~~~~~~~~~~~~~

I have no idea how I managed to close the door.

The Germans downstairs, Heidenreich here, the porter with a grain of sand in his eye. This case too was crystal-clear.

If I'd been an impulsive man of the belligerent type, I would presumably have been at Heidenreich's throat in a second. And would've had a bullet through my body—he sat, as I discovered later, with a pistol in his hand. But I'm not that sort of man. When my fear becomes great and real, as it was now, I notice it first by the fact that all the internal organs plunge down through my body. I remain motionless, stiff as a poker, and when I can move at last, all my movements are inhibited and slow; but at the same time my brain races along, seeking refuge in comparisons, figures and logic.

In a flash I thought I hadn't been so frightened since that time in the spring of 1941 when I was waiting at Victoria Terrace. But that time all went well, the whole thing seemed a joke—I wasn't even beaten, he only banged his writing table. True, when I got out again I was a widower and childless. Childless? Well, I believed I was anyway.

During the hours I sat waiting that time I tried to keep calm by doing sums in my head. I multiplied by four. Four times four is sixteen, four times sixteen is sixty-four, four times sixty-four is two hundred and fifty-six.... I got up into the millions and the billions, but had to stop when the numbers became too long for me. Then I multiplied by three, and after that again I combined multiplication by three and four. I sat there figuring and figuring, all the while trembling with fright. But it helped.

I had no time for anything like that now. My eyes fastened upon the ashtray on the table, it was something tangible. I counted quickly: Eight stubs. He'd been waiting for quite a while.

Why was Heidenreich here? That slip of paper. His son, that is. Why was I in this town? That same son—his espionage had led to this assignment. And how had be become... But that was my fault. Had I been more of a man that week or day in September 1921, this would never have happened, my son would've been my son and stood on the right side, Landmark and Evensen wouldn't have been arrested, and I not sent down here and therefore also not arrested. It was my own past come back to haunt me, it was I myself who'd spied on me, and in reality it was I myself who sat there in the chair keeping a watch on me. A perfect circle.

People say one can dream a long dream in a tenth of a second. It happens that thoughts move just as fast in a waking state, but then a dreamlike feeling arises.

Now Heidenreich spoke, and I thought, still logically, People do not talk in dreams, not in real dreams.

"Nice to see you," Heidenreich said.

I replied that I wished I could say the same.

"But you can!" he said. "It's *very* nice to see me. And it will get even nicer."

He spoke calmly, in the same ironic tone, his voice slightly nasal, as in the old days.

"Oh yes," he said, "I've been waiting awhile, as you can see. But you can never wait too long for a good thing!"

With short, stiff sidelong steps I had slowly approached the window, where the blackout curtain had been drawn. The room was only on the second floor. The blackout paper would protect me a little from the glass splinters, there was a chance—

"I don't think I would try that," Heidenreich said. "First, I do have *this*!" And he showed me the pistol. "But second, there are a couple of men on the sidewalk below. You see, I'm not the only one who thinks it will be nice—very nice—to meet you."

"So you're carrying a pistol?" I said.

He replied that as a rule he was not. This was a peaceful town. The pistol was just a little toy he took along on occasions such as this.

"And now I think we'll go," he said. "The others might get impatient."

He stood up. A single well-aimed blow—but he was on his guard and just gave me a friendly smile.

There was nothing more to say. I preceded him through the door. In a flying fraction of a second I recalled the fights in my boyhood and the strange numb feeling in my nose when it was hit by a blow. Now I had that feeling in my whole body.

We walked down the corridor in the direction of the stairs. I knew he had the pistol in his hand. My thoughts no longer worked logically. They flew in all directions at once, like a frightened flock of birds.

One couldn't be sure it was Inga's note. Was it my house in Oslo? Had someone been caught at the border? Had there been a raid? What did they know? I had to alert Andreas, Dr. Haug, the bank manager, Garmo—I could no longer alert anyone. My lab in Oslo, what about that? A notice in the papers some day when all this was over: He was forty-four years old ...

But at the same time I thought with stumbling eagerness that when all this was over I would rejoice in life as never before; I would enjoy every hour, every minute, rejoice when I went to sleep and when I woke up, rejoice in every breath—just think, to be able to breathe freely, talk with friends, work, sit in my lab and measure and weigh, sit in my office and turn the pages of some nice documents smelling of dust, stretch out on the smooth rocks by the seashore, walk in the woods, smell the resin and the sun-baked evergreens, dry twigs snapping underfoot, a long walk ending at a chalet meadow, cow dung on the path, bells and moos—sit yourself down—

He was forty-four years old ...

When we reached the lobby five men got up—the Gestapo officer I'd seen in the square and later on in the winter garden, behind him two Gestapo agents, and behind them again, over in the shadow, two young guardsmen. One of them was Heidenreich, Jr.

Carl Heidenreich turned to the officer. He spoke to him in German and asked if he should get his car. But it was so nearby.

The officer answered shortly, "Wir gehen!"

He made a sign to one of his men. The next moment I had handcuffs around my left wrist.

We started off. At the head went the officer and Carl Heidenreich, then the first Gestapo man and I. Behind us, the others. The two guardsmen brought up the rear.

I tried to be brave and ironic. I thought, Almost as long a procession as this afternoon!

But I stumbled as I thought this—my legs didn't remember the distance to the floor.

The two men behind the counter stood still, moving neither hand nor foot. But I saw the look in the eye of one of them and knew that someone would be notified.

Then we were outside, in utter darkness. The Gestapo man at the rear turned on a powerful flashlight and lighted the way. We walked along the slippery, uneven paving of the square, passed to the left of the fountain and turned down a street, also to the left. A few steps down that way and we had arrived.

I tried to picture to myself how this little group appeared from above—let's say, as seen from a plane high up. Would they be able to see from there that one was a captive and the others his guards?

I thought, Thousands are at this moment in the same situation. There was comfort in that thought.

My being so weak-kneed, I thought further, feebly, like the shadow of a thought, was perhaps due to the fact that my strength was divided among three—or was it four—persons. I was myself, I was an observer walking alongside, I was young Heidenreich who walked at the rear. And with a certain part of me I was also Carl Heidenreich, whose contours I could see in front of me now and then.

He had waited many years for this. How did such a triumph feel?

How did it feel to be the son of such a man? How being married to him?

The Gestapo officer unlocked the door for us.

A voice from the darkness behind me, "Do you need me now, Dad?"

Carl Heidenreich exchanged a few words with the officer. Then he said, without turning around, "Thanks. But we don't need you anymore now."

What happened during the next few seconds is not entirely clear to me. I think we walked through a hallway and on through a guardroom with benches and tables in it, and then through an anteroom with a writing table and chairs. Finally we came to a quite large office.

There were no people anywhere.

The Gestapo officer gave a sign again and the handcuffs were removed.

He and Heidenreich sat down side by side behind the writing table.

Behind me stood the two Gestapo men.

"Sit down!" said the officer, pointing. He spoke Norwegian throughout when he addressed me. Quite good Norwegian too. But he and Heidenreich spoke German to one another.

It felt good to be able to sit down.

They used the usual method—a sharp light focused directly on my face. But the questions were only of the preliminary sort. Date of birth? Occupation? Address? Business in this town?

They both laughed when I mentioned my business in the bank.

"We shall have to find out whether those who commissioned that business were in good faith," said the officer in German. Heidenreich nodded and noted down something on a pad.

Those who had commissioned me *were* in good faith. For a moment I felt a huge relief. This would be sure to turn out well, they would end up laughing on the wrong side of their mouths. I thought, like a sort of spell, I've got away from them before, I've got away from them before!

I became fired up with hope and faith. Now afterward I know that it was the same sort of hectic optimism that fills the heart of a mortally ill patient when the doctor gives him a ray of hope.

"And you have no other business in this town?"

I had no other business.

They both nodded, as if they accepted my answer.

With this the preliminaries were over.

At a sign from the Gestapo officer, the two men pulled me roughly out of my chair.

I was hustled out the door, down a staircase, through a door, across a room, and through another door.

A glance sufficed. This was the workshop. It was here it would take place.

It had probably been a laundry room at one time. The concrete floor sloped from the sides toward the middle, where there was a drain covered by a grate. By one wall there was a large sink. A long red rubber hose hung over the faucet, and on the floor stood a bucket. On the opposite wall was a large cupboard, and between the cupboard and the sink a big table. There the instruments were laid out one after the other, neatly arranged in German fashion. Some of the things I recognized offhand—rubber clubs, sticks and whips of different sizes and lengths. A few of the instruments I wasn't familiar with. There was also a number of articles of shiny metal lying there.

In the other part of the room was a bunk bed, a table, and a few chairs.

There was something more—an indefinable, nauseatingly bad smell. Here people had screamed, moaned and cried, here they had bled and vomited, here bowels and bladders had been voided, here strong men had been transformed into maundering babes—and all this had been observed by dull or glittering eyes.

All those big words about the Third Reich, the promised millennium— this was what they boiled down to, this was the stuff at the bottom of the pot.

This was what awaited me now.

But the same thing had happened to millions, and it was happening to thousands at this very moment. In that vast drama I was just a walk-on, so small that I could barely be glimpsed, like a tiny speck.

It was a comfort to feel so small.

At first nothing happened except that the two Gestapo men took off my raincoat and my jacket and tied my hands and feet with a rope. They laced it incredibly hard. Then they must've been given a signal, because suddenly they were gone and the door closed behind them. I was alone with Heidenreich and the Gestapo officer.

I had a feeling of being somewhere deep underground.

I know now, afterward, that it was the expression on the faces of Heidenreich and the German that gave me that feeling. In reality I knew, of course, that we had only gone down one flight of stairs. And high up on the wall there was a window covered with a grille. We weren't any deeper.

It must've been this window that made them use the sofa cushion later on.

It was Heidenreich who spoke to me first.

"I've requested the honor of taking part in this interrogation," he said. "I thought I might be of some use, inasmuch as I knew you, Sir, at one time."

He was addressing me formally at this point. However, that changed as the evening progressed.

Then he made a speech, partly aimed at me and partly at the Gestapo officer. I had been a cultural Bolshevik from my youth on, and a secret enemy from the first day of the Occupation. They knew all about me. The documents from the interrogation of 1941 were in the office upstairs. At that time the case was dismissed for lack of evidence, and I got away with two weeks in jail.

I thought, How were they able to get those papers down here so quickly? By train or by car? Were they picked up or sent?

The question seemed to me very important.

"This time the case will not be dismissed!" Heidenreich said.

They knew I had dined at the bank manager's, that the two of us had gone together to Dr. Haug, that there we had met with Garmo and Colbjørnsen—

So it *was* Inga.

I thought again, You must make sure to alert them!

Then it struck me that right now other things came first.

They knew all about us, he said. Every bit. He mentioned several things. Quite many, in fact. They were incredibly well informed. That fact alone was uncanny enough. But then, like an ice-cold wind, came the thought that when he told me all this—which no Norwegian should know that they knew—it meant—it meant—

He was forty-four years old ...

I was no longer three or four persons, but I tried with all my might to remain two—a calm observer who was above trifles, and a more accidental fellow who was soon to get a good licking.

Now they only wanted to have my formal confession, Heidenreich said. If I let them have that, nothing more would happen to me just yet.

So, what was my business in this town?

His face had changed. I'd never seen such a face before. It flashed through my head that those fellows at Victoria Terrace had, in fact, been extremely sedate and courteous.

I had some difficulty in speaking, but I did manage to say that my business down here was to go through certain papers in the bank.

Slowly and carefully, Heidenreich and the officer undressed to their shirt sleeves. They did so without mutual agreement, and I thought—or the observer thought—that Heidenreich must have participated in such things before.

But that thought was in a strange way weightless and shadowy. Now it was all about me. And another thought came to me, sharp and painful but still holding some comfort: He has every reason for doing this. Now you're paying an installment on your debt.

In the course of the last half-hour, this thought had occurred to me many times already, and it had strengthened me every time. I was scared, to be sure, I was sick with fright, bathed in a cold sweat, my heart pounding, knees trembling. But I knew that, without that thought, I would've felt a great deal worse.

His speech, his talk about the interrogation in 1941, the question about my business in town—all of that affected me as quite irrelevant, something pertaining to another case. This was a private settling of accounts between Heidenreich and myself. And there it seemed to me that the man was largely in the right.

There was also another voice. It said, mockingly, "Remorse and guilt feelings! Christian thinking!"

But that voice was feeble and came from far away, it didn't get through.

They bent me forward over the back of a chair.

Some months ago I had taken in a man who'd been badly tortured but managed to escape. His back was covered with scars and sores. But he said, "The anxiety beforehand is the worst part of it."

The anxiety beforehand was the worst part, and now I was through with it. It—

The officer struck with a long black rubber club, Heidenreich with something which I think was a rubber hose wound about with metal wire and with tarred bands on top of that again. It was that which inflicted the greatest pain.

There is no point in going into particulars. The whole thing was actually very monotonous. Question, "What was your business in this town?" Answer—or no answer—whereupon they whacked away.

I must've screamed horribly. In any case they took a sofa cushion and strapped it to my face. It had an unpleasant, sour smell of old vomit, and I had a fleeting recollection of cabins deep below deck, high seas, and nausea. My screams sounded so strange against the cushion, it was like walking in a dense fog shouting for help.

They removed the cushion several times and asked, "What was your business in this town?"

They weren't satisfied with the sofa cushion as a muffler, they also turned on a phonograph. It played, shrilly and deafeningly, an American swing record, *I can't give you anything but love, baby!* It had to be an electric phonograph with some special device, for it played the record over and over again without stopping.

234

The sofa cushion nearly suffocated me. That may have been one of the reasons why I fainted a few times. I came to again lying on the floor, my face swimming in cold water, which streamed down the sloping concrete and through the drain in the center.

They mostly struck at my back. But once one of them missed and hit the back of my head. I imagine I was out for quite a while after that. When I came to again, once more with cold water running past my face, I felt really rotten and just lay there vomiting awhile. Then it started all over again.

I cannot give a coherent account of the thoughts that went through my head while it was going on. I suspect there wasn't very much coherence in my thoughts anyway.

I know I thought several times, when I looked at the distorted face of Heidenreich, Well, I owed you this!

But I also thought, How stupid of you to collect that debt.

Somewhat later I thought, Now we are quits.

A long time after that again I thought, Now I owe nobody in the whole world anything—now I'm free.

Afterward it seems strange to me that my thoughts circled around guilt and debt to such a degree. But perhaps it was because they were simple thoughts, easy to think.

Very early on something inside me got jammed. From that moment on I knew, Let them do what they will, let happen what may, I'm safe.

It was a strange feeling, verging on the highest happiness.

But previous to that I had remembered Hans Berg, at the time he was eleven years old and was flogged by his father. I thought, What a little Nazi boy could stand, I can certainly stand!

He wasn't a Nazi boy then, of course, but that didn't occur to me.

My strength was ebbing away. I could tell by several things. I think my sensitivity to pain decreased; my breath grew weaker, my screams grew decidedly weaker. I was still two people, but the observer began to be blurred. For a while I fortified myself by thinking of things I'd loved, and things I still loved and intended to return to when all this was over. I thought of a trip I'd made to the summer dairy as a child. It had rained, and in the end I was so wet that I couldn't get any wetter; then I waded in the brooks and made little runs off the road and waded in the swamps, making my boots squish. I'd made lots of trips to the summer dairy, most of them in nice weather, I have no idea why I thought of that one in particular. Then I remembered how, as a boy, I was once sitting on the chopping block in the woodshed at home; it was evening, there was a smell of resin and sawdust and pitch pine, and I was happy. Later I thought of a cottage I had up in the Østerdal valley. I pictured myself standing on the flagstone in front of the door early one morning looking at the grass, which was gray with dew. My boat lay a short way off, half pulled ashore. I was going out to draw my nets.

Actually I'm not sure whether I thought all these things or whether some of them were things I dreamed while I was slowly coming to after a faint. But I clearly recall hearing myself cry out "Kari! Kari!" up against the cushion once.

I had fainted again and came to once more in running water. But meanwhile the two men must have agreed to call it a day. They were getting dressed. Finally the Gestapo officer went up to a small mirror hanging on the wall. While he was busy before the mirror, making faces and arranging the part in his hair, Heidenreich stood watching me. I lay motionless, looking at him with almost closed eyes. I don't know whether I could have moved or not; in any case I didn't dare to. I'd never seen such hatred in a face before. Suddenly I was grateful for the fact that the Gestapo officer was present in the room. I became almost fond of him, feeling that he was my protector and friend. But he seemed glued to that mirror, the part in his hair was never nice enough, he straightened it out over and over again. And all along Heidenreich stood watching me.

I noticed that they had loosened the ropes somewhat, the blood began circulating in my hands and feet again. The pain was excruciating; I moaned, and Heidenreich realized I was conscious. "This was only the beginning," he said, friendly now. "This was only a little warm-up. Remember, the real thing will come tomorrow. Then we'll proceed more scientifically. More methodically. Can you hear me?"

He bent forward toward me.

"Tomorrow you'll come to regret you were ever born, that your parents ever saw the light of day, that your family ever emerged from the darkness where they belonged. I've canceled the hospital for tomorrow. You are my patient now—can you hear me? I'll take care of you. I'll nurse you, never fear. Your nails—can you feel the nerves under your nails? I'll teach you to feel them! I'll teach you to feel—but we'll come to that later."

He drew a deep, trembling breath. At that moment I realized that the man was mad.

He bent over still more, getting closer to me. "What was it you said to me once—'may you yourself have children where you do not want them, and none where you do! May everything around you wither as if you were an outcast on the face of the earth!'

"By the way, what's the story—I believe I heard you'd lost your wife and your little son. My heartfelt condolences!"

He straightened up and bowed twice.

236

"Unfortunately I have to state that the withering is all around *you*—as if *you* were an outcast on the face of the earth. *I*, on the other hand, I have a *son*! He's a joy to me every day, every minute of the day. Nobody has a son like that. Nobody! He—"

I realized one more thing as I lay there—he both knew and didn't know that the boy was my son.

"Na! Kommen Sie?"

It was the Gestapo officer. He'd finally finished making the part in his hair and glanced in our direction, slightly irritated. He thought, no doubt, that things were becoming a bit too private.

"Einen Augenblick."

Heidenreich straightened up, rushed over to the mirror and hastily tidied his hair and tie—his crown was balding, but he tried to hide it by wearing his hair long and making the part far over on one side.

The moment he stepped in front of the mirror the man underwent a change. His face turned smooth, a faint smile appeared on his lips, he was suddenly calm, superior, a man of the world cynically smiling at all those sapheads who, for the lack of sense, let themselves be guided by their wretched feelings.

"Fertig!"

He still walked over to me and gave me a kick in the back, painful too. Then they were gone, and the door closed.

They left the light on.

They were gone. I could scarcely believe it. I drew a deep breath, changed my position a little, moaned, drooled a bit, drew another deep breath. My heart was pounding, my whole body ached, my back burned like fire.

But I felt at peace.

I was happy—I hadn't thought I would ever be that happy again in my whole life.

I may possibly have slept awhile, I can't say for sure. But I don't think so. I think it was then, without a pause and without any sort of transition, that it began—that singular state which I've since privately called *the vision*.

The starting point was Heidenreich standing in front of the mirror and suddenly turning himself into quite a different man from what he really was.

How funny to watch people when they look at themselves in the mirror. They make faces, put on airs, look lovingly in the mirror and strike a pose—to themselves.

They don't know how they really look. They have a dream about themselves and try to resemble it. They draw themselves up, make faces, straighten their necks, make their mouths firmer and more determined—or ironically smiling—smooth out their eyebrows or wrinkle them—what a helluva guy!

An unsuccessful corporal looked at himself in the mirror, and looked at himself in the mirror. Until he saw himself as lieutenant, captain, major, colonel, general, field marshal, army commander, a leader of the people, the lord and master of the world, trampling with his jackboots all the kneeling peoples of the earth.

He looked in the mirror and looked in the mirror, until he was hypnotized. Until he hypnotized others into seeing him as he saw himself. Until eventually—for them as for him—he was no longer a little corporal with an absurd little mustache and an extremely murky relationship to himself, but a great man, a ruler, a superman. Until they began to tramp in step at his command and were happy to tramp in step, thinking, We can tramp in step! Nobody can tramp in step like us! We can tramp in step, fight in step, subjugate in step, trample others in step, trample the world to rubble in step!

That was our present situation.

And then, when all was said and done, it was only the corporal's boots that liked to tramp. And the corporal's face was only a corporal's face and always would be, and his plan was a corporal's plan and always would be, only magnified to gigantic dimensions, because there proved to be so many corporal brains around in high places.

*

That was the first, sober beginning. Then it rolled on.

My brain was light and free, as though all hindrances were gone; racing off, it rushed through chains of thought, solved problems or swept them aside, gathered and arranged old observations, viewed them from a fresh vantage point, rose higher to new perspectives, rose higher, ever higher.

I understood myself, my own youth, why I fell short so easily, and how easily I could have held my own. I understood the others who had fallen short. I understood Kari and myself, Heidenreich and myself, my son and myself. But all that was nothing but details in a drama that embraced all and everything in the present, the past, and the future. I rose higher and saw further—class struggle and war, madmen on the throne and wise people in the dungeons, religions that changed, grew up and died, *I don't believe in God!* as a new religion, fixed ideas which made for happiness and happiness that made for fixed ideas, groups and peoples that reeled blindly forward— and then the solution, it was somewhere, the deliverance and the light were somewhere, and I saw the deliverance, glimpsed the light, could almost see the solution, pursued it, almost had it in my hand, the light grew brighter, I had it—almost certainly—I had it!

It has been written about this or that man of God that he saw the heavens open before him. I did not. It was the earth I saw, and the life of people on earth. But I saw it in such a way that it filled me with ecstatic happiness.

That vision is the real reason for my continuing these notes here in Sweden. But now that I'm approaching it, now that I've reached it, I notice that I'm backing away. I don't have the courage to—

It's not fear. It's a kind of awe. Of course it's fear. For I know, after all, that if I try to reproduce what I saw and don't succeed, then I'll tear something to pieces, then I have once and for all destroyed ...

It will have to wait.

But I can say this much about the state I found myself in: I wept from gratitude more than once.

I was in the land of the blessed.

Kari was an important part of the vision, in a way it began with her. But it seemed almost disturbing, like a glimpse of everyday reality, when the door opened and Kari herself stepped in.

Shadows from the Past

~~~~~~~~~~~~~~~~~~~~~~~

One of my eyes was closed from a blow, and the other may not have seen very clearly. It took some time before I understood that she was real, and then some before I recognized her. She was differently dressed than I remembered her.

I discovered shortly that she hadn't really changed very much. Well, twenty years mean something for everybody, but she was to a surprising degree the same—her figure, her features, her voice, everything. Her smile I never saw.

She did have a few streaks of gray in her hair. A little later I noticed that she had wrinkles around the corners of her eyes, not from laughter alone.

She looked at me with such a strange expression in her eyes. Afterward she told me she wasn't certain at first that it was me.

She stood motionless just inside the door awhile.

I was still partly in my own world. My visions continued to roll by, but fainter, paler. They might be compared to a magnificent pageant you once saw as a child—it goes on and on, one display bigger and nicer than the one before, the jubilation rising around you, you are part of the jubilation, you are sheer jubilation. But eventually it has gone by, it rolls on, it's not quite past but almost past, you can still make out the last riders, you hear the jubilation rising farther away, still farther away, and then, slowly, it's over and you draw a deep sigh.

I tried to sit up. It was excruciatingly painful and I fell back again with a groan.

She had recognized me now.

"Oh!" she exclaimed. Then she spoke my name. In a moment she was leaning over me.

She managed to loosen the ropes. She rubbed my hands and feet. It felt like razors cutting into you. She shuddered once or twice and her hands shook; there were tremors about her mouth, but she didn't cry. She had seen my back. I had my shirt on, but I knew I had bleeding sores on my back, that the blood had soaked through the shirt and that it had gotten stuck to my skin.

"Oh!" she murmured several times. Otherwise she didn't say a word. Nor did I.

240

I was able to get up on the bunk. She asked me if I had a handkerchief, but I couldn't frame an answer. Then she found one in my raincoat and another in the pocket of my jacket. She went over to the sink, came back and washed my face.

Once or twice, when she had her back turned, her shoulders twitched. But not for long. She worked quickly and effectively. Then she asked me if I was able to stand up.

I tried and made it. I was slightly dizzy but could stand. Then came something more difficult—putting on my jacket. But she helped me, and that too worked out.

"I'll take your raincoat over my arm," she said quickly. "It isn't raining anymore."

There wasn't much strength left in me, and I nearly took a couple of tumbles.

I had a bump on my neck, it was incredibly sensitive. And now I noticed that I had a splitting headache. I also felt nauseous.

She asked me if I thought I would be able to walk.

"Though I don't think we'll risk anything by taking our time—I'll explain later. But we'd better get out of here."

I said I would be able to.

She supported me, and it went better than I had expected. The stairway had infinitely many steps, but it did end at last.

She locked a couple of doors behind us. Then we were out in the street.

It wasn't quite so dark any longer. After leaning against a wall awhile, I could see that the sky was only partly overcast. A few stars peeped out, and one could make out the streets and the walls of the houses.

She took my hand and guided me along.

We hadn't walked many steps before we came to a car.

"We'll have to use the car," she said. "We may have to go quite far and you aren't up to walking."

She helped me into the front seat, beside the steering wheel, while she herself remained outside.

She had to drop by the office for a moment, she said. It would only take a few minutes. If someone came—nobody would, I could rely on that—but *should* someone come, and should they shine a light on me and ask me something, I just had to say, I'm waiting for Dr. Heidenreich. I ought to say it in German. But it was very unlikely that anyone would come. And besides, everybody knew the car.

Then she was gone. I sat there in the darkness, leaning forward and holding on to the door handle so that nothing would touch my back. Some time passed. Once or twice people passed on the sidewalk and I said inwardly, like a jingle, Ich warte auf Dr. Heidenreich. Ich warte …

But they were all civilian steps; they died away and all I saw were shadows disappearing among shadows.

Then she was back again. She had a parcel in her hand, opened the back door and placed the parcel on the seat. She sat down behind the wheel.

"Has anyone been here?"

"No, no one."

She turned on the lights. The narrow strip that wasn't blacked out cast a faint light along the street. We drove off.

Without turning her head she asked, "How do you feel now?"

"Much better, thanks."

And it was true. It had been helpful to get out into the open air and have new things to be scared of. My nausea had subsided. My heart was somewhat unruly, and the bump on my neck beat like clockwork; otherwise I was all right.

She drove carefully, looking right and left. She wasn't quite as confident as she let on.

I clung to the handle of the car door, but I still felt every turn and every unevenness in the street down my whole back.

Then we began to talk. It was mostly she who did the talking, I lacked the breath to say much, nor did I have much to say. I didn't hear all she said, I was too tired. It became part of the whole picture that, when I finally met her again after twenty-two years, I could barely speak and was too tired to hear or take in more than fragments of what she said.

At some point I managed to ask her, "How did you know that I…"

She replied that she'd heard her husband and her son saying I was in town and that I was an enemy. Later, this evening, her son had told me I'd been arrested. "Well, he doesn't know that I know you, of course," she said. A little later still, when her husband dropped by, she had understood some more. Though not from anything he'd said.

Actually she didn't use the word "husband." She called him Carl. Her son she called Karsten.

I believe I came up with a rather stupid question—why she had saved me or something like that.

I didn't comprehend the full significance of her answer till later. "I didn't want him to turn himself into a murderer," she said.

The rescue itself hadn't been a problem. The Germans were having a party tonight, and both her son and her husband were there. There were only two men on guard in the basement. She had let her son go down with a drink for them before he went to the party.

"There were sleeping tablets in it," she said. "Such things are available in a doctor's house. Besides, I suffer from insomnia."

The rest was like nothing. She had an extra set of keys to the basement. No one knew she had them. After a suitable interval she let herself in. Sure enough, the two of them were fast asleep. And then—

"A mystery story!" I said.

She said, "Most of what happens nowadays is a series of mystery stories!"

I need not be afraid that she would be discovered. For she had been lucky. The two guards had eaten their supper down there, and the leftovers were still on the table. She had mixed a good dose of sleeping powder into the leftovers and rinsed the mug that had contained the drink, to be on the safe side. It had been emptied to the last drop.

And just in case—in case I should be caught again, she added, dryly and matter-of-factly—she'd better let me know a few more things. When she'd taken me to where I was going, she intended to drive back again and break a pane in the basement window. If I were caught a second time and questioned, I could just say that someone had thrown me two keys, two keys, remember, and a note with the words, *Let yourself out.*

"They will think it was one of their own people," she said. "The sleeping powder in the food, the keys they must think were duplicated, and one thing and another. It will give them lots to do."

At some point or other I must've asked her how Heidenreich had become a Nazi. Because I remember she tried to give me an explanation. But she did it slowly, gropingly, and with pauses, as if she felt on shaky ground. Anyway, I heard only part of what she related.

They didn't talk together very much, she said. Not during the last few years at any rate. Then he talked about such things only with Karsten.

But it began, I believe she said, during a couple of periods when he was studying in Germany. This was before Hitler. He made a number of friends among physicians down there. Some of them were Jews, by the way. And one of those Jews had stayed with them later on. That was in Hitler's time; he'd lived here while waiting for his American visa.

That Jew was such an exceptionally engaging man, and Carl had thought very highly of him. Later she had once asked Carl what his opinion was of the persecution of the Jews, knowing there were such people as his friend Abraham. But he just said, Life is merciless! He'd often said that in recent years.

No, she really didn't know how it had happened.

Perhaps the fact that he felt slighted and unjustly treated here at home was part of the answer.

I must've shown a certain surprise. For she grew eager and said that all his friends had misunderstood Carl. They thought he was a cynic, but in reality he was a very sensitive and vulnerable man.

"Well, I can't expect you to believe that, of course," she said.

He was extremely ambitious as a medical student and had dreamed of a career in research. But when he applied for a fellowship for further study, it was given to the son of a professor.

"I think a wrong was done him there," she said. "I don't really know, but..."

In any case, that incident became decisive. He gave up research.

"He took it very much to heart. And Carl had difficulty getting over things like that. He would brood over an insult for years."

When the war came he was pro-German and had been so for many years. But he was not a Nazi. His Jewish friends—for he had several ...

But he used to speak about the corruption here at home. And he had allowed Karsten to spend several vacations in Germany. And he was completely enthused by what he saw.

At this point I asked, "And you? You did nothing to prevent—"

"I didn't feel I had any right to," she said. And she repeated, as if to herself, "Everything considered, I didn't feel I had the right."

When the Occupation came he didn't join the Nazi Party. On the contrary, at first it looked as if he would turn in the opposite direction. It was only when—

She was silent a moment. Then she said, "It's just as well that you should know about it. I think that your attitude carried some weight with him—in the sense that he felt like doing the opposite. We heard about you in the spring of '41. Shortly afterward he joined the Party."

Again she halted a moment. "He hated you with a curious hatred!" she said.

"Did he know—"

"*No!*"

She said that one word with a sudden hard tone of voice that I'd never heard before. Then she continued again, tentatively, gropingly. I could hear that these were things she had thought about a lot and been unable to grasp.

"I believe that, for some reason or other, he thought exceptionally well of you in the beginning," she said. "I mean—at that time, in his student days. That he looked upon you as a younger brother, or something of the sort. But then you must have hurt him frightfully some time or other. He never told me what it was, but I noticed that he brooded over it. And it grew bigger and bigger as the years went by.

"By the way, he practically never mentioned your name."

I told her I'd gone to him to ask him to help us. That he had said no and that I had called him a cowardly bastard.

She remained silent for a while.

"You went to Carl?"

"Yes."

"And you called him—"

She seemed to consider something for a moment.

"I may just as well ..."—she tossed her head in a way that I recognized.

In a way Carl was a fearful man, she said. But he didn't want to be—nor was he when you came right down to it. His nerves were fearful but not his will. He would rather die than admit being fearful. In fact, he risked his own life more than once to avoid admitting it.

Suddenly she said, "When did you say that thing? Can you remember what day—what day of that week—you were in his place?"

I told her.

"And what time of day?"

I remembered that too. It was at two o'clock.

"I was in his place at twelve o'clock!" she said.

"To—to ask him to help you?"

"No. To ask him to marry me!"

She had again that hard tone of voice.

She was silent awhile.

"I think I understand a little more now," she then said. "I'm afraid I understand a great deal more now."

She said no more. The car nosed its way forward, like an animal with luminous eyes. I thought I recognized the direction and asked where we were going.

"I'm taking you to a certain Dr. Haug. You must have medical attention. Previously..." She hesitated, but went on, "Previously he was a good friend of ours. But now... He is what you and your people call a good Norwegian. Anyway, I'm not sure he's home."

She drove carefully on. I clung to the door handle. My arm was stiff, and I seemed to feel every stone of the pavement in my back.

We drove along the cemetery wall and on. Then we reached Dr. Haug's garden gate.

She got out of the car. "I must see if he's home. It'll only take a moment. If somebody should come, you're still waiting for Dr. Heidenreich."

She was gone again. I was alone in the car.

The whole town was dark and silent, as if it were a ghost town. There wasn't a glimmer of light to be seen from Dr. Haug's villa either.

What time was it? I put my wristwatch up to my sound eye, but discovered that the crystal was broken and the hands gone.

Not a sound. No, someone was coming. There, in the back. Hobnailed boots. There were several of them, marching to a heavy, tramping beat.

My escape could very well have been discovered by now. What if someone had been sent down to the watch with beer or wine? What if Heidenreich and the Gestapo officer had felt in a jolly mood and were minded to pay me a nocturnal visit? What if …

I felt nauseous again. My heart was acting up. An iron fist gripped my stomach and turned it upside down.

The steps came closer.

Ich warte auf Dr. Heidenreich. Ich warte auf Dr. Heid—

They were walking on the other side of the street. They didn't use a lantern. They clumped by. *They walked on!* I slumped down in my seat, leaned my back against the back rest, groaned with pain, and discovered that I was soaking wet with perspiration.

Then, there she was.

"Dr. Haug wasn't home!" she said shortly. "The family had left for the country. I'd half expected it. Now we must drive to Garmo's. But he's probably left too."

She got in and turned the car around. We drove off. First backtracking a bit, before she turned. She made several turns. We drove slowly. And yet— well, I'd never dreamed that this little town could be so big. And it consisted almost exclusively of turns.

It was during this part of the trip that I asked her if she would be kind enough to explain to me—well, she was sure to know what I meant.

She didn't speak for a moment. When she answered, I could tell by her voice that she, too, was very tired.

"It's all so long ago."

She sat for another moment. "I'd been together with Carl before I knew you. Or rather, he was the one I'd been with—been living with. You understand?"

It was hardly possible to misunderstand her.

"And that I didn't tell you my name and such … I wasn't afraid for myself. It was my mother. You understand—I had a stepfather."

Come to think, I had guessed that much.

Her mother was dead now. Her stepfather too. Her own father had died when she was quite small. She barely remembered him.

"All graves now, nothing but graves," she said. "And here we are, you and I—you know, now and then I feel I'm just a shadow of something that once was alive. And when I'm a bit unhappy every once in a while, it's just because I haven't quite found peace in my grave yet."

She told me the story of her youth. Actually, it was very commonplace, as is often the case with life's adversities. A kind but weak mother. A strong and strict and half-mad stepfather. A spirited and defiant child. She didn't want to say anything bad about her stepfather, he meant well, no doubt. He was what people usually call a man of character. Work, duty, discipline, punishment. The punishment was mostly for her. He would go into fits of rage and then he beat you. Properly, with a cane. This continued until she was fifteen. Then she bit his hand.

"And I had sharp teeth!" she said.

She refused to put up with corporal punishment any longer. She had noticed that it excited him in a special way. "Women notice such things," she said. "Already as children we notice things like that."

After that he never beat her again; he took it out on her mother if he thought the daughter misbehaved. And her mother couldn't defend herself, she feared and loved him as Luther wanted us to fear and love God.

But I mustn't think he was any sort of monster. He could be kind, too. Only so unbalanced ever so often. By the way, there was mental illness in the family.

How had Heidenreich entered the picture?

He was a relation of her stepfather. A kind of nephew. Well, a bit further removed. And the year before Kari and I became acquainted, he'd lived in their house. And then the stepfather had—

She stopped dead.

"He arranged it!" she said at last.

"Arranged what?"

"For Carl to have me. Well, it came to a kind of engagement, first. We would get married as soon as Carl had finished his studies. But—"

It was a difficult subject.

"My stepfather simply worshiped everything having to do with ancient Norway," she said. "He thought there had been nothing but degeneration since then. And he said that marriage as we knew it was just some Christian nonsense. In the old days, when a man was betrothed to a woman, he could have her—that way. But it was really more complicated. I believe that—"

Another pause.

"He—my stepfather—was so fond of Carl," she said. "He looked upon him as a son, even perhaps as something more. Carl was studying medicine, as he himself had wanted to do but couldn't afford. And—well, I believe he felt Carl was himself, in a way. Himself reincarnated as a young man. They looked alike too and came from the same part of the country, and—

"Yes, I do believe—it's odious to say it, and besides he's dead—but I do believe that …that he felt somehow he himself had me when Carl had me."

The relationship had lasted for a year. Then she rebelled.

"It wasn't that I had anything against Carl. He was in love, and he was kind—to me anyway.

"But—I was too young. I was not in love. Not that way. And I thought it was revolting—to have been sold, or given away, or … And so one day I said no."

The upshot was that Heidenreich moved out. And the engagement, if there had been an engagement, was broken off.

"Or postponed," she said. "I had to stretch a point on account of Mother. I had to promise that when Carl had finished his studies we would come back to the matter, as you men are in the habit of saying."

Pause.

"Poor Mother!" she said suddenly.

She herself had thought of moving out. She worked in a law office and made enough to get by in a pinch. And besides she had a small inheritance. Her guardian made her an offer to move to his place. But she couldn't bring herself to leave her mother.

"What a strange home!" I said.

"Yes. But aren't most homes strange in some way or other?"

All this, the crisis that is, took place almost a year before she met me.

"So, all that time you didn't see—Carl?"

"Oh sure," she said. "At dinner every Sunday. That was a clause in the peace agreement, or whatever you'd like to call it."

"But—"

"He would come, sit there for a few hours, and leave. That way he got to see me at least. When a man is in love he'll put up with a lot. And I put up with it because of Mother.

"It was during that year you became acquainted with Carl, wasn't it? There were some affairs and things, I believe. I knew all about that. He told me about them to make me jealous."

Another pause.

"Poor Carl!" she said. "And poor you, who got involved in all this. And— well, poor all of us maybe."

248

The evening she met me, she and her friend had just accompanied Carl to the West Country steamer. It was on her way back from there that—

"It all seemed so strange to me," she said. "I had agreed to go to the pier with him to have a little peace at home. And so I met you. I was as happy as a lark already beforehand, and then... Well, it did seem like a sign."

We were now in a different part of town, with low buildings, row houses of some sort as far as I could tell. She stopped in front of one of them, got out and vanished in the darkness.

It took longer this time.

The street was dark, quiet, dead. Not a soul, not a sound.

Then they came. Clomping boots in step. They were getting close.

Ich warte auf Dr. Heidenreich. Ich warte—.

All of a sudden, my heart pounding in my breast, I was beset by panic. Was *warte auf* correct? Didn't that mean to 'wait on?' I'm waiting on Dr. Heidenreich? *Erwarte* was the right word. Ich erwarte Dr. Heidenreich. Nonsense! *Warte auf* could mean both. A colloquialism. Ich warte...

They had come much closer. And they were walking on the near sidewalk. But they weren't running, they were walking. If it had been discovered, they would've been running and carrying lighted lamps, which they would flash at everything they saw—

A lamp was switched on.

Ich warte auf Dr. Heidenreich... Ich erwarte Dr.—

They flashed the light at the car. The cone-shaped beam entered by the back window, silhouetting my head against the windshield.

One of them said something to the others.

They came level with the car. There were four altogether.

It's the end. Ich warte... Ich erwarte...

One of them turned his head.

They didn't stop. Now they were already far up the street.

I sat there clinging to the door handle with all the strength I had left. My arm was stiff and as tender as a boil. I thought to myself, The third time I won't be able to take it, I'll scream or fall flat, or—

Then she was back again.

"Has something happened here?"

"No, it was just a patrol passing by."

She got in.

"Garmo has also left for the country. I spoke to his housekeeper."

She sat for a moment.

"You'll have to be bandaged. I could drive back and do it at my place. But...Or we could go in and do it here—I have bandages in the car and the housekeeper could help me. But I would rather drive you to the others right away. Can you take it?"

I thought I could.

We drove off again. Out of town this time, on a bumpy country road. But out of town.

The houses disappeared. I dimly perceived trees beside the road, and fences. Now and then I could make out a private road which joined the country road.

She drove slowly and carefully. The car still seemed to nose its way forward. She kept a lookout on the road ahead of her and to both sides. Her face was tense.

We came to a crossroads. Suddenly I saw her face change, becoming calmer, restful. She relaxed a little behind the wheel.

"Now I think we can feel safe," she said. "They haven't discovered anything, otherwise they would've been at that crossroads."

It was now, as we were driving out toward the hide-out, that she told me the conclusion to her story.

"Are you really interested?" she said. "It's so long ago. And you already know most of it. That fortnight in August and the beginning of September— my stepfather was in the hospital during that time. He was there the following week too, but then he was to be discharged in a day or two. It was this that— that gave me a pretext to go to Carl.

"I told him I couldn't stand my stepfather any longer. That he turned my life into a living hell, and my mother's on account of me, and—and that I hadn't understood it fully until now, after being rid of him for three weeks, and—

"I told him that, if he wanted me he could have me. But I wanted to get married now, right away. I said, 'You can do as you like. I can drown myself too, if that's what you prefer!'

"He agreed to our getting married right away. He asked for nothing better. But I could see he found it strange. After all, I didn't tell him I loved him."

"But how could you—without as much as a word to me—"

She was speaking quite softly now. But bitterly. How many times hadn't she gone over this herself!

"You never mentioned marriage. I didn't think you even regarded it as a possibility. I would have drowned myself rather than propose that to you.

"I had that money. It wasn't very much, though you could have finished your studies. But I couldn't come right out and buy you either."

I didn't answer. I could perhaps have answered something. But to what purpose? I was tired, dead tired.

It was she who began talking again.

"I saw how frightened you were. And then *I*, too, became really frightened. Oo—I don't think another human being has been more frightened.

"And then I thought—about you: I'm abandoning him. But hasn't he already abandoned *me?*

"And I thought: I'm fooling Carl. But didn't he fool me first?"

Again she spoke in that hard tone of voice. And she'd lost her temper, as if defending a cause she didn't quite believe in herself.

"Why, how many women, do you suppose, haven't thought and done the same thing?"

Suddenly she wept. "I thought what I did was for the best."

Pause.

"At any rate I thought that I thought so."

Another pause.

"Now I no longer know what was the best or the worst. I don't even know what I thought at the time. I only know I've felt guilty toward him every single day since we were married. I have—tried—to make it up to him, but it has just gone from bad to worse."

I sat quite still beside her, hanging on to the door handle. It was important to sit perfectly still, without moving. Everything hurt less then. I remembered that day in my room when I'd sat still in my chair, not daring to move for fear of getting crushed—crushed under the weight of my own dread.

That dread was no more. It was dead and gone.

Too late. Everything was too late.

When I continued the conversation, it was mostly out of politenes.

"But the child?" I asked. "When you thought of the child that was coming— you had to assume, didn't you, that he …"

Her answer came very slowly. It looked as though she had to make an effort and track down her thoughts in dark corners.

"At first—I don't really know what I thought at first. I was so confused. But later, when we were preparing to get married and everyone was so happy, I thought, You have to talk to him about it! At once! But I put it off and put it off, from one day to the next.

"I was afraid. He was capable of flying into a dangerous rage, he was like my stepfather that way.

"I think I can swear it wasn't myself I was afraid for. My own life was quite indifferent to me at that time, nothing in the world seemed more indifferent. Why can't I get sick? I thought. But I didn't get sick.

"It was you I was afraid for. I still believe there was no way of knowing what he would have done. And I thought I had done enough harm. And—and—"

She stopped for a moment.

"And I was still in love with you—then!" she said.

She was still in love with me—then. And she didn't want him to turn murderer—now.

What a crazy hope I'd been nurturing for twenty-two years! I felt my heart sink and my body go numb, as when I entered my hotel room and stood face to face with Heidenreich.

I heard her continue. "And so I didn't tell him. And then we got married and it was too late. I hoped and prayed—to something or other—that I would have an accident, so that the child would never be born. But no accident occurred. And then, as the time drew near, I prayed desperately that it would be stillborn."

Again she was silent a moment. Then she whispered, "An expectant mother who has such thoughts is bound to bring punishment on herself!"

"And then?"

"Well, what then? Oh yes. When finally my time came I remember thinking, If it lives I'll tell all—come what may! I no longer cared, one way or another.

"But when I held the child in my arms, something changed. Then, *he* was suddenly the only thing that mattered. Everything else was indifferent. And so—well, I just couldn't say anything."

"But what about *him*?" I managed to say. "What about Heiden—what about Carl? When the child came prematurely and—"

"Doctors can fool themselves about less complex matters than that," she said.

"But when the boy grew up—the resemblance—it's so striking?"

She hesitated awhile. When she replied, it was as though her voice had a shade of the old ironic gaiety for a moment. "Is it possible you haven't noticed how alike you and Carl are?"

I had noticed nothing of the sort. I didn't say a word, I had to collect myself.

Her gaiety—if it had been there for a moment—didn't last. She sat like a shadow beside me. I could hear her mumble, "And yet he has had a suspicion. All along. That I can see now."

"But—hasn't he ever—asked you—"

"No, never," she said. "Not a word. And again I can see why—now. The fact is—well, time has borne it out—Carl and I can't have children together. I don't know what the reason is."

"And he hasn't looked into the reason why? Medically, I mean?"
Pause.

"Maybe he hasn't dared take that risk," she then said. "Perhaps he preferred to remain in a state of uncertainty.

"But it was unavoidable—I see that too now—that as the years went by and we didn't have any more children, his suspicion should grow stronger and stronger once it had been planted. But at the same time he became more and more fond of the boy.

"As things turned out, you see, Karsten became his son far more than mine. That, too, is my fault. I pushed him over to Carl, in a way, from when he was quite small. I may have seen it as a sort of atonement for something. Oh dear! I'm so tired! Sometimes I feel that I'm nothing but the shadow of a bad conscience!"

At last she was no longer talking about her everlasting Carl. She began to tell me about Karsten.

Then I noticed in earnest that I was tired myself. The tiredness crept up on me so badly that I no longer understood what she was telling me. I sat there in a sort of stupor, and what she was saying turned into fog. Only a sentence here and there reached me—tree tops sticking out of the fog.

"...Carl was fantastic with him...

"...I became an outsider. Especially these last few years. But in a way that was how I wanted it...

"...but then I felt even more guilty...

"...Carl has always treated Karsten as an equal...

"...I didn't feel I had any right to interfere. Karsten was *his* son, much more so than if he had really been...."

Her words came to me from far away. Her voice was merely a faint hum blending in with the sound of the engine. I tried to pull myself together. I said to myself, Listen now! It's about your son, it's about *you yourself* she's talking. You as you might have been if ...

But it carried no weight. I pinched my arm. It didn't help. This is in keeping with everything else about you, I thought. You fall asleep in your own Gethsemane.

But irony didn't help either, its sting got wrapped up in the fog as in cotton wool.

"Are you asleep?" she said. "Poor thing! But we're almost there now."

Suddenly I realized it wasn't out of politeness I had continued this conversation. I was deadly afraid of being separated from her. On and off I had dreaded every sentence she uttered. But most of all I dreaded the moment we would arrive and she be gone, without a chance of seeing her anymore.

She turned on a small flashlight and looked at her watch.

"It's nearly one o'clock. You've still got four or five hours' time. If Dr. Haug drives you, you may be in Oslo before anyone here knows anything."

She turned toward me—imploringly, "One thing—you mustn't think that

253

Carl is all bad. At bottom he's not bad at all. But you probably can't understand that—after what you've experienced tonight. It's just that—"

She gave up.

I thought, No living being is all bad.

The king cobra is not bad. It falls in love and dances lovely, gliding dances with its beloved. Afterward it defends its young. But to us it's bad—so bad and dangerous that its head has become a symbol of evil.

She turned toward me again. "We've only talked about me and—and mine. But you have also gone through much. You lost your wife and your little son—three years old, I heard. And it was the Germans, wasn't it, who—"

"Viewed superficially," I said, "the Germans were to blame. In reality, I'm afraid, I was to blame. I married her because I was lonely and she loved me. But I didn't love her as much as—well, as she deserved. I've never forgotten you, and—I believe I used you as a shield against a new love. I shut myself up with my thoughts of you. I guess it was a sort of escape from life. She noticed it and rebelled. Our marriage began as a false paradise and ended as a minor hell. She loved and hated me, suffered fits of remorse and grew more and more nervous. At times we had to have a nurse. And I shut myself up more and more—and thought of you. Then the Germans came and arrested me. They hadn't got very much on me, I had just refused to follow orders. But she thought it was something much worse, and expressed such fear that the Germans *thought* it was something worse. When she discovered that, she went out of her mind. She wrote a letter to the Gestapo and drowned herself and our boy."

I sat there listening to my own words as if someone else were uttering them.

I hadn't even known I harbored such thoughts. I had believed that, in my marriage at least, I had been blameless.

I suddenly felt as though I'd been walking uphill since time immemorial. Hill after hill after hill. My strength had given out a long time ago, but I walked on, hill after hill. However, this one, the last, was a few feet too much for me. I managed to climb it, but then it was over. I didn't have the strength anymore, couldn't bother. In reality I was already dead. I couldn't have been more dead if I'd rested beneath six feet of earth with a stone over my head. He was forty-four years old....

She touched my arm lightly. "My friend!" she said softly.

I asked, "And what do you plan to do now?"

She hesitated with her answer. "I don't know. I really can't see myself going on with Carl after what I know now. But—if I leave him it'll all be plain as day. And I still don't feel he has deserved that. Not that it would matter terribly much. But Karsten——."

I suspected rather than saw that she was weeping silently beside me.

Neither of us spoke again.

A moment later we turned into a yard. She helped me out of the car. It took a bit of time. I'd grown stiff, as if I were frozen solid. We went up to the door and she knocked.

No one came. She knocked again. Twice, three times.

Finally there were footsteps inside. And then I heard the doctor's voice, "Who is it?"

I said who I was.

I felt a fleeting touch of her hand. I knew it meant goodbye.

Flight
~~~~~~~~~~~~~~~~~~~~~~~~~~~

Dr. Haug said what people are likely to say on such occasions, "In heaven's name, man, you do look a mess! Jesus Christ, how did you get out? They're hard on your heels, are they?!? Oh, it's you, Maria! Well, we did suspect … By Jove, I became quite nervous when I heard a knock. For I must tell you—"

What he wanted to tell us had to wait. The room was spinning, and again I found myself on the floor.

There followed an unpleasant half-hour while the doctor pulled off my shirt, washed and disinfected me and wrapped me up in bandages. I think I fainted a couple of times, but each time I came to the doctor was cursing just as robustly and heatedly. "Damn sons-of-bitches! What? Heidenreich was part of it! That he shall pay for! And in the neck too! What the blooming, blazing hell… Have this drink! Sit still now!"

I managed to tell him the main thing. He became frightened.

"But how on earth—they know *that* too! But then we must …"

Betweentimes he told me some things.

They had learned about my arrest after less than half an hour. From then on things happened thick and fast. Inga and Colbjørnsen and …

The bank manager and Garmo were in hiding some other place. He himself had just arrived. So many things were happening at once. Inga broke down and eventually had to be given a shot, she would be dead to the world for at least twelve hours. His wife also broke down—Inga was like a daughter to her. She was with that damn wretch of a girl at the moment.

And Colbjørnsen had shot and killed himself.

He wasn't sure I had taken it in, so he repeated it. Colbjørnsen had shot himself. It was just too much for him. He had confided in Inga up to a point— he simply had to tell her *something,* he said, because he was using her as a spy. Against whom? Well, would I like to take a guess? Sure enough, against himself, Dr. Haug, and the bank manager! Top that one if you can!!

The doctor continued, while oaths and curses streamed from his lips like Bengal lights. "Colbjørnsen claimed he'd told her next to nothing. Only what she *had* to know, as he said. And her spying stint itself—against us, that is— proved, after all, that she was reliable! Said he. Top that one too if you can! But the son of a bitch was madly in love with the girl and had completely lost his head."

He took a deep breath.

"And Inga!" he said. "Hmm, well, Inga …"

She had played sweetheart to Colbjørnsen by order of young Heidenreich, who was himself secretly her sweetheart! Top that one too, whoever can! What a devilish fellow, a damn out-and-out cad!!! And this was the boy the doctor had at one time …

But anyway, Inga had been a frequent visitor at Colbjørnsen's place. When she wasn't at young Heidenreich's, of course! And evidently she'd heard something and seen some papers maybe, and then she'd put two and two together—after all, she was no dumbbell, the troll!

But had ever a living soul heard about the likes of that damn Colbjørnsen, absolute idiot that he was! An intelligent man, too! Well, one shouldn't speak ill of the dead, but what a perfect dunce!

Oh yes, Colbjørnsen went straight home—there broke out a minor thunderstorm at the meeting, naturally—and put a bullet through his head. Dead as a herring instantly.

"I came from there only an hour ago," the doctor said. "Poor devil! Can you imagine his last moments! And afterward, you know, I had to pack a few things.

"And there was no help to be had from my wife. She just sat bawling at Inga's bedside."

When he was through bandaging me, I felt as though I were armor-plated.

He also dug out a fresh shirt for me. "Wear it in good health!" he said. "It's the last shirt you'll see in Norway!"

Suddenly his thoughts took another direction. "Mrs. Heidenreich!" he said, and was silent for a moment. "Poor, poor Maria!"

He sagged as if under a burden. Then he straightened up again.

"Tragedies grow around us as thick as toadstools on a tree stump," he said. "And all because of that greenhorn, that seven times accursed pup! Who can he have gotten it from? From Heidenreich, of course! But even Heidenreich… If I didn't know Maria so well, I could almost believe the devil himself had planted his seed there."

He left the room for a moment and returned with a suitcase. "Enough chatter!" he said. "Listen! Can you stand up? You have to get to Oslo as fast as my car can drive you! Let's see—we should have plenty of time. But we must count on their getting on the telephone to alert the Gestapo in there as soon as they find out about… Christ, what a life!"

He stopped for a moment, snapping his fingers. "We may just as well take Inga and the missus over to Garmo and the bank manager—we'll be passing right by there anyway."

What happened from now on for a while is somewhat unclear in my mind. I sat in the front seat of the car. I believe the doctor and his wife carried Inga down. Mrs. Haug sat in the back seat, beside the bundle that was Inga. She didn't look at me and didn't say a word to me. She was anything but ecstatic about me, I understood that much.

We went full blast, spattering mud as we drove along.

"If anyone stops us, we are on our way to Ullevål. An accident, blood transfusion and things!" the doctor said.

We stopped somewhere en route and the doctor got out. Some shadows came up to the car, I believe I shook hands with the bank manager and Garmo. Later on, in Sweden, they claimed that I spoke sensibly and coherently to them. The only sign of fever was my insistence I'd been rescued by someone named Kari.

Then the doctor and I were alone in the car, whooshing through the nocturnal darkness. Nobody tried to stop us. If they had, it would probably have been the end—the doctor had a pistol on his lap and I one in my hand.

Dawn was just breaking as we reached Oslo.

Up till now I hadn't officially known Andreas; I don't think he even knew that I knew who he was. But here minor considerations had to be pushed aside. We drove straight to his house and kept knocking on his door till a scared maid appeared, before he himself showed up. It was four-thirty in the morning. We could still count on having an hour or two. And one thing: Heidenreich hadn't mentioned Andreas by name.

It took just a minute for Andreas to be fully up on the situation. "That means your house goes to hell!" This was the first thing he said. And the next was, "Strange, actually, that nobody has been there yet. They really haven't— I think so anyway. Do I dare make a call? I'll risk it."

A call and a few innocent words showed that everything was in order.

Andreas got the wind up when he heard about all the things the Germans knew. He looked sharply at me. "These aren't feverish dreams, are they?" he said. "Seeing how horribly you've been treated, you must be running a fever."

He looked at me with an air of sympathy (him showing sympathy!): "Are you sure?"

I was sure. Whereupon he became so busy that he forgot us for several minutes. We were minor characters now—people to be gotten rid of. Everything had to be organized afresh down there, that was the main thing.

My own thoughts were elsewhere. I was restless and wanted to get home— that is, to drop by.

At first Andreas protested, but even he had to give in.

I had the fixed idea that I must take my papers along, even if it were to cost me—well, almost whatever it might cost me.

And so I was in a car once more, being driven in the direction of my house. I had already been told the address of the hide-out. The driver, who was a member of the group, had it as well.

"What a pity you can't go into hiding in your own place," Andreas said. And he sighed, "All that fine workmanship!"

The car stopped at a corner one block above the house. It would wait for me there. It was five-thirty. This was the moment for the bombshell to explode down there in the little town. In half an hour or maybe an hour ...

I stumped my way in, exchanged a few words with my permanent tenant, Andersen as we called him. For that matter, he had perfectly legal—but false—papers in that name. The password I'd brought with me was: Instant pullout. Andersen was already packed—his luggage consisted of a small parcel which he stuck in one pocket, and a pistol which he stuck in the other. Andersen's motto was: Travel light. He'd awakened the maids, they were both dressed. The new maid wanted to come with us, but the old one refused to leave the place.

"Not on your life!" Antonia said. "This is where I've lived, and this is where I'll stay. Someone must remain and look after things. And believe me, nobody can be as stupid as I in a pinch. They won't fool me!"

Strangely enough, we had no one in hiding at that moment. Every once in a while one was lucky.

It took me ten minutes or so to dig up the papers and put them in a small traveling bag with a few other trifles. Then we were ready, the three of us.

So far there were no signs of danger. No bells, nobody to be seen from the window. We should be able to walk calmly and peacefully out through the gate.

I don't know what made me go up to the periscope we had installed in the board fence. I peered out.

At that very moment they came. Two cars. They stopped a little way below my house. Out of the first car jumped young Heidenreich. Three or four men in civvies swarmed out behind him. At the same time, four or five men had emerged from the other car. My dear son directed and distributed the men. The house was to be surrounded.

It was strange to see oneself in action.

We conferred for a moment there in the backyard. We quickly realized we had one chance, and one only.

In the toolshed hung a paint-smudged overalls, and a paintpot had been left behind by the latest workmen. I slipped on the overalls and picked up the paintpot. Andersen took my traveling bag. I was the painter's apprentice, Andersen the master painter. He was younger than I, but that was all right. It was still rather early in the morning, but we would have to take that chance. Leaning up against one of the old apple trees was a small ladder—we were in the middle of the apple harvest. I took the ladder on my shoulder. The girl—we called her Olava—had no blind. We decided she ought to come along to make it more difficult.

Then we just had to open the extra door facing the houses of the Germans, and stroll calmly through the open space between the two apartment buildings as if it were the most natural thing in the world. Andersen pointed up at something on the wall a couple of times, otherwise he kept his hand in his pocket. Olava pointed too, and I nodded to indicate that I understood. By then we had already reached the sidewalk, where a sentry was posted, but no one else. They hadn't dreamed we might come out that way. The sentry looked at us for a moment and then averted his eyes. We calmly crossed the sidewalk and entered the street, before casting one more glance back at the house to check on the paint, and one thing with another. Nobody in sight. Then we crossed the street, went around the corner and up to the car.

Antonia came to Sweden all the same. She got fed up with the obligation to report to the police, she said.

It was from her we learned what happened afterward. A few minutes after we were gone the bell rang. Antonia went to open. Five men stood outside, all in civvies; but the moment she opened the door the muzzles of five pistols were pointed at her.

"I felt real proud!" Antonia said.

Well, they went in, looked around, and ended by questioning her. The one who did the questioning was a very young man, a Norwegian by the way. The other four were Germans, as far as she could make out. When she told them I'd dropped by briefly but had taken a suitcase and left for the country, they all became so hopping mad that they cursed and swore for several minutes. The angriest of them all was the young Norwegian. He jumped up and down on the floor, waving his arms and screaming! And then—it was in the so-called inner office, my laboratory, that this took place—then this Norwegian grabbed the nearest glass flask and smashed it into a thousand pieces on the floor. But that wasn't enough, he took the next flask, and the next, and smashed them on the floor. Afterward he grabbed whatever instruments he could lay his hands on and smashed the whole lot on the floor—until one of the others spat out a word—*genug!* or something.

"It was a horrible sight!" Antonia said. "But it was fun too, in a way."

Postscript 1947

The Anthill

~~~~~~~~~~~~~~~~~~~~~~~~~~

On May 12, 1945 I came back to Oslo. The Germans had lived in my home for a year and a half. I won't try to describe the scene that confronted me, but I thought as I walked through the rooms, What on earth—did they wage war *here?*

The builder who, long ago now, had sold me the house was just working out an estimate of the damage to the two apartment buildings. And now he was getting an additional assignment from me.

If I hadn't known it was the same man I wouldn't have recognized him. He had become thin and gaunt. His skin was loose and floppy, like a too large suit of clothes, and his complexion was no longer a fiery red but a dull grayish-yellow.

He had become so quiet. "Yes ...," he said. "Yes ...," he said a moment later.

He didn't hear very much of what I said. He'd gotten into the habit of letting his mind wander. When he thought nobody was watching, his eyes took on an expression like that of a sick animal.

He had lost both his sons since I saw him last. One had fallen during the fighting in Norway in 1940, the other had died a prisoner in Germany. He'd been informed of the latter a couple of days ago.

That his son had lost his life in a gas chamber at a *Nacht und Nebel* camp, the authorities had mercifully omitted to tell him.

This quiet man, who'd been so loud and cheerful six years ago, gave me a sort of bad conscience. I'd thought myself I could never really be happy again. But one day back in Norway sufficed. When you go around and see nothing but people who are so happy that they walk on air, three feet above the ground, you end up by walking on air yourself, a miserable inch or so from the ground.

Quitting the street to drop by at the builder's was like coming from a sunny day in May into a quiet, semi-dark room.

"Yes ...," he said. "Yes ..."

On May 15, Dr. Haug called me. He too had come home—to a totally stripped house. The only thing they hadn't taken with them was the telephone. But what the hell! Everything was wonderful—that is, except for Maria. Her husband had committed suicide, her son was arrested, and she herself didn't show her face to anybody. Wouldn't I come down and try to talk with her?

I telephoned her right away. Sure, she would be glad to see me.

I had managed to get my car out of the barn where it had been in storage for several years. It had stood on nice, dry ground and hadn't suffered very much damage.

The following day I drove down to the little town.

First of all I called on the doctor and the bank manager. We'd spent some time together in Sweden, and I now counted them among my friends. We dined at the bank manager's. His house had escaped without damage, the German commandant had moved in there; but his wine cellar had gone the way of all flesh, naturally—except for some extra fine items in a secret place which those blockheads hadn't discovered.

"And in their hurry they forgot to take along twenty bottles of cognac and thirty jugs of old Dutch gin of their own stock!" the bank manager said. "Under the circumstances I'm afraid I shall forget to report the matter to the authorities. Skoal!"

We had a good time at the bank manager's. But I sat on pins and needles. I was going somewhere else, as soon as I knew the essentials.

They weren't able to tell me very much.

Dr. Heidenreich and his son had been belligerent up to the very last day of the war. The wife hadn't been seen much by anybody.

On May 7, in the afternoon, news of the liberation began to spread. In the evening flags appeared on the verandas, children paraded in the streets, carrying little flags, the banned radios suddenly turned up all over the place, and news reports and music streamed out of the open windows. People burned their blackout curtains in the town square and in the streets round about, and then they gathered around the fires to sing. Later they began to dance—in the square, in the streets, on the docks. The members of the Home Front appeared on the scene in their windbreakers. No official announcement had yet come through and the Germans were still in town, but they mostly kept to their barracks.

Through this crowd of people walked Dr. Heidenreich. Silence fell around him as he advanced—he was hated by everybody. But nobody did him any harm, nobody spoke to him. "His face looked so strange," someone said afterward. "I almost believe he didn't see us."

He followed the streets toward the harbor, straight out to one of the piers.

Down there he was accosted for the first time. "Hey, you!" someone called. "This is the end for people like you!"

It was impossible to know whether he heard it or not. He had reached the edge of the pier just then. He jumped straight in and disappeared at once. They didn't find his body until two hours later. He had several kilos of lead and other metal in his pockets, mostly shot and such, but also a large lump of lead.

He hadn't notified anyone beforehand. Not even his son, as far as one could tell—he was extremely distraught when they brought the body and cried out several times, "Why did you do it, Dad!"

That he hadn't told Maria was easier to understand, perhaps. Their relationship had been rather lackluster lately, it was rumored—nobody knew anything for certain, naturally.

The following day they arrested the son. He simply stood there smiling with screwed-up eyes when they picked him up.

A few days later Dr. Heidenreich was buried very quietly.

All this happened before the bank manager and the doctor returned, on the thirteenth. They came alone, their families were still in Sweden, Garmo too. This story was one of the first things they heard. And one of the first things they did, both separately and together, was to call Maria. They figured she might need help now, and they felt she had more than earned it.

But she didn't want any help. She was managing perfectly well, she said. Thanks, but she had everything she needed. It was extremely nice of them, but... She very nearly hung up on them.

"Then I went to see her," the doctor said. "Something I won't do again. Well, she wasn't discourteous, far from it. She was just so distant. I understand, of course, that she has a lot on her mind. But there must be limits to everything. She was not *present*, if you see what I mean. She reminded me—yes, she reminded me of a religious fanatic I once met who was forced to sit and talk about the weather!"

Well, then they called me. That was all.

Shortly afterward I was on my way to her house.

Walking through that town, where I had once spent two days, was a strange experience. It was like walking on familiar ground. The square with the fountain, bringing to mind the Nazi meeting that fall day; the two myrtles in front of the hotel entrance, making me think of Inga with her slip of paper, now married in Sweden; and look, there was that old house of granite and red brick where I'd spent a few hours in a basement.

All these thoughts were nothing but attempts at escape. I was as nervous as a youth before a tryst.

She herself opened the door. She gave me her hand but said nothing. Without a word, she led me into the living room.

The hallway had been in semi-darkness. When we came into the bright living room I backed away a step. She had changed in a way that frightened me at first.

She had grayed during those eighteen months. But that wasn't it. She had grown thinner and was very pale; she didn't look well. But that wasn't it. Something about her, one thing or another, fairly jumped out at me, but I couldn't say what it was. I only knew: she had become a stranger. It was—it was something about her eyes, something about her mouth. It hadn't been there before.

She looked as though she were utterly indifferent. No, that wasn't it either—her eyes were smoldering and her mouth was set in a way that—no, she was not indifferent, anything but.

She smiled when she saw the expression on my face. A wan smile. But—and I cannot explain this—it affected me more deeply than any smile I'd ever received. If only I could have said to her, "I and all that I have is yours!"

But one doesn't make such offers in a crematorium.

I said nothing. And when she spoke herself it was only to utter a few ordinary words in an even voice. She just said, "Quite a bit has happened since we last met."

Then we each sat in our chairs, talking sensibly.

No, she didn't need any help. Yes, financially she would be all right, as far as she could see. Anyway, she had money of her own. She'd had some money from the start and later a bit more, and Carl had set aside some for her from time to time. This house was in her name. Whatever happened to what Carl left behind, there was no reason to worry.

No, Carl hadn't told her anything beforehand. "He hardly ever spoke to me—after that night," she said. "He didn't come out and say so, but I think he had his suspicions about that too."

All things considered she was glad, for his sake, that he had done what he did. "Isn't it strange?" she said. "In a way I was relieved, and a little proud too. He went all out. He stayed the course to the end."

But it was terrible for Karsten. That, too, on top of everything else.

With this she had broached the subject around which all her thoughts were churning.

It would be pointless to repeat all she said. Nor was there any clear sense to her thoughts. She was confused, helpless and despairing, and chased in circles around the same thing over and over again.

"At one time I thought he would become the rarest thing of all—a happy human being!" she said. "But those last few days—I don't think I've ever seen such despair.

"He was liked by everybody—once. And now there's only me—and a few young girls here and there."

It was almost *en passant* that she told me about Hans Berg. His daughter,

Erna, had completely lost her head over Karsten. That daughter was everything to her father. He joined the Party so that his daughter could get close to her sweetheart. The mother was desperate.

She continued to pursue this train of thought. She clung to it for a while. "You see—the girls were crazy about him. He was far more dangerous that way than you ever were."

The last sentence came like a flicker of her old gaiety. She wanted to tease me; but she was also proud of her son.

That flicker remained the only one.

"But something was wrong there too," she said. "In reality he didn't give a hoot about any of those girls. The only thing that interested him in the end was something he called *the cause*."

She pursued that train of thought awhile. She told me, not without a certain pride, that Karsten had been able to create a quite strong youth movement in the town.

I recalled the meeting in the square that afternoon and had to smile. She saw that smile.

"Well, relatively strong," she said. "I know, of course, that you saw that meeting in the square. But there was an extra foray into the woods just then. They were looking for something—which they didn't find, incidentally."

But to Karsten it wasn't so important whether he spoke to many or just a few. He would gladly sit all day and all night talking to a single person. And then he made a strangely powerful impression on people. Hypnotic, almost. She'd seen it herself.

I thought, There, in him, is the revolutionary force! Twisted, sure, but it's there. While I was paralyzed by the cowardice that calls itself respectability and—partly maybe—by a certain respectability that is often called cowardice.

"He couldn't forgive me for not *believing*!" she said. "I lost him because of that.

"Oh, why must you men believe so intensely? Karsten believed so strongly, I would sometimes get scared.

"People become hard from believing!"

Suddenly she turned toward me. It was as though she were beseeching me. "You don't think, do you, that he was *completely* mistaken? It can't be possible, can it, that he's wrong in *everything*?"

I couldn't help her. And I don't think she expected me to.

Suddenly her set face relaxed and her eyes filled with tears. She covered her face with her hands and wept without a sound, as women can do after long practice. But her shoulders were shaking.

I sat there beside her unable to help, unable even to comfort her.

Strange to think—one evening not so terribly long ago I'd looked upon that son of hers with fear and loathing, paralyzed by the thought: That thing could've been you!

Now I was far away—I knew that, even if I wanted to, I wouldn't be allowed to have even the remotest share in him. And I wasn't sure whether I wanted to either.

She raised her head again, grimy with tears and with an expression of fanatical defiance. "Come to that, I don't give a damn about right or wrong!" she said. "If I could win him back I'd be willing to believe in anything! Anything whatever! Do you hear me? I wouldn't stop at murder—if only I could win him back."

And I sat there and knew: To no avail. You will never win him back. He has wandered too far into the stony desert of fanaticism.

"Woman, what have I to do with thee?" That was a word ascribed to Him they called the Savior. Had he really said it?

The thief could also have said it.

About her who sat there a few feet away from me, but separated from me by a wall I wasn't able to climb—about her I knew there were no limits to what she would be willing to do out of pious deception.

Which would lead nowhere.

"No, no, no," she suddenly cried out, like a wild protest against me, although I hadn't said a word. "I can't have anything to do with you! He's the only one that matters, he alone! I can't betray him a second time!"

There isn't much more to report from this conversation. She said things over again, contradicting herself, and once more said things over again. For a while she reminded me unpleasantly of a marten I'd once seen in a zoo. It was in a cage but refused to see it. The slim, lithe wild animal ran and ran without stopping, tearing at the bars now and then but continuing to run in circles, one after another—there had to be an exit somewhere! What was it thinking of? The woods, freedom, a mate, a lair with young? I don't know. I only know it was painful to see the noble animal running around, with tame human beings gaping outside.

And thanks for coming! she said at last. It had been helpful to speak her mind.

I thought, For how long? An hour perhaps. Then the churning would start afresh.

But we'd better not see each other, she said as she showed me out. If she needed me, she would write. But apart from that—well, she would have to get through this by herself.

*

As agreed, I dropped by at Dr. Haug's afterward.

He opened the door himself.

I could only tell him, "We must let her go her own way awhile."

He showed me into the living room. "This place is nothing to brag about right now," he said. "But I managed to borrow a few chairs, a table and a couch, and—"

A woman got up from her chair as I came in.

Every once in a while you have a feeling that the world is about the size of an average glee club. The woman who'd gotten up was the one whose name I'd forgotten and whom I called Ida.

Dr. Haug introduced us, "...Mrs. Marie Kjelsberg..."

"Wife of Major Kjelsberg," he added for the sake of clarity, letting me know at the same time that the woman's husband was among the Norwegian armed forces in England. He was expected home any day now.

So she and Lieutenant Kjelsberg had actually married.

Her name was Marie. Of course, I'd known that all along. And in some way or other I'd known that Kari's name was Maria. Then and there a brief notice in the paper from prehistoric times flickered in my memory: "Maria Steen, daughter of ..., was today married to Carl Heidenreich, a medical student."

The circle was closed. Self-knowledge and the struggle against self-knowledge, repression, drowning in the river of oblivion ...

If the notice in the paper was real, that is. If it wasn't just something I imagined afterward.

Anyway, it was a matter of indifference. Total indifference.

She was remarkably unchanged and looked much younger than her forty some years. With a smile she explained to Dr. Haug that she already knew me—though only superficially, as she said, and terribly long ago, but...

We sat talking awhile all three of us.

It was with a certain relief I noticed that, as far as I could see, she didn't feel any bitterness toward me. She thought she remembered we'd had a tiff. She couldn't remember what it was all about, but she must almost certainly have been right, as she said with a coquettish little smile.

I nodded. Most certainly!

I also noticed—without many words being said—that she had only a pale recollection of our little love affair of so many years ago. She was married now, happily married to a war hero. She had no past from before her marriage.

"Major Kjelsberg was one of the original members of our club," Dr. Haug explained.

That too. So she and Kari had lived in the same small town.

Had they recognized each other? Impossible to know. They'd seen each other for a brief moment in the shadow of a kiosk one dark evening.

I was absorbed in my own thoughts for a while and didn't hear what they were saying. When I came back to reality again they were talking politics, and Mrs. Kjelsberg was holding forth.

Fancy Ida talking politics!

Order had to be restored again after all these lawless years. Slogans had to be broadcast, and ...

A nation must have confidence in its leaders. A nation must look up to its führers. What kind of future would a nation have if the respect for authority had broken down? Her husband had often said that ...

She hadn't grown very much older in her upper story either.

Dr. Haug sat listening to her with a faint smile. He had obviously given up speaking about difficult matters with her.

But I couldn't help myself. "Hitler thought the same," I said.

"Hitler?" She didn't understand what I was driving at. She just said, "Yes, that awful Hitler!"

She left shortly afterward, and the conversation took a more serious turn.

Dr. Haug was deeply absorbed by some documents he'd gotten hold of concerning a number of scientific experiments carried out in a large German prison, or possibly a concentration camp, which included Jews, male and female, besides Poles, Gypsies, and members of other so-called inferior races. The experiments were as follows:

A young Jewess would be informed that sentence had been passed on her. She was to be executed, or she would be transported to an unknown place— and she had good reason to believe that this also meant death, or the proverbial fate worse than death. Then observation was made of the effects of this information on her various biological functions, for example, her menstrual cycle. It became apparent that such psychic shocks had a distinct effect, in purely biological terms. In some cases the period would come ahead of time, in others it failed to occur. And so forth.

Or convicts were exposed to different kinds of pain, which ended in death. In such cases subsequent microscopic and chemical-biological examination of heart, kidneys, adrenal glands and other internal organs showed that the pain, fear, and particular form of death agony had brought about certain characteristic and very interesting changes.

I asked Dr. Haug, "Do you believe this is true?"

"I *know* it's true that the Germans carried out such investigations," he said.

Getting up, he added, "I've often asked myself: has the German people fallen prey to some kind of spiritual cancer? Remember, we don't have to do with ordinary Nazis here. But with scientists, with…Devils, pure and simple!"

Again a strange coincidence: I was given the same room at the hotel as the last time.

There I stood over by the window, there went Colbjørnsen, there sat Heidenreich, in the chair.

This may partly explain why I lay awake till well into the night.

I did, as a matter of fact, have a good deal to think about.

Kari—or Maria, which I had to try and call her now. Dr. Heidenreich. Karsten. And once again Kari. And Kari over and over again.

That latest conversation had been goodbye. Was that to be my lot in life from now on—to say goodbye, and again say goodbye?

I realized I couldn't give up hope. I would continue to hope as long as I lived.

One despairing human being—but there must be some way out!

Well into the night I noticed, without knowing how it had happened, that Dr. Haug's story was more and more pushing its way into the foreground.

Many despairing human beings—with cool gentlemen studying their despair.

Possibly I was running a mild fever. Possibly it was hopelessness eventually venting itself in revolt.

Dr. Haug's story just wouldn't let go. I lay awake struggling with it well into the night.

This latest thing is the worst of all, I thought. With people who make use of such a situation for that kind of experiments—with such people I renounce all kinship. If they are to be called humans and to be judged as such, I henceforth, and for all future time, renounce my claim to that name. Boorishness—all right. Bestial behavior—all right. Crude, unvarnished sadism—all right too; we all know—the world having made us what we are and we the world—it's there. But this! Such a calm, objective coldness when faced with human suffering—there can be nothing worse. So come into my arms, you coarse, stinking Gestapo hangman. You are a swine, scum, an undying shame to the father who begot you, to the mother who bore you, the village or city you grew up in, the land that educated you and used you. But I can see that, with all your evil, you are still a human being. If I could I would trample you under foot, wipe you out from the number of the living; for I know you won't ever become a decent human being: you will lick the boots of those over you and torment those that fate has delivered into your hands. And what's worse—if you get the chance, you will form your children in your own accursed image, so that misery shall never perish from the earth. You are a tumor produced by a sick time, and the only right thing is to burn you out of the body that we call the world.

But to you, stinking, repulsive, evil as you are, I say, Come into my arms! You are a human being, and you don't pretend to be any better than you are. And come into my arms, you pimps, thugs, murderers and criminals of all stripes, you are what you are. But *you*—you fine, anointed gentlemen with titles and honors, scientific culture and academic decorum, strolling self-importantly through white hospital wards, sitting with a dignified air in immaculate offices—which you turn to such uses! Never! Never! There is no bridge between you and me! If I have my way, the earth shall not harbor both of us at the same time!

I'd fallen asleep at last but woke up again. I'd dreamed something, and somehow or other I was awakened by the dream.

I had dreamed about an anthill. But it was no ordinary, confused dream, it was a fragment of a recollection.

Lying awake, I relived something that had happened at some point in that everlasting and famous year 1921.

A small party of us were visiting a mutual friend in the country not far from Oslo. It was a weekend in early spring, at the end of April, I believe. The birches had already begun to put forth leaves, like tiny mouse's ears. Can you show me anything purer, more chaste and innocent than the Northern birch when it gets swathed in green, as if by a light, almost invisible veil? It was that time of year. And Sunday morning we were taking a stroll through that early, delicate spring landscape, following sodden paths, crossing old footbridges, and walking along old, rickety rail fences, through thickets and past fields. It was the kind of Sunday that for some reason or other is connected in my mind with the word Palm Sunday, the harbinger of Easter. But it must've been later.

Yellow coltsfoot grew along the roadside ditches. An anthill sat beside our trail. The sun was already baking hot and the ants were out in great numbers welcoming the spring. They were busy as ants always are—snuff-brown and unemotional, dutiful and dumb. Thousands of them ran back and forth on top of their mound, sniffing at pine needles and at their peers; the place was teeming with life. We stood still and watched, ants are always entertaining. One of us held his hand over the mound and smelled it afterward—sure, it smelled sour. In short, we had turned into innocent young boys doing science again.

One of us lighted a cigarette and inadvertently tossed the match onto the mound. The outer layer of pine needles had already had time to dry, and a tiny little fire flared up there.

Then you should have seen the ants! What a fire squad! One, two, three, ten, twenty, a hundred threw themselves into the flames, using their body fluid to put them out. That was how it appeared. That must've been the thinking of those tiny brown workmen. If they were capable of thinking—which is, of course, doubtful.

It was an interesting little spectacle. And when the fire had been put out, we wanted to see more. We looked about us that fine, sunny spring day, and in no time at all we found an old discarded newspaper lying useless by the fence. Now it would be of some use! We fetched it, tore off a few pages, rolled them into a cornet, stuck the point into the mound and lighted it.

What a commotion! Ants by the hundreds, by the thousands, flocked together and climbed up the newspaper, crawling straight into the flames, where they got crumpled up by the heat and fell back on the mound like a piece of sour brown coal. But more followed, more and more! Until the paper cone was burned up, leaving behind only a small black patch on the mound.

But we had to see more. A fresh cornet, slightly thicker this time—down into the mound with it, out with the matches for a reprise. As it flared up, the ants plunged into the flames, we could see how some of them got sucked in and blown into the air by the draft the small fire produced. More and more ants threw themselves into the flaming mass and were consumed, or they fell down again with burned-off legs—and fresh ones threw themselves in. Until the last page of the newspaper had burned itself out and all that remained was a big black patch in the middle of the mound. The rest of the ants—hundreds, thousands—were running around more busily than ever, tidying up, straightening out, smoothing over, dragging the dead bodies away and putting the mound in order again.

We didn't say very much to one another as we rambled on along fences and fields, through thickets and past birches with that light, virginal green veil over them—on to a drink by the fireplace followed by Sunday dinner: veal roast, red wine and caramel pudding.

Of us four, one was later sent to the Grini camp. One was a prisoner in Germany. I was the third. The fourth was Carl Heidenreich.

"Cancer," Dr. Haug had said. What was it I had read about cancer?

Cancer occurs when an ordinary cell for some unknown reason begins to grow and multiply without restraint, at the expense of the other cells in the body!

Next morning I was awakened by church bells and the sounds of a brass band. It was May 17. The first Independence Day after five long years.

Shortly afterward I was driving toward Oslo.

It was pouring.

But nothing could dampen the joy of Norwegians on this day. There were people all over, on every road and path—grownups, but mostly children with flags in their hands. My worn heart leaped up. Soaking-wet figures with the water pouring off them. Flags like flowers along the road. And faces shining with happiness.

The Fourth Time
~~~~~~~~~~~~~~~~~~~~~~

It's not very pleasant to tell oneself at the conclusion of a task: I didn't carry it off.

But that's where I am.

Three times I've failed in this task. The first time in Norway in 1943, the second time in Sweden in 1944, and the third time now, in 1947, going through and organizing my papers.

During those August days in 1943 when I first began my daily notes, a plan was smoldering someplace or other inside me, a plan so wild and ambitious that I didn't dare admit it even to myself.

I know, or believe I know, that certain situations recur in the lives of most people. Often in such a way that one might be tempted to believe in the law of eternal return. If, as someone has said, the destiny of a human being resembles a web, it's strange how often the same pattern is repeated—to the point of monotony, in fact. Well, of course this only applies to those people who *have* a destiny. And that, again, means those people who have soul. Defective, maybe, with chips, holes and flaws, but soul all the same. Many people lack that. For reasons we cannot determine, but which are always deplorable, it was broken at an early age, so that it cannot resonate or sing, cannot store up and refine what it experiences. Those people are to be pitied, as are those who get involved with them.

But in the lives of those who have soul you will find that one and the same pattern recurs. Disguised, distorted maybe, but it recurs.

What's the reason?

I doubt whether we'll ever be able to pin it down to perfection. But if we take a person we know particularly well, someone we have known for a long time, and follow that person's life back to its starting point, we find at the beginning a number of threads—characteristics and experiences so early that they fade away in the obscurity and oblivion that envelop the first and most important part of our lives. We may guess at part of what is hidden back there, but we can never know anything for certain about it. That's what I believe anyway. And I further believe that these threads already contain the germ of that which is to become the pattern of our lives.

I realize, of course, that these threads do not determine everything. They are only the warp in the web. Then there are the external events and all that we call fortuitous occurrences, which interweave with it in all directions, happily or unhappily, luckily or unluckily.

But not so fortuitous all the same. For these original threads are no ordinary threads. They are magical, magnetic. There are forces in them, they have their own will, desires, demands, wishes and fears. They go their own way in the web, often in defiance of—even in direct opposition to—our plans, our calculation and our will. They have the power to repel certain experiences and attract others. And thus we—many of us, even the smallest among us—largely determine our own fate.

But as a rule differently than we would want, and without our being aware of it. We are subject to forces and wills in our own psyches that we can never get to know, a thought that is somewhat uncanny.

But I have another belief that runs counter to this. I believe that, if we could examine a person's life closely and steadily enough, if we could follow the pattern with a sufficiently clear, loving and comprehensive understanding from hour to hour, day to day, year to year, then we would eventually be omniscient as far as this one person was concerned. Then we would also, from our knowledge of his past and present, be able to glimpse his future. And we would be able to feel our way back to the starting point, to where the threads were twined, with this person's happiness or unhappiness as a consequence. Most often unhappiness, alas. But we would accomplish more. We would grasp the unifying principle in this person's life, but at the same time something else and larger—the unifying principle of the life around him. Indeed, if we could apprehend the whole gamut of one person's life, from top to bottom, we would understand the unifying principle of all human life, the life of families, groups, communities, *everything.* And if we could put this life in black and white, then whoever read that book and had the mental capacity to grasp what he read, would understand not only this other person's life but his own as well. And it would have the effect of a rebirth.

Consider what that word means. A woman carries a life inside her. It causes her many worries but also secret joys, a silent delight that is pain, hope, fear and bliss all at once. And by her delivery, which is pain, agony, fear and delight all at once, she gives birth to new life.

We all have a latent life within us, joyous and agonizing life from the time behind the horizon, the time of infinite agony and infinite joy. When we succeed in redeeming some of it we feel connected to ourselves—ourselves as we were at the beginning—and to all and everything. Remember, at that time we lived at the source of things, we hadn't branched out or specialized, nor isolated ourselves. We hadn't yet covered ourselves with bark and armor and thorns, but were flesh of everybody's flesh, life of everybody's life. Look at a little child playing with a puppy or with a cat—or with a dead thing, for that matter. You can see that this child doesn't yet feel as something separate from the cat, the dog, the doll or the teddy bear. It's at one with everything. It lives in the great unity that we later lose in part, but that we always—if we have retained our soul—long to achieve, and which we experience afresh during a great love, a great sorrow, and what some call being born again.

Connectedness, unity, insight, rebirth—in my groping way I was looking for all that. With what imperfect tools, alas! With a memory that constantly failed and constantly led me astray, because it wasn't searching for truth but let itself be guided by my own secret wishes and anxieties. With an understanding as cloudy as a frosted windowpane. With a sensibility which, at best, could only perceive bits and pieces, bits of a melody, pieces of a happening.

It was with miserable tools such as these that I poked around and searched, in the mad hope of being able to recreate a picture I wasn't even certain had ever been a reality; for I couldn't see it, of course, being myself in the middle of it. In any case, the picture couldn't help being incomplete, vague, distorted and falsified. Nevertheless I kept hoping—ah, what a mad dream, what a forlorn hope—that it would give me a feeling of something essential behind all that fortuitousness, a hint of connectedness, a shadow of redemption.

And in my heart of hearts there was perhaps a wild hope of a new life, like refreshing rain upon a dry and dust-covered meadow. Rain, tears and sun …

I didn't succeed, nor could I have succeeded. I didn't find the pattern in my own life, much less in the lives of the group I tried to depict, as those lives were lived during a brief period a number of years ago. Anyway, if I had seriously believed myself capable of solving that problem, I would have been a certified megalomaniac. Anyone who was to follow a person's life in the way I have indicated above would need, first of all, to have several years at his disposal, and secondly he would have to be a superman. I was and will always be a common man, and I didn't have years, just days and weeks.

Nevertheless I had that plan, not as a responsible thought but as a wild, presumptuous dream. Maybe I thought there was a short cut to my goal. I ought to have known that, in the world of the spirit, there are no short cuts.

And then life stepped in, released me in its own way from my original task and embarked me on another—which was still somehow the same. By describing what happened to me, I tried to attain the imagined or real clear-sightedness which in the end I did experience.

I failed again—I was bound to fail. That vision—if it was a vision, that is, and not just a feverish dream—was organically related to my mental state at the time when it occurred. And that mental state, whether it was madness, delirium, or the kind of clear-sightedness that a person is said to experience during great crises or just before death, didn't return on command.

Miserable, I stood before a door that closed the moment I'd hoped it would open wide.

That was in 1944.

Then I tried again, now. Even more fruitlessly. Three more years had gone by, and that mental state, whatever it should be called, was further away from me by those very three years.

To my own eyes I look like someone trying to recall a dream he had the previous night. As the day wears on, he moves further and further away from it. Saying to himself that this dream told him an essential truth doesn't help a bit. The pictures fade, turn into fog, disappear.

Or I'm like a fugitive who has escaped from a beloved, ravaged home and boarded a ship that will carry him to an unknown port. He stands on deck looking back. Then it doesn't do much good if he thinks, *That* I should have taken along, and *that*, and *that*.... The ship carries him off, he moves farther and farther away from it all. Soon the coast is just a few faraway blue hills.

I didn't succeed. I'd better repeat those bitter words a few more times.

And yet I have retained a faint hope, wilder and crazier than any other.

I have a thought: When I originally conceived the idea of describing people's lives as a constantly recurring pattern, wasn't it because, for a moment, I thought I dimly perceived such a pattern? And when I subsequently tried to attain the vision through writing, wasn't it because, deep down, I had some inkling of the content of that vision?

I lost the pattern—if there was one. I didn't find the vision—if it ever existed.

But, I think—and this is my fourth try—that maybe others can see what I myself am unable to see. Is there a pattern all the same, and is there a logical sum total—call it vision or whatever you will—of that which I experienced? Is it all there before my very eyes, the reason why I cannot see it being that I've looked for it so eagerly and so long that I'm dazzled by it?

Anyway, here are the papers. If there is a pattern, others will have to find it.

But I understand enough to know that, if others are to attain the vision, they will need all the help I can offer them.

It isn't much of a help, I'm afraid.

I know I felt I had gone through a unique experience. It was composed of past cowardice and present malice, of crass coincidence and an iron nemesis.

What emerged from these elements was almost unbelievable.

But didn't something absolutely central and valid emerge at the same time?

I felt it did when I had the experience. Or rather, when the experience composed itself, took on form and focus—became a vision, madness, feverish dream, sacred knowledge, or I can no longer tell what.

Vision or not, it filled me with rapture, so that I thought, Go out and tell all nations—

I remember thinking, I've just solved the riddle of the universe!

I remember thinking, Did I have to go through all that in order to arrive at this?

I remember thinking, lying there on the basement floor, bloody and miserable, with a feverish pulse, Praise the Lord!

I know I wasn't normal. Maybe not quite sane. The situation wasn't normal, to put it mildly.

But did I *see* anything?

Did the abnormal situation cause veils to be swept aside, the fog to lift, light to fall on dark places?

I don't know. After all, I can't relive it. I remember only fragments, but fragments of a vision do not make a vision. What creates the vision is precisely that ungraspable element which binds the parts together into a unity.

These fragments are like cold, stiff slag of something that was for one intense moment molten, incandescent metal.

They all stem from the first part. Of the finale, the harmonization, the last big resolution, I have no clear recollection.

Here they are, those fragments.

It was youth and the life of youth that I saw—in a world led and governed and driven into the abyss by old men.

Those old men lift their trembling fingers and say, It's a sin, it's a sin! All that your body and soul desire is sin. Remember, you are bad and all you desire is bad. Therefore you must control yourself. Look at me! I'm controlling myself. Difficult, you say? Impossible, you say? Oh, no! You just have to control yourself for some twenty or thirty years, until you turn fifty or sixty, then it will be easier, and in the end it will run by itself, you have mastered self-control and are on the verge of perfection, which, to be sure, you will only attain in the grave. The end of life is death.

The old men raise their fingers once more and say, Get into line! Stay in school till you are old and gray, then you'll have a chance to become like one of us—withered, powerful, and rich. The end of life is the vanity that sprouts and grows in you when you've killed your pristine life through poring over books.

And again they lift their fingers to speak:

By its very nature the world is wide and rich and free, with happy hunting grounds for all.

But that's just the trouble. For that freedom is the lowest form of freedom, it's dangerous, its name is chaos and licentiousness. And you do not wish to be licentious, do you? But then you must go in for our planned, well-organized higher freedom. And in order to achieve that we have to build fences and walls and barbed wire barricades and impediments and cubicles around you and within you—national borders and customs barriers and class distinctions and class arrogance, and associations with bylaws and statutes with sections, and rules for everything you must do and not do, say and not say, think and not think, feel and not feel, and prohibitions against most things, punishment for almost anything, and fear of everything. The end of life is dignity. That's the highest form of freedom, and it consists of your no longer being able to move.

Old men. A whole forest of old men with raised fingers.

Love? No, career. Joy? No, duty. Zest for life? No, patience. Adventure? No, school. Rebellion? No, obedience.

And the young are docile. They betray love. It hurts, but they betray it. Too late do they discover that if you betray love you betray everything. Then you bring trouble both upon yourself and others. And you lose your own youth—the more you cling to it the faster you lose it, because youth is only another name for the time of love.

And then the wheel starts turning. The third name for youth is vitality. And if the vitality is not used, then it's misused. If it's not allowed to display itself in love, it will display itself in hatred, resentment, envy and suspicion. Fences, cubicles, prohibitions, fear, war and portents of war, malice, cruelty, revenge and thoughts of revenge ...

Another fragment. I saw Nazism as our bastard child. Begotten blindly and cowardly, betrayed in its mother's womb and abandoned to itself, totally neglected.

And I saw us, the spotless and self-righteous ones, watching this creature, child of our own flesh and blood, and saying, "We do not know you!"

And the cock crowed.

And I saw him, our son, change his lineaments and become the thief Barabbas. And I saw him bare his teeth at us and grin and say, "You didn't know me, did you? Quite right! Be false and cowardly! That suits you best!"

I saw us one more time. It was the present and the future that I saw.

We lay asleep behind our fences, inside our walls, each in his or her cubicle. Then we were awakened—we thought—by some terrible thing that was happening. We were awakened in such an exceptional way. But all went well and then it was over, it was really just a bad dream. And now we were awake, thank God, and it was only a dream. And now we are awake, we think, having turned over in our cubicle and going on sleeping.

But the thing changed—it wasn't just us, it was all, everybody. Lying there, each in his separate cubicle, each behind his separate wall. Asleep. Now on one side, now on the other.

And someone says but isn't heard, "Wake up! We must find the answer now! We must see now! We must understand now, lest we never understand, lest the same happen again, but bigger and more devastating than before. And then some day a dull, sleepy humanity will rouse itself half awake, rub its eyes and say, "What's up?"

It could be the day before the world ends.

GREEN INTEGER
Pataphysics and Pedantry

Douglas Messerli, *Publisher*

MASTERWORKS OF FICTION
Green Integer Books

Masterworks of Fiction is a program of Green Integer
to reprint important works of fiction from all centuries.
We make no claim to any superiority of these fictions over others
in either form or content, but contend
that these works are highly enjoyable to read and, more importantly,
have challenged the ideas and language of the times
in which they were published, establishing themselves over the years
as among the outstanding works of their period.
By republishing both well known and lesser recognized titles in this series
we hope to continue our mission of bringing our society
into a slight tremolo of confusion and fright at least.

Books in this series

José Donoso *Hell Has No Limits* (1966)
Knut Hamsun *A Wanderer Plays on Muted Strings* (1909)
Raymond Federman *The Twofold Vibration* (1982)
Gertrude Stein *To Do: A Book of Alphabets and Birthdays* (1957)
Gérard de Nerval *Aurélia* (1855)
Tereza Albues *Pedra Canga* (1987)
Sigurd Hoel *Meeting at the Milestone* (1947)
Leslie Scalapino *Defoe* (1994)

*

Books Published by Green Integer

History, or Messages from History Gertrude Stein [1997]
Notes on the Cinematographer Robert Bresson [1997]
The Critic As Artist Oscar Wilde [1997]
Tent Posts Henri Michaux [1997]
Eureka Edgar Allan Poe [1997]
An Interview Jean Renoir [1998]
Mirrors Marcel Cohen [1998]

The Effort to Fall Christopher Spranger [1998]
Radio Dialogs I Arno Schmidt [1999]
Travels Hans Christian Andersen [1999]
In the Mirror of the Eighth King Christopher Middleton [1999]
On Ibsen James Joyce [1999]
A Wanderer Plays on Muted Strings Knut Hamsun [2001]
Laughter: An Essay on the Meaning of the Comic
Henri Bergson [1999]
Operratics Michel Leiris [2001]
Seven Visions Sergei Paradjanov [1998]
Ghost Image Hervé Guibert [1998]
Ballets Without Music, Without Dancers, Without Anything
Louis-Ferdinand Céline [1999]
My Tired Father Gellu Naum [2000]
Manifestos Manifest Vicente Huidobro [2000]
Aurelia Gérard de Nerval [2001]
On Overgrown Paths Knut Hamsun [1999]
Displeasures of the Table Martha Ronk [2001]
What Is Man? Mark Twain [2000]
Metropolis Antonio Porta [1999]
Poems Sappho [1999]
Suicide Circus: Selected Poems Alexei Kruchenykh [2001]
Hell Has No Limits José Donoso [1999]
To Do: Alphabets and Birthdays Gertrude Stein [2001]
Letters from Hanusse Joshua Haigh [2000]
[edited by Douglas Messerli]
Suites Federico García Lorca [2001]
Pedra Canga Tereza Albues [2001]
The Pretext Rae Armantrout [2001]
Theoretical Objects Nick Piombino [1999]
Yi 痏 Yang Lian [2002]
My Life Lyn Hejinian [2002]
Book of Reincarnation Hsu Hui-chih [2002]
The Doll and *The Doll at Play* Hans Bellmer
(with poetry by Paul Éluard) [2002]
Art *Poetic'* Olivier Cadiot [1999]
Fugitive Suns: Selected Poetry Andrée Chedid [1999]
Across the Darkness of the River Hsi Muren [2001]
Mexico. A Play Gertrude Stein [1999]
Sky Eclipse: Selected Poems Régis Bonvicino [2000]
The Twofold Vibration Raymond Federman [2000]
Zuntig Tom La Farge [2001]
The Disparities Rodrigo Toscano [2002]
The Antiphon Djuna Barnes [2001]

The Resurrection of Lady Lester OyamO [2000]
Crowtet I Mac Wellman [2000]
Hercules, Richelieu and Nostradamus Paul Snoek [2000]
Abingdon Square Maria Irene Fornes [2000]
3 Masterpieces of Cuban Drama: Plays by
Julio Matas, Carlos Felipe, and Vigilio Piñera
Translated and Edited with an Introduction by
Luis F. González-Cruz and Ann Waggoner Aken [2000]
Antilyrik and Other Poems Vítězslav Nezval [2001]
Rectification of Eros Sam Eisenstein [2000]
Drifting Dominic Cheung [2000]
Gold Fools Gilbert Sorrentino [2001]
Erotic Recipes Jiao Tung [2001]
The Mysterious Hualien Chen I-chih [2001]
Across the Darkness of the River Hsi Muren [2001]

Green Integer EL-E-PHANT books:

The PIP Anthology of World Poetry of the 20th Century, Volume 1
Douglas Messerli, editor [2000]
The PIP Anthology of World Poetry of the 20th Century, Volume 2
Douglas Messerli, editor [2001]
readiness / enough / depends / on Larry Eigner [2000]
Two Fields that Face and Mirror Each Other Martin Nakell [2001]
Meeting at the Milestone Sigurd Hoel [2002]
Defoe Leslie Scalapino [2002]

BOOKS FORTHCOMING FROM GREEN INTEGER

Islands and Other Essays Jean Grenier
American Notes Charles Dickens
Prefaces and Essays on Poetry
William Wordsworth
Confessions of an English Opium-Eater
Thomas De Quincey
The Renaissance Walter Pater
Captain Nemo's Library Per Olav Enquist
Partial Portraits Henry James
Utah Toby Olson
Rosa Knut Hamsun
Selected Poems and Journal Fragments
Maurice Gilliams